COCKNEY DIAMOND

Also by Elizabeth Waite

SKINNY LIZZIE
COCKNEY WAIF
COCKNEY FAMILY
SECOND CHANCE
THIRD TIME LUCKY
TROUBLE AND STRIFE
NIPPY
KINGSTON KATE
COCKNEY COURAGE
TIME WILL TELL
A LONDON LASS

COCKNEY DIAMOND

ELIZABETH WAITE

A *Time Warner* Book

First published in Great Britain in 2003
by Time Warner Books UK

Copyright © Elizabeth Waite 2003

The moral right of the author has been asserted.

*All characters in this publication are fictitious and any
resemblance to real persons, living or dead, is purely coincidental.*

A CIP catalogue record for this book
is available from the British Library.

ISBN 0 316 72464 5

Typeset by Palimpsest Book Production Limited,
Polmont, Stirlingshire
Printed and bound in Great Britain by
Clays Ltd, St Ives plc

Time Warner Books UK
Brettenham House
Lancaster Place
London WC2E 7EN

www.TimeWarnerBooks.co.uk

I wish to thank all my readers who, having read *Cockney Waif* and *Cockney Family*, took the trouble to write to me.

So much interest has been shown in the characters of Patsy and her family that I was asked to write a third book in the series thus completing the trilogy.

Hopefully *Cockney Diamond* will create as much interest as the two previous books.

FAMILY TREE

FLORENCE HOLMES AND ALEXANDER BERRY

Florence and Alexander befriended Ellen Kent from the day Patsy was born. On the death of Ellen Kent the authorities were all for committing Patsy into an institution. These two people were granted custody and in reality became surrogate parents

ELLEN KENT

Born 1885 in the West End of London – died 1918 – never married – one illegitimate daughter, Patsy

PATSY KENT

Born 1904 in Tooting – married Johnny Jackson 5.12.1921 at Wandsworth Town Hall, South London – divorced 1931 – married Edward Owen in 1931

=

EDWARD OWEN

Born 1899 in Colliers Wood, Surrey – married Patsy Kent 28.12.1931. Patsy and Edward had 4 children

ALEXANDER OWEN

Born 2.4.1924 – married Vicky Baldwin in April 1950, had two children

DAVID OWEN

Born 20.8.1926 – married Valerie, a war widow, who already had a son, Timmy, aged 6 years. David adopted Tim so he became Tim Owen. They had no children of their own

ELLEN OWEN

Ellen and Emma were twins born 10.10.1929. Ellen, the elder by ten minutes, married Robert Dellor – Emma married Donald Langford, double wedding 1950. Ellen and Robert had no children – Emma and Donald had three children

EMMA OWEN

JAMES OWEN
Born 1953

FRANCES OWEN
Born 1954

EDWARD LANGFORD
Born 1951

THOMAS LANGFORD
Born 1953

SAMUEL LANGFORD
Born 1955

BOOK ONE

Reminiscence

Chapter One

Patsy Owen was in a very thoughtful mood today. She fingered the two gold rings that had belonged to her husband's mother and that he had placed on her finger so many years ago. The memory had her smiling.

It was the day that she and Eddie had received the official papers stating that henceforth she could be known as Patsy Owen. God, what a relief that had been! To be able to shake off the surname of Jackson and to shake off her disastrous marriage to Johnny Jackson.

As Eddie had placed the two rings on the third finger of her left hand he had quietly said, 'Now you are Mrs Owen, from this day forth till death do us part.'

If only that could have been true!

Changing one's name by deed-poll and being known as Mrs Owen didn't make it so. If only they could have been married, so many heartaches could have been avoided. Johnny, and indeed all the members of his family, had adopted a dog-in-the-manger attitude. They didn't want her, but they made sure that Eddie couldn't make her his wife.

Eddie had sworn that some day soon they *would* be

married. Unfortunately, it had taken years before he was able to fulfil that promise.

During those years they had been blessed with four children. As was only natural, the subject often came up amongst friends as to how long they had been married. Inwardly Patsy had cringed and evaded the subject whenever possible. Never had she felt able to give an honest answer.

Eddie always insisted that she was too sensitive. Well, it was different for men, wasn't it? Not for the world could she have openly admitted that she was living in sin. Yet the bond they had formed was strong, and their love for each other would last their lifetime.

She laughed out loud at this. She had always thought, and did to this day, that God had sent Eddie Owen to her to compensate for all the trials and tribulations she and her mother had had to endure when she was a child.

It was a long time since she had allowed herself to dwell on the events which had led Ellen, her mother, to leave her well-to-do family and end up on the doorstep of number 22 Strathmore Street, in Tooting, south London.

From that day to the day that she died, her mother had not set eyes on her parents, let alone received help of any kind from any member of her family. It had to be said that her father had not turned her out of house and home; she had left of her own free will, but he hadn't given her much of an alternative. He'd been more bothered about his own reputation. His big house and servants, the sheltered and privileged life he and his wife lived.

He would allow no daughter of his to bring shame to his family by giving birth to a baby on the wrong side of the blanket. Pompous to the last, he'd shown no kindness or understanding. Either Ellen remained hidden in the top part of the house until the baby was born, and agreed to have it whisked away immediately by a charity that dealt with the adoption of unwanted babies; or else she was on her own.

4

How could she even think of disposing of her child? The baby was not unwanted.

Just three days after her nineteenth birthday, her father had broken the news to her that her fiancé had been killed in a hunting accident. Ellen hadn't been able to take it in. She saw herself looking down from her bedroom window, watching Peter walk down the drive and at the gates turning his face up to her to wave. And now she was being told that she would never again see him walk into a room or sitting astride his horse, her heart swelling with pride at his straight back, broad shoulders and handsome face.

Patsy wrapped her arms across her chest to stop herself from trembling, and sighed heavily. Even after all these years she could feel for her mother. Two more weeks and she would have been married.

Word for word she could remember how Mother had explained the situation to her. She must have been about ten years old. Patsy sighed at the recollection.

Such was their love for each other, their lovemaking had been frantic. Her mother had told her that with hindsight it was as if Peter had known that his life was to be cut short. Neither of them had reckoned on her being pregnant.

When the truth came out, life for Ellen had been unbearable. So much shouting. So many horrible accusations.

'My father's eyes were black as coal, his face purple with rage, as he yelled, "Just keep yourself out of my way. The very sight of you sickens me,"' Ellen had sadly told her. The tedious weeks of imprisonment had almost broken her spirit. Only allowed out under the cover of darkness, and then heavily cloaked and ordered to stay within the grounds of the family home, she had had plenty of time to think. Constantly she had turned the alternatives over in her mind. She could stay with her family and be well looked after, which meant giving up her baby, probably without ever having set eyes on it; or she could leave home and have to fend for herself and her child.

Finally she had made her decision and abandoned her family.

But the truth was, each and every one of them had abandoned her, weeks previously.

She had taken with her only what was hers. Quite a bit of valuable jewellery, and a good many gold sovereigns, making sure she had sufficient money to tide her over for a while. Patsy's eyes brimmed with tears as, after all this time, she recalled her mother's words: 'The moment I walked out of that house, I made up my mind I would adopt a new identity. I would become Mrs Ellen Kent. I decided to stick with my own Christian name. The surname I chose was entirely fictitious and the "Mrs" a courtesy title.

'Only once did I pause to look back at the house. Although within easy distance of the city, it stood in beautiful grounds. Just for a moment I wavered, filled with a longing, a yearning that was almost unbearable, to turn back to become part of my family again. My sadness and the feeling of loneliness was awful, but I knew Father would never relent. His decision had been made. My unborn baby was a bastard. It had to be put up for adoption or be placed in an institution. He didn't care which, just so long as he never had to set eyes on it.'

Even after all these years it hurt Patsy so much to remember how her mother had suffered.

Yet God had been with Ellen that day. Having boarded a tram and bought a ticket to the end of the line, she had alighted to find herself at Tooting Broadway. It had taken her a while to familiarise herself with the noisy hustle and bustle that was going on around her. Spotting a carefully printed card pinned to a board which was displayed in a shop window, she heaved a sigh of relief.

It stated: ROOMS TO LET.

The owner of the shop could not have been more helpful. Having listened to Ellen's enquiry, he smiled and told her to be seated on the chair which stood beside the counter. Then he had written down a name and address on a sheet of paper and handed it to Ellen, telling her, 'That's Mrs Holmes. Not everyone's cup of tea, but take my word for it, you'll go a long way to find a more decent, clean lodging and a woman with a bigger heart.' Then, turning to the only other customer in the shop, he had added, 'This gentleman is Alexander Berry, better known to everyone around 'ere as Ollie Berry. He's a neighbour of Florrie Holmes; he'll show you where she lives.'

The two men had given each other a knowing glance. This was no common woman. She was heavily pregnant, and by the look of the clothes she was wearing certainly not from around these parts. Her skirt and jacket were well cut and must have cost more than most men from these parts could ever dream of spending on their wives. And to say her speech was different would have been putting it mildly.

Ellen had told Patsy that at the time she had guessed what they were thinking and she had been scared. Very scared, and with good reason. More so when Mr Berry had placed his hand beneath her elbow, picked up her suitcase and made to steer her across the busy Tooting High Street.

Tooting was very much a working-class district. There were barrow boys shouting their wares, poorly dressed women bustling along with kiddies clinging to their skirts, tram cars rattling along the middle of the road and huge great horses pulling dray-carts. Ellen had been unprepared for all this hustle and bustle, and the obvious signs of poverty. She had breathed a sigh of relief when Mr Berry said they were almost there.

Strathmore Street was narrow, with dingy-looking back-to-back houses almost pressing against each other. As Mr Berry opened the front gate of number 22, Ellen had failed to see a cracked raised flagstone in the path of the small front garden. Catching it with the toe of her boot, she was unable to stop herself from falling, and ended up lying on the ground in an ugly heap, her skirt caught up under her swollen belly.

Even during the telling of all of this to her young daughter, Ellen's face had flushed with embarrassment. It had got worse as she had continued, and Patsy's heart still ached at the thought of how her mother must have suffered. Ellen hadn't been able to pick herself up; searing pains were shooting through her stomach, and then, the last straw, she was vomiting.

A fat woman, with swollen ankles and badly veined legs, had come shuffling out of the house and in a voice that had scared the wits out of Ellen had roared: 'What the 'ell's going on 'ere?' Then, catching her first glimpse of Ellen still sprawled in a most unladylike position on the ground, her voice had softened.

With great difficulty Florrie Holmes lowered herself to Ellen's side. Sliding her arm under Ellen's shoulders, which enabled her to raise Ellen's head slightly, she wiped the vomit from her lips, using the hem of her wraparound overall and all the time whispering, 'You'll be all right, luv. We'll get yer inside and sort yer out some'ow. Then, turning to Mr Berry, she shouted, 'Don't just stand there like a duck out of water; git yerself over to Gran's an' see if one of 'er boys is 'ome, 'cos we'll need a bit of 'elp to get this poor woman inside.'

Three men soon appeared with Mr Berry, and with Gran'ma Day, who lived directly opposite Florrie, issuing orders left right and centre, and Florrie Holmes adding her two pennyworth, it wasn't long before Ellen was safely seated in a tatty but comfortable armchair.

Many was the time after that day that Ellen had admitted to Florrie that she had never felt so low or found herself in so small a room, and Florrie would recall how touched she'd been to see the tears welling up in Ellen's eyes and trickling down her cheeks.

But what had troubled Florrie most at the time was the awful state of her kitchen. From the high mantelshelf hung a ragged cloth, and the hearth was covered with wads of old newspapers; three weeks ago Florrie had ordered the sweep to come this morning and sweep her chimney, and he hadn't turned up. 'Lazy sod! Probably 'ad a win at the dogs an' don't need the money. Still, he'll be round, and when he does he'll be sorry he messed me about. If I wasn't so fat I'd climb up that bloody chimney meself an' soon shift the soot. Never mind. Later on t'day I'll set light to some paraffin rags an' shove 'em up the chimney. That'll do the trick, an' I'll 'ave saved me money.'

The times over the years Patsy had heard that story.

Ollie always said he'd had a hard job to stop himself from laughing, but he knew why Florrie was gabbling on so. She had been trying her best to put her unfamiliar visitor at ease. Moving at a speed which belied her bulk, Florrie soon had them all seated round a well-scrubbed kitchen table with steaming cups of tea in front of them. Ellen told often how she'd laughed as she watched Florrie slicing bread from a long crusty loaf which she held pressed against her big soft belly whilst cutting it into thick slices with a saw-like knife. Ellen couldn't believe how much better she felt after having drunk the hot sweet tea and eaten new bread liberally spread with butter and jam. Although she'd eaten better fare, and off far better china, it was a long time since food had tasted so good or the company had been so friendly.

Another thing Ellen had been fond of saying was that she couldn't have known it then, but that first day in Florrie's home was to form the basis of a life-long friendship and great love between these three ill-assorted people.

Patsy would go along with that. One hundred per cent.

Indeed, every member of her family owed their success in life mainly to her mother's first meeting with Alexander Berry and Florrie Holmes.

Patsy laughed again. Eddie was always telling her that she was reliving the past more as she got older. And it was true.

So many years since Ollie had literally dragged her mother over Florrie's doorstep.

Even though Ellen had worked hard, taking in sewing jobs and working on the stalls in Tooting Market, jobs for which she had never been trained, she was always the first to admit that she could have travelled a lot further and fared much worse. Her baby had been born almost before she had had time to settle into Florrie's two upstairs rooms and get her bearings, never mind make any arrangements to go into hospital.

Sighing heavily, Patsy knew only too well that, but for Gran and Grandad Day and their family, her mother might never have survived in this working-class area, and she herself would almost certainly have ended up being sent to live in the workhouse or some such institution; which was what her grandfather had wanted in the first place.

It was Gran who had assisted Florrie in delivering Ellen's baby.

From the moment Gran'ma Day had told Ellen she had a little girl, it was as if Gran's big heart had opened to include Ellen. Over the years Gran had watched out for her as if she were one of her own daughters. As for Patsy herself – she chuckled at the thought – she couldn't put a foot wrong. The whole tribe of Days loved her.

Very quickly Patsy and her mother had learned that with the Days for your friends, you were lucky indeed. As enemies, they were a different kettle of fish entirely.

Hurt one and you upset them all.

There were so many of them, Ellen, nor indeed many other folk, had never really worked out the final total. Gran and her husband Jack had five sons and one daughter. To them had to be added the daughters-in-law, son-in-law and fourteen grandchildren, all living in Strathmore Street. In adjoining streets lived nephews, nieces, uncles, aunts and cousins.

Compared with others in the district, this family was quite wealthy. It was a safe bet that they owned ninety per cent of all the stalls in Tooting market. Gran presided over the entire brood with as much command as any queen, and God help the daughter-in-law whose views differed from her own. Yet for all that she wielded a rod of iron, she was loved by sons, daughter, grandchildren and in-laws alike.

Patsy had always felt extremely lucky that her mother, and she herself, had been included in this love that knew no bounds.

Patsy bit hard down on her lip as her mind went back to Mother's early days of living in Tooting. Soon after Patsy had been born, Ellen's stock of sovereigns had run out and most of her jewellery had been sold. If it hadn't been for Florrie and Ollie, they would have starved. Although Ellen had applied for numerous jobs, she had had no luck. Even in the offices of a builder's yard she had been turned away. 'Too genteel' had been the boss's reason.

Then, one particularly bad day, Gran had sent for her.

The thought of what her mother had told her in later years had Patsy once again laughing out loud. Gran's kitchen had been full of children: boys wearing trousers which were far too big for them; pretty little girls with long hair that could have done with a good brush and comb, and all of them looking grubby. Yet for all that, they greeted Ellen with squeals of delight and hugs and kisses, all of them happy as Larry and fit as a bunch of fleas. Gran didn't need any telling that Ellen hadn't been able to find employment; the sad look on her face was enough. The truth was, she spoke too posh-like for folk around these parts.

11

'Right.' The word burst from Gran's mouth like a cannon being fired, and she wasn't going to brook any argument. 'You're gonna work for my boys, an' I want no beating about the bush. The matter is settled.'

In a daze, Ellen came back to Florrie and told her that the thought of working on a market stall absolutely terrified her. It wasn't that she was too proud; she just feared that she would not be able to do the heavy work.

Gran had followed her across the road. 'Did you 'ear me?' she bellowed.

Ellen was at a loss for words. Moneywise she knew that she had to do something, and do it quickly. She had no option. This new life she had chosen was full of pitfalls. She needed coal, the rent had to be paid every week, food had to be bought, and her baby needed so many things.

She wanted this job so badly, but could she do it?

Were the Day family just sorry for her? She was sure that was the reason this job was being offered to her. Emotion clogged her throat. She hadn't expected to feel grateful for charity.

As if reading her thoughts, Gran had spoken softly.

'It's not charity that my boys will be giving you, Ellen. Bleedin' 'ard dirty work, that's what it will be. All hours that Gawd almighty sends, and grubby, grimy jobs. And don't you dare go thinking I don't know what I'm talking about. I worked on that market long before it 'ad a roof on it. Yeah, an' I 'elped my Jack push a barrow round the streets of an evening.'

Ellen's face must have been a picture.

Florrie's cheeks were wobbling with laughter. Ellen was so slender, beautiful, but like a flipping rake she was, her hair always groomed so that it shone like silk. Her pushing a barrow! It was hard to imagine.

'Gawd's truth I'm telling yer,' Gran carried on. 'Had t' put a stop t' me grafting for two reasons: first, me legs

12

swelled up like balloons; and the second was my Jack. Put me in the pudding club regular as clockwork. He only 'ad to 'ang his trousers on the end of our bed and I'd end up with another bun in the oven.'

Just when they thought Gran had said all she had to say, she added, 'My only worry is that you'll slip down the drain 'oles between the stalls.'

And that remark had all three of them in fits of laughter.

Gran had rubbed at her eyes, and this time her voice sounded serious as she said, 'My Queenie will see you're all right. She's a good 'un is my Queenie, you'll see.'

And that was how it all came about.

Ellen Kent had worked for the Day brothers in Tooting market from that day until the day she died. She was the first to admit she had cause to be eternally grateful to the fat, coarse, common woman known to all as Gran, whom she had come to love so dearly. Patsy still held the memory of how Mother would come home each evening with dirt-grimed fingernails and her eyelids drooping with exhaustion. Nevertheless, it had been a good life: caring company, rough cockney humour, and not many dull days.

Life had continued along those lines for fourteen years.

Big, strong Alexander Berry, and Florrie Holmes, rough and ready as they came, had become not only friends but their family.

Then Ellen had died of consumption. Too young. Far too young.

Patsy's big green eyes clouded as she recalled so vividly that period of her life. 'Poor Mum. Poor Mum,' she murmured.

Over the whole of that weekend, Ellen's body had lain in an open coffin upon a trestle table in Florrie's downstairs front room. Florrie had insisted to the undertakers that she be brought home. Neighbours, friends, stall-holders from the market and even barrow boys had come to pay their last respects. They came in a stream, old and young alike. All agreed Ellen was laid out nice. Florrie kept candles lit, day and night, at the head and foot of the coffin.

Ollie too had done Ellen proud. If it hadn't been for him, she would have been buried in a pauper's grave. He had paid the entire cost of the funeral.

The glass-sided hearse was drawn by two grey horses, a black cloth draped across each of their backs. Folk lined the street. Men removed their cloth caps, folding them in half and clutching them in their work-stained hands, and bowed their heads.

Florrie, dressed from head to toe in black, her best hat stripped of its usual flower adornment and replaced by a wide black ribbon, looked exactly what she was: a good, kindly working-class woman.

Ollie Berry always looked smart because he worked at the Town Hall. The day they buried her mother, Patsy remembered how exceptionally smart he'd looked. Holding tightly to Patsy's hand, he'd walked tall and upright, in dark suit, white shirt and black tie, and there was never a moment during the service that his eyes had not glistened with tears.

A long, long, sad day that had been.

So many tears shed for one lady.

One day had become much like another. Patsy remembered she had cried a lot, but there had always been the arms of Florrie or Gran that she could throw herself into. Each day when Ollie came home from work he did his best to make up for all the sadness and pain.

Then came the shock.

The district relieving officer and a man who stated that he was from the Shaftesbury Welfare Society were standing on Florrie's doorstep. Florrie sent Patsy flying to fetch Ollie, refusing to allow either of the two gentlemen to step over her doorstep until Gran and Ollie were present, because she needed no telling the reason for this visit.

Once inside, the nightmare had begun. Maybe the adults had been expecting it, but never for as long as she lived would Patsy forget the shock that rippled through the whole of her body that morning.

The relieving officer had addressed himself to Ollie. 'The crux of the matter is that this child is now without parents. Either she goes to an orphanage, although I fear she may be too old for that, or to an institution.'

It had seemed to Patsy, who was cowering in a corner, that the whole room had exploded with noisy disgust.

'Take 'er to the workhouse! Over my dead body yer will!' In desperation Gran had reached for one of her walking sticks and was waving it menacingly.

Wild horses wouldn't have kept Florrie quiet. 'Not while I've got me 'ealth an' strength does that kid leave this 'ouse. It were me an' Gran what brought 'er into this world, an' we've cared for 'er an' her mum ever since. We ain't about to stop now. So sod yer bits of paper, don't even think about taking our Patsy anywhere. This 'as always been her 'ome an' it still is. You got that?'

Even Ollie's usual calm was forgotten. Throwing caution to the wind, he made his fury known in no uncertain terms. 'I shall apply to be the child's guardian. No harm will come to her, she will continue to live with Mrs Holmes, and I will see that she is adequately provided for. No workhouse commitment order will ever be served here, I promise you that.'

Even today, as Patsy gazed around their office, she felt the relief surge through her body. How different her life might have been!

Gran and Florrie would have fought like demons to keep her safe amongst the good-hearted cockney people she had grown up with. But would they have been able to win against the authorities?

Ollie was different.

Men looked up to him, he was respected. Besides, he loved her. So did Florrie and Gran, but with Ollie it was a sort of belonging.

'Can any one of you claim to be a blood relative of this child?' This question had been falteringly asked by the man from the Shaftesbury Society.

'Or have you legal guardianship, as required by law?' asked Mr Litchfield, the district relieving officer.

'No.' Ollie answered for all of them. 'But that doesn't mean we are about to stand by and allow you, or any other body, to take young Patsy off to the workhouse.'

'Oh come now, Mr Berry.' Mr Litchfield shook his head in frustration. 'Conditions today are not that bad, I assure you. Patsy would be given every care until she reached the age of sixteen.'

'Yer can say what yer like, wave all yer legal papers till the cows come 'ome, but we're telling you again, she ain't going nowhere.' Gran couldn't keep her nose out. 'She'd end up being nuffin' but a bloody drudge. Anyway, my boys will back Mr Berry in anything he sees fit t' do. So that's it. Patsy's staying 'ere, where she's lived from the day she was born.'

Suddenly Patsy felt chilled to the bone and she shuddered as that man's answer came back clearly into her mind.

'Madam, raising your voice won't help in the least. You cannot block the system. This child is a waif without kith or kin and with no visible means of support or shelter.'

Florrie's outburst had been fierce. 'That's a damn lie. You've just been told, she's got a good 'ome upstairs where she was born and where she's lived all her life. As to no support, Mr Berry's just told yer he'll see she don't go short, an' there ain't one person in this whole street that would see our Patsy starve.'

By now Ollie was trembling with temper. Quietly but

16

firmly he stated, 'I shall fight every inch of the way to keep Mrs Kent's daughter here among people who love her and will willingly care for her.'

Patsy remembered how she couldn't have taken much more. Frightened to death as to what might happen to her, she was quietly sobbing.

Ollie had stretched out his arms, bringing her forward to stand between his knees. His words were still etched in her mind: 'It will be all right, Patsy, you'll see. I'll move heaven and earth if I have to, to keep you here where you belong. That's a promise.'

And by God, Patsy now muttered to herself, Alexander Berry had certainly made good that promise. Year after year he had proved just how much he loved her. Florrie too. A second mother and more she'd been. And Gran Day and all her large family, they never let the wind blow on her if they could help it. One way and another she had fared far better even than her own mother could have imagined.

The final outcome had been a long time coming, and all the time Ollie had reproached himself. Why hadn't he proposed to Ellen and legally adopted Patsy? Why? Why? God knows he had loved Ellen from the first moment he set eyes on her. In the end, the courts made their decision.

Patsy Kent was to be left in the partial care of Mrs Florence Holmes, and Mr Alexander Berry was delegated to be her guardian.

Patsy could never remember not loving Florrie and Ollie, but on the day that the courts made their final decision known, she loved the pair of them a hundred times more.

Chapter Two

HOW MANY TIMES HAD Patsy wished that Danny Day and his brother Blower had not arranged a street outing to Bushy Park and Hampton Court.

Not that it hadn't been a lovely day out. She and her friend Peggy had so enjoyed the fair. But it was there, on that day, that she had first set eyes on Johnny Jackson.

If only we could put old heads on young shoulders. She had been flattered by his attention and fallen for him hook, line and sinker.

Johnny was a gypsy, the like of which she had never met before. He looked like a foreigner. Dark-skinned, his hair black as coal, a mop of tight curls. His body was firm and taut, his brawny arms heavily tattooed. Oh, he was such a handsome lad, and his happy-go-lucky way of looking at life was infectious. He had pursued her relentlessly, appealing to her to be happy and to laugh with him. The mere sight of him had set her heart pounding, and yet she'd never been able to define exactly what her feelings for Johnny Jackson had been.

One evening, as they walked on the common, his lips had brushed her ear and he'd whispered, 'Will you be my girl?'

She couldn't believe that he was so interested in her. Without any hesitation she had said, 'Yes, I will.' And so years of torment had begun.

During the summer months she'd promised Florrie time and time again she wouldn't meet him. If only she had kept that promise. Sometimes he was so loving towards her. Other times he was horrible, so smug, smirking at her, taunting her for being a virgin: 'A little girl that doesn't want to grow up,' he would mock her.

She was thrilled to have a boyfriend. Someone who constantly told her he loved her. But Florrie was never going to understand. Ollie was worse; he made his feelings well and truly clear.

As for every member of the Day family, their opinion of the Jackson tribe did not bear repeating. 'Lazy bloody tyke' was Gran's name for Johnny, if she referred to him at all; mostly she just sniffed when Patsy was getting ready to go out.

As she remembered all of this, Patsy hated herself and for the umpteenth time regretted that she had never listened to her elders' advice. The Days employed her, just as they had her mother, and to them she was part and parcel of their huge family. So why had she let them all down?

That question had haunted her for years.

Her biggest mistake had been to give in to Johnny's pleading and go to Kent with the whole Jackson tribe to pick hops.

One week she had lasted! She couldn't stand the days, never mind the evenings, when drink was more important than food and the family were drunk well before the pub's closing time. Finally, on the seventh day, Johnny had forced himself on her and that had been the last straw. She left the hop-fields, walking along lanes and across green pastures until at last she found the railway station. What a journey. Guilt was eating away at her. How could she go back? Why hadn't she listened to Florrie or to Ollie's advice? How could she face them? And what about Gran and the job she'd walked out on?

In the depths of despair, she had told herself she had nowhere else to go.

What a sight she must have looked when she arrived on the doorstep. Florrie had taken one look at her. It was enough for her to be able to tell that her beloved Patsy had been to hell and back. Every ounce of love and affection she felt for Patsy had come to the surface. She opened her arms wide. No reproaches, only heartfelt love and rough red hands that shook as she patted Patsy's back with a steady rhythm, just as she had when she'd been a baby.

Her Patsy was home. Nothing else mattered.

Every morning for over a fortnight Florrie had stood at the bottom of the stairs listening to Patsy vomiting. Then it dawned on her. Oh my Gawd, she's pregnant! Oh, the poor kid. It's got t' be that bloody Johnny Jackson. I swear I'll end up swinging for him.

Gran had been even more furious, if that was possible. 'You poor bloody mite. You're still only a child yerself. Why the 'ell didn't we do more t' stop you going hop-picking?' Seeing the look on Patsy's face, Gran's temper lessened. She'd opened her arms and Patsy had flown into them to be rocked back and forth.

Daily Patsy had called herself a daft cow, and that was exactly what she had been. Mad. Utterly mad.

Then she'd made matters ten times worse.

Finding Johnny waiting at the market entrance one evening when she'd finished work, she'd told him about the baby and asked him if he would marry her. She wanted the baby. Had convinced herself that Johnny would be different if they were man and wife. Had completely deluded herself that she could make it work.

God, she'd taken some stick from everyone! But she wouldn't budge. Against all the protests, she and Johnny were married.

A vivid picture of that morning came now into Patsy's mind, and her eyes stung with unshed tears. How could she have been so foolish?

No flowers. No new dress. Yet everywhere had looked extra special that Wednesday morning the first week in December. The roads were white with frost. She was wearing a navy blue skirt and a pale blue jumper, and it was cold, but her winter coat had been too shabby to get married in. Ollie and Florrie had been the only two witnesses. Johnny, being twenty-three, had needed no one's consent. Patsy, still not quite seventeen, had had to apply to the county court for permission to be married, as she was still under their jurisdiction.

Very reluctantly, Florrie had agreed that Patsy could bring her new husband to live with her upstairs in her house. Choked with apprehension, Florrie had said, 'At least that way I can keep an eye on you.'

In less than three weeks Patsy had been asking herself if this husband was really the Johnny with whom she had walked, laughed and been happy. It hadn't taken long for her to realise that Johnny was lazy, selfish and cunning. He didn't wash as often as he should, and, worst of all, he was a liar.

He was in bed when she went to work in the morning, and still lying there when she came home at lunchtime. Evenings she never saw him. The crunch came when he turned up one night, nearly midnight, very much the worse for drink. When she refused to let him make love to her, he hit her, again and again, but it was what he kept saying that had hurt the most.

'How do I know it's my bleeding kid? My family, especially my brothers, they don't think it is.'

21

The weeks turned into months and Johnny changed into a raging bully. The straw that broke the camel's back was when Florrie had reluctantly mentioned that Patsy hadn't been leaving her the rent money.

The bottom had fallen out of Patsy's world; she needed no telling what had happened.

'Don't beat about the bush,' she had ordered Florrie. 'Tell me. How many weeks?'

'Well,' Florrie had pondered, 'you see, luv, the first time it wasn't on the hall table I thought you had forgotten. Then a fortnight ago I guessed you were a bit short an' didn't like to bring the matter up, but I couldn't go on paying the whole lot. I didn't have enough.'

'So how many weeks do I owe?'

'I paid the first two weeks, but today I've had to tell the landlord I'd make it up as soon as I could. I wouldn't 'ave mentioned it now, but he's getting a bit impatient.'

Inwardly Patsy had been seething. She wouldn't do that to Florrie. It was a filthy trick. But at least now she knew why Johnny always came home on Sunday nights though he mostly stayed away the rest of the week.

How heavily she sighed now, and with hindsight she knew she should never have gone near that family. It had not been a wise decision. Anger was the only thing that had given her courage when she had arrived outside the hoardings which surrounded the ground on which the Jacksons lived. She hadn't been prepared for the sight of this place. It was unbelievable. On a huge area of waste ground stood several Romany-type caravans. None appeared to be in a state of good repair. Originally, most likely, they would have been gaily painted, but now the paintwork was cracked and chipped and the front steps broken and dangerous. Beneath the vans, chickens and ducks were picking over what appeared to be rotting fruit and vegetables. The ground was littered with animal droppings. Within seconds of her having stepped through the gate, half the Jackson tribe were grouped around her.

'What the bloody 'ell do you want?' Mrs Jackson grinned wildly.

Patsy had known she was on dangerous ground and was determined to stay calm.

'I'd like to see Johnny, please.'

'Would yer now?' Mrs Jackson said sarcastically. 'Well, I doubt he'll want t' see you, but his van is over there.' A bony finger pointed the direction.

Patsy trembled as she remembered how warily she had had to tread because two scruffy boys were deliberately driving several pigs, scuffing and grunting, towards her.

Johnny stood in the doorway of his van, looking down at her, contempt showing in his face. 'Well, well, well, and what can I do for you?'

She had tried so hard to be bold as she'd said, 'I've come for my rent money, Johnny.'

'Don't know what you're on about,' was what he'd said, but by God, he'd had the grace to look sheepish.

'Please.' Much as it went against the grain, Patsy heard herself plead. 'Don't play games with me. You know very well I always leave my rent money out every Monday morning.'

'So what?' he'd bawled at her.

'So not including the two weeks that Florrie paid for me, it's been missing three weeks. I have to have it back, Johnny, I don't earn enough to lose that kind of money and Florrie can't afford it.'

'Are you calling my son a thief?' The suddenness with which Mrs Jackson had sprung forward had terrified Patsy. 'No son of mine stole your bloody rent money, you cheeky bleeding bitch.'

Frightened half to death, Patsy had done her best to stand her ground. 'There isn't anyone else that could have taken

23

that money. Why won't you admit it, Johnny? You know I can't afford to lose it.'

'Piss off,' was all he'd said.

She'd known from the start that she was wasting her time. Johnny had no principles. She was turning to leave when all hell broke loose. She was being pushed from all sides. She missed her footing and down she went. As she lay on the ground it seemed that every female member of the Jackson tribe was leering down at her. Such vile obscenities, and the malice with which they were being uttered had shocked her.

'Ain't our Johnny's kid; why should he be lumbered with it? Plenty of others were knocking you off. An' another thing, none of us believe our Johnny married you, he wouldn't be so daft.' These accusations were coming from all directions.

Worst of all, though, was Johnny's mother. The words she uttered rankled still, and Patsy knew they would for as long as she lived. At times they felt like a knife being twisted in her heart. 'You're no better than your bloody mother was. A brothel-bred git, that's what she was, an' you're no better. If you're not off my land in two minutes I'll set the bleeding dogs on yer.'

Johnny was now standing looking down at her. 'Please, Johnny,' she'd begged as she struggled to get up on to her knees. His hand whipped out, striking her hard across the side of her face. She hadn't been able to get up. Everyone was hitting her, until she was half senseless, then two men grabbed her and frog-marched her across the ground to the gate and literally threw her on to the pavement. Lying there, she could still hear obscenities ringing in her ears.

How she made it home she never knew. She had vomited down the front of her coat. One eye was so swollen she couldn't see out of it. Her legs and the bottom of her skirt were covered in filth. She had to walk and the time it took her to reach Tooting seemed endless. There was no way a conductor would allow her to board a tram, not the state she was in.

24

The sight of her had broken Florrie's heart. 'Wish I'd never let on about the blasted rent money,' she'd berated herself as she helped Patsy through to the kitchen.

It was to Ollie that she had poured out her heart. The blood had rushed to his face as she had repeated what Mrs Jackson had said of her mother. 'None of them believe it's Johnny's baby I'm carrying either,' she moaned.

Ollie had gasped in horror for more reasons than one. The whole of one side of her face was cut and bruised, showing signs of turning black and blue. Near to her ear were deep lacerations. His anger had become uncontrollable. Florrie had watched in dread as he went into her scullery. His hamlike fist slammed against the wall and deep guttural sounds came from his mouth. Half the street must have heard the threats he was shouting.

'By Christ, I'll see he pays for this! Him and his whole rotten tribe. If it takes to the end of my days, I'll make him sorry he ever laid a finger on my Patsy. And as for letting his mother call my beloved Ellen a brothel-bred git, I'll cut the bastard's tongue out for that.'

Gran and Florrie between them had gently bathed Patsy, put her into a soft clean nightdress and got her into bed.

It was three o'clock in the morning when she'd woken up. Her legs felt as heavy as lead and her shins burned as if hot rods were running through them.

She stretched her feet and screamed. It was cramp, so she'd thought. She had managed to light a candle, and that was when she saw the blood stains. She still remembered how she had groped her way towards the head of the stairs, and then suddenly, without any effort, she was going forward and downward.

She had lost the baby. She had truly thought that Johnny had loved her. He hadn't been forced to marry her. Probably never would have done if they had not gone to the registry office without telling his family.

As always, Ollie, Florrie, Gran and the rest of the Day family had been absolutely marvellous to her. They saw to it that she wanted for nothing.

Except that the one and only thing she really wanted, no one could give her.

She so badly wanted her mum.

Chapter Three

A FREEZING SNOWY WINTER had given way to a long hot summer.

Patsy had stopped wallowing in self-pity and had no more tears left to shed. All the heartaches had faded and there was a maturity about her now. Her life had got back to normal, working six days a week on the market, spending Sundays doing her washing and ironing, and taking long walks in the evenings.

It had been coming up to the August bank holiday weekend when Eddie Owen had come into her life. At this thought she felt herself smiling thankfully; it was a fact that she had appreciated every day that she had since lived.

Eddie was presentable, well dressed, nicely spoken; in fact, when she had first been introduced to him, Patsy had been flustered at meeting this big, unusual man with his cultured voice. However, his movements were awkward. He had been born with a club foot, leaving one leg much shorter than the other. Consequently an ugly iron structure, about three inches in height, had been mounted on to the bottom of his right boot.

Because Danny Day had been taken ill, Eddie Owen had

offered to help the Day brothers out during such a busy period. Blower Day had accepted his offer gladly, suggesting that Patsy accompany Eddie on the delivery rounds.

'You know the places Danny calls on, and I know you've helped him with his books many a time. You could nip up to the big houses, get the orders and run them back to Eddie, couldn't you, Patsy?'

Eddie hadn't been a bit put out by the implication that his club foot would slow him down. 'It would be a good solution, that's if you wouldn't mind.' He had spoken as if he genuinely did want her to go with him.

She and Eddie had worked well together.

At one o'clock they had pulled off the road. Eddie had put the nose-bags on the two horses and left them to feed, while he and Patsy sat on the grass and ate their packed lunch. Patsy recalled how happy she had felt as she told Florrie all about it at the end of that first day.

Next morning, as Eddie had come towards her in the yard, he looked even taller than she had thought he was. His shoulders were so broad and his muscles moved as he walked. But his eyes! The darkest brown, and so large, they dominated his whole face. When he had smiled at her, she'd felt it was such a warm, friendly smile.

They quickly got into a routine. Each lunchtime Patsy sat close to him, her knees pulled up to her chin, learning all about him, engrossed in what he had to say.

One day she'd told him about herself, about Johnny, about the baby she had lost and how Kent was no longer her legal name but she couldn't stand the thought of being known as Patsy Jackson. She talked of Florrie and Ollie so much that Eddie felt he not only knew them, but liked them.

Patsy was at ease with Eddie and had talked to him more than she'd spoken to anyone for months. What few questions

28

he had put to her were asked in such a way that she knew he wasn't being nosy, but that he cared.

Come the holiday Monday, Eddie had asked her if she would like to go out with him and back to his home, which was above a general shop his father owned, to meet his dad and have some tea.

Patsy had hesitated.

'It doesn't matter if you'd rather not,' he had added quietly.

'No, no, it isn't that,' she had quickly protested. 'I always go somewhere with Florrie and Ollie when it's a bank holiday. Only a tram ride, or something like that. Flo especially will be looking forward to it.'

Eddie's face had brightened.

'Listen, listen to me. Why don't you go out, but bring them to my home for a late tea? My dad would be pleased to have the company.'

Patsy grinned to herself as she remembered how she had warned him that Florrie was a bit of a character.

'I can't wait to meet them. You will come, won't you?' And he'd laughed, not knowing what he'd let himself in for.

It had been the beginning of a great friendship. Florrie's first impression had been that Frank Owen and his son Eddie were good 'uns, and her opinion hadn't altered in all these years. Naturally, having seen the Owens' lovely home, which to Flo's amazement even had a bathroom, she had to start thinking about match-making.

Ollie was far more cautious. He fully agreed that Eddie was a fine young man and his father a good, likeable gentleman. How he wished things could be more straightforward for his Patsy. It was, and always had been, his heart's desire to see her happy.

Things had to be allowed to take their course, but lurking in the background was Johnny Jackson – and legally she was still married to him. Ollie couldn't help feeling that Johnny might adopt the attitude that even though he didn't want Patsy, he'd make it damn difficult for anyone else to have her. Taking into account that the Owens owned a thriving business, and their home alone proved that they weren't short of a bob or two, if anything came of a relationship between Eddie and Patsy, Johnny would smell money. Ollie told Florrie he'd stake his life on it.

Funny, Patsy was thinking now, how things had turned out. At that point in time there was no way that Ollie could possibly have known how accurate his premonition would turn out to be, or to what lengths Johnny and his tribe would go.

Life had become good and Patsy had been happy.

She and Eddie became firm friends. They went for walks, picnicked by the river and occasionally went to Brighton, where Patsy watched, fascinated, as the sea rolled in.

Eddie told her he had been born in the main bedroom above the shop. Because of his withered leg, his mother would not allow him to attend the local school, preferring to send him to a private establishment where he had received a good education. Even so, he had to endure taunts from the other boys, who would call him cripple-boy, gammy leg, or iron foot. Because he was unable to take part in school sports, he had become withdrawn, living his life under his mother's protective wing.

It had been from his father that Patsy had learned more intimate details.

Frank Owen told her that his wife was to be pitied more than blamed. True, she had cosseted and molly-coddled Eddie, but he stressed that it had been a traumatic experience for her when, at his birth, the doctor had informed her that their son had a withered, shortened leg. Mrs Owen's mind had immediately registered 'cripple', despite the fact that he was otherwise a fine, healthy baby. She'd rejected all suggestions that her son should be seen by a specialist who could possibly operate on his foot.

Since the death of his mother, Eddie had stretched himself more. He had enrolled at college for several courses and proved himself to be academically very bright.

By now Eddie was a regular visitor to Strathmore Street. The Day family approved of him, and Florrie was more than content. Ollie had taken pleasure in constantly hearing Patsy laughing, but he still had misgivings. The fact remained that Patsy was already married.

Sadly, one Sunday afternoon in April, Frank Owen had suffered a stroke, slipped into a coma and died peacefully.

The reality of his father's death didn't hit Eddie until after the funeral. His visits to Patsy stopped, and she was unable to understand why.

After Eddie had been absent a full week, Ollie had made the decision to take Patsy and Florrie to Colliers Wood to visit him. On arrival they got a shock. Eddie not only looked upset; he looked really ill. Florrie had thought it best to drag Patsy off to the kitchen and leave the two men alone.

'Have you thought about opening up the shop?' Ollie had started the conversation apprehensively.

Eddie made no reply.

'The perishable goods will have to be thrown out.'

'So what?' Eddie's reply was sharp.

His tone of voice saddened Ollie. 'Try telling me what your plans are,' he encouraged him.

Florrie had deliberately left the kitchen door ajar, and as the time passed and Eddie finally opened up to Ollie, both Patsy and she wept silently. It hurt even now to recall Eddie's words, and yet at the time they had made Patsy's heart swell with love for this great big lonely man.

Eddie had heaved a great sigh before saying, 'It's Patsy

31

really. I love her so much and my dearest wish is to marry her. I know it must sound daft, but I fell in love with her the moment I set eyes on her in that market yard. She was so different. So small; beautiful rich copper hair and green eyes. I was captivated from that first moment. My views have never changed. She *is* different. She has a kind nature, she's fun to be with, it never seems to bother her that I have a deformity and she never pities me. I can't stand pity. I know we can't be married, yet I can't stand the thought of living without her.'

Ollie had thought hard for a moment before saying, 'Well, why don't you seek professional advice?'

'I'll think about it,' Eddie had promised. Then quietly he added, 'Ollie, you really do care for Patsy, don't you?'

'As if she were my own flesh and blood,' Ollie assured him.

He had known for a long time that Eddie loved Patsy – it was in his every action and every look – yet he wasn't quite prepared for Eddie's next decision.

'I'm going to ask Patsy if she will marry me. If she says yes, I'll take her to the solicitor's and we'll see what he has to say about her getting a divorce.'

Mr Topple, partner in the firm of London solicitors who had taken care of the Owens' affairs over a long period of time, studied Patsy's face and then took the bull by the horns.

'Divorce for you, Mrs Jackson, would be the obvious answer. Unfortunately, as the law stands, that could prove to be difficult. Unless of course you are very rich. Very few working-class women have been known to bring a petition.'

Patsy had looked so bewildered that Mr Topple had felt at a loss.

'Oh yes,' he had continued. 'You may not want to believe it, but the law can work entirely differently for the rich.

Unfair, I know, but true, I assure you. There was a time when the church courts dealt with all matrimonial matters and those who wanted a divorce had to obtain a special Act of Parliament. The law has been changed slightly to allow a husband to obtain a divorce, but only on the grounds of his wife's adultery. A few society ladies have been known to engage a barrister to plead their case to the church courts, but even then there is only one ground on which she may do so, and again that is proving the act of adultery.'

Patsy had had to swallow hard before she could reply.

'My husband left me, Mr Topple. He never wanted me, he never provided for me and he was very cruel. Yet unless he agrees, I have to stay tied to him for the rest of my life. Is that what you're saying?'

'Have you approached your husband on the subject?'

Before Patsy could answer, Eddie spoke up clearly. 'No, but I have, and to sum up Mr Jackson's attitude is easy. He doesn't want Patsy but he's going to do his damnedest to make sure that no one else is able to have her. His whole family were adamant. No divorce.'

When Patsy heard that, she looked at Eddie with even greater admiration. He had faced the Jackson clan, on his own!

'There is something more pressing that has to be dealt with.' Mr Topple was now all businesslike. 'This only concerns you, Edward.'

Patsy had made to rise.

Eddie checked her. 'Stay, Patsy, please. All my future plans include Patsy; if you've no objection, Mr Topple, I would like her to stay.'

'In that case, you should consider reopening your late father's business with her help.'

Each of them had shown a different reaction to this bombshell: while Eddie's face glowed with enthusiasm, Patsy's eyes showed doubt.

Mr Topple pressed the point. 'If, at a later date, you decide to sell the property, which is entirely freehold, the market value would be greatly increased were the business functioning. On the other hand, should you be so unwise as to leave the premises lying idle, the property would deteriorate, thereby diminishing in value. Another point to consider is that there would be no good will to sell. If you were both to decide to reopen the business, it could add considerably to your resources.'

Very quietly Eddie had asked, 'Are you suggesting what I think you are?'

There had been a long pause before he got his answer.

'Well, yes, I suppose I am recommending that you set up home together.' Then, looking directly at Patsy, the solicitor asked, 'How would you feel about changing your surname? Whereas divorce seems out of the question, there is no earthly reason why you should not take Owen as your surname.'

Patsy had had to take a deep breath before she could look directly at Eddie, and then to her shame she had blurted her thoughts out loud.

'I might just as well call myself the Queen of Sheba. The neighbours would still know me as Patsy Jackson, and can you imagine what my life would be like? Married to one man and living in sin with another!'

Mr Topple had been kindness itself.

'Patsy, we would use a formal method of legalising your change of surname. A legal deed and you would become Mrs Owen.'

Even all these years on, the memory made her temper rise.

Oh, if only it had been as simple as that.

Patsy agreed to move to Colliers Wood, live with Eddie and help to run the shop.

'Gawd help yer,' was Gran's only comment.

Not Florrie; she arrived, removed her hat, donned her floral pinafore and took charge. Around Patsy's waist, Florrie pinned a coarse sack. Eddie was ordered to wear a khaki-coloured dust coat. Between the three of them, wonders were performed. Shelves were scrubbed, cupboards cleaned out, windows washed inside and out. Old stock was thrown away. The counter was polished until it gleamed and the floor was scrubbed until Florrie announced, 'Good, you've used elbow grease; anyone could eat their dinner off that floor.'

At last a cup of tea, and when their cups had been drained, Eddie went and stood by Florrie's side. 'Thanks, Flo . . . for everything.' He emphasised his words by pressing her hand tightly between his own.

Each knew what the other was thinking. Eddie wasn't just saying thanks for all her hard work. He was telling her he was grateful that she hadn't made a fuss over Patsy coming to live with him.

It had been a good day. A good beginning.

The next day they opened the shop for business.

They had deluded themselves. The straightforward blissful life they had each imagined was not to be. In those days it was not unheard of for a man to live with a woman without marriage, but it was rare, and although grossly unfair, it was always the women that were made to feel shameful. Patsy had expected a measure of bad feeling, but nothing like on the scale which she received.

'You got one 'usband already. You've only cottoned on to Owen because he's got money. Why else would a hussy like you take up with a cripple?' These and far worse were the kind of taunts she had to put up with daily.

For a whole month Patsy had done her best. Sworn at, spat at, kicked and robbed. What chance had she stood? She finally gave up when the Jacksons came into the shop, demanded to see Patsy, then laughed in Florrie's face when she told them Patsy wasn't there.

Customers had joined in what had turned into a right old schemozzle, which had ended up with Florrie getting arrested.

Enough was enough.

Eddie boarded up the shop. Florrie took Patsy home with her and Eddie accepted the offer of a room in Ollie's house.

Realistic as always, Ollie had sighed in despair and asked, 'Did either of you really believe it would be any different? Right from the start I warned you that Johnny Jackson is jealous. He begrudges Patsy any happiness, let alone prosperity. Neither he nor his tribe is going to let you or your customers forget the fact that no matter what name Patsy goes by, he, not you, Eddie, is her legal husband. He holds the whip hand by refusing to agree to a divorce, but his day will come. I'll see t' that if it's the last thing I ever do.'

That was not the end of it. Johnny and his brothers made Patsy's life hell. In the end Eddie came up with what he considered the perfect solution. They would leave the country. Emigrate to Australia. Once there, he assured her, they would be able to live openly as husband and wife with no one being any the wiser.

Every last detail had been dealt with.

The people of Strathmore Street and the market traders had given them a never-to-be-forgotten party. At this point the memories she was recalling became too much for Patsy and she had to shake her head and wipe away the tears. Years had passed, yet it was all so vivid in her mind, it might have happened yesterday.

She adored Eddie. Still did to this day. Had wanted to spend the rest of her life with him. Yet on that last day, when they were all ready to leave, there had been a but!

Such a big but.

How on earth could she walk away from all these kind folk? The huge Day family who regarded her as one of their own. Rough and ready they certainly were, but each and every one of them had a heart of gold. But the overriding factor had been Florrie Holmes and Alexander Berry. They were the only family she had ever known. How could she put thousands of miles between her and the two people who had loved and cared for her from the day she had been born?

Australia!

All she knew was that it was on the other side of the world.

She couldn't do it. She just couldn't.

Eddie had been absolutely marvellous. Freed her from all feelings of guilt.

They had stopped at the corner of the street to turn and wave goodbye. Eddie had looked into her eyes, still enormous and brilliant green, but brimming with tears.

He couldn't do it either.

One gentle push and she was running back to Ollie, Florrie and Gran.

Several times during that day, Eddie assured her that come what may, they were staying where they belonged. How could they not? All the women were hugging and kissing her, while Eddie's hand had been shaken and his back slapped so many times that he'd begun to feel dizzy. 'Good on yer, lad. No one ever won a battle by running away,' seemed to be the general opinion of the men.

Grandad had the last word. 'Just settle where it suits you, boy. Take care of our Patsy an' you'll be all right. Don't let the Jacksons get the better of you. We'll sort the lot of them out, when the time is right. Bloody load of thieves and rogues the lot of them.'

Eddie had told her afterwards that he'd had to struggle to keep a straight face as he pictured the Jackson tribe in full flight with the whole of the Day family in hot pursuit.

Bringing her thoughts back to the present for the moment, Patsy said aloud, 'It was the right decision to stay put.'

Chapter Four

SOMETIMES PATSY HAD TO pinch herself. They had settled down to such a good and happy life. She'd had a hard job to believe it was all true.

Eddie was sure no man had ever loved a woman more than he loved Patsy. He had only one regret, a regret that was equally shared by Patsy. If only they could be married. To legally be husband and wife was their dearest wish.

Having sold the shop, Eddie had bought a large house not far from Clapham Common. Navy Street was a short side road with tall houses that had spacious rooms spread out on three floors. There were two inside lavatories and a bathroom.

The top floor was let to a single lady, referred to by the estate agent as a sitting tenant, and because the premises weren't being sold with full vacant possession, the asking price had been that much lower.

Life is full of strange surprises. The tenant, a lady named Kitty Palmer, turned out to have been at school with Florrie Holmes.

Kitty had been worried as to who would buy the property. Florrie had soon put her mind at rest over a cup of tea.

'Two of the best,' she'd declared. 'You'd go a long way to find a better couple than my Patsy and her Eddie.'

It had worked out great for all of them.

Kitty wasn't lonely any more and Patsy soon found her to be a good, kind, caring lady. Life was wonderful, and even more so when on 2 April 1924 their first son, Alexander Frank Owen, was born. But the fact that she wasn't legally Eddie's wife in the eyes of the law still hurt. Patsy shuddered at the memory of the times she had changed the subject when the question of how long they had been married came up.

Two things stood out in Patsy's mind about the year 1926. One was the general strike, which lasted only nine days yet brought unbelievable suffering to the poor miners. It had been several months before the pits were working again, and then only on the employers' terms.

The other event had her smiling. On 20 August she had given birth to another healthy son, David Edward Owen.

By the time the boys were old enough to go to school, the family had grown with the addition of twin girls, one to be named Ellen after her dear mother; and because they thought Emma went so well with Ellen, that was the name they gave to their other daughter.

How grateful they had felt, and still did. Two sons and two daughters.

It was getting towards Christmas 1928 when Ollie had received the first of a series of letters from a law firm based in Liverpool informing him that his brother, Mr Jack Ronald Berry, had died in New Zealand.

Both Patsy and Eddie had fired questions at Ollie, but he hadn't known all the answers himself.

'Jack was very much older than me,' he had told them. 'He left home, went to sea when I was still a lad.'

'Did you never hear from him?' Patsy was eager to hear

the ins and outs of this missing brother who had never turned up since she had known Ollie, and was now dead.

'Yes, we did for a while. Coloured postcards from all around the world. I'm sure I showed them to you, Patsy, when you were a little girl.'

'Well, what happened?' Eddie had quietly asked.

Ollie had shrugged his shoulders. 'We seemed to lose track of him. When my parents died, I did everything I could to trace him, but all my attempts came to nothing.'

That first letter certainly opened up a can of worms!

Although Jack Berry had died in New Zealand, he had had business interests in many countries. Ollie had been advised to contact the the firm of solicitors in person. Apparently there were a lot of legal formalities to be gone through, and as Jack Berry's only surving relative, Ollie's signature was needed on several documents.

Ollie was away in Liverpool almost two months.

Dinner the night he came home was a happy meal, a real family gathering. Naturally Florrie was there. She not only wanted to know what had kept Ollie in Liverpool for so long, she wanted to know every last detail when it came to discussion of Jack Berry's affairs.

Ollie was strangely uncommunicative about giving details. 'There's not much to tell,' he had insisted. 'Heck of a lot of sorting out for the legal fellows to do. Seems Jack really did see the world. Had his fingers in all sorts of pies in all sorts of places. That's about as much as I know at the moment.'

Further than that, he would not be drawn.

It was from a Peter Crawford, who had flown over to England from Australia, that Ollie learned the most about his brother's affairs. Jack had made Peter manager of J & B Enterprises years before. He had trusted him one hundred per cent. Peter spent hours going into details with Ollie and explaining that although the company's interests were pretty scattered, the main offices were in Melbourne. One piece of information, which Ollie later relayed, made them all laugh. One of the main reasons why, as the only beneficiary, Alexander Berry's inheritance would be so great was that a gold mine owned by his brother and long since written off had suddenly struck a rich seam.

Ollie had not been aware of it when Peter had made that first visit, but as the years passed Peter proved himself to be not only an invaluable businessman, but a great friend of the family.

Christmas Eve, 1930. The sky looked full of snow, but it had been far too cold for snow and Ollie had remarked that it was more than likely that everything would freeze.

Patsy remembered that morning so vividly. She had been bending over the cot, loosening the covers, checking that the twins hadn't got their noses pressed into the pillows.

'Look, will you stop fussing and sit down?' Ollie had spoken to her as he used to when she was a child. 'I need to talk to you seriously.'

She had straightened up, turned to look at him, her eyes full of questions.

Speaking very sternly, Ollie had said, 'Now there's no need to look at me like that. Just come and sit at the table, and listen to what I have to say.'

Placing a large manilla envelope on the table between them, his voice was very firm as he said, 'We have to talk about the Jacksons.'

Even today, remembering, she felt the colour drain from her face. She had felt so resentful. Why in heaven's name had he to bring that dratted family up? At that moment in time, how could she possibly have dreamed what a great gift her darling Ollie was offering her, or to what lengths he had gone to make it possible?

He had drawn an official-looking document from the

envelope, and without giving her the chance to say so much as a word, he started to talk.

'This document is a land deed. You remember the waste ground at Mitcham where the Jacksons lived?'

Patsy hadn't answered. She didn't want to be reminded of Johnny and his family. Not then. Not ever.

'That ground belonged to the Coal and Coke Company. The Jacksons may have lived on it for years, but they were squatters.'

'So?' Her curiosity had been roused by then.

With a straight face Ollie continued: 'The company decided they had had enough. They put the land up for sale, and I bought it.'

'What?' Patsy recalled how she had hissed the word out. 'Whatever for? What can you possibly want with a piece of rotten old waste land? If you're thinking of revenge by throwing the Jacksons off that land, how are you going to go about it? You said yourself that the Coal and Coke Company have been trying for years to evict them. If a great company like that couldn't get them off, how are you going to manage it?'

'There is more to tell,' he confessed.

'Well, come on then,' she grinned at him. 'Let's have the rest of this story.'

'I had a contracting firm close off the part where the Jacksons had their caravans, and on the other part of the ground, the bit that lies well back from the road, I've had three houses built.'

Patsy didn't need to be reminded of how she had stared at him in total disbelief.

'I never revealed my identity. The Jacksons have no idea who the purchaser was. Mr Topple conducted all the legal transactions for me. He also asked the courts for an eviction order against them.'

Patsy had still kept quiet. Yet inside she was laughing

43

merrily. What a man Ollie was! He'd sworn years ago that he would pay back all the hurt she had suffered at the hands of the Jacksons.

It seemed as though Ollie had been able to read her mind, for he now savoured the rest of the telling. 'The courts didn't refuse the application because I offered the Jacksons alternative accommodation.'

Now her mind raced ahead of him. He was mad! He had to be. He'd evicted the Jacksons from what was now his land and put them into brand-new houses. She couldn't see the point. They'd never pay the rent.

'Does Eddie know what you've done?'

'Yes, he does. Mind you, when I told him this morning what I was going to do today, he did say rather you than me. In fact, he told me to be ready to duck!' Having said that, Ollie unfolded the document and laid it flat between them.

Now Patsy was crying softly as in her mind she could still hear the love that had been so evident in Ollie's voice as he had told her: 'Rightly or wrongly, Patsy, this is my Christmas present to you. The whole thing, land and houses, notarised in your name. That tribe that were so cruel to you are now living in houses which belong to you.'

The silence that followed had seemed to go on for ever.

Finally Ollie had spoken. 'Take your time, my love. All my instincts told me I was doing right. Now, my darling girl, it's up to you. Sit tight for a while, give it a lot of thought, is about the best advice I can give you.'

They had got to their feet and Ollie had kissed her. Just a peck on the cheek, but that small action said it all. Except he had softly added, 'Just remember, Patsy, you owe the Jacksons nothing.'

Christmas had come and gone.

Patsy had lost count of the number of times she had asked

44

herself could she do it? If she could make the deed justify the end then she had to!

She'd been having trouble breathing when she finally found herself standing on the very spot where the Jacksons had lived for so long. Tall hoardings no longer enclosed the site. The ground was covered in stubbly grass and stinging nettles grew everywhere. Her heart had been thumping against her ribs. She'd told herself not to panic. Not now she had come this far. Treading warily she had walked along the narrow lane until the ground sloped downwards. From where she had stood she could look down on three two-storey houses. They hadn't looked in any way pretentious. They were just solidly built ordinary dwellings.

She heard the sound of dogs rushing towards her before she saw them. They came charging at her, three of them, all Alsatians, and skidded to a halt forming a semicircle around her. The noise of their barking was deafening and their fangs had terrified her.

'Down, down, I say, and stop that blasted racket.'

Thank God for that. Patsy had breathed a sigh of relief as a man came into sight. As he drew nearer he'd yelled again, 'Down! Down, I tell yer.' The three dogs dropped down on to their bellies, their front paws spread flat each side of their heads, their ferocious eyes still focused on Patsy. She hadn't dared to move.

The man was very close now, and every instinct told Patsy that he was a Jackson. He was scruffy-looking, his collarless shirt open almost to his waist showed a heavily tattooed chest, and black braces hung loosely down over corduroy trousers.

She trembled now as she remembered just how frightened she had been.

'It's yer own damn fault, whoever you are,' the man had yelled at the top of his voice. 'You've no sodding business being on this land. You're trespassing! Me dogs are only doing their job.'

'I'm well aware that this is private land,' she'd said as bravely as she could. 'I'm here to see Johnny Jackson.'

The man had looked perplexed as he stared at her. She was very well dressed, her tone of voice was one of authority, and by the look of her she wasn't hard up.

'Well?' was all that she'd managed to say.

The man thrust his chin out towards her. 'Who the bloody 'ell are yer? Here t' see my bruvver! You've got nerve, I'll give yer that, but take my advice an' sling yer bleeding hook. We don't 'old with the likes of you around 'ere.'

He had raised his voice and shouted the last few words, which had set the dogs off snarling again, but they lay where they were, making no attempt to move.

Doing her best to keep her voice steady, Patsy had said, 'That's what your family told me nine years ago, that they didn't hold with the likes of me.'

'What!' he'd scowled. 'Don't know what you're on about. Go on, clear off, before I really set the dogs on you.'

Patsy managed a cynical smile. 'Your mother used the same threat when I was here last. Now, are you going to fetch your brother or shall I walk down to the house and find him?'

'Who the bloody 'ell are you?' he asked again, but a lot of the boldness had gone from his tone.

Patsy would have loved to walk past him, and she might have done if it weren't for the three dogs that still lay so alarmingly close to her. Instead, she'd stood up straight and, sounding a lot braver than she felt, told him, 'I'm Patsy Kent, that was. A brothel-bred git, according to your mother.'

He rushed at her, letting out a deep growl, and grabbed her.

Patsy had truly believed her time had come. He was going to kill her, and if he didn't the dogs would. She had felt his hot stale breath and felt his fingers digging into her neck.

The dogs were out of control now, leaping up in the air, snarling and panting. She really had thought she was fighting for her life as she kicked and struggled to break free.

'Cut it out! Do you 'ear me? Cut it out.' The shouts were coming from down the lane as another man came tearing towards them. He stopped suddenly, as if unsure what to do. 'Let go of her,' he ordered, grabbing the other man, who was still holding on to Patsy, and pulling him away. 'Now lock those dogs up. Go on, lock them away, before they really hurt someone.'

Patsy staggered as the first man released his hold. She'd had to fight to get herself under control and she still had to gasp to get her breath. Her assailant gave a low whistle, turned and went back the way he had come, the dogs racing ahead of him. She found herself suddenly free, and as she looked at her rescuer, she knew without a doubt that she was facing the man who legally was still her husband. Johnny Jackson.

Time had not dealt kindly with him. His thick black hair still grew long at the sides and back of his head, but the crown was shiny and bald. His once good-looking face was different; he must at some time have broken his nose and it had failed to heal properly. For a while he watched her. Then a look of total disbelief came to his face.

'You . . . Patsy?' he stammered.

'Yes, Johnny, it's me,' she'd snapped.

A gloating smirk had spread about his mouth as he eyed her up and down from top to toe.

'Ain't done bad fer yerself, 'ave yer, Patsy?' His voice was filled with sarcasm, and when he threw back his head and roared with laughter, her hand had itched to swipe him around the face, but she was too busy trying to wipe away the blood that was trickling down her legs from where the dogs had dug their claws into her.

'You should 'ave known better,' Johnny said, still grinning.

'Remember? We always guard our land with dogs.'

Without stopping to think she said sharply, 'It's not your land!'

'Oh yeah,' he'd sneered, 'and what would you know about it?'

'A lot more than you think,' she told him firmly, and had the satisfaction of seeing the grin disappear from his face and a baffled look come into his eyes.

Keeping her voice as steady as she could, Patsy had pressed her point home.

'I own this land!'

Johnny Jackson might have been only a fairground worker, but he was no fool. Instinctively he knew she was telling the truth. She'd given him no time to react to her statement. Boldly now she added, 'I also own all three houses which you and your family are living in.'

It had been a real joy to watch his face explode in anger.

'You bitch, you bloody bitch.' His words came out as a snarl, and his arm came forward and upwards with his fist clenched tight.

Patsy had moved quickly, her manner as ferocious as his now because she knew she held the upper hand. 'You lay one finger on me,' she'd screamed, 'and I'll have the police here so fast you won't know what's hit you. I'll also see that every damn one of you Jacksons are evicted from my properties.'

'Jesus Christ Almighty!' He brought his clenched fist up again, but it was his own forehead he thumped. 'You bloody vindictive cow!' he'd roared at her.

'Vindictive! Well, if that's not a case of the pot calling the kettle black, I don't know what is. For years you've never wanted me but you've made damn sure no one else could have me. I don't give a monkey's what you or your family call me now, but I'll tell you this, Johnny, you'd better mark every word I say. Either you do, to the letter, everything I'm going to ask of you, or I'll see that neither you nor one single member of your family goes on living in my houses.'

They were both shaking with anger, but it was his eyes that fell away first.

'Right,' Patsy said, with a confidence she was far from feeling. 'Now that we understand each other, shall we go down to one of my houses and have a talk?'

As she walked down the lane behind Johnny, Patsy had shuddered, knowing there was probably worse to come. But she had dug her hands deep into her coat pockets and renewed her determination.

Patsy had looked around the messy room in disgust.

'D'yer want t' take yer coat off? Looks expensive but yer won't get it pinched.' There was laughter again in Johnny's eyes and she knew he was mocking her.

She refused his offer. He had already removed his own coat. They sat down opposite each other and the sight of him had sickened her.

His calico shirt had no collar, but a brass stud hung limply from the top buttonhole. His sleeves were rolled up beyond his elbows, and the well-remembered tattoos were visible on his forearms. His eyes, especially when he laughed, still held some of that boyish charm that had captivated her so long ago, but his body had run to fat.

He had given her a roguish grin, but Patsy had felt that it was sheer bravado when he'd said, 'Me missus 'as got her eye on you.'

Patsy had trembled as the thought struck her that maybe his mother was in the house. She certainly didn't want to come face to face with her.

Twisting her body round, she'd seen a woman lolling against the door-jamb, lighting one cigarette from the stub of another. She was no beauty, and certainly not well groomed. Her body was thin to the point of scrawniness.

Her rough red hands were dry and knobbly. Long ginger-coloured hair was parted at the centre and scraped back into a plait. Her face had a pinched look, and it was obvious she wasn't going to trust Patsy further than she could throw her. However, compared to Johnny she appeared clean, respectable and tidy.

The woman spoke first. 'I was about t' ask who the 'ell you are but I guess I don't 'ave to. You're the biddy who tried to foster her bastard off on Johnny. What d'yer want this time? From the look of yer, there ain't much that you're in need of.'

The woman deliberately blew a cloud of smoke in Patsy's direction and Johnny threw back his head and laughed uproariously. Then, in what sounded like a proud declaration, he nodded at Patsy and said, 'That's Mary, me wife.'

It was Mary who shouted now. 'Yeah, an' we've got five young 'uns, all legal Jacksons. So whatever bloody trouble you've come 'ere to stir up t'day, you can damn well forget it an' sling yer bloody hook.'

Patsy considered this statement and inwardly smiled. It was more than she could have hoped for. Mary and Johnny had played right into her hands.

Mary stubbed her cigarette out in a tin ashtray and her voice was frightening for Patsy to listen to. 'Don't let my skinniness fool you. I'm tough enough to 'andle a couple of big bruisers any day. An' you . . . I could kill yer as quick as look at yer, an' I will too if you don't soon state what you've come about, and then get going back t' yer sodding fancy man. Anyone's only got to look at yer to see some poor bugger is keeping yer. You've got two minutes before I take yer by the scruff of yer neck an' throw you out of my 'ouse.'

To this day Patsy had never known just how she had managed to hold her temper in check. She had felt furious.

'Tell her, Johnny!' She rapped the words out sharply at him.

Mary came forward, fists clenched.

Johnny jumped to his feet and stood between them. His features were twisted with anger as he snarled at Patsy, 'You tell 'er.'

No emotion showed on Patsy's face. She had remained outwardly calm as she said, 'I am still to this day Johnny's legal wife. But more to the point, this is not your house that you are threatening to throw me out of. It is *my* house. In fact, all three houses in which the Jackson family are living are owned outright by me.'

You could have heard a pin drop. Mary reached for her packet of cigarettes and box of matches and threw one word at Johnny.

'True?'

He only mumbled gruffly, 'Would seem so.'

Patsy allowed the silence to linger. She made sure her words had sunk in before she spoke again, and when she did her voice had let them both know that she meant every single word.

'Seeing as how none of you have bothered to pay me any rent for almost six months, I will be quite within my rights to have the whole lot of you evicted from my properties.'

Patsy flinched now as she remembered Mary's reaction.

'Yer whore! On the game up in the city knocking off all the rich guys. How else would yer 'ave got the sodding money to dream up this airy-fairy idea to get yer revenge on Johnny 'cos he couldn't stand the sight of yer?'

She really was out of control, and as frightened as Patsy had been, she still felt a little bit sorry for her.

She had braced herself and told them both straight, 'Where the money came from is no concern of yours, and my airy-fairy idea, as you call it, is for real. That much you had better believe. If the whole tribe of you wish to go on

51

living in my houses, then Johnny has to agree to allow me to divorce him.'

'What d'yer wanna a divorce for, after all these years?' Johnny had sounded furious. 'We were never wed properly anyway. Sorry an' all that, but you ain't dragging me through no law courts. Not on yer life you're not. Can't be bothered. Just 'cos yer come into a bloody fortune you ain't getting me mixed up with lawyers an' such like.'

'That's telling 'er,' Mary had encouraged him.

Patsy had sighed heavily before saying, 'All right. But you can't have it both ways.'

'And what's that supposed to mean?' Johnny's voice had been heavy with sarcasm.

Patsy opened her handbag, took out a business card and held it out until it almost touched the tip of Johnny's nose. 'This is the name and address of my solicitor. You have a choice. Either you pay him a visit before the end of this week, do exactly as he asks, sign any documents he puts in front of you, or come next Monday morning I will have the bailiffs here and every last one of you will be cleared off my land and out of my houses.'

Johnny had come to his feet like an uncurled spring. Anger flamed his cheeks, his clenched fists beat the air and his voice was sheer blood and thunder as he had roared at her, 'You bleeding cow! You mean it, don't yer? You'd put us, our kids and all the family, out on the streets. Gawd above, you've turned out to be a spiteful bloody bitch an' no mistake.'

Patsy hadn't been able to resist having the last word.

'Just tell your mother that this brothel-bred git will expect her rent to be paid regularly on the dot every week from now on. That's if she wants to remain living in one of my properties. And by the way, the same goes for the tenants of all three of my houses. Goodbye, Johnny.'

Mary had been strangely quiet as Patsy had made her way

down the short hall and let herself out of the front door.

Men, women, teenagers and children stood huddled in the doorways of both the other two houses. Hatred was apparent in the eyes of the adults, but the time when that family could browbeat her was long gone. All she had wished for as she walked away was to be shot of the lot of them. To wipe clean away the period of her life that had been entwined with theirs. Ollie had had the forethought to give her the wherewithal for this scheme. Would it work? For the rest of that week she had never stopped praying that it would. All she had ever wanted, from the moment she had set eyes on Eddie, was to be his wife.

Once Johnny had indeed visited the solicitor, both Eddie and Ollie had done their best to reassure her that there would be no further complications. Eddie, in his usual practical fashion, had said, 'How many more times do we have to tell you, my darling, money speaks all languages. This barrister is costing a small fortune and that is why you can be sure that there will be no last-minute hitches.'

Nevertheless, Patsy had spent sleepless nights worrying over what ordeals she might have to face in court.

When, finally, the day arrived, Ollie was there by her side, holding on tightly to her hand, and she had soon found out that she had no need to get upset.

Earlier, in the lobby, her barrister, in what had seemed to Patsy almost a conspiratorial whisper, had informed her that he had asked the court's discretion as to her own adultery. Her cheeks had flamed up as he had patted her arm and said, 'Far better to admit to cohabitation now than to have some busybody coming forward, claiming to show cause as to why the decree nisi should not be made absolute.'

Johnny had admitted that he had cohabited with an Irish woman named Mary Best for seven years, and that they had five children.

It had suddenly all been over quite quickly, and the judge had granted her a decree nisi.

And then had come what seemed the longest wait of all.

On New Year's Eve 1931, the world had been in a deep depression; there was wholesale unemployment, bringing with it the evils of poverty and poor health among the working classes. But that night the crowd that had gathered in Strathmore Street hadn't cared. They were there to celebrate with Mr and Mrs Owen, who had been married that day.

As Big Ben had rung out the old year and brought in 1932, Eddie had whispered to his wife, 'Not many folk have their four children in their wedding photographs.'

Patsy had felt so happy, yet she had burst into tears. She could hardly believe it. She really was Mrs Edward Owen.

Gran and Florrie had looked at each other in amazement.

Patsy told herself that she would never, as long as she lived, forget what Gran had said that night.

'Well, I'll be buggered! Supposed to be the happiest day of her bloody life, and what does she do? She stands there bawling.'

BOOK TWO

1964

Chapter One

PATSY'S THOUGHTS CENTRED ON her children as she returned to her desk, put her reading glasses on and stared at the pile of papers that lay in front of her. Just then the door swung open and her daughter-in-law Vicky entered bringing Patsy back from her musings with a bump.

Right from the very start the whole family had taken to Vicky Baldwin. She was a girl who had had a rough start in life if ever there was one. Brought up in an orphanage, without a single clue as to who her parents had been, she had been turfed out to earn her own living as soon as she had reached the age of sixteen. She had lived in one hostel after another. Yet she had taken all the knocks that life had thrown at her and had still come up smiling. It had been a good day when Ollie had offered her a job and she had come into their lives. Such a happy person was Vicky. Fairly tall, with light brown hair and a freckly face, her pale blue eyes sparkled with merriment whenever she showed off her cheeky grin.

The war had forced all the children to grow up before their time.

From the age of fourteen, Alex had learned to manipulate any situation to his own advantage. Always dragging his younger brother David along with him. Shortages for the family had been greatly eased because of their conniving. But it wasn't only me and mine that benefited, Patsy reminded herself. Alex had always seen that neighbours, especially old folk, were given a share in whatever he got his hands on, but then that was part and parcel of day-to-day living during those dark, terrible war years.

Londoners helped one another. That applied in particular to Gran and what was left of the Day family. Most of Gran's boys were in the Services; her youngest son, the one they'd always called Sonnie, was never far from their thoughts. He had been drafted into the Air Training Corps. During the awful months that followed when London was relentlessly bombarded by German planes, Churchill had said it was the RAF's finest hour, but as families had daily listened to the evening news on the wireless most folk thought it was a case of triumph and tragedy. Sadly it was the latter for Gran and Jack Day because their son never came back home.

During the war years Gran's daughter Queenie and all her daughters-in-law had no choice but to carry on the business to the best of their ability, despite the shortages of fruit and vegetables as well as a good many other commodities.

Thinking back, Patsy tried to remember when she had first noticed that Grannie Day suddenly seemed to have aged. She couldn't pin-point the date but at least Gran had lived to see the end of the war and life return to some sort of normality.

Come February 1952, sadness struck the nation, and Patsy herself, in a very personal way. A brief bulletin on the railings of Buckingham Palace announced that King George VI had died peacefully in his sleep. Princess Elizabeth, who had served in the ATS during the war, was now Queen Elizabeth.

On the day when the funeral procession of King George VI was on its way to Windsor, Grannie Day died peacefully in the front room of her house in Strathmore Street. When Eddie came home and told her, Patsy hadn't been able to say a word. To this day she remembered the sense of utter loneliness. She couldn't imagine how life could go on without Grannie Day. She had been the head of a large family, loving, kind and generous – she'd give you her last shilling if she thought you needed it more than she did. For all that she was never slow to speak her mind. What was it one of the Day children had said one very cold winter's night when they had all been living in Strathmore Street? Suddenly the incident was as clear as a bell in Patsy's mind.

Florrie had told them that Gran was doing the dinner for everyone that evening. Oh the memory! Coal fire burning half-way up the chimney, adults sitting shoulder to shoulder around the huge kitchen table and a great many children squashed together on the floor. And the dinner? Neck of mutton stew, thick with vegetables and dumplings which were as light as a feather, thick slices of crusty bread to mop up the delicious gravy.

The intimacy of comradeship that night was something that Patsy felt she would never forget as long as she lived. And to sum that night up one of Gran's teenaged grandsons had wiped his plate clean with his piece of bread, sat back with a satisfied grin on his face and said, 'Gran, you're a bloody diamond!'

'No she's not,' piped up his brother. 'Gran's got bread pudding *and* apple pie with custard for our pudding and that makes her a double diamond.'

No one was going to argue with that!

Every man and woman had bawled their eyes out as they sat in the church at her funeral and Patsy had prayed then that she herself might turn out to be as good a grandmother to her grandchildren as Grannie Day had been to all of them.

Alex had volunteered for the army the minute he was eighteen and Vicky had gone into the WAAF. Absence had only made the heart grow fonder, and come peacetime, Vicky and Alex were married. Happy as any pair had ever been, they now had two children, James, who was almost ten, and Frances, who was just nine years old.

Funny how life turns out, Patsy thought. Her own life had been made so much better by the folk of Strathmore Street and the loving care they had so freely given. They never had much in the way of worldly goods but what they did have they shared.

Much the same had happened to Vicky. Thank God Patsy and her family had been able to do as much for her.

Things had changed now, and it was hard to believe how well they had all prospered.

Today Vicky was, as always when she was at work, fairly conservatively dressed in a dark grey suit, though Patsy knew she could make herself look much younger and even sexy when the occasion arose.

'You're bright an' early this morning, Mum,' Vicky smiled. 'Shall I make us a cuppa before we get down to business?'

'Oh, yes please, Vicky,' Patsy answered quickly. 'I did put the kettle on when I first got here but I never got around to making a drink. I've been letting myself wander down memory lane.'

'That's what old age does for you,' Vicky grinned. 'I'll only be a few minutes.'

'You're a right cheeky madam, yer know that, don't you?' Patsy called after her, but she was smiling to herself.

'Thanks, luv,' Patsy said as she took a cup of tea from Vicky's hand, then watched as her daughter-in-law sat down in the chair which stood in front of the desk opposite.

'Did you enjoy your week off?' Patsy asked, when she'd drained her cup.

60

'Yes, I did. I spent a couple of days shopping with Emma.'

The telephone rang in the outer office, and Vicky quickly set down her cup and went to answer it.

Emma and Ellen. As always, Patsy sighed as she rolled the names of her twin daughters around in her mind.

Emma was settled so happily, married to Donald Langford, described by most as a good bloke. Independent, that was for sure. A bricklayer by trade, he had been working on the hospital's rebuilding programme when Emma had first met him. Both the twins were doing a nurses' training course at the same hospital. Now Donald was about the only member of the family who didn't work for the firm. Instead he owned his own business, had about thirty tradesmen on his pay-roll and made sure that his wife and three sons wanted for nothing.

If only Ellen's life could have turned out half as well.

Ellen! Kind and loving, she saw wrong in no one. Too trusting by half.

She had fallen for a junior doctor, Robert Dellor, and right from the first meeting Patsy had been at a loss to describe exactly how she felt about him. Too smooth and sure of himself.

Florrie had thought along the same lines and she'd voiced her opinion loud and clear. 'He fancies his luck a bit too much for my liking. He'd suit Emma more than our Ellen . . . she'd see through him in no time.'

When their brother David had been asked his thoughts on Robert, he'd just been cautious, saying, 'Well, there's something about him that doesn't ring true.' But he wouldn't be drawn further than that.

Their elder brother, Alex, who'd had a wise head on his shoulders from an early stage in his life, merely said it was none of his business. Ellen had made her choice and his mother should stop acting as if she were a broody old hen afraid of losing her chicks.

When the twins were twenty-one they'd had a double

wedding. Making all the preparations should have been a happy time, but Robert Dellor had still given Patsy sleepless nights. She just had not been able to trust him. Even on the morning of the wedding she had asked Eddie, 'Do you really believe Robert's parents live in Geneva? Surely they could have sent a telegram, or written a letter to Ellen. As far as I can fathom he's got half a dozen mates coming to the church but not a single relative.'

With hindsight, Patsy's fears had been well founded.

Once married to Ellen, Robert Dellor's true colours had soon come to light. He had got himself into some very bad situations. That was when he started pulling diabolical stunts to get out of the scrapes he found himself in. Even today Patsy had to beat down her panic as memories flooded back.

Finally Robert had got on to a path of self-destruction. The main trouble was his drinking and his gambling debts, and because there was nothing of any value left in the house to sell he had gone for Ellen. By now she was used to him ill treating her, but this time he had beaten and kicked her so hard that she had had to do something to ward off the blows and had grabbed the nearest thing to hand, which happened to be a knife. She had only managed to slash his arm. Really badly, though.

Robert had phoned the police and told them his wife had gone berserk and tried to kill him. Ellen had crawled to the bathroom, locked herself in and cut the veins in both of her wrists.

The long and short of it was that Ellen was almost beyond help. She didn't want to live. She wouldn't eat, drink or speak. There had been no option. She was detained in a mental home.

The first time Patsy had been allowed to visit Ellen had been such a shock that she still suffered nightmares about it. Her lovely Ellen, with her sunny, outgoing disposition, the exact replica of Emma, without the tomboy mannerisms yet with the same mischievous green eyes and shiny dark brown hair that held chestnut glints. To think that she should have been incarcerated in a lunatic asylum.

Ellen had been placed in a single room. It had no furniture other than one armchair discreetly placed in the farthest corner. The bed, in the centre of the room, could scarcely be termed a bed. It was just a thick mattress raised only inches from the floor. The walls of the room had been padded and covered with a soft pale blue fabric.

Ellen had lain like a dead thing. Her forehead was bandaged, her face the colour of alabaster. Her lips were cut and swollen and her cheeks severely bruised. Her closed eyelids were ringed around with black and blue discoloration, all the more stark because of the strange whiteness of her skin.

Patsy had pleaded aloud, 'Ellen love, open your eyes.' No response whatsoever, and Patsy's tears were blinding her.

With two fingers, she had lifted the edge of the sheet which was all that covered Ellen. Her daughter was naked, not even a nightdress. She had almost choked as she stared at Ellen's bruised body.

Nothing had prepared her for this.

She had had to make a supreme effort to quell the queasiness that had risen in her throat. Carefully she had laid the sheet back over Ellen.

She no longer wanted to cry!

Anger boiled up inside her. Blind rage. Hate for Robert Dellor. All these emotions had been tearing away at her insides. Her head between her hands, she had prayed. Prayed like she had never done before in the whole of her life.

Please, please, God, don't take Ellen. Please don't let her die.

Why, oh why, had all this had to happen when Eddie and Ollie were thousands of miles away in Australia dealing with the businesses that Jack Berry had left?

* * *

63

Day after day, week after week, Patsy had made the journey to Belmont. The very chill of that place had eaten into her bones. And every day she cursed Robert Dellor and wished that Ellen had never met him.

Then light had dawned. Patsy had an idea and she was going to act on it. Ellen would never recover unless someone could convince her that there was a life for her outside of these walls, and that it could be a good and useful one.

It had taken a good deal of persuasion to get Ellen to come out of the noisy visitors' room, put on a coat and allow her mother to tie a scarf over her head; and quite some time to convince her that it was safe to go for a walk in the grounds. It was a struggle, with Ellen resisting strongly, but Patsy was determined and after a while they were seated side by side on a bench seat.

'Ellen,' Patsy began cautiously, 'if you could have one wish, what would you wish for?'

Ellen had sat perfectly still, studying the ground at her feet. She'd looked so miserable that Patsy had scarcely thought it worthwhile continuing. But after letting a few minutes tick by she had said, 'All right, Ellen, you needn't talk if you don't want to, but I want you to listen to me.'

Still Ellen hadn't moved.

Doing her best to speak calmly, Patsy had begun. 'Do you remember, love, when Vicky and I went down to Ramsgate to view the Gloucester Hotel? At first we thought we'd had a wasted journey. Then we met Mrs Wright and all her old genteel friends that were being turned out of their rest home because the owner wanted to sell the premises. It was the second time they had all been made homeless, and Vicky and I felt so sorry for all of them. I came home and persuaded your grandad, Ollie, to purchase the Maplehurst.'

She paused, hoping for a reply but getting nothing.

'I made a whole lot of promises to those old folk. Weren't we all excited when your grandad told us everything was settled, the company now owned that rest home and the old folk had somewhere safe to live for the rest of their lives? It was a kind thing to do, wasn't it?'

Still there had been no reaction from Ellen.

Anger had flared up again in Patsy, fierce anger. In that instant there had been murder in her heart, and God help Robert Dellor if she could have got hold of him at that moment.

'I mustn't give up,' she'd muttered to herself.

'Don't you think, Ellen, with your nursing experience, you'd be such a great help down there? We'd all be happy to know that we had someone on hand that we could rely on if any of the residents were taken ill. Of course you could have your own flat, your own bit of privacy. We'd be down to see you often. Doesn't take long to get to Ramsgate; you'd probably get browned off with the sight of us all.

'Emma thinks it's terribly funny the way your Aunt Florrie and Mrs Wright have become great buddies. Mrs Wright is a bit frightfully-frightfully, but the pair of them get on like a house on fire. You'd have your Aunt Florrie on your doorstep more often than you'd want. Come t' give you a helping hand, is most likely what her excuse would be. Your dad and me wouldn't want to be strangers, so perhaps you'd better take over the job of getting Sunday tea for everyone, say once a month? Give me a rest from the job and make a nice change for yer dad.'

After all that there was still not a movement from Ellen.

I mustn't fail, thought Patsy, but what else can I say or do?

Now, again with hindsight, she knew that if she hadn't persevered they might just as well have thrown the key away. Ellen could have been spending all these years in that God-awful place.

She had reached the end of her tether when the miracle had happened.

Gentle fingers were plucking at her sleeve. She hadn't believed it. A gurgling sound was coming from Ellen's throat, her eyes were screwed up tightly, her hands were fluttering, beating the air with such urgency that Patsy had been frightened.

It had seemed to take ages for this spasm to pass. Then suddenly Ellen had become still. Very, very gently, Patsy drew her daughter into her arms, and for the first time Ellen made no resistance.

It was as if all Ellen's grief and fear had come to a head at once and was bursting from her in tears. Patsy cradled her, smoothing her hair back from her damp forehead. Then Ellen's tears changed to racking sobs, and Patsy pillowed her head on her shoulder, all the time patting Ellen's back and rocking her as if she were a baby.

Gradually she became quiet. They both stayed still. Neither of them spoke. They held on to each other as if afraid one would collapse without the support of the other.

This was the answer to all of Patsy's prayers. More than she had hoped for at one time.

At last they had drawn apart. Ellen's eyes were still shining with tears, but her mother could see beyond into their depths, and was instantly reassured.

It had been her turn to weep floods of tears, but they were tears of relief.

'That was Ellen on the phone,' Vicky said as she came back into the main office. She was smiling reassuringly at her mother-in-law because she was fully aware of her concern for Ellen's well-being. 'She's laying on a special surprise party for one of her lady residents who will be ninety. She wants to know how many of us will be able to turn up.'

Patsy sat up straight and decided that the past was best put to rest even if it could never be entirely forgotten.

All these memories had Patsy longing to speak to her

daughter. While the thought was uppermost in her mind, she was going to ring Ellen back.

She felt a tightening in her throat. Why did she still need to worry over Ellen so much? Ellen had a good life now. Or did she? Thirty-four years old, divorced, and no signs of any man in her life. Her twin sister, Emma, was so happily married, with three gorgeous sons: Edward Junior, who had been their first grandson and was now twelve years old; Thomas, who was ten; and cheeky young Sam, who was nine.

Didn't Ellen ever feel a twinge of envy? Or even regret? She always assured her brothers and sister that she was perfectly happy, but look at the company she had. Day in, day out, she lived with elderly folk. That couldn't be right for one so young. It had been a godsend when Ellen had at last come out of hospital and had agreed to take on the job at the Maplehurst, but that was eleven years ago!

'Hallo, Ellen dear,' Patsy said as her daughter picked up the phone on the first ring.

For the first five minutes Patsy entertained her daughter with snatches of gossip about the family, and, as usual, Ellen found them hilarious, especially when they concerned her father and her grandfather Ollie, and most of all her dearly beloved Aunt Florrie. Patsy was aware that she was chattering on, but she just wanted to keep her daughter in close contact with what was going on in London, because Ellen very rarely left Ramsgate. The family went to visit her, never the reverse.

Suddenly Patsy veered away from what she had been saying and launched into how thrilled she'd been to hear that Ellen was putting on a party.

'It's got to be special, Mum, Mrs Brookes is going to be ninety. I'm hoping to put on some extra-special entertainment.'

'Sounds good t' me, luv,' Patsy said, delighted to hear the eagerness in Ellen's voice. 'I'm positive the whole family will be coming. I'll get yer dad t' see about booking rooms for all of us. As the party is going to be in March, the Gloucester shouldn't be busy and we can take over the whole place for the weekend.'

Patsy was thrilled to hear the laughter in Ellen's voice as she said, 'When Ollie and Dad started up the Ace Trading Company and bought their first charabancs to do day trips to the seaside, who'd have thought we'd end up owning hotels?'

'Not me, that's for sure,' Patsy agreed. 'But it's all turned out very well, hasn't it? I still can't always bring myself to believe how much the business has spread. Especially when I think it all started because of Jack Berry, who lived in Strathmore Street just the same as we did.'

'Mum, last time Grandad came down here on his own, he spent some time telling the residents how his older brother had got into trouble with the police when he was a lad, and that's how he came to leave home and end up in Australia where he made his fortune. Kept the old folk enthralled, he did.'

'Well, luv, it is quite a story of bad lad makes good. Only sad that he never lived long enough to reap the benefits.'

'But Ollie said his brother *did* in many ways. Jack was twelve years older than Ollie so he wasn't so young when he died, and what with his dealings in New Zealand as well as Australia he must have been mighty proud of himself.'

'And we've all got good reason to be grateful to him,' Patsy answered softly.

'A good many more people than just our family, eh, Mum? If you hadn't convinced me it was right for me to come here to live, God alone knows what I would have done with my life. Probably sat in a room somewhere and taken up knitting.'

'Like hell you would!' Patsy said in her typical blunt fashion. 'Anyway, I'll talk to you again soon. Oh Lord, what am I going to bring down as presents for all the old 'uns, especially Mrs Wright and Mr Stapleton, and God above, I mustn't forget the special birthday girl!'

'You'll come up trumps. You always do, Mum, though you'll probably moan like hell about what a hard job it is.'

'I don't believe my kids,' Patsy answered loudly. 'This morning there was Vicky giving me a load of old madam, an' now there's you telling me I'm a moaner. What did I do t' deserve you lot?'

'Get on with you, Mum. You know darn well you love each an' every one of us,' Ellen said, blowing a kiss down the line before replacing the receiver.

Chapter Two

THERE WAS A TAP at the door, and without waiting for Patsy to call out, it swung open and her elder son, Alex, entered. He was on time, but then wasn't he always?

Alex was tall, lean and trim in build, with his father's good looks, his huge brown eyes with the same long lashes. He also had Eddie's disposition, making him a happy man and kindly with it, even if he was a devious rascal when it suited him. He was wearing a well-cut dark grey suit, a crisp white shirt and a burgundy silk tie, all of which tended to make him look older than his forty years and a darn sight more serious than usual.

'Morning, Mum,' he said, striding towards her. Reaching her desk, he leaned over and planted a kiss on her cheek. 'You've taken great pains to make yourself look businesslike today. Meeting someone you want to impress?' he asked cheekily.

'Morning, Alex. We'll 'ave less of yer sauce, and by the same yardstick, you're well turned out t'day. Some dolly-bird you want t' make an impression on?'

'Hey, we are on the ball this morning, tit-fer-tat, eh? If you must know, Mother dear, I think I've come up with a

70

solution as regards putting more coaches on the road. What I want to ask you is may I pinch my wife off you just for this morning? I have an appointment at Vauxhall and I promised Ollie I'd take notes.'

'Oh, I see. For one thing you can't be bothered with the paperwork, and for another, Vicky's shorthand is so good she won't miss a trick.'

'Got it in one, Mother dear. So, please, is it all right?'

Patsy wanted to laugh at the expression on his face. He knew damn well she could read him like a book and also that she rarely refused him anything. But she stifled her laughter and nodded her head before saying, 'You know Ollie is upset the way a couple of hotels have let us down, and that both he and yer father were thinking of laying off some of our drivers.'

'Yes, Mum, but you know what those two are like, they hate to have to make decisions when they know someone is going to get hurt.' He shrugged his shoulders. 'Sometimes it's inevitable, but if my solution is found t' be workable, maybe we can take on more men rather than cut our workforce. Even I hate to see men permanently laid off, but if we 'ave to . . . well.'

'You get off to your meeting, the pair of you, and you can tell us about your solution at Friday's meeting when we're all together. And don't worry about the men who might have to be laid off. They will be all right, really they will.'

She hesitated for a moment before quietly adding, 'But there is one thing I would like you to bear in mind.'

'Oh yeah, sounds serious, but come on, spit it out.'

'Ellen is putting on a special party in about a month's time. Vicky will give you more details; she took the phone call. Your sister has given us plenty of notice, so do your best to come down for that weekend, and make sure you bring Frances and Jamie.'

Alex hid a grin and remained silent, watching his mother closely. This old folk's home in Ramsgate that she had persuaded Ollie to buy all those years ago really was her pet venture. More so because Ellen had retreated there, almost shutting herself away from the outside world.

Not that he blamed his sister. God, she'd had a terrible time with that bastard she'd married, and at least she seemed happy living down there in Ramsgate. But eleven years was a long time, especially for someone as young and lovely as Ellen was.

'We'll be there, Mother, and so will every other member of the family if they know what's good for them. And our two kids won't need any persuading either,' he grinned.

'Humph, so you think the family are afraid of me, do you?'

'No, of course not,' he quickly replied, doing his best to keep a straight face. 'They'll all turn up because they know how dear t' yer heart those residents are. And as for the old folk, they'll be thrilled to see all of us, but most especially you. They all worship you, but then you know that. They never tire of telling tales as to how they were turned out of their home and would have had nowhere to go if you hadn't stepped in and persuaded Ollie to buy the place.'

Patsy wagged a finger. 'Don't exaggerate, and don't you dare take the mickey either, or as big as you are I'll box yer ears.'

Alex laughed and went round the desk. He hugged her to him and kissed the top of her head. 'You've a heart big enough to take in half the country, but I'm glad you're our mum. And I'll tell yer something else. On that score, David, Emma and Ellen have always agreed with me.'

'Oh, so it's a dose of flattery that I'm getting now, is it?'

She looked across to where her daughter-in-law was putting on her jacket, and thought to herself, You marrying my son was the best thing that could have happened to him.

72

Then, with a smile at Vicky, she said, 'Take him off or I'm never going to get any work done today.'

In the weeks that followed, several company meetings took place, or at least that was how Ollie and Eddie described them. But as the majority of these 'meetings' were held around her kitchen table, and more often than not Florrie was present, Patsy was unable to take whatever matter was under discussion too seriously. So many interruptions from Florrie, and her comments, fuelled by her vivid imagination and her cockney humour, always had Patsy in fits of laughter. More than once both Eddie and Ollie threatened that if Florrie didn't behave herself she'd be banished to another room.

That threat only made her ten times worse.

Having everything running well, Ollie lost no time in taking Alex's suggestion seriously. More so because his brother agreed wholeheartedly that it was time the company expanded. It was decided that they would lose no time in being on the look-out for suitable hotels to buy so that the company could offer more choice of holidays further afield.

There was a time when Patsy used to believe that the only one of her children that she had to worry about was Ellen. Now, suddenly, thinking to herself that David had been unusually quiet tonight, she wondered, not for the first time, what had gone wrong between him and Valerie.

Valerie had lost her first husband during the war; she had given birth to Timmy six months after she had learned that he had been killed. It must have been a terrible time for her. Young Timmy had been barely four years old when David had first brought him and Valerie home to Sunday tea.

The whole family had taken Tim to their hearts, and he was calling Patsy and Eddie Gran and Grandad even before his mother and David had wed. He had been thrilled to have David as a father and had grown up to be a really nice young man whom David was proud to have for his son and who was highly regarded in the family firm. Sadly Valerie and David had not been blessed with any children of their own.

Patsy heaved a great sigh. During the last two years Valerie had pushed her patience to the limits, gallivanting around the dance halls and nightclubs while David stayed at home. She had also stopped coming to family gatherings, which was an embarrassment for David and for Tim too.

It had almost become a rule that no one would pass comment on Valerie's absence. Her behaviour was baffling when one thought about how good David had been to her. Patsy knew better than to interfere, so all she could do was hope and pray that things would sort themselves out.

Chapter Three

IT WAS TEN O'CLOCK on Saturday morning. Patsy sat at her kitchen table, still in her dressing gown. She looked around this big room, at the old dresser with its display of china, at the black-leaded grate with its bright coal fire, at Eddie's huge armchair by the hearth. At each end of the brass fender was a leather-topped box which held the kindling for the making of a fire. How her grandchildren loved to sit on these boxes, their feet and legs far too near the fire, toasting thick slices of bread on a long-handled toasting fork.

Patsy smiled happily. She loved this big old house in Navy Street.

How many times had Eddie done his best to get her to agree to move out to Surrey? To be nearer the children, he pleaded. No, was always her answer, firm and definite. She was a Londoner and this was where she wanted to be. She had felt sad when Kitty, who had lived in their top flat, had died. Then, since all the children had moved out into homes of their own, she and Eddie had rattled around this big house like two peas in a colander.

But now Florrie was permanently installed in the large ground-floor front room. Eddie and Ollie's joint efforts had turned it into a bed-sitting room with a side door leading into a bathroom and toilet which had been built on to the side of the house. Really impressive, everyone agreed.

Ollie now lived upstairs in what had been Kitty's flat, and Tim, who at the age of twenty had left home, rented Ollie's Strathmore Street house from him. Ollie's parents had bought the freehold of that house many years ago, whereas the house Florrie had lived in had only been rented. It was so good to have Florrie and Ollie under the same roof, and there weren't many weekends when some of the family didn't turn up for one of Patsy's roast dinners. Wouldn't have it any other way, she grinned to herself.

'Hallo, you in, Mum?'

'Oh, good,' Patsy called in answer. 'I was hoping you'd drop in, Emma.' Then, seeing her daughter was on her own, she asked, 'Where are the boys?'

Emma loosened her coat as she came into the warmth of the kitchen, kissed her mother's cheek and said, 'Donald left me the car this morning so I dropped the boys off at the yard. We picked James up on the way. Vicky said she was going shopping, but she and Frances will be coming here later on this afternoon.'

Patsy laughed loudly.

'What with your three and Jamie, your dad and Ollie will be made up. Suppose they'll all be off to a football match this afternoon.'

'Mother! Don't you know anything? It's not just any old football match. The Gunners are at home to Chelsea, and wild horses wouldn't keep our menfolk away from Highbury today.'

'In that case I suppose David and Tim will be joining them.'

'More than likely. By the way, Mum, why aren't you dressed?' Without waiting for an answer she added, 'I'm gonna put the kettle on, I'm gasping for a cuppa.'

Ten minutes later, with a steaming cup of tea in front of

them, Emma and Patsy were chattering merrily away about family matters. The party her twin sister was hosting down at Ramsgate was top of Emma's list.

'Everyone thinks it will be a great weekend. Haven't had everyone under the same roof for a long time,' she mused.

'I wish I thought *all* the family would be there,' Patsy murmured half to herself. She was wondering if she should keep her own counsel or take the bull by the horns and pay Valerie and David a visit. Would she be doing more harm than good?

'Mum, you're not listening to me!' Emma shook her arm impatiently.

'Oh, sorry, dear. You were saying it would make a nice break having a long weekend at the Gloucester.'

'Oh, for God's sake, Mum, that was five minutes ago,' Emma cried. 'I was telling you about Valerie.'

'What on earth has she been up to now?' Patsy asked, sounding annoyed.

'Much as usual,' said Emma sadly.

This reply made Patsy sit upright in her chair and she stared hard at her daughter before saying, 'I know I've always told you a still tongue makes a wise head, but surely things are getting out of hand. Poor David, all these rumours must be getting back to him.'

'That's just it, Mum. They're not just rumours. But I wouldn't worry too much about David, he can take care of himself.'

Patsy sighed deeply. 'Why is Valerie gadding about so much on her own? After all, she's no spring chicken, is she? She's asking for trouble. Big trouble. Do you think she's found someone else?'

'Well, I'm not in Valerie's confidence, and I don't know anything about her love life except that she and David are not getting on so well these days. But if I had to take a guess I'd say she feels she missed out on a lot of things.

After all, she was only sixteen when she first married, and she had Tim before she was seventeen. Then she was a war widow. Maybe she just wants a good time. Nothing permanent. More like one-night stands.'

'Emma! That's a terrible thing to say. Is that what Tim thinks? Is that why he left home?'

'I don't know. I'm sorry, Mum.' Emma dropped her eyes. 'It's just what I feel. I didn't mean to shock you.'

'Hmm. I've lived long enough not to be shocked at most things. But Valerie out on the loose, that's going too far.'

'I know. It's not nice. But you asked me what I hear, so I've told you. By all accounts Val is going to some rough clubs and dance halls. Perhaps she thinks our David is a bit of a stick-in-the-mud and she's making up for lost time.'

'She doesn't know when she's well off. As far as I'm aware, she has never known what it is to need a shilling in her whole life. Let's hope she comes to her senses before it's too late.'

It probably is too late, Emma thought with a twinge of sadness. Poor David, what a terrible mess. Stifling a sigh, she finally said, 'Go get yourself dressed, Mum, and we'll go shopping together.'

As she walked quickly up the long hallway and mounted the stairs, Patsy was deep in thought. Maybe she would make a point of getting Valerie on her own and asking her outright just what was going on. Surely she must have been upset when Tim announced he was leaving home. A pretty sad state of affairs, she thought ruefully. I'll do whatever I can to help if only Valerie will let me. But that young lady has a mind of her own, as we all know too well.

I'll bide my time for a bit, she decided.

Chapter Four

EVERYONE SAID EDDIE OWEN was the odd one out when it came to the Ace Trading Company. He certainly wasn't a cockney. He'd had a private education because his mother had believed he wouldn't be able to stand up to the rough and tumble of the local school.

As a teenager Eddie had been made aware of his disability far too often. His mother had used it as a means of keeping him close to her, and he had sought to escape through books.

Meeting Patsy had given him self-confidence. The heavy iron attached to his boot had never worried her. She had altered his whole attitude to life. He adored her, loved her as no other person could understand. Eventually, having an operation and subsequently being able to dance with his wife had been a dream come true.

Now, at the age of sixty-four, there was an air of prosperity, even glamour to Eddie Owen, that sprang not so much from his good looks as from his character and personality, not to mention his huge dark brown eyes, which drew the ladies to him even though he had eyes for no one but Patsy. Equally he had good male friends, mates who trusted him and on whom he knew he could rely. Like Ollie, his father figure and friend from the day they had first met, he could be hard-headed, objective and outspoken, but always honest. He and Alexander Berry made a good pair, both in family matters and where business was concerned.

Eddie often thought back to the day when Ollie had formed the limited company, making himself and Patsy equal partners. He had put his arm around the older man's shoulders and said, 'Thanks for *everything*, Ollie.'

The reply had been short and to the point.

'Oh, lad, it's a pleasure. You make my Patsy happy and that's good enough for me.'

Now Eddie was pondering on the suggestion that Alex, his elder son, had put forward: 'Stop relying on private hotels for our holiday breaks; let the company reach out, buy more hotels, go further afield, put in reliable managers and trained catering staff,' he had urged.

The suggestion had received approval from Ollie and the boys hadn't let the grass grow under their feet. He himself hadn't had any qualms about Alex and David setting out for the West Country to sound out a few estate agents. He was pleased also that they had decided Tim should go with them.

Tim had worked for the family firm since leaving school. He didn't have a specific job, and Patsy called him a busy-body, a name she meant in the nicest sense. Tim was his own man, although he was never shy of telling Patsy and Eddie how much he appreciated being part of such a loving family. In the office he never needed to be told what to do, had his fingers into everything and never seemed to be out of his depth. He thrived on the idea of sending people away on holiday, rather than just running day trips. He saw to it that both clients and the company were well covered by insurance, that people were booked at the hotel of their choice, that their rooms were suitable for their needs and that their luggage did not go astray. Indeed, he made himself responsible for the paying customers' well-being at all times.

And he did it brilliantly.

Alex often teased him with the fact that he wanted to please everyone. Tim always quickly retorted that that was hardly possible.

All in all Eddie felt he had a good working relationship and a most special friendship with both of his sons and all of his grandsons, which gave him a great deal of satisfaction and pleasure.

As to his daughters, Emma couldn't be more happily settled. Her husband Donald was as straight as a die, and the fact that he worshipped the ground that Emma walked on made him a great guy in Eddie and Patsy's book. In addition to this, Emma and Donald had provided them with three healthy grandsons. Who could ask for more?

His other daughter, Ellen, was a different kettle of fish. He sighed heavily, thinking of the sleepless nights he and Patsy had spent anguishing over what to do for the best where she was concerned. What wouldn't he give to see her happily married to a decent bloke.

There were times when he thanked God that he and Ollie had been in Australia when his darling daughter had been practically killed by Robert Dellor. If they had been home at the time he was pretty sure that one or both of them would have been facing criminal charges of grievous bodily harm. If not murder!

Poor Ellen. She hadn't stood a chance against that slimy brute.

The fact that Patsy had spent week after week visiting Ellen in a lunatic asylum was something that still tortured him today, because he knew only too well that his wife still suffered nightmares because of it. There had been many a night when he'd done his best to calm Patsy, to reassure her that Ellen was safe and well. At his wits' end sometimes, he'd sworn that he'd live to have his day with that bastard.

To this day he didn't feel entirely satisfied with the way things had turned out.

Ollie had spared no expense. When Ellen had refused to bring charges against her husband, because she was too scared to face him in court, Ollie had sought advice from the best legal minds in the country. The long and short of it was that Eddie proved to the court that his daughter was too ill to fend for herself, and as her father and guardian it was he himself who instigated the proceedings. Robert Dellor was struck off by the General Medical Council and given a term of six years in prison. Six years! Ellen and her mother were still suffering the effects more than eleven years later. At the time Eddie supposed it had been some consolation. More so when Ellen had obtained her divorce without too much trouble. But in his bones he'd known that was never going to be the end of the matter.

Nothing had been heard of Robert until a week ago. Then Ellen had phoned him, sounding terrified. She had received a letter fom her ex-husband asking for financial help. God help us! The cheek of that beggar was unbelievable!

Within hours of Ellen's phone call, both Eddie and Ollie were in Ramsgate.

The postmark on the envelope in which the letter had been sent was Edinburgh. Ollie straight away said, 'He could have got any truck driver to post it.' Robert had given no return address; simply asked that Ellen give the matter some thought and said he would contact her again soon.

They had moved fast. Engaged a firm of investigators to find out where Robert Dellor was living and to keep an eye on the Maplehurst. Ellen had made them both swear that they wouldn't tell her mother that Robert had found out where she was living. That was proving difficult for Eddie. He talked everything over with Patsy, but this time he knew he had to keep his promise. For more reasons than one. Patsy would go mad. She'd want to get down to Ramsgate and be by Ellen's side morning, noon and night. It would also revive all the living nightmares that Patsy had had to endure when Ellen was lying at death's door. And that was something that he was going to avoid at all costs if he possibly could.

But just let that bastard turn up in Ramsgate and start pestering Ellen, and he'd have him like a shot and bugger the consequences. This time he'd make sure Robert Dellor knew he wasn't dealing with a woman on her own. He wasn't going to get away with it. Not this time.

Oh, what the hell, he thought, becoming impatient with himself. I'm not going to spend the next few days worrying about Robert Dellor's intentions. We'll find out where he is and we *will* deal with him.

Pushing horrible thoughts to the back of his mind, he rang Patsy at home. Although he'd kept his promise and not confided in her over this matter, he needed to talk to her. He felt a rush of relief when he heard her voice and she was equally pleased to hear his. Even after all these years there was still that spark between them.

They talked about the weekend that the whole family were going to spend in Ramsgate. Patsy told him who was coming for dinner this Sunday, and as usual laughed as she said, 'That's not counting those that will turn up on the off-chance.'

Finally Eddie said, 'I'll try to be home by six. Bye, luv.'

He replaced the receiver and walked to the gates of their yard at Vauxhall. Being the first week in March, they had only two coaches out on day trips and two smaller ones that were doing their regular school runs. Once they were safely in and the yard locked up, he could head for home.

The very thought sent a warm feeling coursing through his veins. The evenings were drawing out a bit, but there was still a damp chill in the air due to the heavy rains which had fallen earlier that week. They'd have a fire halfway up the chimney, and he and Patsy would sit opposite each other and relax. That was if she hadn't brought any of the grand-children home with her. He laughed at the thought.

He loved having them just as much as she did.

Alexander Berry was no less worried than Eddie was.

He loved Ellen dearly and regarded her as his grand-daughter. To learn that Robert Dellor had had the audacity to turn up again after all this time was almost unbelievable!

Of course Ellen was unhappy and frightened. She had good reason.

He wasn't quite sure how they would deal with Robert Dellor this time, but deal with him they most certainly would.

Ollie let his thoughts wander back over the past.

He had never married. With his parents both dead and only his older brother living in Australia he had become a lonely man.

Then his life had taken a turn for the better when in 1904 he had met Ellen Kent. She was alone in the world and heavily pregnant. That she had been high born was obvious. Yet she had settled down in a working-class district, had her baby and devoted her life to bringing up the child. To feed and clothe both the baby and herself, Ellen had done any menial task that brought in a few shillings. A family of costermongers had employed her to work on their stalls in Tooting market. Even that heavy, dirty work hadn't changed her.

Ellen Kent had been so different from anyone else he had ever met. She was unique. Such a slight lady, with bright grey eyes and a pleasant face with fine bone structure. It was, however, her smiling, loving quality that seemed to draw people to her. Every person that came into contact with this gentle lady agreed that to know Ellen was to love her. It was as if she had been a breed apart.

When consumption had racked her body and she had died an early death, he had the greatest regret that he had never plucked up enough courage to ask Ellen to marry him. Having been on the scene from the day the baby had been born, he accepted responsibility for the child. In every thought and deed Patsy became his daughter, and he'd loved and respected her all these years.

Patsy finally marrying Eddie Owen and having four children had given him a wonderful family. First grandchildren and now great-grandchildren. And there was nothing in this world that he wouldn't do for each and every one of them.

All those years ago he had never imagined in his wildest dreams that he would inherit a vast fortune from his elder brother Jack. He had done his best to share his wealth with Eddie and Patsy, to provide a good living not only for them but for all the men and women who were now in his employ. He would also see that his grandchildren's kiddies had the best advantages. Not that that would mean spoiling them. Oh no! They would learn at an early age that money had to be earned to be appreciated.

Although he would be eighty-two this year, Ollie wasn't ready to sit back and take life easy. Forming the company had been great fun *and* profitable. With four coaches catering for Londoners' day trips to the seaside, they had moved on. Bought two hotels and the Maplehurst rest home in Ramsgate.

He chuckled heartily at the very thought.

Whoever would have thought that that purchase would be the means of all us here in London having an extended family down there in Ramsgate?

Because that was what it had become.

Never mind whether the Maplehurst showed a profit. It was a happy place. One had only to enter the front door to feel the welcome and the love that abounded between the walls. It had been like mixing oil and water, and whoever said it couldn't be done had never been to a party in the Maplehurst!

Take their very own Florrie. A cockney to her backbone and she didn't give a toss who knew it. Rough and ready, bawdy even at times, with a voice that could stop a man in his tracks if it suited her. Yet the family would flay anyone alive that hurt their Florrie. To them, and all her many friends, she was a queen with a big heart.

Against her you could compare Mrs Dorothy Wright, the lady who had urged Patsy to help the old folk find a permanent place in which they could safely live. Mrs Wright was refined, genteel, spoke the Queen's English and was never known to raise her voice. Yet she and Florrie, opposites from entirely different worlds, were the best of friends. None more so.

A gathering at the Maplehust had to be seen to be believed. Again Ollie threw back his head and laughed out loud. According to Ellen, there was shortly to be another birthday party at the home, and all the family were invited. And if Patsy's orders were obeyed, the family would be there not just for the one day but to take over the Gloucester Hotel and make a long weekend of it!

He himself was looking forward to it. Very much so.

But before then he hoped against hope that the whereabouts of Robert Dellor would have been found. That beast of a man had to be taught that the past was the past and he could not come crawling out of the woodwork whenever he thought fit.

Even now, whenever his mind turned to that man, Ollie's whole body heaved in protest. What he had done to their gentle Ellen just didn't bear thinking about.

He wasn't ashamed to admit it. He hated Robert Dellor's guts.

Chapter Five

THE MANSE: THAT WAS the name carved into the brickwork over the main oak doors. The property stood at the bottom of a small hill, at the edge of the village of Mawgan Porth, about halfway between Newquay and Trevose Head.

A deep, wide river ran through the grounds, which boasted huge old oaks and sycamore trees. The property had originally belonged to the church, and at one time, many years ago, might even have been used as an abbey.

Alex, David and Tim looked at each other and grinned broadly.

It was the fifth property the three men had looked at, and so far the only one they had given a second glance. What made this manor-like building different would have been hard to explain. It was charming, especially so with the bright spring sunshine and the greenery all around showing signs of new life and the promise of a good summer to come. But they couldn't get away from the fact that it was dilapidated and rambling. Made of good stone, it had half-timbered frontage, tall chimneys and many leaded windows.

Alex and David agreed straight off that were the company

to buy this property, the badly ruined parts would have to be rebuilt. Tim's point was that the kitchens would have to be tackled – they were bound to be much too old-fashioned – and what about bathrooms? Since the end of the war, folk were a lot more choosy. Probably a good few more bathrooms would have to be added. And what about the wilderness which covered the neglected grounds? If they ever got around to using this place as a hotel, guests would need to be able to walk the grounds in safety.

'Not like you t' be so pessimistic,' David told Tim. Then quickly he added, 'Though I do think we are all of one mind. A great deal of time and energy plus specialist workmen would be needed to renovate this property up to the standard required before Ace Trading Company could use it as a hotel.'

'Yeah, but what a challenge!' Alex cried, already in love with this old building.

Half of the same mind, David said quietly, 'Don't see a queue of folk wanting to purchase, but all the same we could ask Dad and Ollie to view this one.'

'Great place, I agree,' Tim said cautiously. 'Be a bottomless pit, though, when it comes to pouring money into it.'

Both his father and his uncle laughed. 'You'll get the job of signing the cheques and the blame if it all goes belly-up,' David warned.

'Yeah, but I'd keep my eye on the ball an' I'd take the credit if – and I say *if* – it did all work out well.' With that, this tall, lean young man threw back his head and roared with laughter.

'What the hell's tickled you?' his uncle asked.

'Well . . .' Tim hesitated. 'I was about to suggest that if Grandad and Ollie do decide to come down and view this property they bring Grandma with them. Great head on her shoulders, has Gran.'

Now it was David's turn to laugh. 'If Mum comes down she'll want to bring Aunt Flo with her; she'll say a trip to the West Country would do Florrie the world of good.'

'Well, what's wrong with that?' Alex queried.

'Nothing,' David said, smothering a grin. 'Except can you see Florrie wandering around this place? I know exactly what she'd say.'

'Go on then, tell us,' Tim urged.

David drew himself up to his full height and, using both hands, pushed at his chest in much the same way as Florrie was wont to heave up her ample bosom. Then, imitating her cockney voice, he said, 'Gawd blimey, who the bloody 'ell is gonna clean this lot up?'

When the three of them had stopped laughing, Alex added his two pennyworth.

'And she'd probably declare the whole place was haunted before she'd got past the first floor.'

'I've just had another thought,' Tim said. 'Gran would want to know where the nearest market is, an' she wouldn't be talking about cattle markets.'

'You're dead right, son,' David assured him. 'I don't think our mum could exist without market stalls and barrow boys. With all that she's come up in the world, she wouldn't dream of doing her weekend shopping anywhere else but up the market. Bantering with the costermongers is life blood to our mum.'

Tim smiled at his father. He loved Patsy, Eddie and Florrie just as much as if they were his own flesh and blood. Being adopted by David had only given him an even greater sense of loyalty. And he was so grateful to Ollie, the man to whom the Owens owed all their prosperity. Ollie was grandfather to all the children, himself included. He was the kind of man you felt you could turn to at any time and know that he would be there; rock-solid was Alexander Berry.

It was from Ollie that Tim had learned so much about Patsy's early life. The struggles she had experienced, the hardships she'd endured, and the loneliness too. He knew only too well that her marriage to Eddie and her children meant everything to her.

The happy life she now led had been hard won.

It was because he had listened so intently to so many fantastic, and often tear-jerking, stories about Patsy that he appreciated the fact that she treated him as one of her own. There wasn't anything in the world he wouldn't do for his grandma.

Tim loved his job, and his whole extended family, which included Vicky and Alex and their children James and Frances, as well as Emma and Donald and their three boys. Not forgetting his aunt Ellen, who was a lovely lady and yet he somehow always felt sorry for her. She had made a bad marriage and paid dearly for it. Now she lived a lonely kind of life.

His only problem was his mother. Just lately he'd had many a sleepless night over her. How could she treat David so badly? He couldn't fathom her out at all these days. Had he done wrong in leaving home? Had he been a coward? Should he have stayed and challenged his mother? Asked her point-blank what she thought she was doing? When it came to rock-bottom, Tim had the most awful feeling that she had found someone else and was going to leave David. What an awful position that would leave him in. If he stayed, would it be like accepting charity, seeing as how his job, as well as everything else, came from the family? Terrible thing to admit, but there were times now when he hated his mother. What she was doing was cruel.

She didn't seem to realise just how well off she was.

'Well, we can't stand here much longer dilly-dallying,' Alex said brightly. 'I suggest we find a pub that does a decent lunch and then return to the estate agent and ask his opinion as to what kind of figure the owners are prepared to accept for this run-down property.'

'Jumping the gun a bit, aren't you, brother?' David asked.

'Not exactly,' Alex said, shaking his head. 'We've got all the details, and if we are the least bit interested the first thing would be for us to get a surveyor's report. For that we need to find a damn good firm, not some fly-by-night that isn't going to earn his fee. But on the other hand, we don't want to spend good money until Dad and Ollie have given their opinion. And if we're going to tempt them to view the place, they'll want to know up front what kind of money we're talking about.'

'I hear what you're saying.' Tim spoke cautiously. 'And it would be as well to be able to tell Ollie what the rock-bottom asking price might be.'

'I can't see any one of them coming down to view for a couple of weeks,' David pondered. 'We've got Ellen's party next weekend.'

The three men looked at each other and knew by the grin that came to their lips that they were all thinking the same thought. They'd all be down in Ramsgate for that, or Patsy would want to know the reason why!

'Do you think all families are like ours?' David asked.

'What the 'ell do yer mean by that?' Alex asked, turning to face his brother and his nephew.

'To tell you the truth, I've never been able to work out just how Mum manages to rule all of us with her rod of iron. After all, there's a lot of us men and we're not exactly small, are we? Then there's her, only five foot two, yet we all do her bidding.'

'That's because she's always got our happiness at heart. She knows what it is to cope with life, remembers her own hardships and suffering,' Alex answered swiftly, then added, 'But because she had Ollie and our dad she overcame all her problems. She knows we all need money to survive, but having loved ones around you is what she thinks really counts in the end.'

David murmured, 'You're right, Alex. Dead right.' Then, searching his pocket for a handkerchief, he blew his nose hard before walking briskly towards the road. Over his shoulder he called, 'Who said something about lunch? I'm starving.'

Chapter Six

EDDIE STOOD AT THE doorway of Maplehurst's biggest lounge. He thought it was the loveliest spot in the entire rest home. It was the last word in elegant comfort. He was looking for Patsy. Usually he had a natural self-confidence and handled himself easily, but today, amongst all these elderly residents, he felt at a loss.

Since he couldn't see his wife, he took a glass of wine from a passing waitress, thinking he'd much prefer a glass of beer, and made a move towards his younger son. David was the only member of the family who did not have his other half with him, and Eddie felt slightly sorry for him.

'Hi, David,' he greeted his son. 'Everything looks very festive, doesn't it? But then doesn't our Ellen always go to great lengths to keep everyone happy?'

'She sure does, Dad,' David murmured, hoping his father wasn't going to comment on Valerie's absence.

Eddie was aware that David was feeling awkward and said quickly, 'I think I'd better go an' look for your mother. I can't imagine what's happened to her.'

David put out an arm to stay his father. 'I haven't had a

chance to ask you, Dad, what did Mum have to say about the Cornwall property?'

Eddie grinned. 'First off? Can't you guess? Too far from London! But then seeing as how Ollie and I both agreed that we'd go down and view the place, she has half-heartedly agreed to come with us as long as we take Florrie as well.'

Now it was hard for David not to smirk.

'That figures. But I'm glad, Dad. I'm not a hundred per cent sure the property would suit the company but it is well worth a visit. It's certainly different, and the asking price seemed pretty low, but as Tim pointed out, repairs and alterations could be opening up a bottomless pit.'

'Well, we'll see, son. Few days' break down in the West Country will make a nice change for us old uns.'

'Not so much of the old uns.' Patsy, coming up from behind, smiling brightly, playfully punched her husband's arm, glanced at her son and cried, 'Isn't this a marvellous party! Ellen never fails to come up trumps, does she? I think it's going to be a great weekend.' But at that moment she saw a man move out of the shadow of the bushes and walk past the far window, and immediately fear clutched at her heart and she felt the colour drain from her face. She turned her head away quickly. Had she imagined it? No, she knew she hadn't. She didn't want to believe it, but there was no getting away from the fact that Robert Dellor was creeping about outside in the grounds.

Had anyone else seen him? Where were her two sons? Her heart was beating nineteen to the dozen!

Patsy's eyes darted around the room and came to rest on Ellen, who was standing stock-still a few yards away, staring back at her and looking terrified. Oh my God! Poor Ellen, and today of all days!

Patsy motioned towards the door with a brief nod of her head. Then, doing her best to smile, she left the party, walking slowly. Within a minute she opened the door to the dining room, went in and sat down heavily on the nearest chair. She was surprised that her legs had carried her this far. She felt sick to the bottom of her stomach. It had been so many years. What could he possibly want with Ellen? Surely he didn't intend to hurt her again, but she could tell without asking that Ellen was absolutely petrified.

Ellen came in a few seconds later, closed the door behind her, and leaned heavily against it. Her face was dead white and she was shaking visibly.

Patsy longed to take her into her arms, but instead she sat still and asked, 'You saw him then? It was Robert, wasn't it?'

'Yes.' Ellen nodded, her voice barely more than a whisper.

Patsy felt the bile rise in her throat. She forced herself to swallow hard. She had to get a grip on herself, close her mind and stop dragging up the awful memories and pictures of when that beast of a man had almost killed Ellen.

She forced herself to ask, 'Did you know he was in the neighbourhood? That he might be coming here?'

'No. Of course not, Mum.' But it was a half-lie, because this was what Ellen had been dreading for the past few weeks.

Patsy looked directly at Ellen, as though she expected her to say more. But Ellen remained silent and Patsy said softly, 'Well, don't look so scared, my luv. He couldn't have picked a better time to show his face. With all our men here today, I think he'll end up wishing he'd never come. I must go an' find yer father.'

'Mum . . .'

'Yes, Ellen?' Patsy stopped dead in her tracks.

'Mum,' Ellen began again, 'I have to tell you. Robert wrote to me, a few weeks ago, asking for money, said he needed it badly.'

'And you never thought to tell us?'

Ellen looked decidedly sheepish, resigned and weary all

at once. 'I didn't want you to find out. You suffered enough last time because of me.' Then, taking a few steps to be nearer her mother, she held out her hands. 'Mum, don't be cross with me. Please. I did tell Dad, and he and Ollie came down here and read the letter. And before you fire a rocket off at them, I implored them not to tell you. Truly, I never wanted you to know that Robert had turned up again after all this time. But now, today of all days, he's decided to put in an appearance!'

Patsy felt stunned. She tried hard to smile as she said, 'Perhaps it's just as well, what with yer dad and the boys being on hand.'

Ellen bit her lip nervously. 'I hope there won't be . . . whatever. Not today, Mum. We don't want the residents upset.'

'It will be all right. There won't be any trouble,' Patsy promised, sounding more confident than she felt. 'You go back to your guests. Must be nearly time for the main meal, and this dining room looks grand. As always, you must have worked so hard.'

Ellen was not going to be put off that easily. 'Mum, I need to know what you're going to do.'

Patsy was rooted to the spot for a moment, staring into the distance, remembering the nightmare of seeing her lovely Ellen battered and bruised and laid out on a mattress on the floor of a padded cell.

The cheek of that man! Twelve years on, and he comes to Ellen because he needs money! However, getting up the wall and spoiling the party for all these dear old folk would serve no good purpose. She must find Eddie. Let her men deal with Robert Dellor this time. She patted Ellen's shoulder comfortingly and urged, 'Put on a brave face, Ellen, and a big smile. You won't have to even see Robert. Your father will deal with him and see him on his way.'

'He's sure to ask for me,' Ellen said, sounding terrified.

'What he asks for and what he gets today will be vastly different. That much I can promise you. Now do as I say and go back to your party, but send your father in here to me.'

'All right,' Ellen agreed reluctantly as she slowly made for the door.

Patsy walked to the windows, staring out at Maplehurst's beautiful gardens. How peaceful they looked in the spring sunshine.

The very thought of Robert Dellor lurking about out there chilled her to the bone. She was sure a man like him would not leave quietly unless he was given what he was asking for. If he was turned away with nothing, he wouldn't leave it there. He'd get his revenge. And that could mean only one thing: he'd try to hurt Ellen again. If not today, who was to say she would be safe in the future, now that he knew where she lived and worked?

She let out a deep sigh. She had no answers. And worrying about what he might do was surely a sheer waste of time.

Eddie burst into the room. Getting right to the point, he said, 'Patsy, don't look at me like that. Everything is under control. Ollie was the first to spot that rotter but he held his temper and invited him into the front office.' Then, having taken a few deep breaths, he wrapped his big arms around his wife and kissed her tenderly, holding her close, before saying, 'I think it's great he's turned up here today. Got a bit of a shock, I'd say, when Ollie opened the front door. I'd have given a lot to see the look on his face. And I'm told he was very reluctant to step over the threshold, more so when he turned tail and found Alex and David coming up behind him. But he was persuaded.'

He laughed a great belly laugh. 'Bet by now he wishes he was anywhere but here.'

'Oh, Eddie, no trouble, please,' Patsy pleaded in a quiet voice, looking up at him. 'There won't be, will there?'

'I honestly can't answer that, Patsy. I want you to go back and stay with Ellen, and when the gong sounds see that everyone gets safely seated here in the dining room. This must be terrible for our Ellen, so it's up to all of us to see that her party proceeds as promised. Leave Robert Dellor to us, and we will be joining you in no time at all. Go on, go now and do yer best to act normally.'

He bent his head, kissed her and led her towards the door.

Slowly Patsy pulled herself together. She took a deep breath and walked briskly across the hall and into the big lounge, all the time asking herself why she should be worried that her sons might hurt Robert Dellor. It had been his own idea to contact Ellen and ask her to give him money. After twelve years, it really was unbelievable, and if his plans were to go wrong and he came out the worse for his trouble, then it was no more than he deserved.

Eddie and Ollie were here this time, not thousands of miles away, and whereas normally they were both thoughtful and fair-minded, who could blame either one of them if today they put a stop to that scoundrel once and for all.

Across the floor of the front office, Eddie Owen, his two sons, his son-in law Donald Langford, and Alexander Berry returned Robert Dellor's angry outburst with a steady, unblinking gaze.

'My business is with Ellen, not you lot,' Robert shouted with a lot more bravado than he was actually feeling. 'The house she sold from under me was mine and I'm here to collect what is rightfully owing to me.'

'Then you've had a wasted journey,' Eddie shot back. He was having a hard job to control his temper. Filled with loathing and hatred for this slimy devious bloke. His big brown eyes blazed as he added, 'You're dealing with us today, not Ellen.'

Robert looked from one to another and sneered. 'Oh, very brave, five against one, great odds, wouldn't you say?'

Eddie thought of his daughter at the mercy of this creep and was pushed too far. He made a ball of his fist and drew his arm back.

'DAD! Don't!' David and Alex both exploded, moving violently towards Robert.

'Don't stop him . . . go on, let him beat me up,' Robert bellowed, his flushed face darkening even more. ''Cos I tell you what I'm going t' do. Go straight to the police.'

'Just a minute, Mr Dellor,' Ollie cut in quickly, his anger running high. 'Today, one way or another, we shall settle you for good an' all. Make no mistake, when you leave here today, matters between you and this family *will* be settled. It can be done quietly. But if you choose not to listen to what we have to say, then on your own head be it.'

'Look here,' Robert shouted. 'You're not being fair. I only want what Ellen owes me.'

'Fair?' Ollie retorted. 'Leaving aside what you did to Ellen, let's deal with the house. First off, her father put a large deposit down on that property, but did you keep up with the mortgage repayments? Like as hell you did. Ellen worked every hour that God Almighty sent, but still she couldn't keep up with your gambling debts, and that's why you half killed her.'

'I still say it's not fair that Ellen walked away with all that cash.' Robert's voice was a horrible whine by now.

'The issues of fair or unfair just don't come into it this time around,' Alex butted in coldly.

'Well, they should do. That house was in my name as well as hers, and the mortgage repayments were like a rope around my neck. Anyway, like I've said, this is nothing t' do with you lot. It should be between just Ellen and me.'

'Repayments my arse. When did they ever bother you?' Donald felt he had stood quietly listening for long enough.

He had watched his wife Emma suffer agonies because of what this scumbag had done to her twin sister. 'You'll be telling us next that you were a good husband.'

Robert took two steps backwards. 'Well, Ellen never pulled her weight, that's for sure. Too busy swanning around London to care what happened to me or our home.'

Eddie had heard enough. His fist went back and this time he planted it firmly between Robert's eyes before stopping to think of the consequences.

Robert staggered forward, trying to grab hold of the desk, but David put his foot out and tripped him up. He fell in a crumpled heap on the floor. David stood over him, breathing heavily. His chest felt like it was going to explode with anger. Robert was looking up at him, his eyes showing how frightened he was, and David knew what he was thinking but decided he wasn't going to let him off the hook.

Slowly and deliberately he said, 'I've never forgotten what you did to my sister.' All the hatred and the urge for revenge were contained in those words. He had forgotten that they were down in Ramsgate for a party, had forgotten everything except the fact that he had good cause to hate this man. Because of him, Ellen had been committed to a mental asylum. Lifting his foot high, he aimed his first kick. Robert screamed, but David carried on regardless. He felt no sympathy. Robert Dellor was a coward, the worst kind, who dished out beatings to a defenceless woman.

Finally David said, 'Have you anything to say before I let my brother have his turn with you?'

Robert just about managed to shake his head. He knew when he was defeated.

Both Ollie and Eddie were shocked by what David had done, but neither of them felt they could really blame him.

Now Alex was bending over Robert. 'I could carry on where my brother has left off and still sleep nights, because whatever happens to you would only be a flea bite compared

100

to what you did to my sister. But I'm gonna leave you be for the time being. Whatever happens next is down to my father and grandfather. Still, I have a promise to make to you.' To make sure Robert was listening, he prodded him with the toe of his shoe. 'Push yer luck once more and you'll end up wishing you were dead. You're damn lucky one of us hasn't killed you stone-dead today.'

Robert's heart sank as he looked up at the faces of these five big men. He was never going to be able to get one over on them. As this unpleasant fact sank in, he grumbled to himself, How come I picked on today to visit Ellen? On her own I could have frightened her into paying up. How the hell was I to know the whole bloody family were here?

He needed money badly, but that was no longer the point. He could feel the naked hatred being directed at him as all these pairs of eyes stared down. His one aim now was to get the hell out of here before they decided to really batter the life out of him.

'Leave him be now.' Ollie decided to take charge. He wanted this over and done with. Any one of them in this room was capable of murder today, and the outcome of that would be a total disaster.

'Sit up.' All Ollie's hatred and knowledge of what this slimy git had done to Ellen were contained in those two words. He crouched down until his face was level with Robert's. Speaking quietly and slowly, the big old man made his presence felt.

'When you so cowardly beat up my granddaughter and left her for dead, you made enemies for life. Her father and I weren't here to deal with you then. But we are here now. You didn't reckon on that, did you?'

Robert closed his eyes and turned his head away.

Ollie straightened up and kicked him in the side. 'Did you? Answer me,' he yelled, all his fury coming to the fore.

'No,' Robert stammered.

'Well now, you listen and you listen good. Money will buy most things, including violence. I never thought I'd live to see this day, but I've come to the conclusion that there is only one way to deal with scum like you. It has become a case of needs must when the devil drives. So I'm going to let it be known to every villain in the whole of London that if they see or hear that you have come within a mile of Ellen, I will pay them a great deal of money to make sure that the only thing you will need from that day on is an undertaker.'

The very tone of Ollie's voice was enough to freeze the blood in Robert's veins. This was no idle threat. He had no doubt that every word that Alexander Berry had said would be carried out to the letter.

Ollie crouched low again. With his lips very close to Robert's face he asked, 'Have you got the message?'

Blood oozed from the side of Robert's mouth, there were men going hammer and tongs inside his head and he was sure he had quite a few broken ribs. But making a great effort he quickly said, 'Yes, yes, yes.'

They didn't bother to see if he was badly hurt. Strong hands dragged him to his feet and frog-marched him down a passageway. Ollie unlocked the back door and Eddie said, 'Put him down behind the potting sheds, lads. He can have a good sleep there.'

'Out of sight, out of mind, wouldn't you say?' Alex laughed.

'If he knows what is good for him, it will be,' was Ollie's serious reply.

Having spent a few minutes tidying themselves up, the five men agreed they had better join the party. As they approached the dining room the door opened and a smiling Frances said, 'Where have you lot been? I've been asked to fetch two more bottles of white wine.'

'I'll get it,' Alex offered.

'All right, Dad.' Then, turning to Ollie, she said, 'Come on, Grandad, come an' join the throng. The food is great. In fact it's a lovely gathering. Weird but lovely.'

The men grinned. Weird was probably the right word.

'Have my boys been looking after you?' her uncle asked.

Frances laughed. 'Come on, Uncle Donald. I'm getting to be a big girl. I don't need minders.'

Don't you? The same thought came to all their minds as they put on a bright smile and went to take their seats. With scumbags like Robert Dellor loose in this world, all young girls needed to be watched over.

Chapter Seven

PATSY OPENED HER FRONT door and stepped back in surprise. It was only a quarter to eight on this Wednesday morning, and Valerie, her daughter-in-law, was standing on the doorstep looking pretty dishevelled. The family had only got back from Ramsgate late yesterday afternoon.

'You'd better come in,' Patsy murmured, as she turned and walked down the passage. She had no idea why Valerie had decided to make this call and she dreaded the thought that it might result in a slanging match. Not that she was frightened of Valerie, even though she was inches taller than Patsy herself.

Still, this matter had to be dealt with, before Val made serious trouble, not only for David but also for Tim; and, when Patsy came to think about it, trouble for the whole family.

The kitchen door was partially open, and seeing Florrie seated at the table, Valerie paused for a moment before going in. The room was bright and cheerful; the table covered with a blue-checked gingham cloth was well laid. Toast in a rack, teapot complete with cosy, milk jug, sugar basin, marmalade, jam and honey. Half-grapefruits in dishes each smothered with sugar, and a huge bunch of bananas.

Florrie's surprise showed, but clearing her throat she said, 'Morning, Val, you're in time for some breakfast. Sit yer down.'

'Hello, Aunt Flo,' Valerie replied coldly. 'I 'aven't come for breakfast.'

Florrie paid no attention to her tone. She could read this one like a book. 'Well, at least 'ave a cuppa,' she said, taking off the cosy and lifting the big brown pot.

'Yeah, all right,' Val muttered. Then, seeing the look that Patsy gave her, quickly added, 'Thank you.'

''Ow are yer?' Florrie asked, passing over the cup and saucer.

'All right, I suppose,' came the surly reply.

'Then what the 'ell are yer doing 'ere at this time in the morning?' Florrie couldn't hold back any longer, but her swift question got Valerie's back up good and proper.

'What's it got t' do with you? It's my mother-in-law I've come to see.'

Val's rudeness and sneering manner were like a red rag to a bull where Florrie was concerned. But looking hard at Val's face, she saw the tiredness in her eyes and the weary lines around her mouth. Val had lost weight, seemed strung up. A bundle of nerves. And the short, skimpy skirt and figure-hugging top she was wearing made her look like a cheap tart. Whatever had happened to the decent Valerie that they'd all known?

'Been out all night, 'ave yer?' Florrie said quietly, doing her best to suppress her anger.

Valerie ignored her and turned to Patsy. She took a sip of her tea before saying, 'I'd like t' talk to you about my Tim.'

This request jolted Patsy, but she half smiled and said, 'Go on then, I'm listening.'

'Well . . .' Val began shakily, 'for starters I'm thinking of leaving David.'

Florrie wasn't having that!

'Only thinking about it? Well, that is kind of yer!'

Patsy shook her head at Florrie, knowing it wouldn't do a bit of good. She'd have her say come hell or high water.

But Val ignored Florrie and continued: 'Between one an' another of yer, you've taken my Tim away from me.' Now her eyes were bright with tears, but she sniffed and went on, 'But it's not only that. It's me an' David. I don't think we should ever 'ave got married.' This last statement was said in a different voice, sounding nowhere near so bitter.

Patsy shook her head in utter disbelief. It had taken Val a jolly long time to come to this conclusion. But there was no point in arguing with her, or reminding her that she had been eager enough all those years ago to have David not only as a husband, but as a legally adopted father for Tim.

Valerie hesitated for a moment and then went on: 'David is such a stick-in-the-mud. Never wants to do anything or go anywhere – well, not with me anyway. He makes me feel that I'm no longer attractive.'

Patsy reflected on this statement for a moment. Was that what all these flings were about? Val fighting to be seen as attractive? To be a young woman again? Well, Patsy sighed softly to herself, wouldn't we all like to turn the clock back? Or was it these so-called swinging sixties that were to blame?

Suddenly life was so different. And the mode of dress! Short skirts, tight skimpy tops showing bare midriffs, and never a decent pair of shoes in sight, only high boots. Loads of make-up and hair dyed all colours. Were young women realising that the war years had robbed them of their youth? Their teenage years?

They had been hard, frightening years. Nothing lovely had been available, everything had been so drab and dreary. No silk stockings. No new dresses. Winter coats made out of old grey army blankets. Underwear all flannelette and fleecy-lined. Now the shops looked like Aladdin's Caves in comparison. Clubs and dance halls were all brilliantly lit up, the blackout forgotten. Real live bands played sweet dance music.

Yes, we did miss so much during those hard years, thought Patsy, especially the young girls who were growing up. Now they wanted to make up for lost time. They were out to attract the men. Come to think of it, the boys were almost as bad, with their strange haircuts and sharp suits. Whereas the young women all wanted to be sex symbols like the film stars they saw at the cinema, the boys yearned to be like The Beatles. And who could blame them.

Patsy sighed wearily. Valerie was not so young; certainly, with a grown-up son it didn't seem right to up sticks and go out and about on the razzle.

'I feel sorry for you, Val,' she said quietly. 'But you haven't stopped to consider how lucky you are. Surely Tim should be the most important thing in your life? He loves you dearly.'

'Oh, come off it, Patsy,' Valerie said with a sneer. 'You've all enticed him away from me good an' proper. Bought him, I'd say, 'cos you've even given him a house to live in on his own. He doesn't love me any more, and he certainly doesn't need me.'

'Yes he does. And if you were t' sit down an' think about it, you'd realise he only left home because your behaviour of late has embarrassed him. He can't face you.'

'I don't believe a word of it,' Valerie said, shifting in her chair. She took another gulp of her tea, then brought the cup down on the saucer with a bang and glared at her mother-in-law. 'You know your trouble, Patsy, you think you can rule everyone. All right, I've made some mistakes, but being domineering ain't one of them.' She leaned forward and practically spat the next words out. 'Every member of this family does what you tell them to or you'd 'ave them out on their bloody ear so fast their feet wouldn't touch the ground.'

Patsy brought herself up in her chair with as much dignity as she could muster, but before she could find words to form an answer, Florrie had intervened.

'I've never 'eard anything quite so ridiculous! You're not only spiteful, you're bloody mad, gal. You 'ave to be t' come out with something like that.'

Valerie laughed. 'I might 'ave known you'd say something like that. Whatever Patsy decides, you're always there to back her t' the hilt. Whether it's right or wrong you don't give a toss. She's the boss, an' you're there t' make sure no one crosses 'er.' Val was really yelling now, her anger and bitterness getting the better of her.

Patsy shook her head from side to side. Matters were getting out of hand. This was exactly what she'd hoped to avoid.

Speaking quietly she said, 'I wish you would listen to me, Valerie. No one is trying to take your son away from you. He is a grown man with a wise head on his shoulders. He makes his own decisions. I just wish you and David would sit down and talk to each other. Try and sort things out . . .' Patsy paused, then added, 'Before it is too late.' Then, taking a chance, she went on, 'I bet if you ask our David, he will tell you outright that he loves you the way you are. After all, he's showing a good few grey hairs himself these days.'

'David's too pig-headed to sit down and talk.' Val was sulking now. 'And you're doing it again, telling me what I should do.'

Patsy shook her head in disbelief. 'I give up. But I would like you t' know I mean well. Myself and Eddie would be really upset if you and David were to split up.'

Abruptly Valerie stood up, shoving the table away from her. 'That's what I came 'ere this morning for. To 'ave a go at all of you for bribing my Tim to leave 'ome, an' to let yer know that I *am* leaving David.'

Florrie reached out and took Patsy's hand. 'Don't let 'er

108

get t' yer, luv. She's made up 'er mind, and no matter what's she's trying to prove, none of this is your fault.'

Val gave Florrie a hideous look as she buttoned up her jacket. 'Like I said, you're the power behind her throne! Well, good luck t' the lot of yer, 'cos I'm off.'

Patsy and Florrie sat in silence, listening to Val's high heels striking down the long hall to the front door. Patsy, ever the optimist, was hoping against hope that even at this late stage Valerie would come to her senses. Florrie, though, was a realist, and she feared the worst.

Chapter Eight

PATSY HAD DECIDED THAT Cornwall was a magical place. It was giving her a sense of well-being. Much as she loved London and adored her children, it was nice to have a change from the daily workings of the business.

She stood outside The Manse, gazing down at the great stretch of overgrown garden, yet not really seeing it, a faraway expression on her face. She was thinking about Valerie. The way they had parted had been dreadful, and she still felt shaken. Sighing, she walked over to stand beneath one of the huge trees. I mustn't bear a grudge, she told herself firmly. And I mustn't let my anger show to the family, and especially not to David or Tim.

Suddenly she smiled to herself, wondering what Florrie was doing with herself this morning. She had refused point blank to come back today for a second look at this old property. 'Once was more than enough,' she'd loudly declared.

Of course, even if this place were ever to belong to Ace Trading Company and eventually brought up to the standard of a first-class hotel, they'd never get Florrie to change her mind. To try and persuade her to live in the midst of all this spacious countryside would be useless. Yet it had been a good idea to bring her for a visit. She wasn't against a bit of good old-fashioned comfort. And Ollie had made sure that she received A1 treatment all the way, including a very large comfortable sea-view room in the hotel. The very thought had Patsy grinning.

When she, Eddie and Ollie had been ready to set off this morning, she'd gone upstairs to tell Florrie they'd be back in time for evening dinner. The bedroom had looked sunny and restful as she watched Florrie pad across the deep carpet to the dressing table which stood in the wide bay window looking over the great stretch of golden sand and beyond to the sea. Still dressed in the white fluffy towelling robe provided by the hotel, Florrie had sat down and started to brush her hair.

'Will you be all right?' Patsy had asked.

Florrie's hearty laughter had rung out. 'What on earth are yer going on about? Course I will, my luv. Get yerselves off, there's no need to worry about me. Yer know what? It's amazing 'ere. I've only got t' pick up that phone an' they bring me anything I want.'

'Even fish an' chips or jellied eels?' Patsy teased.

'If that's what I ask for, dare say they would.' Florrie didn't sound at all doubtful. 'You get off an' do what yer 'ave to. I'll see you all tonight.'

'If you're sure,' Patsy had said slowly, not really comfortable at leaving Florrie on her own for the whole day.

'Penny for them.' Ollie cut into Patsy's thoughts.

'I was just wondering if I did right to leave Florrie.'

'Stop worrying about her. Believe me, she'll be having a wonderful time,' Ollie said, laughing loudly.

'Stop worrying about her? You're a fine one to talk. You don't let the wind blow on our Florrie,' Patsy said, laughing with him.

They heard Eddie's footsteps as he came around the side of the building.

'Hello, luv, everything all right?' Patsy asked, as he came down the four stone steps towards them.

'All settled,' he said. 'Surveyor is coming out at nine o'clock tomorrow morning.'

'Where did you phone from?' Ollie asked.

'Nearest pub. About a mile away. Great bloke, the governor. I said we'd pop in for a drink and a snack later.'

'You haven't wasted much time,' Patsy cried.

Eddie shrugged. 'We like the place. As the lads said, it's got potential, so we're getting a full survey. That's all we can do at the moment.'

'I thoroughly agree.' Ollie smiled broadly. 'Now we might as well enjoy the rest of the day. Lead on to the pub, Eddie.'

Patsy said nothing as they walked to the car. Several nagging questions were buzzing around in her head. This was a grand place, but oh, it was such a long way from London. She settled herself comfortably in the back seat, and looked down at her hands, curled in her lap, fiddling with her wedding ring. She was so lucky really. Whatever her men decided, she'd go along with them. She certainly wasn't going to let them see how doubtful she felt, but . . . She leaned forward and tapped Ollie on the shoulder.

He turned his head and Patsy looked at him carefully. 'I want to ask you something. You might not like it, but I feel compelled to ask it.' She waited, still watching him closely.

He smiled. 'Patsy, my luv, whenever did you not feel able to be straightforward with me? What's the question?'

She caught Eddie glancing at her in the driving mirror, but she took a deep breath and pressed on. 'D'you think it's a bit over the top buying a place to run as a hotel so far away from London?'

Ollie twisted round and looked at her in astonishment, then he laughed. 'Anyone would think Cornwall was the other side of the world. Anyway, it was the lads' idea to branch out, and after all the company will be mainly theirs

112

before too long. I don't want to hold them back. They know what they're doing.'

'But we've always dealt with Londoners. Bought places where they like to go. Can you really see a coachload of East Enders staying in The Manse? Never mind what they'd find to do of an evening. I can't help wondering if we're getting a bit above ourselves.'

Ollie shook his head. 'Patsy, at my age I'm certainly not worried about making loads more money. Nor am I ambitious for higher things. Actually, everything I do and plan is for the family. In a manner of speaking, your children and their children are mine. It has always been that way, just as surely as if we were of the same blood line. All I want is for each and every one of them to have a secure and happy future. Not to have to scratch a living as you and your mother did. Now isn't that what you want?'

'Yes, I suppose so,' Patsy admitted sheepishly. 'I trust Alex and David and if at all possible I like to go along with their ideas. They both work hard and do a good job.'

'Well there you are, then.'

It came to her then that there was no point arguing with him any further. She might own a third of the company's shares, and this was supposed to be the era of women's rights and all that, but when it came down to rock bottom it was still largely a man's world. At least in business it was.

Eddie straightened his shoulders. 'We're almost there. Next point on the agenda is what you would like for your lunch.'

'Trust you.' Patsy grinned. 'All problems get shelved when food is about.'

That evening Patsy and Eddie took Florrie for a drive, leaving Ollie to enjoy a glass of port and his cigar. Eddie stopped the car and Patsy, who was sitting in the back beside Florrie, lowered a window. A young man and a woman were running up the beach, their hair wet from their swim. She was wrapped in a towelling robe and they both looked fit and happy. Further over were two boys, weatherbeaten and bare-legged; they were painting the sides of a dinghy, getting her ready for the coming season no doubt. Eddie had said that if they did buy a place in Cornwall, he would buy a boat and teach his grandchildren to fish. That set Patsy thinking. Not only of the grandchildren but also of her grown-up children. What with the war and its aftermath, when had they ever got away for a real holiday?

Picnics on the sands. Cornish cream teas. They could explore all the tiny coves, swim in the sea. Oh, so many things she'd be able to do with them if they were to come to Cornwall.

She might even find time to stand and stare.

She looked at Florrie and grinned. 'I was thinking about all the things we might do if we brought the kids down here for a couple of weeks.'

'What! The lads would be bored to tears, and as for Frances, she's a town-bird if ever there was one.'

'Don't you think they'd like The Manse?'

Florrie raised her eyebrows. 'Oh, they'd find it interesting enough. All those staircases leading up an' down, no two rooms seem to be on the same level once you get past the first floor. And on the top floor there's so many tiles missing off the roof they could lie in bed an' see the sky.'

'All that would be put right,' Patsy said, doing her best to sound convincing.

'Hmm, take a bloody army to get that place in working order. An' even then they'll 'ave an 'ard job convincing folk it's like London by the sea. It ain't a bit like Southend either, is it? No sausage an' mash, nor cockles and whelks, and definitely no funfairs.'

Patsy had to laugh at her stern face but Florrie didn't mind, and suddenly the pair of them were laughing fit to bust.

114

Eddie waited until a silence fell between them before he turned round. 'Nothing but doubts from you two, eh?'

It took a minute or two before Patsy could form an answer. 'It's a big decision, Eddie,' she said at last. 'I know we'll have lots of discussions with the boys before we sign anything, and there are so many questions we'll have to find answers for, aren't there?'

'Of course there are, my luv, and nothing will be decided in haste, I promise. You and every member of the family will have plenty of time to put forward not only all their ideas but all their objections as well. You'll see.'

Florrie reached to take hold of Patsy's hand, and the look that passed between them said that each knew full well that their thoughts were running along the same lines. They might have their own opinions, and of course they would be listened to, but if the men were in complete agreement, they might just as well give in from the beginning.

A few seagulls flew overhead. Patsy opened the car door to watch their graceful flight, and she felt in her bones, in that moment, that she would be coming back to Cornwall again in the not too distant future.

In spite of all her misgivings.

Chapter Nine

FIVE WEEKS LATER, PATSY could not believe how Eddie and Ollie had managed to get so much done since they'd come back from Cornwall. They'd worked wonders, accomplished so much in that short space of time.

The Manse, for better or for worse, was well on the way to being owned by the Ace Trading Company. Patsy felt much more settled in her mind now, confident that her men knew what they were doing. She had finally given in gracefully, even though Florrie was still moaning like hell and telling her far too often that she should have put her foot down much harder. To Florrie, Cornwall was the other end of the world!

No, it wasn't the business that was niggling away at her. It was members of the family.

Valerie had done exactly as she had said she would: upped sticks and gone. Both David and Tim were terribly upset. Then there was Frances, her only granddaughter. There was something really wrong with Frances. Patsy didn't know what it was, but in her heart she just knew everything was not well with that young lady.

Patsy had always possessed that highly sensitive mind

116

which born survivors are often blessed with. A sort of sixth sense that enabled her to pick up on things, both good and bad, but especially bad. And then of course there was her gut instinct, which she had come to trust, to rely on without questioning, knowing she was almost always right. For some time she had felt Frances wasn't easy in her company, which was a hard thing to accept, because being the only girl, she had been the apple of everyone's eye, and Patsy had always felt close to her – spoiling her rotten if the truth be told. But these days Frances seemed awkward, and so far Patsy had been unable to put a finger on anything in particular.

Sitting back in her chair, Patsy couldn't decide whether or not to discuss her feelings with Eddie. She wondered if she should broach the subject with Vicky. Surely if there was something wrong with Frances, her mother would be the first to pick up on it.

Or maybe it might be better to talk to Emma.

She started sorting through the morning post, but it wasn't long before Emma's happy face appeared round the door.

'Morning, Mum, early start, eh?'

Patsy nodded her head. 'Yes, your father and Ollie were up an' out real early, so I thought I might just as well come into the office. There's always plenty of paperwork t' be seen to.'

'You were wearing a worried frown when I came in. Are you feeling all right, Mum?'

'Yes.' Patsy reassured her, and gave a small smile as she got up to put the kettle on. 'It's just something that's been niggling away at me for about a month now.'

'Like what?' Emma asked, then quickly said, 'Come on, Mum, you always say a problem shared is a problem halved.'

'Who said anything about a problem? It's just a gut feeling I have that all is not well with our Frances.'

'Oh? Well, have you spoken to Vicky? Surely she could tell you if there was something wrong.'

'I've thought about it. But it doesn't do to be too sure on that score,' Patsy warned her daughter. 'Parents are often the last ones to know.'

'Funny, you and Frances are so close. If she were to tell anyone her problems I think it would be you. She's always going on about how great her gran is.'

'I feel the same way about her. Only girl amongst the boys an' all that. We all tend to make a fuss of Frances.'

'Have you asked any of the boys about this, Mum? They're all so protective of her. Mind you, she charms them all the way. Has each and every one of her cousins – and her brother – eating out of her hand most of the time.'

Patsy raised her eyebrows. 'That's true. And the same goes for her uncles, and Grandad and Ollie. She plays them all to the hilt.'

'Nicely, though,' Emma commented.

'Oh, I'm not saying different,' Patsy quickly said. 'A nicer girl than Frances you'd go a heck of a long way t' meet. I can't see any major difficulty in her life, and yet . . .' She left the sentence unfinished.

'What about last Sunday, Mum? Surely you didn't think anything was wrong with her then, did you? She looked great. Lovely dress, pretty shawl, colourful sandals.'

'Yes.' Patsy nodded her agreement. 'But that's my point. She's growing up far too fast for my liking.'

Emma began to laugh. 'Are you thinking she's got herself a boyfriend?'

'Well, the thought did enter my head, especially with the grown-up way she seems to want to dress these days. But when I asked her what she'd been up to lately, she was a bit cagey with me, an' that's not like Frances. She's always talked to me, as you well know.'

'Oh, Mum, you know how young girls are these days. It's all flower power an' freedom. Or so they tell me.'

Patsy bit back a smile. 'You don't have to defend Frances

to me, Emma dear. I know she's a good girl, and as for what the youngsters tell you, you're not so old, and if you think you are, what does that make me?'

'Now you're fishing, Mother. You've never looked better an' you know it.'

To herself Emma was thinking her mum was probably right to be concerned about Frances. She'd had a sneaking suspicion that her niece wasn't happy for a while now. She'd even broached the subject with her husband. Quiet and reliable as always, Donald hadn't had much to say on the matter.

It was a difficult situation. Emma didn't want to be seen to be prying, but if she got the chance she felt it was about time to sound Vicky out.

That was if she could find the right moment.

A sudden thought came to her and she immediately voiced it aloud to her mother. 'It could be that our Frances is upset because Peggy Stevens is moving away from here.'

'Oh, I didn't know they were moving,' Patsy answered thoughtfully.

'Yeah, apparently there are some new blocks of flats and maisonettes that have been built up near the Elephant and Castle – you know, where that landmine landed and they cleared the whole site after the war.'

'Yeah, but I fail to see how the Stevenses qualify for a new place.'

'Can't answer that one,' Emma said, 'though I do know that they have relations still living in the East End.'

'Ah well, good luck t' them. But I shall be sorry t' see them go, nice family, and Frances and Peggy have grown up together. Even though Alex and Vicky decided to move out to Tolworth, those two girls have still remained friends. Whenever Frances stays here with me she spends much of her time round Peggy's house. You could be right, Emma, that's probably what Frances is upset about. Still, she can always visit, and I wouldn't mind having Peggy to stay here sometimes; she's very well-mannered.'

Emma nodded her agreement, hoping against hope that that was all that was worrying her niece.

Chapter Ten

PATSY, OLLIE AND FLORRIE had had the house to themselves for two weeks. It had been great, and the time had flown by. It had reminded them all of the days when they had lived in Tooting, and when Florrie and Patsy never had more than a shilling or two left in their purse on a Monday morning.

Now, on this warm and pleasant Sunday morning, Patsy felt happy at the thought that by this evening her menfolk would be back from Cornwall and their families would all be here in this house for their evening dinner. The icing on the cake was that Ellen would also be here, for two whole weeks, the first time she had taken a holiday away from the Maplehurst since she had taken on the job. Another added bonus was that Peter Crawford, Jack Berry's manager, had been in London for the last three days and he too was invited for this evening. It was promising to be one of the most beautiful days of midsummer in more ways than one.

The door burst open and Thomas and Sam appeared. Patsy looked at them and gasped. 'My God, what on earth 'ave you two been up to?'

'We've only been on the common, Gran,' came the cheeky reply.

'Looks like you've tried t' dig half of it up. Now upstairs quick,' Patsy said, glaring at them. 'You look like a couple of street urchins. I want you out of those dirty trousers and shirts and back down here clean and tidy before your mother gets here.'

'What shall we put on, Gran?' Sam asked warily.

'Don't give me that!' Patsy yelled. 'You know very well there's plenty of clothes in the airing cupboard on the landing. And don't forget to wash behind your ears and brush yer hair. I've seen you dirty before, but it's Sunday today and you should never have got yerselves into such a state. Now get going.'

'All right, Gran,' Thomas murmured meekly.

Watching Emma and Donald's two youngest sons disappear upstairs took Patsy back years to when Alex and David had been small boys. So young myself then, she thought, too young. Suddenly a smile lit up her face as images of her boys came to mind. Two right little beggars they had been, but so loving.

There were no dramas in Navy Street that evening. Patsy's traditional Sunday roast progressed without a hitch. After the huge meal had been served and eaten, Emma and Ellen made and passed around the coffee. Watching Ellen closely, Patsy thought her daughter had indeed changed. So close now, so quiet and withdrawn. She supposed that living with elderly folk all the time, it was only to be expected. She was so thankful that Alex and David had persuaded their sister to come home and be part of a family gathering once again.

A happy mood seemed to settle over everyone as the children went out into the garden and the adults settled down to chat – or in Florrie and Ollie's case to doze. Patsy had thought Ellen would feel strange, slightly out of it, but was relieved that she had chatted to everyone and was now deep in conversation with Peter Crawford.

Peter was well aware of how badly Ellen's husband had treated her. Keeping in touch, as he had over the years, with the family, both for business reasons and because of the great friendship he had formed with Ollie and the entire Owen family, he was also aware that Ellen had practically withdrawn from the outside world.

This evening he had quietly studied her. His conclusion was that she was a truly beautiful, gentle lady. So like her twin, Emma, yet lacking the vitality and spontaneous gestures of her sister.

He took a deep breath. Ellen stirred feelings in him that left him unsure of himself. There were so many factors to be considered. For a start there was the age difference, and no matter which way you looked at it, it was vast. And since the car accident he had been involved in, which had taken Jack Berry's life, his life had altered considerably.

He laughed to himself at that thought.

He had been a proper little urchin when Jack Berry had taken him under his wing. Twenty-five years he had stayed close to Jack. He had worked hard, watched and learned, and in return Jack had made him a rich man. More than that, they had given each other respect and loyalty in every way possible.

He had made a remarkable recovery from the injuries he had sustained in the car crash, though he still suffered pain and consequently lived a quieter life. But he kept himself fit, his mind active and he had the income to dress well and to travel the world.

From what he had learned, Ellen had suffered as much as he had and more. She had not really lived her life since that awful period when she had been committed to a special hospital. She had shut herself away. Doing good for others, taking care of the elderly. Surely she deserved better than that? A life of her own?

He felt he could give her that and more, yet caution was the word that was staring him in the face. Ellen was timid, even frightened at times. If only she would let him, he would do anything to give her back at least some of the self-confidence and happiness that her twin sister enjoyed.

People said he didn't look his age. He hoped it was true, but would Ellen see him as an old man? He sincerely hoped not. He took a deep breath and took the plunge.

'Will you let me take you out for a meal, or maybe get seats for a show? Please, Ellen?' Ellen stared at him, her expression troubled. He hastily said, 'I don't want to rush you. We just seem to hit it off OK and I wondered . . .' He gave her a reassuring smile. 'Will you think about it?'

Patsy, watching from across the room, glanced at Eddie. Had he noticed that Peter was taking notice of Ellen? Had she imagined it? Oh dear God. For someone as good and kind as Peter to love and cherish her lovely Ellen would be the answer to all her prayers.

Peter tried again. 'Please, Ellen?'

'I wouldn't be very good company,' Ellen half whispered.

'Yes you would.' Moving away, Peter lifted her face, looked into her eyes. 'I know you don't trust men, with good reason, but I would never hurt you. Please say you will let me take you out, if only for a meal.'

'I would like that, Peter, but . . .' Her voice wavered and stopped. Her eyes filled up.

'Hey, come on, Ellen,' he said. 'We'll be good for each other, you'll see.'

'Yes, all right.' She brushed her eyes with her fingertips, forced a cheerful smile. 'It's just that it's been so long.'

'I know, I know. All the more reason to live a little while you are here in London.'

'I can't help feeling it may not be fair to you. I'm not used to going out.'

He laughed. 'Well, being an Aussie, I'll be the one to entertain you. So, will you trust me?'

'Yes, thank you. I'll look forward to it.'

At that moment Peter Crawford felt very protective and wanted more than anything to wrap his arms around her and hug her fiercely.

Ellen just couldn't help wondering why Peter Crawford was being so nice to her. She had been struck by him the minute he had taken her hand to shake it as her father had introduced them. She had been taken with his incredibly smooth tanned skin, his deep blue eyes and even the faint smell of his aftershave. He certainly looked sharp, every inch a businessman. Fair hair turning to silver at the sides, as tall as her father and brothers, he wore an immaculate grey suit obviously hand-tailored. He was a man of the world, well travelled, used to financial deals and by the looks of him willing to spend what he earned with style. When he spoke, it was very quietly, very calmly, with occasional flashes of humour.

There was no cheeky chappie or even a hint of an intention of double-dealing about him as there had been with Robert. She quickly told herself that comparing the two men was not a good idea. Robert had never showed he really cared for anyone other than himself; he was always loud-mouthed and brash. Whereas Peter seemed to bring his professional values into his everyday life. Summed up in one word, Ellen would have said he was classy. He was treating her as an intelligent adult, and that fact alone meant a lot to her.

Later that night, Ellen stood in front of the mirror on the dressing table in her bedroom, staring at herself but not really focusing. Instead, she was thinking of her mother, whom she had always adored. Ellen was absolutely certain there was no one quite like Patsy Owen. Her mother was a one-off, loving, generous and kind. She usually gave everyone the benefit of the doubt and tried always to see the best in people. With one exception: hurt her children and she would fight like a demon. Hadn't she proved that when Ellen herself had been so ill? To be honest, Ellen was well aware that there had been a time when she had lost the will to live. It was her mother who, day after day, hour by hour, had urged her to fight back, get better and start to live again.

For twelve years Ellen had made a new life for herself. Grabbing at straws, she had accepted her mother's suggestion to take over and be in charge of the Maplehurst. It had been a good time, quiet but good. The old folk were charming and the rewards of knowing that they were safe and happy finishing their days in a secure home were great.

Now she had come home for a short holiday, and on the very first evening Peter Crawford had been there. She had been attracted to him and he to her. With that thought she became agitated. Suppose he wasn't all he seemed? Once she had adored Robert, trusted him, and look where that relationship had got her!

She must not panic. She wasn't a child, though she felt as if she were. A lost child. She would talk to her mother. Patsy had suffered in her younger days, until Eddie had come into her life. 'He was my salvation', her mother was fond of saying. She might even have a word with her father. He had always been there for her, so who better to turn to now?

Patsy and Ollie were having a rare evening on their own. Eddie and the boys were off chasing another contract. They'd eaten their evening meal and cleared away. Ollie had poured himself a glass of port and was busy lighting a cigar, while Patsy had a glass of Bristol Cream sherry in front of her. The two of them were soon engaged in a discussion about the past, which Patsy noticed Ollie seemed to enjoy quite frequently these days.

Suddenly Ollie leaned forward and said in a conspiratorial whisper, 'Do you think Ellen is getting along all right with Peter?'

'I can't tell, not for sure,' Patsy murmured, 'but by God I'd give my front teeth to see them two make a go of it.'

'Everyone else is married, settled well, except for David, although Tim did mention that his father had received a letter from Val asking if the two of them could meet.'

'Really?' Patsy cried in disbelief. 'No one told me.'

Ollie laughed loudly. 'Perhaps Tim didn't want to find out what your reaction might be.'

'Come off it, Ollie. I've not been against Val. It depends on what she wants to see David for.'

'I know no more than you do . . . yet. Anyway, I thought we were discussing Ellen and Peter Crawford,' Ollie complained, sounding unusually put out. I've hoped and longed to see our Ellen settled and happy before I die, and Peter might be just the right man to grant me that wish.'

Patsy threw him a chastising look and tutted softly. 'What's got into you tonight? You're the one who's forever telling me you're going to live to be a hundred.'

'All the more reason for me to want to attend Ellen's wedding before I take to a bathchair.'

Ignoring this comment, Patsy said, 'If it is to be it will happen without us interfering.'

'Yes, I suppose so.' Ollie drew himself up in his chair, a look of helplessness spreading across his face. 'This generation . . . I don't know, Patsy, the youngsters baffle me at times. But Peter, how old is he? Never married, and there's Ellen who has made such a mess of her life, or so it seems to me. You'd think they'd both grab at the chance to find happiness together, especially at their age. Loneliness as one gets older can be a terrible thing.'

Ollie fell silent, and Patsy froze, watching him closely. Surely he wasn't feeling neglected? She leaned over and patted his hand lying on the table. 'I suppose only recently having got to know each other makes them cautious.'

'Yes, more than likely, but wouldn't it be lovely if they do feel great about each other and eventually decide to get married?'

'Yes, oh yes, Ollie, it would, as you say, be wonderful. Both Eddie and I have longed for Ellen to be happy. For her to have someone to really care for her.'

Slowly Patsy got up and went to the sideboard. She poured a brandy for Ollie and another sherry for herself. They sat in silence for a while, as companionable tonight as they had been for as long as Patsy could remember. Eventually Ollie roused himself.

'I think it's time I was away to my bed.'

Patsy gave him a grin as she bent over to kiss him goodnight. 'Sleep well,' she said, quickly adding, 'Don't lie awake match-making.'

'Hmm. Hark who's talking. Still, I suppose we two and Eddie will always worry over the children. Always thinking we know best for each and every one of them.'

'Well, we do. Don't we?' she teased. 'With the old heads we have on our shoulders, and Florrie always in the background to tell us where we're going wrong, we have to get it right. Well, most of the time, anyway.'

BOOK THREE

1966

Chapter One

A FEELING OF EXCITEMENT ran through Patsy.

The Manse was open for business. Two years it had taken, but there it was, with the familiar and distinctive lettering above the door, 'The Manse Hotel', and in smaller lettering underneath, '(Ace Trading Company)'.

She grabbed Eddie's arm. 'I know it's only a hotel, but I feel so proud, Eddie. I do wish Florrie could have been here for the opening.'

Eddie looked across to Ollie, who stood gazing out over the lawns, where a fountain played in the centre. Flowerbeds added bright splashes of colour around the edges of the smooth clipped grass.

The two men nodded at each other, each knowing what the other was thinking. Pride of ownership, gratification at a job well done, a sense of tremendous satisfaction.

Together they all went up the steps and in through the main entrance, and Patsy caught her breath. This area was cream, with lots of small tables and comfortable chairs, and the floor was laid with cream and coffee-coloured carpet tiles. The staircase which led to the upper floors looked magnificent.

'Oh, Eddie, and you Ollie, you've outdone yourselves this time,' Patsy exclaimed.

They both gave her a delighted grin, and turned to introduce her to Russell, the man they had selected to be the manager, and two assistants who were also on duty. Patsy chatted to them excitedly as she was given a complete tour. The young men were pleasant, suited well to their smart uniforms, and well informed about the business of running a hotel. Patsy found herself relaxing as they showed her the various bedrooms, many with their own bathrooms, then the public rooms and back downstairs to the kitchens, which were absolutely unbelievable. All that shiny equipment, and the staff!

The dining room was paradise, every table a picture, with white linen cloths, serviettes folded to stand up in high peaks, shining cutlery and sparkling glassware. The head waiter, in his dark suit, white shirt and black tie, introduced three other waiters, all smartly dressed, and Patsy's eyes darted from side to side, taking in every last detail.

'Well,' said Eddie. 'Fancy staying here for a few days? Did you bring a bucket and spade?'

'No, and it's silly, I know, but when I come down again with the kids I would like somewhere a bit more homely for us. I'd be frightened to death to let our tribe run loose in this place.'

Eddie put his arm around her shoulder, and kissed the top of her head. 'I knew you'd come out with something like that, and so now's the time to tell you that Ollie and I have a big surprise for you. We three are going to stay here for a couple of days, and this afternoon we'll take you out. Let's go up to our room and get changed, shall we?'

Their bedroom, on the first floor, was beautiful.

The windows were open, causing the flimsy voile curtains

to stir gently in the soft breeze. The only sounds were the birds in the trees and the faint distant roar of the sea.

Eddie picked Patsy up and laid her on the bed. 'Come a long way, haven't we, Mrs Owen?'

'We certainly have,' she whispered.

He began to kiss her face while loosening her clothes, and she wallowed in his tenderness. How wonderful he always was, even after all these years. Whenever they made love she felt completely loved, even adored. It had always been the same. Being loved by him was an experience beyond words. He made sure she knew he had made her his for now and always.

Some time later, the jangling telephone at the side of the bed pierced the silence. Eddie, startled, snapped open his eyes and gaped at Patsy. 'God, we've both been asleep.'

Sitting up, Patsy smiled. 'Maybe you'd better answer it.'

Eddie lifted the receiver. 'Hallo, Edward Owen speaking.' Then he laughed. 'It's Ollie, wants to know if we're coming down to lunch!'

'Oh!' Patsy tugged at the sheet, covering herself.

Eddie began to chuckle. He put one hand over the mouthpiece. 'He can't see you lying here naked, you daft 'apporth.'

Patsy made a face. 'But I feel funny.'

Eddie spoke into the phone. 'Give us half an hour.' Then he hung up, looked at Patsy and burst out laughing. 'Come here, you!' he cried, dragging her up and wrapping his arms around her. She struggled with him, laughing and rumpling his hair, and they rolled over and off the edge of the bed, falling to the floor with a bump.

'Give over, Eddie!' Patsy cried. 'I need to wash and dress. You told Ollie we'd be down in half an hour.'

'Time enough for more lovely passion,' he pleaded.

'Of course there's not!' she shrieked, beating her fists against his chest.

133

He caught her wrists, held them tightly and peered down into her face. 'I'll never cease to wonder how you came to be mine, Patsy. I love you more as the years go by, if that's possible.' He released her suddenly and sat up. Patsy did the same.

'Can't believe we're rolling about on this lovely carpet in a hotel which belongs to us.'

Eddie kissed the tip of her nose. 'I'll wash first and get dressed, and you can come downstairs when you are ready.' He sprang up and pulled her to her feet. 'And don't look so darned happy or Ollie will guess what we've been up to.'

'Oh you . . . rotter!' Then her tone changed. 'Anyway, if he doesn't know how randy you can be by now, then he's not all there.'

'I'll tell him you said that, shall I?'

But Patsy had beaten him into the bathroom and locked the door.

Eddie kept his hand firmly on Patsy's arm as he led her down the flagged pathway of Primrose Cottage. The sound of the door being opened made Patsy jump. Ollie stood there with his hand on the latch, smiling at them.

'There you are, my luv, come away in and see what you think of your future holiday home.'

Patsy moved forward and, sounding surprised, said, 'You two are devious. What you get up to behind my back is nobody's business.'

Ollie laughed and opened the door wide, and Patsy grinned as she walked past him and into the main room. She stood at one end, her hand pressed tightly against her cheek. The sun was shining through the windows and she felt as if she were dreaming. This was almost too good to be true. She turned about and walked to a big chair placed beside the open-hearth stone fireplace and sat down. At one time this must have been two, maybe three rooms. Now, with great care and imagination, it had been converted into one large room that took in the entire length and breath of the ground floor of this cottage.

The area she was sitting in was restful, chintzy covers over comfortable armchairs. The far end boasted a huge table with six chairs placed around it, and an open door led to a small kitchen.

Oh! Already, in her mind's eye, she could see her grand-children eating, laughing, talking in this gorgeous room.

She sat forward in her chair, and looking around the sunlit room, dreaming about the future, Patsy thought how lucky she was. This cottage would be absolutely ideal for real family holidays. She felt she had seldom been happier.

'Don't you want to see the upstairs?' Ollie broke into her day-dreaming.

Patsy turned her gaze to Eddie. He was openly laughing at her.

'Come on,' he said. 'Want me to carry you up? The staircase is very narrow.'

'No I don't,' she told him, thrusting him gently out of the way.

Under a high sloping roof there were three bedrooms, each with mullioned windows. No need for lace curtains, no one to overlook; nothing but beautiful countryside as far as the eye could see. The back garden was small but cottagey; a few daffodils still bloomed. The green of the grass and the colour of the flowers and a few shrubs caught Patsy's eye immediately.

'Oh, this is unbelievable,' she exclaimed with pleasure.

'Well, I hope you and the kids have a great many good holidays here,' replied Eddie, putting his arms around her. 'You are so easily pleased,' he added.

The old-fashioned bathroom had her laughing loudly. The huge deep bath was set on iron claw feet, and a shining copper geyser was mounted on the wall above two giant brass taps. The toilet was covered with planks of well-scrubbed wood, with just a hole set dead centre.

'I expect you've noticed most of the furniture is old,' Ollie said. 'It was all here, came as part of the sale. It's good stuff, too good to throw away.'

'It looks so well cared for,' Patsy replied, peeping again into the largest of the three rooms. The smell of lavender filled the air.

'There's a couple live up the lane at the nearest farmhouse. The wife looks after this cottage and is still willing to do so,' Eddie informed her with laughter in his voice. He looked out of the window. 'Funnily enough, she's almost here now.'

'That figures,' Ollie grinned. 'She don't miss a trick.'

'She's a funny body but she means well.' Eddie laughed outright as they watched a plump middle-aged woman bustle up the path.

'Co-ee!' she called from the foot of the stairs.

The moment Patsy shook her work-worn hand, she knew she was going to like this kind countrywoman. Her greeting was warm and comforting. Eddie brought a tray of tea and biscuits, and as she listened to Daisy Button's Cornish accent, a warm glow of satisfaction came over Patsy. She knew without a doubt that they had found a treasure.

'You just drop a postcard or ring, 'cos we're on the telephone now, mi dear,' Daisy stated, 'and I'll have ee provisions all in and fresh-baked scones and a fruit cake in yer larder by the time you arrive with your grandchildren.'

Patsy couldn't wait to bring the children down here. What a holiday they would have. Never in a million years would she have taken any one of them to stay at The Manse. She'd have been on tenterhooks as to what the little beggars might say or do.

Ollie and Eddie knew her so well, and this cottage was

a find indeed. To think that they actually owned it made her feel secure and happy.

She asked no more from life except to be with her family, her grandchildren being an added bonus. Holidays in a place such as this were something she hadn't even dreamed about.

Three days later, as they left the dining room, the head waiter told them there was a telephone call for Mr Owen and would he take it at the reception desk.

Ollie led Patsy to a window table in the lounge and ordered coffee and liqueurs. They sat in pleasant silence for a while until, with slow steps, Eddie came back. Instantly Patsy was on her feet; one look at her husband's face and she knew something was dreadfully wrong.

'What's happened?' she pleaded, grabbing hold of Eddie's arm.

He shook his head slowly. 'Come on, luv, let's sit down,' he begged. 'Please, Patsy.'

Patsy sighed deeply as she seated herself. 'I wish you'd just come out with it and tell me what's wrong. Is it one of the children?'

He took her hand, squeezed her fingers. 'No, it's not any of the kids,' he whispered hoarsely. 'It's Florrie.'

'Oh my God,' Patsy said in a voice that shook. 'She's died, hasn't she, and I wasn't even there with her.'

'I'm so sorry, Patsy. Emma and Donald were with her. They said she went to sleep ever so peaceful like.'

Patsy's tears now really began to flow.

It was after midnight. When they arrived home, they found that nearly all the family had gathered together in Navy Street.

Emma was inconsolable. She did not turn nor did she move at all when her parents arrived; merely went on sitting there in what had been Florrie's room, staring into space.

Patsy flew to her, put her hand lightly on her shoulder,

bent over until her face was close to her daughter's. 'I'm here, Emma, so is yer dad and Ollie.'

She made no answer.

It was Ollie who took her hands in his and brought her slowly to her feet. Big as he was, his actions were very gentle. Emma finally lifted her face to look up into his, and then she began to weep. Ollie took her in his arms and held her close, soothing her.

'I miss her already and she's only just died,' Emma said with a sob that almost broke Patsy's heart. 'The doctor said we had to let the undertakers take her away. I'm so sorry, Mum, I wanted to keep her here till you and Dad got back.'

'Ssh, luv, ssh,' Patsy murmured. 'It's all right. We'll go together to see her in the morning.'

Eddie's throat was thick with emotion and he was unable to check his own tears.

'All my life, every single day,' Patsy whispered, 'she's been there for me, and I wasn't here for her when she needed me.'

Ollie glanced at Eddie. For once in their lives they were at a loss as to what they could do to help their beloved Patsy.

Florrie had, thank God, had a peaceful end, with Emma and Donald there to comfort her, but it was going to take a long time for Patsy to forgive herself for not being there.

'Come on,' Eddie said quietly. 'Let's go and join the others and have a cup of tea.'

Patsy sighed a very long, slow sigh. She couldn't speak; she was staring at a photograph which stood on Florrie's mantelpiece. It was a picture of herself with Alex and David and the twins, standing in Florrie's front garden in Strathmore Street. Florrie stood behind them, her arms stretched wide to encircle them all.

Ellen arrived the next morning in time to go with the family to the chapel of rest.

They stood in a group and gazed at Florrie's face and saw how peaceful it was in death, and then one by one they leaned forward and kissed her withered cheek.

At the door Patsy faltered, turned and went back to stand alone by the coffin. Again she bent low, and, her voice barely a whisper, began to talk. 'Oh, Florrie, it was a lovely way for you to go, but what about me? We never even had a chance to say goodbye. Thank you, for being my second mum and always my dearest friend.'

Eddie had to come back and lead Patsy away. She was blinded by tears.

Chapter Two

'YOU DON'T THINK THINGS are moving too quickly between our Ellen and Peter, do you?' Patsy asked, staring at Eddie, who sat opposite her on the sofa in the front room.

Eddie gave a hearty chuckle. 'There's no pleasing you, is there? One minute you're praying like mad that they will get together, and now that it looks that way, you're telling me that you're uneasy.'

Patsy bit her lip, then said in a rush, 'You said yerself that he'd stayed over here in England a lot longer than he intended. You also said we never really know about other people, not even those that are closest to us, and let's face it, Eddie, we don't know Peter all that well. We never spent a lot of time with him.'

'You're right. But Ollie knows him well enough, and he is the shrewdest person we know, and brilliant at reading people. If there was anything underhand about Peter's feelings for our Ellen, Ollie would have spotted it ages ago.'

'Oh, I do hope you're right,' Patsy answered quietly.

Eddie *was* right.

One hundred per cent.

★　★　★

Ellen was bewildered.

The very fact that everything between herself and Peter seemed so right frightened her. The whole relationship seemed too good to be true. When she met Peter now she would go without hesitation into his eager arms. They would be like two youngsters as they sighed simultaneously, looking into one another's faces, wondering if there was any change that might have taken place since they last met. Had doubt crept in? He would lift her off her feet and kiss her again and again and she'd cling to him as if her very life depended upon it.

She was relaxing a little more every time they met; he was aware of it and so was she. But away from him she would start to question things.

Surely Peter loved her, how could she doubt it? His every action told her so. They had done no more than hold each other so far, though Peter's kisses told her he was hungry for more. Could she let herself go? Believe that happiness with this wonderful man could be hers?

When her thoughts went back to those terrible years during which she had been married to Robert, she became agitated, even frightened. She found it difficult to believe Peter when he told her how much she had come to mean to him.

They spent a great deal of time just talking. So far he'd stayed in Ramsgate for three weeks and there wasn't a day or an evening that they had not met. Tonight they had dined at The Gloucester and he had walked her back to her flat at the Maplehurst.

Once inside, she had been taking off her jacket when she heard him move across the room, his footsteps almost soundless on her thick carpet, and then he was directly behind her, so close she could feel the warmth of him. His arms closed around her and she began to tremble. He held her, not fiercely but lovingly.

'Ellen, my darling, isn't it about time we told each other how we feel?' His voice broke and she was moved at the emotion in it. 'We are not children. I'm pretty sure we are both aware of our feelings for each other, but I want to tell you . . . ask you . . . do you have the slightest idea of how much I love you? I think I loved you from the moment I first saw you.'

He paused, brushed his lips over the back of her head before saying, 'Dear Ellen, please turn round, face me and look into my eyes, and realise I'm telling you the truth. What can I say or do to make you trust me? I want you to marry me. Please say you will be my wife. But if you are always going to feel that you can't trust me, say so, then I'll go away and leave you alone.'

She turned slowly, swaying a little, and all she managed to utter was, 'Oh, Peter.' She lifted her face, and when he placed his lips on hers, so gently, barely more than the merest touch, she felt as if she were floating. His kisses became warm, ardent, and her whole body glowed. She moaned, and once again murmured, 'Oh, Peter.'

She wanted so badly to believe that he loved her. What could she do? What should she do? It had been such a long time. Years. Years during which she had firmly believed she would never give herself to another man, never again be able to trust a man enough. Not after all the abuse she had suffered at the hands of Robert Dellor.

Was Peter being honest with her? At this moment did she care? She had been so alone, so starved of love, for so long, could she now tear herself away from his strong arms? His mouth and his hands and his powerful body were telling her he wanted her, needed her, loved her.

She was only human. Her body was on fire and she no longer felt afraid. All that mattered was that they should come together now.

Brushing her forehead with his lips, Peter guided her from

the living room, across the hall and into her bedroom. Placing her on her bed, he knelt down beside her and slowly undressed her. Then he hastily shrugged out of his own clothes and lay down beside her. Slowly and with great care his hands moved over her body.

Much later she slept, her head on his shoulder, his arms wrapped tightly around her, his face resting against her hair.

He did not sleep, for his thoughts were busy. He had had other women in his time, but never one he had wanted to marry. Ellen was entirely different. He sighed. She was to him so very, very different. He wanted her for his wife. This beloved woman who had previously been so ill treated; he wanted above all else to make her happy, keep her safe and close to him. He had to persuade her to marry him, share his life for as long as they both should live.

Otherwise his life would have no meaning.

It was seven o'clock the following morning. Ellen lifted the coffee pot and poured Peter a second cup. She gave him a broad smile before saying, 'Why the rush? I've said I will marry you, but by special licence and within seven days doesn't sound very attractive to me.'

'So, my darling, when would you like our wedding to be?'

She pondered for a moment, then quietly said, 'Christmas is not too far away and it would give the family time to get used to the idea.'

'I suppose Christmas it will have to be then,' Peter answered slowly and reluctantly. 'Do you want it to be a huge affair?'

'We won't be able to keep the family away, but I'd like it to be a quiet wedding because . . .' Ellen's voice wavered. 'Well, it is the second time around for me.'

Startled, Peter said, 'We're all entitled to make mistakes. You were very young and far too trusting.' Then, softening his tone, he added, 'Ellen, you mustn't dwell on the past. Look to the future. Our future. Together.'

'How about your relatives? And will you want to live in Australia?'

Peter didn't hesitate. 'My parents both died in a car accident when I was only a few months old; they had been married less than two years. From the day I started my first job with Jack Berry he became my family. That's one of the reasons I love your big family, and Ollie being Jack's brother, well, it all seems very fitting to me. I shall have to go back to Australia to wind things up, but after we are married my globetrotting days will be over.'

Ellen looked at him in disbelief, totally at a loss for words. She put her coffee cup down on the saucer and continued to gape at him. It was a while before she found her voice and was able to say, 'But your whole life is tied up in Australia. You might not like living here. Besides what will you do . . .' She didn't finish the sentence, but sat up very straight in her chair.

'My darling,' Peter laughed, 'you should have used the past tense. My life *was* tied up in Australia. Not any more. I have you now. You will be my wife and I will be here to love you and to take care of you.'

'What about your work?' She was dumbfounded that he had made such huge decisions so quickly.

'Don't get so upset,' he urged. 'You know full well Ollie has sold off the main parts of the company both in Australia and New Zealand. Working for strangers hasn't been the same. Besides, I am not a poor man. Jack was more than an employer. He paid me well and he taught me when and when not to buy shares. I feel very attached to Ollie. I know I can work here with him, indeed with all the family, no problems at all. I promise you.'

Ellen felt her cheeks redden. 'I can't believe this,' she muttered. 'Are you seriously telling me that you've discussed with Ollie marrying me and living here in England? Have you talked to anyone else?'

'Of course not,' he quickly protested. 'To tell you the truth, I have been building up the courage to ask you to marry me for weeks. Ollie, being the wise old owl he is, guessed as much, and if I'm not very much mistaken he's discussed the pair of us at great length with your mother and father.'

Ellen's laugh stopped him short. 'You know, I can well believe that. It doesn't take much imagination to realise that all three of them have been match-making. They've thrown us together at every opportunity.'

'Well, they haven't done too badly, have they? I'm more than thrilled that you've taken to me enough to say that you will marry me. So shall we tell them it's to be a Christmas wedding?'

Ellen sighed happily and nodded her head. Then, smiling broadly, she said, 'Oh, Peter, I do love you.'

'And I love you, Ellen,' he answered, getting to his feet. 'And from now on that is all that matters. We shall be together for the rest of our lives.'

Gently he pulled her to her feet, took her in his arms and kissed her.

It was a long, lingering kiss that drove away all her doubts.

Chapter Three

THE WHOLE FAMILY WERE absolutely delighted that Ellen and Peter were going to get married. A Christmas wedding at that!

The ceremony was to take place on the twenty-third of December. Peter and Ellen were not going away on honeymoon. Navy Street was to be the host house for the festive season and Patsy, Eddie and Ollie were looking forward to it immensely, even though they knew the house would be bursting at the seams. What a festive Christmas it would be. On the fifth of January, the newly married couple would be flying to Australia for three months. Patsy smiled thankfully to herself and sent up a silent prayer of thanks not only that things were turning out so well for her beloved Ellen, but also that their permanent home was going to be here in England.

She was also grateful that Ellen had managed to find someone to replace her at the Maplehurst. Julie Taylor was aged about forty, and her husband had recently died. She had been coming to the Maplehurst every day for the past two months, and was to move into Ellen's flat and take over her job the first week in November. The residents had taken to her and she to them. Ellen had assured them all that she would visit often and that the whole family would still be greatly involved in the running of the Maplehurst.

Patsy was beating eggs in a bowl, preparing to make a huge fruit cake ready for the weekend, when she heard her front door open. She stared hard as Alex and Vicky came into the kitchen. A deep frown was knitting Vicky's brow.

'Something's up, isn't it?' Patsy said. 'Don't usually see you two out together mid-week.'

Vicky said quickly, 'Before we explain, we just want you to understand that's she's all right, otherwise we wouldn't have left her.'

'Who's all right? Are you talking about Frances?'

'Yes, sorry, Patsy. You know it's half-term holiday for the schools and Frances pleaded to go and stay with Peggy Stevens. We weren't too sure and we suggested that Peggy come down to stay with us, or even for the pair of them to stay here with you. They want to visit different places in London 'cos they've to write essays, and they think Tolworth is too far out for them to get about. We gave in when Mrs Stevens telephoned us and assured us she would take good care of Frances. To cut the story short, we've just taken her up there and we're not too sure we've done the right thing.'

'I think she's worrying about nothing,' Alex cut in.

Patsy untied her apron, took it off and hung it on a hook on the door. 'Vicky, go and put the kettle on, and while you're busy with that, Alex can tell me why you're so upset.'

'It's something and nothing really, Mum. The Stevenses have a nice enough home and you'll never guess who lives right opposite them: Lily and George Burton!'

'Well I never!' Patsy cried. 'Lily's mother and I went to school together and she used to work up Tooting market with me at one time. We lost track of the family when they were bombed out.'

'Yeah, well, her mother and father are dead and gone,

but George is a smashing bloke. I liked him the minute he shook my hand.'

'What's all this got t' do with Vicky being upset about letting our Frances stay up there?'

'Well, they all live in Ariel Court, in Kennington Lane, not far from the Elephant and Castle, and as I say, the Stevenses' and the Burtons' flats were clean and well kept, but not everyone is like that. On the same floor, quite a bit further along, there's a family with nine children. The woman had a mouth like the Blackwall Tunnel and her language wouldn't be tolerated at a football match.'

'So why did you leave Frances there?'

'Mum, the Stevenses were so nice and the Burtons were thrilled to see me, asked all about you and Ollie. The Stevenses made us tea and had a home-made sponge cake ready, an' they got out their best china. Rotten neighbours aren't their fault. I felt terrible when I heard this family rowing out in the corridor but I hadn't it in me to say I wasn't leaving our girl there.'

Vicky pushed the door open with her foot and placed a tea-tray on the table. 'What would you have done, Patsy?' she asked her mother-in-law.

'I honestly don't know, love, but I'll tell you what. Ellen's coming up tonight for the weekend. I'll get her to come up there with me tomorrow. We'll make some excuse, see how the land lies, and if there's the slightest doubt we'll 'ave Frances in the car quicker than you could say Jack Robinson.'

'Oh, Mum, bless you. I'll sleep much better tonight, and anyway we left Frances loads of coppers and told her to telephone us if she wanted to come home. Day or night, Alex impressed on her. There's a public telephone box right by the main entrance to the flats.'

Patsy was pleased that she'd said the right thing. Vicky usually called her Patsy, but on the occasions she called her

Mum, it always gave Patsy a good feeling that she got on so well with her in-laws.

Patsy and Ellen were hardly out of the car before they had the doubtful pleasure of meeting the noisy family that Alex had spoken of.

Both Lily Burton and Alice Stevens were standing at their front doors, their faces beaming, because they had seen the car draw up and their visitors arrive.

'You don't mind us dropping in on you like this?' Patsy asked as Alice Stevens ushered them into her front room.

'Not a bit of it, thrilled t' see yer, and don't you go,' Alice shouted after Lily Burton. 'Stay an' 'ave a cuppa with us. All gals together,' she laughed. 'Me ole man has taken the gals to the Tower this afternoon. Don't know what time they'll be back, but your Frances is all right. Mind you, 'er and our Peggy stayed awake 'alf the night nattering away nineteen t' the dozen.'

They were all settled with tea and biscuits before Alice said, 'You saw an' 'eard our neighbours as you arrived, didn't yer? I'm sorry yer son an' daughter-in-law 'ad t' hear them going at it 'ammer an' tongs when they were 'ere.'

Ellen looked at her mother, and such was the face she pulled that all four women burst out laughing. The family in question were named Newton. The wife, Rose, was a huge, heavy-breasted, scruffy woman. Bert Newton was a very tall, well-built, upright sergeant-major type who could be heard yelling at his kids a mile off.

'Wanna know what he does for a living?' Lily asked, still laughing.

Patsy swallowed a mouthful of her tea and nodded her head.

'He's manager of the transport division of the Marmite factory.'

'So that was the funny smell.' Ellen voiced her thought

149

aloud. 'I couldn't fathom it out when I got out of the car.'

'You wanna be 'ere when the wind's blowing in this direction. When the factory opens the vents it's not a smell, it's an absolute stink. But we 'ave t' laugh. All the locals who live almost on top of the factory come out into the street and holler to each other, "ALL WINDOWS SHUT!"'

The time passed quickly as the women reminisced about the old days, and Patsy was surprised when her grand-daughter burst through the door saying, 'I wondered what Auntie Ellen's car was doing outside; you haven't come to take me home, have you?'

'No, of course not,' Patsy reassured her. 'When yer dad told me Mr an' Mrs Burton were living right opposite to Peggy's mum, your aunt and I thought it would be nice to come up to London for a change. See our old neighbours. We've known each other for a good many years.'

'Oh,' Frances murmured, not sure that her gran was telling the whole truth. But at the same time she was thrilled to see all the women getting along so well. She was having the time of her life. She'd seen Tower Bridge opened twice and she'd been inside the actual Tower; she'd certainly got plenty to write about when she got down to doing her essay.

'Well, we'd better be making a move,' Patsy said to Ellen. Then, turning to face both Lily and Alice, she added, 'You've really made us very welcome and I don't remember when I've laughed so much. Thanks ever so much. We'll keep in touch now we know where you are. We'll make a point of seeing more of you.'

Patsy didn't know just how true that pledge would turn out to be.

Chapter Four

It truly was going to be a white Christmas.

Away from the high street and main shopping centres where the barrow boys were flogging holly branches, wreaths and mistletoe, and the fruit stalls had tangerines wrapped in red, blue and gold paper, snow-covered shrubs helped give the snowy scene a festive feel. On the common and in the parks the drifts of newly fallen snow were virgin white.

Everything for the wedding was going well. Too well, Ellen sometimes thought. How could she be so lucky?

'We still have so much to sort out, decisions to make,' she exclaimed one evening when Peter was saying how he wished the twenty-third would come quicker.

'Let's enjoy the next few weeks, and then whilst we're in Australia we'll have long talks, thrash things out. Together we'll decide where we're going to buy a house and how we're going to proceed. What do you say?'

'Yes, all right. We'll leave things until we're away on our own. It's a good idea. For now we'll enjoy this precious Christmas with all our loved ones around us.'

Peter Crawford, orphaned when only a baby and raised by an elderly aunt, had always been lonely as a child. He was finding that he thoroughly enjoyed being part of Ellen's large family. At first it had been a novelty to him. Now he counted himself very lucky. He nodded, poured out two glasses of wine, passed one to Ellen and they clinked glasses. His eyes showed tenderness as they gazed at her.

After a while he said, 'I love you so much, Ellen. I hope I can make you happy.'

She looked at him in surprise. 'You already have,' she murmured, and as her eyes met his she saw the depth and strength of his feelings for her.

'Everything is going to be all right. It really is, Ellen, because we shall have each other,' he promised.

At that moment Ellen was amazed at just how much she loved this man. She had thought a life of caring for elderly folk was all she had to look forward to. Now she knew she had been wrong. More than anything else she wanted to spend the rest of her life with Peter. She had been frightened, even terrified to admit she was in love with him. Now that she had, the future held so much for her.

The day had arrived at last.

Wandsworth Registry Office was filled to capacity, almost bursting at the seams. Family occupied the front chairs and friends and neighbours were crowded in closely behind, for they had turned out in full force to honour Ellen, who had suffered so much in her earlier life. Everyone present silently prayed that she had at last found safety and happiness with this handsome Australian.

The ceremony began. Peter's responses were loud and clear as he vowed that he would forsake all others, holding Ellen dear to his heart for as long as they both should live. After they had been declared husband and wife, most of the women were crying with pleasure, while the men clapped Peter on the back and queued to kiss the bride. Both her father and Ollie, her adopted grandfather, in turn held Ellen gently in their arms, and each had to sniff away his tears. It certainly was an emotional scene.

Afterwards they all filed into the waiting cars and went back to Clapham parish hall to partake of a very special lunch, which Eddie had ordered a London firm of caterers to arrange. He had also booked a popular dance band to play during the evening. One other thing he had made sure of was that a case of champagne and a tier of the wedding cake had been safely delivered to the Maplehurst rest home. The elderly residents would never have forgiven the family if they had not been included in the celebrations.

What an attractive family I have, Patsy was saying to herself, her eyes lighting up with pleasure when Peter led Ellen on to the floor for the first waltz while everyone in the hall stood up and clapped their hands.

They do look so well together, she thought. He so tall and broad-shouldered, Ellen so slender and elegant. Having changed from the linen suit she had worn for her wedding, she was wearing a calf-length dress of midnight blue wool-crepe with a matching bolero that was edged with silver beads. Round her neck hung her only piece of jewellery. It was the gold locket and chain that her father had bought, one for her and one for Emma, on their twenty-first birthday.

She looked radiant.

Like all mothers, Patsy knew that each of her children had a very distinct personality. Alex was her first born, and if she were honest she still had an extra-special love for him. He had been named after her beloved Ollie, who had cared for her from the day she had been born, so perhaps she was entitled to love him just that little bit extra.

David was so very much like his father that she felt it was a bonus to have been given him for a son. He was not so ambitious as Alex, more contented. He asked nothing more of life than that which came easily. It was so sad that things had gone wrong between him and Valerie. Still, Tim had stuck by him; great mates those two were.

Ellen and Emma. She had certainly been blessed to have been granted two such beautiful girls. Emma's life had run a truly good path. No one could wish for a better husband than Donald, and the pair of them had three lively, healthy sons. Happy as the day was long, that little family were.

How differently life had treated her twin . . .

Suddenly Patsy shook her head hard. Today was not the day to be remembering that awful period.

'Come on, Gran, we're going to do the conga.' Sam, her youngest grandson, was tugging at her arm. 'You get in line behind me, Dad, then Gran only has to put her arms round your waist and follow what everyone else in the line is doing.'

Patsy was given no option. More willing hands were grabbing her and the music was getting faster and faster. Out of one door, through the corridor and back into the hall through another door. Legs flung out, feet stamping, much laughter, voices raised.

Patsy had almost decided she was too old for this when the music stopped and she breathed a sigh of relief.

Eddie came towards her, red in the face and panting. 'Here, let's sit down and enjoy this,' he said, handing her two glasses and holding up a bottle of champagne.

With the bottle uncorked and their glasses filled, Eddie looked at her. 'I never thought we'd live t' see this day,' he said.

'Neither did I,' Patsy readily agreed.

'Well,' Eddie smiled, 'here's to our children and our grand-children, and may we live to see our great-grandchildren.'

They clinked glasses and Patsy drank gratefully. Then giving him a smirky look she said, 'Jumping the gun a bit, aren't you, Mr Owen?'

'I don't think so,' he laughed. 'You watch our eldest two grandsons and the way they're flirting with the girls. And to see them dance to a slow tune, well, it would never have happened in our day. They dance so close together you couldn't put a fag-paper between them, that's if you can call it dancing.'

Patsy had drained her glass and held it out for a refill. 'Jealous, are we?' she muttered cheekily.

'Too true I am, but also relieved that we can go home to the comfort of our big double bed. These children, even these young adults, are not our responsibility any more.'

'Oh, so you're going to wipe them out of our lives after today, are you?'

'You know darn well I didn't mean that,' Eddie protested.

'Just as well,' Patsy told him sternly, 'because you can bet yer last dollar that more than 'alf of them will still turn up for their Sunday dinner next week.'

'And I'll have t' do the washing-up,' he muttered almost beneath his breath.

'I 'eard that. Anyone would think you were hard done by! Tell you what, though, Eddie, we won't half miss Ellen an' Peter. Three months is gonna seem a long time.' Then a thought hit her and she quickly asked, 'You don't think that when Peter gets our Ellen over there he'll persuade her to stay and live in Australia, do you?'

'Oh, no!' Eddie groaned. 'They've only been married a few hours, they're not going for a while yet, and you're worrying yourself that they might never come back home again.'

'Well?'

'Well, nothing. Peter is a man of his word and he's told us straight what they intend to do. So, Patsy, will you do me a favour and stop worrying over daft things. Here, give me your glass; drink a bit more and then you might start to enjoy yourself.'

Christmas morning, and in the church the whole family filled three pews. Frances glowed in her new red coat with

155

a little fur-trimmed hat perched on her curly hair and her hands tucked into a neat little muff. David sat at the end of one pew, Tim next to him. Alex and Vicky's son James sat with his cousins, Edward Junior, Thomas and Sam. The lads looked uncomfortable, so neat and clean and having been told over and over again to behave themselves.

Patsy had left the turkey roasting slowly in the oven with a leg of pork on a lower shelf. The vegetables had all been prepared the day before, and two huge puddings slowly bubbled away in a steamer on top of the stove.

If only Florrie could still have been with them. Her presence, not to mention her bulk and her banter, would always be missed whenever the family had a gathering. How she would have loved to have been at Ellen's wedding! To know that at last the second twin was coming out of her shell and hopefully, please God, going to lead a full and happy life from now on.

Patsy stood to join the congregation in the singing of Christmas carols, but first she had to brush away a tear. There would never be a day that she didn't think of her dear loving Florrie. Now there was a rustle through the church as folk knelt. Time for prayers. Time to give thanks that our Lord Jesus Christ had been born on this day.

Patsy prayed to be given faith, enough faith to believe that life did go on after death and that they would all meet their loved ones again.

Chapter Five

IT WAS MORE THAN two years since the Stevenses had moved up to Kennington Lane, during which time Frances had twice spent a few days with them, and twice both girls had stayed in Navy Street. Having them to stay with her pleased Patsy no end because the house became alive when youngsters were about.

Now Frances was sitting in her kitchen, having just been collected by her father and brought to see her gran.

'Well, what was your weekend in London like this time?' Patsy asked curiously.

'Really nice, Gran, but . . .'

Patsy had a sudden sense of foreboding. 'I knew it,' she muttered to herself. Whenever Frances came back from staying with the Stevenses there was something fishy about her. She was quiet, almost secretive, not a bit like her normal jolly self.

'But what?' Patsy demanded to know. 'Is it Mr an' Mrs Stevens that you don't like?'

'Course not,' Frances quickly protested. 'They're ever so nice and so are your friends Mr and Mrs Burton.'

'Yeah, well, go on, because I don't have t' be psychic to

know that something's happening up there that's upsetting you. I'm going to get to the bottom of it if it kills me. So, are you going t' tell me, or do I have t' take myself up there and ask a few questions?'

'Oh, Gran, I wish you wouldn't keep on. I have a smashing time, I really do, it's just those neighbours.' Frances hesitated and heaved a sigh. 'It's nothing to do with us, but this time Mr and Mrs Burton did interfere and Peggy's mum and dad backed them up. Me and Peggy thought there was going to be a right old bust-up, and there was a bit.'

'Frances,' Patsy yelled in desperation, 'will you please tell me what you are talking about, 'cos you're not making any sense.'

Again Frances sighed. 'All I know is that it's all over the Newtons. You know, that noisy lot that live at the end of the corridor, the family that has all those children.'

'What you're telling me is they were arguing and fighting again.'

'No, Gran, nothing like that. Well, not at first. Mrs Newton has recently had another baby, it's ever so tiny, and the council have given her another one.'

'What!' Patsy shouted in disbelief. 'You mean that the council exchanged her baby just because it was small?'

The look on her gran's face made Frances grin. 'Don't be so daft, Gran. It's not like that at all. Peggy's dad is furious. He thinks the council asked the Newtons to look after this other baby and are paying them to do it.'

'Christ Almighty!' Patsy shook her head and stared upwards. The Newtons asked to look after someone else's newly born child? It beggared belief. From the little she had seen of that family they couldn't take proper care of the nine children they already had. Now she had two more babies. It couldn't be right. Terrible thoughts were running through Patsy's head. Supposing the babies were being neglected . . . supposing . . .

Frances cut into her gran's thoughts. 'Peggy's dad said he'd never heard the likes of it in all his life and he wanted to fetch the police, but her mum said they'd better go down to the town hall and talk to the council first. Then Peggy and I heard her mum talking to your friend Mrs Burton, and she said that whatever wrong-doing Rose and Bert Newton had got themselves into it was ten to one they'd wriggle out of it.'

Frances was observing her gran out of the corner of her eye. She looked as if she was planning something, and when Gran started on something she always made sure she finished it to her liking. Perhaps she shouldn't have told her about the Newtons having two new babies.

'Your dad's back,' Patsy said, having heard her son's car pull up. 'I'll walk out with you.'

'You two had a good old chin-wag?' Alex asked, planting a kiss on his mother's cheek.

'You could say that,' Patsy answered thoughtfully. Then, wrapping her arms around her granddaughter, she hugged her close. 'Don't you go worrying about what you've just told me. It will all come out in the wash, you'll see. 'Bye, my luv, see yer soon. Give my love t' yer mum, and tell that brother of yours it's about time he popped in to see me.'

'I will, Gran, we all love you loads.'

Patsy stood and waved until the car had turned the corner. Then, as she turned to go back inside the house, she made a snap decision. First thing tomorrow morning she was going up to Kennington Lane. Strictly speaking it was nothing to do with her, but curiosity was getting the better of her. Besides, there was another point to consider. These things were always best sorted by getting the facts straight right from the start.

And that was exactly what she intended to do.

★   ★   ★

Patsy drove slowly. She was on a road which she felt was familiar to her. It was wide, and trams were trundling along on tracks laid in the centre of the road. In south London most of the trams had been done away with and replaced by trolley buses which ran on overhead cables. She signalled and turned into a narrow street, and knew she had done right. Ahead of her was a block of flats, and the name plate on the end wall showed it was Ariel Court. All the flats were identical, rows and rows of them on at least ten or maybe even twelve floors, all with wooden front doors painted in bright colours. To the right of the entrance were two rows of maisonettes.

Patsy parked her car and walked along the first corridor until she came to number 18. Having rung the bell twice and got no reply, she heaved an impatient sigh.

She was about to retrace her steps when she suddenly remembered that Alex and Vicky had told her that Lily and George Burton lived right opposite the Stevenses. She pondered for a moment. All the front doors were so close to each other. Then she took a chance and rang the bell of the one immediately facing the Stevenses' flat. Relief flooded through her as the door was opened and a familiar face smiled at her.

'Oh my Gawd, am I glad t' see you,' Lily Burton exclaimed as she practically dragged Patsy over the doorstep. 'Only I 'ope you 'aven't rushed up 'ere because of something yer granddaughter has told you.'

Patsy laughed. 'Well, t' be honest, that's exactly why I'm here. Frances told me such a garbled story that I not only didn't believe her, I didn't understand half of what she was saying.'

'Curiosity killed the cat, didn't it, George?' Lily called out to her husband. 'But while you're out there in the scullery put the kettle on, will yer, luv, and I'll start at the beginning and tell Patsy all what's been going on.'

George put his head around the door, grinned and said, 'Wotcha, Patsy, great t' see you. I'll 'ave a cuppa ready for yer in two minutes.'

The most striking thing about George Burton was his eyes. They were big and brown and very bright, and they shone with life and laughter. Otherwise he was an ordinary working-class man who got on with most people. He would do odd jobs for the elderly and help anyone in need, but most of all he loved kids. He'd lay his life down for his own two. He was also very fond of dogs, and his only regret was that they were not allowed to have a dog whilst they lived in these flats.

Settled round the table with a steaming cup of tea in front of each of them, Lily began her story.

'Every morning I walk part of the way to school with my Julie and Jack, just t' see that they get safely across the main road, though Jack is always moaning at me that they ain't kids any more and I shouldn't go with them. And Julie's even worse, just like your Frances and young Peggy Stevens. All of a sudden they think they're grown-up young ladies.

'After I leave them I do my bits of shopping, sometimes in the Walworth Road and sometimes in East Lane, depends on what kind of a mood I'm in.'

George had been vigorously stirring a load of sugar into his cup. Now he banged the teaspoon down into the saucer and bellowed, 'For goodness' sake get on with it, gal. At the rate you're going, Patsy will 'ave to stay a blinking fortnight before you get to the point.'

Lily gave him a sharp stare before she turned to face Patsy again.

'One morning about a fortnight ago it was raining 'ard an' I decided t' take a short cut and go out through the back entrance to these flats, which meant that I passed Rosie Newton's flat. To see her place from the outside is bad enough; dirty windows with ragged curtains. This day her

161

front door was wide open and I could see right through to her living room. It was unbelievable. About four kiddies sitting round a table that was littered with so much rubbish you couldn't have put a cup down. One little girl was naked and she was sitting on the floor, which was so dirty it would take you a month of Sundays to clean it.'

Patsy closed her eyes, then opened them again. She had had a mental picture of how she and her mother had lived upstairs in Florrie's house. God knows they'd been poor, but never dirty!

'Well, that same morning I caught up with Rose and we walked together to where the barrow boys were setting out their stalls. Rose was, as usual, pushing a pram and I was surprised – no, shocked is a better word – to see that it held two babies. One was little Ernie that I knew was about two or three months old, but at the top end of the pram lay a baby that looked almost new-born dressed in a frock and a bonnet, so I presumed it to be a little girl.

'Without stopping t' think I said, "Where the 'ell did yer get that one from?"

'Rose stopped dead in her tracks. Really annoyed she was. "Not that it's anything t' do with you, Lily Burton," she screamed at me, "but the council 'ave asked me to foster this little girl for about six months and then she's going up for adoption."

'I had to bite my lip. I was absolutely appalled. But I knew I daren't say too much or like as not Rosie would smack me in the mouth. I couldn't help it, though. The questions were buzzing round and round in my head.

'How had this situation come about? Who in God's name had given permission for a family such as the Newtons to be put in charge of such a wee baby? It's common knowledge they can't cope with their own brood.

'Patsy, I didn't even stop t' do me shopping. Me feet flew over the ground. I couldn't wait to get home and talk to

162

George. Thank God he was on late turn – he works for the Post Office, does shift work. I was so angry by then that I couldn't get the words out to tell him.'

'I thought she was 'aving me on,' George chimed in. 'It stands t' reason the council couldn't know the slightest thing about Rose and Bert Newton or they would never have passed a wee mite over into their care.'

Silence reigned for a few minutes before Lily took up the story again.

'Over the next two weeks I purposely made myself become friendly with Rosie. I took her in a home-made bread pudding and made a huge saucepan of soup filled with grated vegetables, enough for all the children to 'ave some.'

'This was all against my advice,' George interrupted. 'I didn't think it was right that baby being there. The authorities should be dealing with it, not my wife.'

'Well, George, we did agree that we'd get our facts straight before we did anything. And so I used any excuse I could think of to get inside Rosie's front door. My main purpose was to keep an eye on that wee baby. She was such a sweet little mite and there were days when I just wanted to pick her up and bring her here to our place for a bath. Honestly, Patsy, it would 'ave broke yer 'eart to see her. Hours an' hours and her napkin was never changed. Time and time again I asked myself the same question. Who on earth had abandoned her?'

'You wanna know what upset me the most?' George asked as his wife took a handkerchief from her apron pocket and wiped her eyes.

Patsy nodded.

'A couple of Sundays ago it was a real nice sunny day. Not over warm but nice, so we wrapped our two kids up, went along to the Newtons and asked if they'd like to bring their children and join us for a day out. Lil said she'd pack up a load of food.

163

'"Where yer thinking of going?" Bert Newton asked.

'"Well, how about Battersea Park, or even Kennington Park, which has an open-air swimming pool and a paddling pool?"

'"It ain't that bloody warm," was all the answer Bert gave me, but surprise surprise, Rosie said it was a good idea and the kids could play ball an' maybe even 'ave a paddle. When we were finally all ready and set to go my Lil asked where the baby was. As to yet it hadn't even been given a name. They all referred to her as "the baby" or just "it", would you believe that?

'"She's asleep," Rose said, too quickly for my liking, and her old man said, "She'll be all right. She don't want t' be lugged about all day."

'My Lil and I looked at each other. The only reason we had asked them to come out with us was so we'd get a chance to 'ave a good look at the child, and 'ere they were preparing to leave her alone in the 'ouse all day on her own. What could I do about it? Bugger all, though I felt like 'aving a go at them there an' then an' I would 'ave done if it 'adn't been for the kids, all ready and looking forward to their day out. We didn't 'ave a bad time, though Bert spent a good hour in the Eight Bells on his own. It was when we got back that I blew my top.

'Lil took our two straight into our place but I was carrying Billy, one of their kids – he's only three and was fast asleep – so I went in and laid him down in an armchair. As soon as Rosie opened her front door we heard the baby screaming, and d'you know where she was? Lying in a cardboard box out in the scullery, and she'd been there all day!'

'Oh my goodness!' Patsy exclaimed. 'How could anyone do such a thing to a young baby?'

'You tell me,' George murmured. 'There has been plenty of gossip about that family and a great many rumours, but the baby's still there and they've given her a name now; they call her Mary.'

'Yeah, the time was going on and it was worrying me sick, so I went along there one morning with a pint of milk.' Lily grinned. 'I said the milkman had left me one too many and could she use it? Then I said, "Rose, I thought you said little Mary was being put up for adoption." Well, I never got no answer. It was as if all hell was let loose. The kitchen door slammed back with such force the whole room rocked. And there stood the dreadful figure of Bert Newton. I tell yer, Patsy, I was terrified. He looked terrible, hadn't had a shave, he was bare-chested, wearing only a pair of trousers, braces dangling, no socks or shoes on his feet. One look at him showed the temper he was in, and I wished I was anywhere but in their flat. He turned to me and said, "Like you, Lil, I'd like a bloody answer. We've got ten of our own t' feed, but that ain't enough for my ole woman. She has t' take on someone else's bastard." He slammed his great fist on to the table top, making the crockery on the dresser rattle. And the way he bawled then they must have 'eard him in the Tower of London. "Well I've 'ad enough, it never stops, crying an' yelling day an' night." Then he lowered his face until it was on a level with his wife's, and he hissed, "For the last time I'm telling yer, get that bastard out of this flat before I come 'ome this evening or I'll throw it in the sodding Thames."'

Lily's eyes were glistening with tears, but she carried on: 'I was shaking in me shoes, Patsy. I longed to pick the baby up, and I almost did, but the smell of ammonia hit me. The clothes she had on needed a good wash and I could see sores on her forehead although a bonnet covered the rest of her head.'

'That's when I made up my mind,' George said firmly, 'that it was my business and I was going straight down to the town 'all first thing in the morning an' if I didn't get some answers there was gonna be hell t' pay.'

Lily was openly crying now. 'I'll make a fresh pot of tea and cut us a few sandwiches,' she sniffed.

Patsy could feel the strain all this was having on both Lily and George, so she asked, 'Have you to go to work today, George?'

'No, I've got a double; that's two rest days.'

'Well then,' Patsy smiled, 'I'm sure there must be a decent café somewhere near here. Why don't we all go and get a breath of fresh air and have a bit of lunch while we're out. We can still go on talking.'

'I dunno,' Lily wavered.

'Sounds good t' me,' George grinned. 'Bert Smith's café is only a couple of minutes away an' he does a great sausage, bacon, egg and chips.'

Less than twenty minutes later and that was what Patsy treated them all to. Plus a plate of bread and butter and a huge pot of tea.

Most of the meal had been eaten and Patsy was dying to know what had taken place at the town hall, but Lily got in first by asking, 'Did your Ellen and her husband ever come back from Australia? Alice Stevens told me they were planning to stay there for some time.'

'Oh yes,' Patsy said, smiling broadly for the first time today. 'They've bought a house at Streatham, not too far away from us, and the family all still meet up fairly regularly. I'm very lucky.' Then she felt she had to ask: 'Is that baby still with the Newton family?'

George's face turned red. 'I'm ashamed to say that it is. We went to the town 'all, me and Lil, for all the good it done us.'

'Oh George, don't lose yer temper. You know they've promised to do something.'

'Do something! Nobody bothered to explain just how that baby came to be fostered with Rosie Newton in the first place. In fact we had to tell at least three different people

166

why we were there before we even got a promise that the matter would be dealt with.'

Lily suddenly laughed. 'Oh, Patsy, you should 'ave been there. It was so quiet an' everyone seemed to speak in whispers. Well, when nobody seemed to be taking any notice of George, he thumped their polished wooden counter with his clenched fist and you'll never guess what he shouted: "If we don't get to see someone who has some authority around here within the next half-hour, I'm getting on the phone to the local paper."'

Now it was George's turn to laugh. 'Pour us out another cuppa, Lil, and I'll tell Patsy what 'appened next.'

He waited until he had put three spoonfuls of sugar in his tea before he said, 'Some sour-faced straight-laced lady haughtily asked me, "And just where do you think that will get you, Mr Burton?" I soon put her straight. "More to the point, where will it get you lot?" I yelled at her. "I'll bring a doctor who will give evidence as to the deplorable filthy state that baby is in. You lot don't give a damn, you wanted that child off yer hands and you placed 'er with a woman who already had ten of her own, the last one being only a couple of months old. I know for a fact that other neighbours 'ave been on to you about the condition of this baby and each and every one of yer says it's not your department. So we'll all get together. The papers will love our stories."'

George had to pause for breath.

'Amazing, wasn't it, George?' Lily said. 'Ten minutes later and we were being shown into a plush office, and my George didn't wait for introductions; he fired off straight away: "Are you going to let us in on what's going on? How come we 'ave to threaten to go to the papers before you even agree t' see us?"'

'All posh-like he was.' George grinned at Patsy. '"Mr Burton, please, we have traced the mother, but it took time. She is not a young gadabout girl. She is twenty-nine years old and over

167

here from New Zealand on an exchange study course. Apparently the baby was the result of a one-night stand. A mistake she deeply regrets. She wants her daughter adopted into a caring family. She doesn't even want her folk back home to know that she has given birth." That's what he had the cheek to tell us, and he was sweating buckets when he'd finished talking, but I wasn't letting him off that easily. Oh no!

"'If you don't soon rescue that baby she won't survive," I told him. "She's dirty, half starved, and her head is covered in sores according to my wife, and she's seen it for herself, which is more than can be said for you lot. Has even one of you visited the Newtons' flat?" He didn't answer and I said, "I thought not. Out of sight, out of mind."

"'All right, Mr Burton," he almost pleaded. "You've made your point and I personally will see that matters move quickly from now on.'"

The silence after that lot hung heavy, and Patsy couldn't stand it. She had to ask: 'And what's happened since then?'

'Nothing, as far as we know,' Lily and George answered together.

'That is the most horrible story I have ever had to listen to,' Patsy said quietly. 'I'm going to write down our address and telephone number, and if there is the slightest thing we can do, please, both of you, ring me. In any case you will keep in touch and let me know what happens to that baby, won't you?'

'Course we will,' George said quickly. 'And Patsy, we do appreciate you listening. We were nearly at our wits' end. Sorry we ain't on the phone, but there's a public box right near the main entrance to our block of flats. We'll call you from there.'

'Well, just ring, give us the number and whoever answers at our end will ring you straight back. Now I must get going or my family will start to worry as to where I've taken myself off to.'

Fond farewells were said, but Patsy had to keep shaking her head to clear it during her journey home.

What had been allowed to happen to that baby didn't bear thinking about.

Chapter Six

EXHAUSTION HIT PATSY AT the end of that long, sad day. She gave a sigh of relief as she lowered herself into an armchair. She looked around the room: at the big dresser with its rows of good china; at the huge sideboard along one wall, the carriage clock on the mantelpiece with photographs of all her grandchildren on either side. Opposite where she was sitting was Eddie's big chair with its velvet cushions. And the whole room had wall-to-wall carpet.

She was so lucky. And so were her children. Indeed, her whole family had so much to be grateful for.

She thought about what Lily and George Burton had told her. Remembered every word again, and then again. She was still sitting there when Eddie came home. She turned to look up at him over her shoulder.

He took one look at her face and said, 'Patsy, you look awful, whatever has happened?'

She tried to tell him but could not find the words. The very thought of what little Mary must be suffering made her feel so angry. She tried not to think about what might be happening to the baby but it kept coming into her mind.

What she had been told would haunt her for a long time.

She managed to give Eddie a scrambled version.

He looked at her in utter disbelief. Finally he said, 'Patsy, calm down and take a deep breath. Do you think that this is what has been worrying our Frances?'

'In a roundabout way, yes I do. Though I wouldn't think she knows the half of it.'

'Neither do I. I'll get us a drink and then you must try and tell me exactly what Lily and George Burton told you. Just stick to the plain facts,' he pleaded.

It was all too much. Patsy was tired out. She broke down and started to cry.

Eddie patted her shoulder, then handed her a drop of brandy. 'Sip it slowly,' he ordered.

It was some time before he managed to get the whole story out of her. Hearing the details left him speechless!

Patsy reached for his hand and in little more than a whisper said, 'Oh Eddie, I feel so helpless. I just can't imagine how anyone could be so cruel, especially to a tiny baby. And what really makes me feel so bitter is that people in authority are letting it happen.'

Eddie sighed heavily. 'I don't like to see you so down in the dumps.'

'I just don't know what I can do to help,' Patsy moaned.

'No, I don't suppose you do,' Eddie said with a rueful smile as he squeezed her hand.

Patsy returned the pressure. 'Thanks for listening. You don't think I'm worrying over nothing, do you?'

'No, I most certainly don't. That's half the trouble today: people see awful things going on but don't want to get involved. Either that or they can't be bothered.'

Thoughtful minutes ticked by as they both finished their drink.

Then Patsy quietly asked, 'Do you think it would be a good idea if I told Ellen an' Emma about this baby? After

171

all, they were both nurses and they might be able to come up with some suggestions.'

Eddie got to his feet without answering, and walked out into what they now called the kitchenette. She heard him fill the kettle, strike a match and place the kettle on to the gas stove. Suddenly she heard him laugh really heartily.

'What's struck you that is so funny?' she called out.

He came to stand in the open doorway, his face still showing a broad grin. 'You tell the twins and it will be like the bush telegraph. Within an hour or two the whole family will have the details and you can bet your life they'll all be up in arms. They'll all want to help. None of them will stand by and see a baby being mistreated.'

Patsy looked at him lovingly. 'You wouldn't mind?'

'Not on your life,' he said determinedly, 'but we won't say anything to anyone tonight. After we've had a meal we'll discuss it a bit more before we decide anything.' He shook his head sadly. 'I just can't believe that in this day and age such goings-on do occur. One thing is for sure: like you, my darling, I couldn't live with myself if I didn't do something to ensure that poor baby is taken better care of.'

It was Sunday, four days since Patsy had been up to Kennington Lane. Almost every member of her family was gathered here in Navy Street. To see them all together never failed to give Patsy a sense of satisfaction. She loved every minute of a day such as this.

Their midday meal passed with a good deal of laughter and reminiscence. The matter uppermost in everyone's mind was set aside until they had finished eating and everything was cleared away. Then everyone seemed to be talking at once and the general feeling was of outrage that a small baby should be farmed out to such an unfeeling couple.

Donald tapped his coffee cup with his spoon, which made everyone stop talking and turn to stare at him. When he had their attention he said patiently, in a soft voice, 'I take it you want to go back, Patsy, and see for yourself what is happening?'

Patsy heaved a heavy sigh. 'Half of me does, and yet I dread to think what I might find. There is also the point that Eddie raised: do I 'ave the right to poke my nose in?'

'All of what you say is understandable, and as you know I never want to interfere unless I can be of some help. But if we all sit back and do nothing . . .'

'He's been like a cat on hot bricks since he heard about that baby,' Emma interrupted.

'Yes, well,' Donald continued. 'My suggestion is that you let Emma and Ellen make a few phone calls, official-like, or at least let the person on the other end of the line get that impression. You never know what they might turn up.'

'Good idea,' was the general opinion.

Donald continued: 'Then I think the two girls should go back with Patsy to visit Mr and Mrs Burton. Hear what, if anything, has been done and do their best to see the baby. That way they can judge the situation for themselves.'

Ollie, who had up until now remained silent, suddenly said, 'I think someone should set about finding the baby's mother. She can't have the child adopted and remain anonymous. There would be papers to sign and she might even have to appear in court. Besides, although she may not want her family in New Zealand to know that she has had a baby, does not even want to acknowledge it, she surely cannot be aware of how badly her daughter is being treated. I am absolutely convinced no mother would have agreed to her child being fostered out to the kind of family that Patsy has described to us.'

All heads in the room were nodding their agreement.

Ellen turned to look at Peter and raised her eyebrows. He knew exactly what she was thinking and inclined his head in approval.

'I'll make some calls, Mum, and I'll go up to Kennington Lane with you,' Ellen said softly.

Emma threw Donald a look. 'Since it was your idea, luv, I presume it's all right if I go as well.'

'I know, and you know, wild horses wouldn't keep you away.' Donald looked at his father-in-law and they both burst out laughing. Which set all the men off.

'I'd like to be a fly on the wall if our mother and sisters find that baby is still being fostered by that Newton family,' Alex said to his brother.

Before David could form an answer, Patsy piped up, 'An' we'll 'ave less of your cheek, young man.'

Peter was the only one who advised caution. He drained the last of his coffee and moved along the sofa to sit nearer to his wife.

'I'm glad you're going with your mother, but don't do anything rash, will you, darling?'

'Like what?' Ellen asked.

'Like picking up the child and bringing it home with you.'

'What makes you think I might do that?' Her expression was very serious as she asked that question.

'Because, my darling Ellen, we've been married almost a year now and I know you so thoroughly and understand you so well. And because you are so kind-hearted that if that child is in a bad condition, you'd not want to walk away and leave her.'

A lump came into Ellen's throat. She was filled with love for this man. What a happy year it had been. Especially the summer months. Sometimes of a morning she woke first, as the sun was coming through a gap in the curtains, touching the brass knobs on the bed-rail and making them glint brightly. Birds were chirruping, perched on the branches of the apple trees in the garden. She would look at Peter; more often than not his head was turned towards her on the pillow, one arm across her body. She would lie still and watch him, counting her blessings. Thanking God that they had found each other. Unable to help herself, she would stroke his hair, smoothing it back from his face. He would open his eyes and smile at her drowsily. Their house was truly a home now, and Peter was settled and successfully working with Ollie.

Emma grinned at her twin. 'You were miles away. I've just said that if you phone the local council I'll ring a few of my old contacts. Like we've always said, it's a case of who you know, not what you know.'

'Yes, all right,' Ellen readily agreed. 'I think Ollie is right. Our main objective once we check whether the baby is all right will have to be to find the mother.'

'But we don't want to frighten her off,' Emma replied cautiously. 'Anyhow, we'll go with Mum tomorrow, and call on Mr and Mrs Burton first, don't you think? Get an update on what Mum already knows.'

'Seems the best idea if Mum agrees.'

'Yes, I do,' Patsy hastily told them. 'But don't take too much for granted. There's no telling whether we'll even be able to speak to the Newtons, never mind get to see the baby.'

'Mum, we'll be guided by you. Take matters as they come. At least we'll be doing our best to make sure that baby isn't suffering.'

Patsy was very moved by just how caring her daughters were. Quietly she murmured, 'Thank you, girls.'

Lily Burton stared in amazement at Patsy Owen and her two daughters standing on her doorstep.

'I didn't expect t' see you again so soon, Patsy, an' I see you've brought reinforcements with you. Well, you'd all better come in. George is at work an' I can guess you've come about little Mary, but I'll tell yer straight off, there ain't much any of us can do to 'elp.'

175

Patsy said quickly, 'Before we get down to brass tacks, Lily, I promise you we've not come t' cause no trouble.'

'I didn't think yer 'ad, luv. Anyway, sit yerselves down an' I'll put the kettle on.'

Ellen and Emma seated themselves but Patsy followed Lily out into the small kitchen.

'Sorry t' call on you like this, Lil, but I 'aven't been able t' get the thought of that baby out of my mind.'

'You 'aven't! How d'yer think me an' my George feel? We're only yards away and can't 'elp 'earing some of the goings-on that come from that flat.'

'Are you telling me that the Newtons still have that baby living with them?' Patsy asked, feeling absolutely astounded. 'After you telling me about your visit to the town hall, I felt sure someone would have visited them and removed the baby from their care.'

'You an' me both,' Lily said, spooning tea into a large brown teapot. 'The thing was, they sent 'er a letter telling 'er which day an 'ealth visitor was gonna call.' Seeing the disbelief on Patsy's face, Lily laughed. 'You've guessed it. All the kids were sent out to various members of their family, and it's my guess that the baby was neat and clean, well wrapped up and fast asleep in the front room when she called. I bet you anything you like the 'ealth visitor wasn't taken into any other room of that flat. I'd go so far as t' say they put something in the baby's bottle t' make sure she was fast asleep.'

'Did Rosie tell yer what the outcome was?'

'What d'yer mean, outcome? They never took the baby away, if that's what you're asking. It's still there now.'

'Did the health visitor say anything?'

'Yeah, she did actually. According to Rosie she said it wouldn't be long before the baby was put up for adoption, but meanwhile they were trying t' make contact with the mother.'

'So they know where the mother is, then?'

'Don't know about that. I'm only telling yer what Rosie told me. Anyway, the tea's made now. I'll carry the tray through but you bring the milk bottle and that plate of biscuits I've put out.'

Patsy told the twins exactly what Lily had told her, and they both looked bewildered.

Emma put her cup down on the floor by her feet, pulled herself up straight in her chair and said slowly, 'When I talked to Grandad Ollie, his suggestion was that we wait until we came back today, and then depending on what news we have we could think about getting some legal advice.'

''Ang on a minute!' Lily shouted. 'Me an' George don't want t' have to appear in no court.'

'You won't have to,' Patsy assured her. 'It's the council officers that will have to give an account of themselves if it comes to that.'

'Is Mrs Newton in now?' Ellen asked. 'It would be nice if she'd let us take a peek at the baby.'

'You're asking something, you are,' Lily said heavily. 'But I'll pop along an' see if she's in.'

Patsy made to rise.

'No, you stay there. I won't be long. But don't get yer 'opes up. She'll more than likely tell me t' bugger off an' mind me own business.'

Lily was back in no time and she was smiling to herself.

'I take it you never got over the doorstep,' Patsy ventured.

'The eldest of 'er boys opened the door and told me his mother had gone up the pawn shop. I felt like pushing me way in and taking a good look at little Mary, but I knew I'd get a mouthful from Rosie if I did and her kids would 'ave got a clout round the ear for letting me in.'

Patsy shook her head. Then, voicing her thoughts aloud, she said, 'What on earth does a woman like Mrs Newton own that is worth pawning?'

Lily looked at Patsy for a long minute, then threw her head back and roared with laughter. 'By golly, Patsy Owen, you 'ave moved up in the world. Forgotten how the other 'alf live, 'ave yer?'

Patsy looked puzzled and her twin daughters even more so.

Lily calmed down before saying, 'It's the first Monday in the month, tally-man day.'

Both Emma and Ellen said, 'What?'

Patsy grinned to herself, suddenly realising that all her children had been brought up in vastly different circumstances to those which she herself had been reared in. They had never known what it was like to be really poor. Never quite having enough to eat, never really warm in winter because you had to make one bag of coal last at least a week. Wearing hand-me-down clothes and dodging the rent collector because you hadn't enough money to pay the rent. Although she wasn't quite sure what Lily was on about, she now had a pretty good idea.

'Gawd luv yer,' Lily said, laughing at the twins. 'It's easy enough t' tell you two were never brought up in the East End. The tally man brings a van full of goods round the streets once a month, all kinds of things. Then he calls every week and folk pay him so much, probably a couple of bob, until the goods are paid for. Or if you're a good customer, pay him regular like, he'll let you have more goods when you've paid about half of what you owed him in the first place. That way you're never out of debt and he's always sure of having customers. It's a dead cert that today Rose Newton has bought a pair of sheets and pillow cases, or some such items from him. But . . .'

Her eye had caught Patsy's and she had to stop talking because they were both now laughing fit to bust. Emma and Ellen were fascinated.

A minute or two later, Lily wiped her eyes on the corner

of her apron and continued: 'She probably sent a couple of her boys out into the street to watch until the tally man had finished working this district, and as soon as they gave her the all clear she's away to uncle's to pawn the new goods.'

Patsy was still laughing. The look on her daughters' faces had to be seen to be believed.

'Why did you say Mrs Newton had gone to uncle's?' Ellen queried.

'It's just another name for a pawn shop.' Patsy was the one to explain. Lily was still laughing her head off.

'So the woman is borrowing money on goods that she doesn't own,' Emma said thoughtfully, then added, 'Well I never!'

Ellen smiled. 'You have to admire her cheek.'

The banging of the front door knocker made them all jump and a voice called through the letter box, 'You there, Lil? My lad said you wanted t' see me.'

Lily straightened her wrapround apron and made to go to the front door, but before she opened it she stopped and cautioned, 'Mind what you're saying. Let 'er do most of the talking.'

She greeted Rose as if they hadn't met for days. 'Come in. There's a cuppa in the pot if you'd like one.'

'When 'ave yer ever known me to refuse a cup of rosy lee?'

My God, Mrs Newton is a big woman! Patsy and her daughters were all thinking the same thing as she came into the living room. She must have weighed about sixteen stone!

'These are friends of mine from the old days,' Lily said by way of an introduction. 'This is Mrs Owen, Patsy t' her friends. She and my mum not only went t' school together, but they both worked up Tooting market. And these twins are her daughters, Ellen an' Emma.' Then, turning her head, she added, 'And this is Rosie, me neighbour.'

'Pleased t' meet all of yer. Lil lived near yer before she got bombed out, did she?'

'Yes, that's right.' Patsy took the initiative.

Rose heaved a great sigh. With one forearm she pushed up her huge bosoms then turned to face Lily. 'What did yer go up t' my place for? Did yer want something special?'

'No, I just thought it would give you a break to come and have a cuppa an' meet me friends.'

'God knows I need one,' Rose said heavily as she plonked herself down on Lily's sofa. 'Did yer 'ear my Bert going on again early this morning?'

Lily lowered her eyes and nodded her head.

'It's this baby. It's just one too many. Bert won't see that the money I get from fostering pays the rent an' then some. If he didn't drink so much but came straight 'ome of a Friday I wouldn't need t' do it.'

Taking a deep breath, Lily said, 'I feel for yer, I really do, Rose. You've enough children of yer own. I understand yer need the money, but it stands t' reason you can't go on like this.'

'I know that, gal, though how I'll get by without the fostering money Gawd only knows. My Bert keeps threatening what he'll do, an' I'm afraid one day he really will hurt that baby.'

'I'll make a fresh pot of tea,' Lily said, getting to her feet. 'I ain't told my friends much, only that you are looking after a dear little girl, but these twins 'ere were both nurses before they got married. Emma 'as three boys but Ellen don't 'ave no kids. You 'ave a word with them. I won't be long.'

Emma was the first to start the ball rolling. 'Mrs Burton told us your arrangement with the council was only temporary, that the baby was going to be put up for adoption.'

'Tell me about it,' Rose Newton roared. 'All I get from them now is they can't find the mother an' foster parents are 'ard t' find. But this morning's ructions with my Bert just about finished me off. I can't take any more. So the only thing I can do is go down to the council offices with the baby and dump her on t' them. That way they'll 'ave t' find another family t' take her. Won't they?'

Lily came back in with a huge cup and saucer filled with a steaming hot brew.

'Cor, fanks, Lil. That's what I like about you, yer never do fings by 'alf.'

Noisily Rose sipped away at her tea, while Patsy racked her brains as to how she could get this coarse woman to allow them to see the baby she was fostering.

As for Lily, an idea was rolling around in her head and she was more than willing to put it to the test, but what would her George say? She never did anything without talking it over with George first.

She took the bull by the horns.

'How about if I give yer a bit of a rest? I'll mind the wee baby for a couple of days if yer like.'

Rose Newton nearly choked on her hot tea. 'Blimey, gal, that's an offer I'd really like t' take yer up on, but I 'adn't better.'

'Why ever not? You said yerself you could do with a break.'

'Yeah, I know I did, but that 'ealth visitor said they'd be sure an' 'ave some news of the mother before long and she promised she'd come straight round and let me know what was 'appening. Best leave things as they are for the time being. I'll give 'em a week, no more, mind. Wouldn't do for them to call on me an' find I 'adn't got the baby. But fanks for yer offer.'

'Do you think we might have a peep at the baby?' Ellen asked in her gentlest voice.

Patsy couldn't believe she had heard right. It wasn't at all like Ellen to be so forward.

'Well . . .' Rose hesitated. They could see she didn't want to offend anyone, but neither did she want them all trooping through her place. 'Suppose yer can if yer like, but I ain't

181

'ad time t' bath an' dress her this morning yet.'

'That's all right, I understand.' Ellen smiled. 'How about if just my sister and I come along with you? When you've finished your tea, that is.'

Patsy looked daggers at her daughter. But she took a deep breath and told herself it was just as well for the twins to see the baby on their own. If she went she'd probably go spare if the child was dirty and uncared for, while Ellen and Emma would keep their thoughts to themselves.

It was a good half an hour before the twins came back.

Patsy looked at each of them in turn, trying to work out what they were thinking. Their faces were pale and their eyes sad. She said anxiously, 'Well, are you going to tell us anything or not?'

Ellen said nothing. She sat down and leaned back in the chair, looking very close to tears.

Emma said, 'I couldn't help feeling sorry for Mrs Newton. The state of that place and the number of children! How the poor woman is expected to cope is beyond me.'

Patsy said patiently, in a soft voice, 'Did you get to see the baby?'

'Oh yes, we saw her all right. The condition she is in is . . . well, indescribable. And her own baby isn't much better. But I still couldn't find it in my heart to lay all the blame at that poor woman's door. Nobody seems to be lifting a finger to help her. They are just leaving her to fend for herself with more children than she can possibly manage.'

'I have to agree.' Ellen spoke quietly, her face still taut with shock. She was wondering how to stop her sister's flow of angry words. 'I don't think there is anything anyone can do until the mother of that baby is found.'

Patsy and Lily stared at each other. 'I do try t' help,' Lily said with a sob in her voice.

'We know you do,' Patsy assured her, placing her arms around her shoulders and holding her close.

What she was thinking was that the sooner she and the twins got out of here the better. Nothing had changed since her first visit and the next step had to be as Ollie had said: take some legal advice and get someone, anyone, on to tracing the baby's mother. Like it or not, her whole family were involved now, and none of them would rest easy until that wee baby was sorted.

A tearful goodbye was said to Lily, and Patsy gave her a firm promise that they would keep in touch.

All the way home Emma was angry. But Patsy felt that Ellen's emotions were different. She had to stop herself from asking too many questions. Time enough for decisions when they got home and their men were with them.

Chapter Seven

ELLEN WALKED SLOWLY DOWN the garden. Winter was at last giving way to spring. Daffodils were shooting up under the trees and in the rough grass at the bottom of the lawn. She should be feeling happy.

It was more than a week since their visit to London, and endless discussions had taken place between the family. Ollie, as always, had used his contacts and got things moving. Apparently the mother of the baby fostered out to Mrs Newton had not been that hard to find. She had readily agreed to a meeting with Ollie's London firm of solicitors, but was adamant she wanted the baby adopted.

For three nights Ellen had turned an idea over and over in her head, and now suddenly she made her decision.

Peter was sitting by the window reading the newspaper when she came into the room and quietly said: 'Would you mind, dear, if we had a serious talk?'

He raised his head and gave her a baffled look. 'Goodness, you do sound serious.'

'Peter, would you consider us adopting this baby?' Ellen asked slowly.

A sudden chill had settled in the room and she found

herself shaking like a leaf. She dreaded to think what his answer would be.

He stared at her but made no answer.

She decided to go ahead and plead her case.

'We've been married a while now, and as yet I haven't conceived. I am afraid that what happened all those years ago when I was so ill may be the cause. Perhaps I am unable to bear children.'

Peter's look now was one of sheer love. He folded the newspaper and laid it down on the floor, then got to his feet and came to stand in front of her. 'Goodness, Ellen, have you been worrying about that? Because there is no need. Not on my part anyway. As long as I have you in my life I am more than content.'

'Oh, Peter, I love you so much, you know I do. But . . . if you had caught even a glimpse of that baby, you would have wanted to pick her up and let her know that someone cared for her, someone loved her.'

Peter was now looking at her with concern.

'No, I don't think I would be as easily moved as you obviously were. We know nothing at all of the child's background. I think you are letting your heart rule your head. Being far too hasty.'

'Yes, I suppose I am,' Ellen admitted in a drained voice.

'Come and sit down, Ellen. I am not dismissing your proposition out of hand, but let me tell you that Ollie and I had a long discussion about this young lady and her baby only yesterday.'

'Did you really?' Ellen asked with the faintest of smiles. She was determined to remain cool and collected. If Peter were to admit that he was dead against such an idea then she would give in and that would be the end of the matter as far as she was concerned.

'According to Ollie,' Peter began, 'the mother is a well-educated young woman, though she would not give any information as to who the father of the baby was. She went to a party, had rather too much to drink and let things get out of hand. Apparently she was horrified when she discovered that she was pregnant. She just wants the baby placed with a caring couple so that she can go back home and get on with her own life. If you really are serious about us having the child, there are a hundred and one things that have to be talked about, even argued about in detail.'

Ellen could not believe what he was saying. There was hope, even if it was only a glimmer at the moment.

Before she could speak, Peter added, 'I suggest you and I pay a visit to George and Lily Burton. Find out if the Newtons have taken the baby back to the council or not.'

Ellen hesitated, and nervously cleared her throat. 'You mean just the two of us on our own?'

'Well, yes. Adoption is a very serious business, and if we consider it at all it will have to be between just you and me. Nothing to do with any other member of the family. Not at this point in time.'

Smiling brightly, Ellen grabbed his arm and cried, 'You really mean it? You'll come and see the baby with me?'

'No, Ellen, what I said was that we'll go to see Mr and Mrs Burton first. The odds are the baby is no longer being fostered by Mrs Newton. Another thought to consider is that another couple may have approached the council, maybe to foster the baby temporarily but with a view to adopting her at a later date.'

Ellen remained silent.

'I'll get us both a cup of coffee while you decide whether we pay this visit or not.' He squeezed Ellen's arm reassuringly before he left the room.

Deep in thought, she couldn't help wondering what the outcome would be. She loved Peter so much, but a baby would enrich their lives even more. She had been so disappointed each month when her period appeared. She was fairly certain that the beating she had received from Robert had had lasting effects. Time was passing, and soon she would be too old to have children of her own. There were times when she envied her sister and brother their families. Even David had had Tim since he was a little boy.

Not only would she be thrilled to have a baby girl to call her own, if they were lucky enough to be allowed to adopt little Mary, but she knew for certain that the child would have a safe and loving upbringing. Peter was a good man, and fine and honourable.

He had said that for now it was a matter to be dealt with entirely between themselves. But what if it did all come right? Mary would soon learn that she not only had parents who would love her for the rest of their lives; she would also have cousins, aunts and uncles, a grandmother and a grandad. And Ollie would have another great-grandchild to add to his list.

Oh, please God, let it happen, she silently prayed.

Determination had won the day.

Ellen could hardly believe that she and Peter were standing in the corridor of a block of council flats just off the Walworth Road.

'No one will open the door unless you knock,' she laughed nervously.

After a moment George Burton stood facing them, a puzzled look on his face.

'Mr Burton? I'm Ellen, Patsy Owen's daughter. My married name is Crawford and this is my husband Peter.' Then turning to Peter, Ellen said, 'This is Mr Burton. For a good many years he and his family were neighbours of ours.'

George thrust out his hand which Peter shook willingly. 'My God! I can see it now. You're one of Patsy's twin girls. Long time no see. Come on in, though whether you've come at a good time or not you'll 'ave t' judge for yerselves.'

Once inside the living room, Ellen stood still, hardly able to believe what she was seeing. Lily Burton had a blanket stretched right out to cover the table top, where a tiny baby lay. She had a pot of cream in her hand and some of it was smeared on two of her fingers. The ointment was a funny yellowish colour.

'Oh my Gawd!' Lily exclaimed when Ellen had introduced Peter to her. 'Sit yerselves down.'

Ellen watched as Lily gently smoothed cream along the baby's thin legs. Then she straightened the baby's petticoat and short dress, wrapped her loosely in a snow-white shawl and, lifting her up, offered her to Ellen. 'Would you like to hold Mary while I make us all a cup of tea?'

Ellen felt such joy as she cradled the baby, but at the same time her eyes filled with tears. She was so thin and tiny, like a small doll.

Peter could hardly bear to look at his wife. She looked so blissfully contented. What had he done? Had it been a good idea to come up to see these folk again? Ellen looked so natural as she nursed the baby, but was he raising false hopes?

When they were all seated and four cups of tea had been poured out, it was Ellen that asked the first question. 'How long have you had the baby, Mrs Burton?'

'Right from the day your mum brought you and your twin up 'ere. And please, if we're to call you Ellen and Peter, then you call us Lily and George.'

Ellen took her eyes off the baby for a minute as she smiled and said, 'All right.'

'Suppose I'd better begin at the beginning, eh, George?' Lily looked at her husband as if asking for his permission.

He nodded his head.

Lilly began: 'After I'd seen you lot off, I started thinking about what Rosie 'ad threatened to do. You remember, take

188

the baby back t' them social workers. Well, I felt ashamed of meself for not doing more t' 'elp, and I got really angry. I mean t' say, that was supposed to 'ave been a child protection officer that came to visit. Right old story that pair must 'ave spun 'er, an' she must 'ave believed them, 'cos she went away and left the baby with Rosie. I couldn't get that baby's sweet little face out of my mind. After all, she never asked t' be born. Poor innocent little thing, being pushed from pillar to post as if she were an unwanted parcel.' Lily paused, picked up her cup and took a gulp of her tea, then turned to Ellen. 'I'll take 'er now, shall I? Lay 'er down in 'er cot. Come and see, it's a nice one. My George got it up the second-hand shop, stripped it down and painted it a pretty shade of pink.'

When the two women left the room, George said to Peter, 'You ain't 'eard the 'alf of it yet, mate. My Lil keeps on about Rosie Newton 'aving done 'er best. Best! Gawd 'elp us, yer should 'ave seen the state that kid was in.'

'I can tell by looking at her that she hasn't been fed properly,' Peter said grimly. 'She's a few months old now, isn't she, yet from the size of her one could be forgiven for thinking she was a newly born baby.'

George wasn't given time to reply. Lily was talking nineteen to the dozen as she and Ellen came back into the room.

'I worked myself up into such a state you wouldn't 'ave believed it. I know I should 'ave talked it over with my George first, but my temper wouldn't let me wait. I went tearing off down to Rosie's an' came straight out with it. "You ain't going down to no council, Rose!" I yelled at 'er. "God knows where that baby will end up. If it's all right with you I'll take 'er right now. There ain't been no time t' talk it over with my George; that will 'ave t' come later. I'll tell yer this, though, he won't see her pushed from one couple to another. He'll make sure that she stays with me

189

until someone in authority decides exactly what is going to 'appen to her. He won't allow that tiny mite to be snatched away by a load of do-gooders. As for the fostering money, Rose, you can go on drawing it until someone cottons on. You need it more than I do. Just remember, I ain't doing it fer the money."

'"You're saying that's what I took 'er in for?"

'I told 'er, quick as lightning, "If the cap fits, wear it." For a moment I thought she wasn't going to let me take the child, but she must 'ave remembered 'er Bert, for she soon changed 'er tune. So I said, "Anyhow, we'll take it one day at a time for now. Wrap 'er up, an' if you've got any bits and pieces for her t' wear I'd be glad of them."'

'And this Mrs Newton handed the child over to you, just like that?' Peter had broken the silence that followed. He sounded shocked to the core.

'Not straight off she didn't. She asked me twice if I were sure, an' when I nodded she heaved a great sigh of relief and told me I was an angel and that I was taking a great weight off her mind. Then she opened one of her dresser drawers, an' you wouldn't believe the clothes she pulled out. I'm telling you, Ellen, the rags I use for wiping up are a darn sight better, and certainly cleaner. There was a vest that had obviously been used for a much older child, a dirty-looking nightdress, a dress that had seen better days and four napkins which when I felt them were as stiff as a board. She bundled them all into a brown paper bag and handed it to me.

'When I bent over the cardboard box in which Mary was lying, the smell of pee nearly knocked me back. I unpinned the soaking wet napkin and left it there. I looked around for something to wrap the baby in but couldn't see anything, so I took me cardigan off and wrapped her up in that.

'Once I got away from Rosie's flat I 'ad to stand still for a minute. I really was appalled at the state of that child and how awful she smelt.'

Lily was out of breath by now, and George took up the story, but not before he had offered Ellen and Peter another cup of tea. They both refused, so intrigued were they by this story. George had their full attention.

'I 'eard later that my Lil had given the baby a quick wipe-over then grabbed some coppers and run to the public phone box. I was in the sorting office when the phone rang. My foreman, a good mate he is, answered it. I could hear a woman's voice yelling down the phone but I never guessed it was my Lil until my mate said, "It's Mrs Burton, isn't it? Calm down, George is right here. I'll pass you over to him."

'As quickly as she could Lil told me what 'ad 'appened and what she'd gone an' done. Good on yer, gal, I said, an' asked if she wanted me t' come 'ome there an' then. I couldn't believe I was 'earing right when she said, "No, no need fer that. Just see if yer can get hold of my sister – after all, she's got seven kids – and then try your brothers and sisters. Gawd knows how many they've got between them."

'I 'ad t' tell her to hold 'er 'orses. I hadn't got a clue as to why she wanted the whole family involved.'

He laughed loudly. 'She called me a dimwit! Said she wanted any and every bit of baby clothes that any of them could spare. Then she said she was going to bath the baby and that as soon as I got 'ome we were going to take her over to the doctor's but she couldn't go till I got there 'cos she hadn't got any clothes for Mary. Course, I 'ad to ask, "Didn't Rose give yer any?" What my Lil said then don't bear repeating, but what it amounted to was if I wanted to see them I'd 'ave t' look in the dustbin, 'cos that's where she 'ad dumped them all.'

Ellen was in a state by now, half laughing, half crying. She couldn't look at Peter. She dreaded to think what he was making of it all.

'I 'ad a word with me gaffer,' George went on. 'He was great. Told me t' get off straight away. So I did the rounds

– thank God neither of our families is scattered too far away – and came home with three bags practically full.'

'Yeah, he did an' all,' Lily piped up. '"You're a good man, George Burton," I told him when he came 'ome. "None better," and he knew I meant it.'

There was a sob in George's voice when he spoke again. 'By the time I did get 'ome, Lil had bathed that baby, and as I looked at her, I just stood and cried. I don't believe that there are many people on this earth that could have looked at that naked little mite and not been moved. She wasn't much better than a skeleton. "Wrap 'er up," I said to Lil, "we can't be responsible for getting her well. Not on our own we can't. Let's get over to the doctor's, see what he 'as t' say."

'We explained the situation to the receptionist and she told us that surgery didn't start for another hour, but that Doctor Benson was on the premises and if we'd like to take a seat she'd see what she could do.

'We only 'ad t' wait about ten minutes, but it seemed ages. Then Doctor Benson opened his office door and told us to come through.' George turned to face Ellen. 'It were my Lil that gently undressed the baby while I held her. Now, I 'ave to tell yer, that doctor is a big bloke. In fact he's huge, with ginger hair and a great big handlebar moustache. His shoulders are that broad a rugby player would give his front teeth to 'ave them. I wouldn't like to upset him.'

'Yeah, but wasn't he gentle with Mary?' Lily was crying openly now. 'I felt so ashamed when he took her and laid her on his couch. I'll never, till my dying day, forget the look on his face. He said he was appalled. Never in all his years of practice had he seen a child so neglected. "Just look at the state of her," he bellowed. And I couldn't look. That day was the first time I had seen her absolutely naked and I felt like saying to that doctor, you should have seen her before I bathed her. But I never said a word. He was so angry he frightened the life out of me.

'"Who the hell was supposed to be looking after her?" he demanded to know.

'I 'ad t' tell him. I 'ad no choice.

'"Mrs Newton?" he bellowed at me. "I know enough about that family; they've got about seven or eight of their own children." I didn't dare tell him and some more. By now, although he was gently going over the baby from top to toe, he was muttering all the time. Things like, "How in God's name was that woman allowed to foster someone else's child? I'd lay a bet it's to do with the amount of money the council pay for fostering."'

You could have cut the silence with a knife when Lily stopped to draw breath. Ellen didn't dare look at Peter, but all the same she was glad that they had come together and that Peter was hearing this all first hand. At least now he knew that she hadn't been exaggerating. She didn't think Lily was going to say any more and was wondering whether she and Peter should be making a move when Lily started again.

'Finally Doctor Benson straightened up and told us we'd better leave the whys an' wherefores for the time being and concentrate on getting this baby into a better condition.'

Then George grinned. 'You might not believe this bit, Peter, but that big man picked the baby up and stood for a minute or two crooning over her, and then he handed her to me. Not to my Lil.'

'He gave 'er t' you 'cos he wanted me to take in all the instructions he was gonna give me.' Lily set George right before turning her attention to Ellen.

'Doctor Benson said the sores on her bottom needed to be dried out, and as often as I could I should leave her lying on a blanket with a nappy spread on top but her bottom bare so's the air could get to it. Then he went and sat down behind his desk, and me and George stood up ready t' go, but he wasn't 'aving that. "Sit still, the both of you," he said. "I want you to use the cream I'm going to give you three times a day on all the sores, but not on her head. Her scalp is in a very bad condition. Use warm water first, then dab at the sore places with cotton wool soaked in a lotion I will also give you."

'When he was sure I'd understood everything, he suddenly asked me, "Do you know how old Mary is?"

'"Five or six months, if Rosie is to be believed," I told him.

'I won't repeat his comments, Ellen, but not many doctors would have sworn like he did. He kept on that we must get some weight on her but that I'd 'ave to go carefully. Give her something like 'alf a Farley's rusk with Oster milk. Little and often, he impressed on me, and if I were to give her vegetables I must put them through a sieve and cover them with a little drop of gravy.'

Lily stopped talking and grinned at Ellen before she said, 'That bloke must 'ave seen the look on my face 'cos he straight away said sorry and I knew what he meant. And what he said next proved it. "You've children of your own, Mrs Burton, and they really are a credit to you, an' here's me sitting here telling you how to feed a baby. I'd say this wee mite has had a rough start in life, but with you and your husband now in charge of her she'll soon improve."

Both George and me said, "Thank you, Doctor," but I felt I 'ad to ask, "What if the council come and say the baby can't stay with us?"

'Well, luv, we didn't need no telling he was on our side. He almost shouted, "You leave the bloody social workers to me. And if you need anything or anyone challenges you, you come straight to me. Day or night. Meanwhile I want you to bring the baby over to me on a regular basis. Say every four days so that I can monitor her progress. And first thing tomorrow morning I will have the chemist deliver a parcel to your flat. Oster milk and Farleys, that sort of thing."'

Lily let out a long-drawn-out breath before she said, 'Well, Ellen an' Peter, what d'yer think of that?'

It was Peter that answered, and Ellen was surprised at the amount of emotion there was in his voice. 'I think you are both to be admired for what you've done in taking that baby on. And as for the kindness and understanding of that doctor, well it goes to show that there are a great number of kind people in this world.'

'You will tell yer mum what's 'appened, won't you, Ellen?' Lily pleaded.

'You bet your life I will,' Ellen replied quickly. 'But how do things stand at the moment? Are you and George going to keep Mary?'

'We've 'ad two visits from the social.' George grinned. 'I was all ready to send them off with a flea in their ear, but it wasn't like that. Not a bit of it. Doctor Benson must 'ave been as good as his word, 'cos they done nothing but praise the pair of us.'

Peter looked very solemn as he turned to face George and asked, 'Has there been any word or discussion on the adoption of Mary?'

'Not to our knowledge there 'asn't. Wouldn't mind taking her on ourselves really. Me and Lil have discussed it for hours, but with our two growing up we only just manage to make ends meet as it is.' He looked across at his wife and grinned. Lily's face reddened. 'There's another reason why, even with the best will in the world, we can't take on Mary for much longer,' George said, smiling. 'We're gonna 'ave another little'n of our own. My Lil only found out she was pregnant a week ago. Came as a bit of a shock at first, but now we're both over the moon, ain't we, gal?'

Lily nodded her head. She was too embarrassed to look at Peter, who had got to his feet and was heartily con-gratulating George.

Inwardly Ellen felt a surge of joy. She didn't mean to be glad that Lily and George hadn't the means to bring up another child. But on the other hand, Lily being pregnant might be taken as a good omen for her and Peter. Perhaps it would leave the way open for them to make an application to become the parents of that sweet baby.

Quickly she glanced at Peter, who, having kissed Lily, was now sitting down again. She couldn't read his face.

And to herself she was saying that it would be a wise man that could read his thoughts.

Chapter Eight

THE FOLLOWING TWO WEEKS were a joy to the Burton family.

Lily's sister and most of George's family, including his elderly mum and dad, were popping in and out constantly. And they didn't come empty-handed. They brought enough decent baby clothes for six kids.

Patsy came up to Kennington Lane to bring her granddaughter to stay with Peggy Stevens, and the whole bunch of them descended on Lily, all taking it in turns to admire the baby.

In the end Patsy had to drag herself away, but at the front door she handed Lily an envelope. Feeling slightly embarrassed, she quietly explained that her whole family admired what Lily and George had done for little Mary, and that this was a small token from each of them. 'Please, Lily, accept it with the good will of us all. There aren't many that would have done what you have.'

'There ain't no need, we're managing fine,' Lily said tearfully. 'But I am grateful to all of you. Thank you.'

Mary's sore bottom and scalp began to show signs of improvement, but there was still hardly any flesh on her bones, and Lily became concerned when she developed a cough. Due for a visit to Doctor Benson that afternoon, she pondered as to whether it was wise to take the baby out. It was by no means warm yet; it had rained earlier on and now the wind had got up and it was biting. She had been up half the night with the baby because her breathing had sounded so chesty.

As soon as her children came through the door at lunchtime, Lily quickly said, 'Don't take yer coat off, Jack, I want yer to pop over to the doctor's surgery and give this note to the lady at the front desk.'

Hardly had Lily set plates of sausages and mash in front of Julie and Jack than Doctor Benson was standing in her kitchen.

With a clean cot sheet spread over her knees, Lily held the baby. The doctor knelt down beside the chair and gave Mary a thorough going-over. When he had finished, he rose to his feet and looked down at Lily, noting her worried expression.

His voice was quiet as he said, 'Mrs Burton, you are to be admired. This baby has come on by leaps and bounds; no one could deny that. However, you must know she is not at all well or you wouldn't have sent for me. I'm sorry to have to tell you she has congestion of the lungs.'

Lily gasped and wrapped her shawl closer around Mary. 'I knew her chest sounded raw and her breathing was wheezy, but I've done me best, truly I 'ave. I've made sure she's been kept warm, honest I 'ave, she's never been in no draughts.'

'Mrs Burton, I have already told you, there is nothing for you to feel guilty about. Quite the opposite: you have done extremely well. The state that child was in was unbelievable. But now . . .' He paused and shook his head. 'I do think we have to hospitalise her even if it's only for a few days. Better to be safe than sorry. I'll go back to the surgery and

198

arrange for an ambulance to come. You'll be able to go to the hospital with her.'

'Can we come?' Jack and Julie were both near to tears after the doctor had gone.

'Not now, my loves. I want yer t' be ever so good, wash yer face and 'ands and go back to school. There's an apple for each of yer on the dresser. You can eat it on the way, an' if I'm not back by the time you come home this afternoon, go into Mrs Stevens. I'll let her know what's 'appening so she'll be on the look-out for both of yer.'

Lily got herself into a strict routine. At least that way she didn't sit and worry.

Each morning at twenty minutes to nine she saw her two children safely across the main road and watched until they had gone through the school gates. From there she went directly to the Royal Waterloo Hospital, where she stayed for the whole of the morning. Her feelings during those hours were mixed.

Had she interfered when she shouldn't have? Didn't 'ave much choice, was what she kept telling herself. Nobody else seemed to give a damn that a small baby was being neglected, and that was putting it mildly. They say every new baby brings its own love with it, she thought. Well, all I can say is that where that wee mite was concerned, no one seemed to even be aware of it. And if they were, they certainly ignored it.

The baby's own mother hadn't even wanted to see her, let alone hold her or be responsible for her.

And as to Rosie and Bert Newton! Each blamed the other, but there wasn't much to choose between them. That baby wouldn't have lived much longer if she'd been left with them. Not the way they were treating her.

Was she going to die now? As Lily sat at the side of the cot and held Mary's tiny hands, she prayed to God that wouldn't happen. So many people had come to love her. Her own two children adored her. You only had to look into her baby blue eyes or stroke the soft fair down that was beginning to grow on her head and she would capture your heart.

George never failed to call in at the hospital every evening. He couldn't have been more upset or loved her more if she had been his own flesh and blood.

One thing did worry them both. How would they feel when adoptive parents were found for her? 'It'll break my bloody heart,' George had said when she had brought the subject up one evening. And that was her own sentiment an' all!

It was two weeks before the doctors decided that the baby was well enough to be taken home.

Lily was given strict instructions that she must attend the baby clinic each and every week. The whole team of staff was pleased with Mary's progress and agreed she looked a different child to the one that had been admitted to the hospital.

Lily felt like saying to them, you should have seen how the poor undernourished wee thing looked when I took matters into my own hands and rescued her from Rosie's flat on that never-to-be-forgotten day.

It was George who was worrying now. Lily had always been a plump, motherly-looking type, but now by the end of the day her legs were badly swollen and already folk were asking if she was carrying twins because she had put on so much weight. It was the uncertainty of the situation that was becoming too much for both of them.

It was this very matter that they were talking about one afternoon when George had come home from an early shift. There was a knock on the door. Lily struggled to get up, but George pressed her back down into the armchair and told her he would see who it was. Lily heard the voices but couldn't quite place them. A big smile spread over her face as Ellen and Peter were ushered into their living room.

They talked about casual things, how the family was, and how much nicer and warmer the weather was turning. Suddenly Lily laughed, looked at Ellen and said, 'I know you're dying t' see Mary yet you 'aven't even asked where she is. Well, she's in her cot in Julie's room if you want to go an' pick her up. She's probably awake by now anyway.'

Peter cleared his throat before saying, 'Much as Ellen would like to do as you say, Lily, I must first tell you there is a different reason for our visit today. We hope, both of us, that you will approve of our intentions and what we have managed to do so far.'

George looked a bit put out. 'Well, we won't know what you are on about until you come out with it. Will we?'

Peter, never usually at a loss for words, was finding this very difficult.

He started nervously: 'Ellen and I have made an application to the county court to obtain the necessary papers which, if approved, would enable us to adopt Mary. We would appreciate it so much if you two would say that you approve.'

The silence that followed was deafening.

Then George sprang to his feet and was patting Peter on the back, and Ellen had her arms around Lily. Both women had tears trickling down their faces.

'Gawd above, we couldn't wish for a better turn-out,' George declared. 'I've written three letters to the social workers and been down the council offices twice. We've been living on a knife edge. Nobody tells us anything. There's always that nagging feeling at the back of our minds that one day a council worker might pop in and announce that they're taking Mary away.'

'Oh, thank God!' Lily murmured, rubbing her eyes with the back of her hand. 'I've lain awake nights wondering what kind of family she would be going to. How would they treat her? Would they love her? When the time comes should we pass over all the decent clothes we've got for 'er? Sometimes it don't bear thinking about.'

Ellen looked puzzled. 'Families that make an application to adopt children are well vetted. Why wouldn't you give her new parents her clothes?'

Lily looked across at her husband. 'You tell 'er, George.'

George got to his feet and wagged his finger first at Ellen and then at Peter, before saying, 'You two don't know you're born. It's a different world up 'ere this side of the river. Like Rosie only fostered that baby for the money, there's many another couple that will milk the system. They'll adopt a child and then plead sudden poverty and you'd never believe the 'elp they'd get then.'

'What has that got to do with whether Lily should hand over the baby's clothes or not?' Ellen sounded thoroughly bewildered.

'A great many reasons, my luv,' he answered her. 'More than likely within days they'd either be sold or shoved in the pawn shop. And you needn't look at me like that, young lady. Just because you've got good parents and been brought up nice an' proper, like, t' know right from wrong. There's buggers round 'ere that would pinch yer eyeballs out of yer sockets t'day an' come back termorrow fer yer eyelashes.'

Ellen didn't know whether to laugh or cry. She looked across at Peter and his face was a picture. His grin stretched from ear to ear.

'It's true, gal,' Lily sighed. 'Me an' George 'ave spent hours going over an' over what's going t' 'appen. Trying to decide whether it wouldn't be possible for us to keep her. Now t' hear you two say that you want to adopt her is the answer t' all of me prayers.'

'Hang on, you two,' Peter pleaded. 'You're as bad as Ellen's mum and dad. When we told them what we were thinking of doing, it was only a few hours before they'd got

202

the whole family arranging the christening party, and you two and Jack and Julie were top of Patsy's guest list.'

'Well, I can't believe this. We wouldn't really be losing her. We'd be able to keep in touch, see 'er now an' again, wouldn't we?' Lily was talking more to herself than to anyone in particular.

Both Ellen and Peter laughed, and he told them, 'I said you had better hold on. Don't take anything for granted or get too excited. We're merely telling you that we've asked to be considered. There may be other applicants that the social workers might think are more suitable.'

'Oh, Peter!' Ellen cried. 'Do you have to say such things?'

'Darling, there's nothing definite at the moment, and as I see it there is nothing more we can do except wait and pray.'

'I'll pray till I'm blue in the face,' Lily sniffed.

George was almost beside himself as he spat out, 'More suitable than you two? Those bloody social workers will 'ave t' go a damn long way!'

Ellen crossed the room to stand beside Lily's chair again. 'I don't suppose you remember Mr Berry from when you lived near us, do you?'

Lily frowned. 'I remember my mum talking about him. Didn't he adopt Patsy?'

'Well, sort of.' Ellen grinned. 'Never legally, but he was made her guardian. Why I've mentioned him is because he is the king-pin in our family. Grandad to me and my brothers and sister, and Great-grandad to their children.'

'I'm with yer,' Lily muttered, 'though I don't see where he comes into it.'

'Oh, but he does. Very much so,' Ellen emphasised. 'You'll see. He's a man who knows a great many influential people, and as the saying goes, it's not what you know but who you know.'

'And you think he'll be able to persuade the court that you are the right people to be Mary's parents?'

'He'll certainly do his utmost, Lily,' Ellen promised. 'He has already set up a meeting with Mary's mother and his solicitors. The legal firm have her written statement that she gives her consent for the child to be adopted.'

'Well I'll be blowed!' George sighed happily. 'Couldn't be a better outcome if we'd drawn it up ourselves. I don't know about any of you lot, but I'm bone dry.' He grinned at Peter. 'Not much of an 'ouse that don't even give a mate a cuppa when he bothers to call, is it? Sorry we ain't got nothing stronger in, not even a glass of beer t' offer you.'

'Tea will be fine,' Peter agreed. 'And if and when we all have something to celebrate, I promise you the drinks will be plentiful and they'll all be on me.'

'Well, if you've all finished,' Ellen said softly, 'please may I go and pick the baby up?'

Even Peter's eyes were brimming as he watched his wife come back into the room cradling Mary in her arms and singing softly and sweetly to her. For the short time he had been married to Ellen, life had been wonderful. Ellen felt safe at last now that she was with him. They loved each other so much and would be together until the end of their days. They truly belonged together, and to be given the chance to have a baby daughter was a gift from heaven.

Peter watched her as she gently rocked the baby. Neither of them spoke.

Each was lost for a while in their own thoughts.

Chapter Nine

EVEN AT HIS GREAT age there was still something of the actor in Ollie. God knows where he inherited the talent from, but he was able to fall back on that skill whenever it suited him.

It did now.

He pushed open the front door of Primrose Cottage, took several deep breaths, bowed low from the waist and waved his arm, inviting everyone to step over the threshold.

Patsy, Emma, Ellen and Frances stood on the brick path, surrounded by suitcases, and laughed as they watched the boys fight as to who should be the first in.

Thomas, Sam and James had decided on the spur of the moment that they would join Patsy and the girls; Edward Junior had stated he was too old to come along.

Today laughter sprang readily to Patsy's lips. She was so looking forward to fourteen days spent at a leisurely pace, and she was hoping against hope that Ellen might also be able to relax. Perhaps being with her sister might help.

The last few weeks had been very trying for Patsy. On the days that she wasn't going to meet Ellen, Ellen would be on the phone to her. 'She's worrying herself sick, and me with her,' Patsy had said irritably to Eddie. 'If only the court would come through with a decision on the adoption. Even knowing they've been turned down would be better than all this uncertainty.'

Of course Eddie had played peacemaker as always. 'Just think, if all this indecision is driving you round the bend, what must it be like for Peter and our Ellen?'

It was then that Ollie had pointed out that the weather was settled, warm and sunny, and a perfectly good cottage was standing empty down in Cornwall.

So here they were! The journey had been long and tiring. Two cars, trying to keep up with each other. The only thing Patsy was grateful for was that Florrie had not been with them. Oh dear, never a day went by that she didn't miss that dear woman, but to have had her along today moaning about how ridiculous it was to have bought a holiday home so far from London would have been the last straw. Anyway, the way she was feeling at the moment, she would probably have agreed with her.

'Are you women going to stand there all day?' Ollie shouted from the doorway. 'Come on in, the boys can fetch the luggage later. I've put the kettle on.'

'Thank God for small mercies,' Emma murmured as she left her twin and her mother and walked briskly down the path.

Never having set eyes on the cottage before, Ellen and Emma were delighted. Roses grew around the door-frame and a thicket of honeysuckle smothered the long wall on one side of the garden. Inside it smelt wonderful: old-fashioned lavender. The living room was huge and so lovely. There was that big table at the far end, the one Patsy had imagined she would one day see her grandchildren sitting round, eating, laughing, talking. On it were several large dishes all covered with white cloths, waiting for the visitors to arrive, and Patsy guessed that Daisy Button had been as good as her word.

Further inspection revealed freshly baked scones and a fruit cake. There was also a big crusty loaf of bread and a note to say that there was milk, cheese, cream and butter outside the back door in the shade underneath a couple of stone flower-pots, and some provisions in the larder. On the windowsill there was a copper jug filled with wild flowers. Daisy had certainly done her best to get the cottage looking great.

Emma roared with laughter as she touched a brass warming pan which hung beside the open-hearth stone fireplace, while Ellen went to the back door to check that the provisions really were there and found herself staring in disbelief at the wooden shed which obviously housed a lavatory and the big tin bath hanging from a nail on the wall outside the door.

Patsy chuckled to herself. She couldn't resist the temptation to let her girls think that was the only toilet and the only means of having a bath. 'Wait until they go upstairs and find the bathroom for themselves,' she whispered to Ollie.

Emma made the tea, while Ellen and her mother made thick sandwiches from the loaf of bread and a piece of boiled bacon Daisy had left in the larder. They ate them sitting round the wooden-topped table just as Patsy had pictured they would. Then they started on the scones, topping them with strawberry jam and thick Cornish cream. Finally Ollie sliced the farmhouse fruit cake. Everyone agreed it was one of the best teas they had ever tasted. Patsy, looking at her daughters and grandchildren, thought this holiday was going to be wonderful.

'Would you like to see upstairs before it gets dark?' Ollie said, smiling to himself before adding, 'There's no electricity, we haven't got round to that yet; it's a bit of a problem because this cottage is off the beaten track.'

The boys stared at him dumbfounded.

'If the property had been the other side of the river we could perhaps have run a supply from Mr Button's farm. As it is, we have to make do with lamps, and I know it's not cold but you boys could light a fire if you want to. That would give a warm glow during the evening.'

Not only the boys but Frances as well thought it was hilarious.

'Right,' Patsy said firmly, 'upstairs first, let's see who is sleeping where.'

One by one they stumbled up the narrow staircase, lugging an assortment of cases and bags.

There were whoops of joy and loud voices laying claim to each bed. Ollie said firmly that they could have all three bedrooms because the sofa downstairs turned down into a bed and that was where he intended to sleep. Suddenly Patsy heard both Ellen and Emma start to giggle. She turned to face Ollie, and they both nodded and said in unison, 'They've found the bathroom!'

When some sort of order had been imposed upstairs, the boys decided a fire was a jolly good idea. They found logs and kindling as well as paraffin in a shed halfway down the garden. There was also a tank which held oil. Ollie explained that it was connected to the big geyser in the bathroom.

Before long the lamps were lit and a fire was crackling in the enormous grate. This huge ground-floor room had looked lovely before. Now it seemed to come to life. Everything glowed: the warm colours of chintz, oak and bricks, and the shining gleam of copper and brass.

'Now, I came prepared,' Ollie said as he lifted a soft-lidded case on to the table. 'Get some glasses from the cupboard, please, Frances; you boys can lay out the games and then we'll sit round the table, have a drink and decide which game you prefer to start off with.' There were soft drinks for the children, several choices for the women, and of course a bottle of rich red port for Ollie himself.

'Oh, Grandad!' the boys yelled, and Frances's face was wreathed in smiles as they each in turn lifted out a different game. There was Monopoly, draughts, Scrabble, several packs of cards and even a chess set with thirty-two finely polished chessmen.

The days passed all too quickly.

They went for walks in the woods, the boys attempting to climb the trees. Frances grazed her knee trying to keep up with them. They went to Newquay, swam in the sea and lay stretched out on the glorious expanse of sand. Lunch that day was eaten in a real old-fashioned pub down by the harbour. But they also spent a lot of time at the cottage. Everybody did a bit of gardening and a bonfire burned almost constantly as they cleared all the rubbish that had accumulated in the outhouses and sheds over the years.

The evenings were great. Everyone played the games and everyone fought to win. Except for chess. That was strictly for the boys and their grandad. Ollie was a good teacher and no one was allowed to interrupt their concentration.

Patsy had brought half a dozen books, so the women were quite content, while Frances took a pack of cards and played Patience, a game her father had taught her.

On the last evening Ellen was alone upstairs. Patsy needed no telling what was wrong. One or another of them had phoned home almost every day from different public telephone boxes just to keep in touch and let the family know they were having a good time and behaving themselves. Today Ellen had spoken to Peter, and she had been in a thoughtful mood ever since.

Patsy tapped lightly on the door of the room that Ellen was sharing with Emma. 'May I come in?' she called.

'Of course, Mum,' Ellen answered, not sounding too happy.

She was sitting on the edge of the bed, and Patsy went

and sat beside her. 'Want t' talk t' me about anything?'

Ellen shook her head.

'Come on now. This is no way to end such a happy holiday, is it? Did Peter give you some news that has upset you?'

Ellen sighed softly. 'I suppose it depends on which way you look at it, Mum. Peter said we've been given a date for a court hearing.'

'Well that's marvellous news, isn't it?'

'Wish I could believe that. Peter also said that the social workers had been driving him mad. Hardly ever off our doorstep, was how he put it.'

'And?' Patsy felt that getting answers from Ellen was like drawing teeth.

Ellen took a deep breath. 'He did say he'd been up to town and paid a visit to the solicitors. Two of them will be in court on the day of the hearing, and Doctor Benson has volunteered to give evidence.'

'Well that all sounds fine t' me,' Patsy said. 'An open-and-shut case, I'd say. One thing, though: how about Mary's mother? Does she 'ave t' appear in court?'

Another heavy sigh escaped from Ellen's lips. 'Yes, she does. And that's what is worrying me. Suppose she refuses to turn up? And even if she is there, what's to say she won't change her mind?'

'Ellen, listen to me. If you and Peter are meant to have this baby and bring her up as your daughter, then that is what will happen. All these social workers are doing their best to see that she is placed where she will be well looked after. They got it all wrong when they put her with Rosie Newton, an' they aren't about to make the same mistake twice.'

'Can't they tell from looking over our home so many times that we are decent enough to be parents? We want that baby,' Ellen said stubbornly. 'I feel in my heart that she belongs with Peter and me.'

210

Patsy looked at her daughter's pale face and vowed fiercely to herself that she would pray every night that the court's decision would be the right one. Ellen had suffered enough in her life.

'Come on now, luv. It's our last night here. Come downstairs and have a drink, and as soon as we get home and Peter shows you all the court papers you'll feel a lot better. Everything will be fine. You two have so much going for you that the court have to allow this adoption to go through. You'll see.'

Ellen couldn't see that her mother had her fingers crossed behind her back, or that she was praying silently that what she was telling her daughter would all come true.

It was the day of the court hearing. For Ellen and Peter the waiting had been unbearable, and now they were about to learn their fate.

Doctor Benson was there when they arrived, and Ellen was never more pleased than to see this giant of a man and his happy face.

'This is Mr Howard,' he said, introducing them to a strong, robust-looking young man. 'He is leading the team of child-care experts,' he explained, doing his best to reassure Ellen.

Leading the team? How many of them were there going to be? Peter wondered. And how could he be the leader? He didn't look more than thirty years old, and surely would be more at home on a rugby pitch.

It would have been hard to say who was the more apprehensive as Ellen was introduced to Mary's mother, Margaret Wilmott. She was tall, slim and extremely sophisticated looking. The suit she wore was charcoal grey and teamed with a high-collared white blouse. She wore black stockings and high-heeled plain black court shoes.

'Miss Wilmott has countersigned the form releasing her from all parental rights. It has been witnessed by two members of our legal firm.' The stern-faced solicitor spoke quietly, glancing first at Peter and then at Ellen.

Peter held out his hand and it was shaken by Miss Wilmott as he murmured, 'Thank you.' Not a word was spoken by either of the women. They merely nodded at each other and turned away.

They both knew the reason for this court sitting today. What was there for them to say?

When the proceedings started, Ellen's heart sank into her boots. All this because they wanted to give a small baby a good home!

If anything, it was poor Lily Burton who had the most questions to answer.

How and why had she taken the baby out of Mrs Newton's care without first at least asking permission?

'Because nobody cared what was happening to that wee child, and if they did care they must 'ave been blind not t' see for themselves that the baby was wasting away.'

Doctor Benson was equally forthright, to say the least. 'Disgraceful,' was how he put it, 'and the child is probably only alive today because Mr and Mrs Burton stepped in and accepted the responsibility.'

'Are you well acquainted with Mr and Mrs Burton?'

'Yes, sir, they and their children are patients of mine. I have great admiration for them both.'

'And how about Mr and Mrs Crawford? Would you say you personally approve this application for adoption?'

Ellen never heard the next word that was said. The blood drained from her face and she slid slowly to the floor in a dead faint. A tall, broad-shouldered policeman carried her out into the fresh air because Peter had been asked to come forward and stand in front of the bench.

It was some time later that Peter, slowly and joyfully, told her that they had been granted permission for the adoption to go ahead.

Ellen felt she couldn't wait for all the legalities to be over and done with. From the day they brought her home the baby would be known as Mary Crawford.

That her second name was to be Lily thrilled George and Lily Burton no end.

BOOK FOUR

London, 1972

Chapter One

'JUST LOOK AT THESE clothes. They are absolutely exquisite,' Patsy whispered to Vicky.

Vicky smiled at her mother-in-law. 'I can't believe that Frances is the top model today. I know it's only a charity show, but it is getting such a lot of publicity and I'm so proud of her.'

Patsy and her twin daughters all laughed. 'We're all proud of her,' Emma said. 'Eighteen years old; can't believe how the years have flown so quickly.'

'I agree,' Patsy said. 'But you've only got to look at our boys. I never for one moment thought they would grow so tall.'

It was one of those events which, right from the outset, was destined to be perfect. Every seat in the hall was taken, and backstage, behind the curtains, it was a sea of activity. Most of the clothes the volunteer models were wearing were brand new, but there were a certain number of dresses and one or two suits which were really old. Lent for this special occasion, they had arrived in boxes, expertly folded and covered with layers of tissue paper. Some smelt of moth balls. Most of the bonnets and hats were old but had been renovated, the original ribbons and velvet bands replaced with new.

So many people were backstage all doing last-minute jobs, sewing on buttons, turning up hems so that the models wouldn't trip and fall over. Ellen was sewing velvet straps to a wide-brimmed bonnet to be tied beneath the girl's chin. 'Wouldn't want it blowing off, would we?' one of the organisers had remarked.

Almost at the same moment that Frances came on to the stage from the left-hand side, her brother James came dashing up the stairs on the right-hand side. They stood facing each other. James cocked his head to one side and stared at his sister with open admiration. She was wearing an elegant honey-blonde wig, and her make-up was immaculate.

'You know, Fran, you look absolutely smashing,' he said. 'What a pity you can't keep that dress. It really looks as if it were moulded round your body.'

'Thank you, brother dear,' Frances said, all smiles. 'But just when and where would I wear it? This is the kind of thing they wore to supper dances, or so Gran told me. Didn't you, Gran?'

Patsy smiled and nodded her head. 'But I'm only going by what I read in magazines or the newspaper. Anyhow, I'm going to leave you all to it and join yer grandad out front before I lose my seat.'

Frances gave a twirl for the benefit of her mother and her aunts. She smoothed the soft material down over her hips. 'I can't help wishing I *could* keep this dress,' she murmured. 'It feels so good.' The gown was the palest shade of blue and had a close-fitting bodice with pin-tucks down as far as the waist line. The skirt was gathered, very full, and entirely covered with beads in shades of silver and gold. As Frances moved, the beads instantly sparkled as they caught and held the light. The effect was dazzling.

'I wonder if our gran ever wore anything like this,' Frances said in an undertone to her brother.

It was Vicky who answered. 'I doubt it. She was very poor before she met your grandad.'

'What, you mean the pair of them never went dancing?'

'Not until later years. You've heard the story of how your grandad was born with a club foot and had to wear an iron lift on the bottom of his boot.'

'Yes.' Everyone in the group nodded their heads; some even remembered seeing a photograph of Eddie wearing that hideous contraption.

'Well,' Vicky looked very seriously at her daughter, 'it wasn't until your gran had a long talk with a young doctor that between them they managed to persuade Grandad to have an operation. It didn't cure the problem entirely, because it should have been done soon after he was born. But the improvement meant a great deal to him, and soon after the operation this doctor ordered him a special pair of shoes and from then on he was able to walk more normally.'

'And then he *did* take Gran dancing,' Frances butted in quickly. 'I've just remembered him telling me about it when I was at school. He told me how proud he was.'

Everyone laughed, but Emma said, 'I still bet Mum never owned a dress anything like the one you're wearing.'

Silence fell until Ellen said sadly, 'Mum an' Dad always saw that we never went without.'

James felt the mood change and quickly took charge. 'I brought a bottle of white wine with me. Shall we all have a glass?'

'Why not,' Vicky answered for them all, quickly adding, 'There is a jug of home-made lemonade if anyone prefers that.'

'Please, I'd love some lemonade,' a small familiar voice said.

All heads turned and everyone gasped in delight as five-year-old Mary Crawford made her appearance.

'Isn't she as pretty as a picture?' Miss Wright, a local school teacher, was here today as wardrobe mistress, voluntarily of course.

Mary certainly looked beautiful. Her dress was of the palest yellow. The full skirt was held in place by a narrow wooden hoop that was sewn into the lining of the under-petticoat. The wide sash that circled her tiny waist was covered in white daisies. The same flowers had been used to trim her poke bonnet, from each side of which were peeping long blonde ringlets. She wore white shoes and socks, and tiny white gloves. She was carrying a flower-trimmed wicker basket filled with sweet-scented rose petals, which she would scatter amongst the audience as she slowly paced the long catwalk that had been set up in the middle of the hall. She had practised this so many times at school that she knew exactly what she had to do. All her family looked at her with pride, but none more than Ellen, her mother.

Emma reached for and held her twin sister's hand. Both women's eyes were brimming with tears. 'You and Peter have done a really good job,' Emma whispered. 'Mary is a credit to you both.'

'Come on, you two,' James said, handing his aunts a glass of wine. 'Smiles only are allowed today.'

'Twenty minutes to curtain-up,' a male voice hollered.

James, having seen that those that preferred wine now had a glass, took a chair, crossed his long legs and lit a cigarette, studying his sister as she accepted a glass of lemonade from their aunt Emma.

Although Frances was of average height, he and his cousins had generally thought of her as being small, perhaps because she had delicate features and was daintily proportioned. So very much like Gran. He was thinking to himself that Frances had turned into a very lovely young lady in the last few years. As children they hadn't treated her at all well, she being the only girl – at least until Uncle Peter and Aunt Ellen had adopted Mary. They had never wanted Frances to tag along with them. Well, not all the time. They had teased her unmercifully, calling her a fat dumpling.

My God, I never realised just how much she has changed!

She no longer looked anything like a dumpling. Today especially she looked like a very expensive china doll.

He drew on his cigarette, quickly stubbed it out in one of the glass ashtrays and drained his glass of wine. Getting to his feet, he squeezed his sister's shoulder affectionately.

'Knock 'em dead, Fran.' He grinned. 'If you like, I'll take you out to dinner this evening.'

'Been stood up by Sybina, have you?' Frances teased him.

'No, I was going to bring her along; you two get on so well. In any case, I presumed you would make it a four-some.'

'Oh . . .' Frances hesitated. 'I don't know whether Luke is coming today or not. I'd like to if he does turn up.'

Her brother sighed inwardly. Luke Somerford! A right Hooray Henry if ever there was one. James couldn't stand the sight of him. His bloody posh voice was enough to set your teeth on edge. He'd never understand what his sister saw in him. Well off? Yes. But in James's book at any rate he was a big-headed spoilt show-off.

Frances used to go out with a decent lad, Alan Yates. They had all known Alan since their school days, and he was always at their house, even got invited to Gran's get-togethers. Ordinary sort but dependable. Shame, he hadn't been around since this Luke had appeared on the scene.

He forced himself to smile at his sister and quietly said, 'Well, if that's what you want, Fran, it's OK by me.'

Frances gave him a grateful smile. 'Thanks, James, it's

221

sweet of you to offer.' She hesitated before adding, 'I spent ages on the phone with Luke this morning but I couldn't pin him down to a definite yes. I'd like to come anyway, even if he doesn't turn up, providing Sybina won't think I'm playing gooseberry.'

'Don't be so daft. You know we'd love to have your company. Just don't hang around too long when the show is over. I'll be in the third row watching you carefully. By the look of things when I came in, a lot of money will be raised today.'

'Will you be watching me, James?' Mary loved the attention she got from all the family, but today she was feeling a bit apprehensive.

'Oh, Mary, I promise I won't take my eyes off you for a moment while you are on the catwalk. You mustn't be nervous. You will be the belle of the ball. You and all the other little girls from your school will get the most applause, you'll see.'

Mary ran to him and held up her face for a kiss, then before going back to stand alongside Miss Wright, she cheekily asked, 'James, shall I shower you with more rose petals than anyone else?'

Everyone burst out laughing at her expression and James wagged a finger at his young cousin. 'I shall be sitting next to your daddy, so you'd better watch what you're doing. Anyway it's time I took my seat. See you all later.' He waved to his aunts and his mother and wished his sister good luck, but as he made his way out front he was still thinking to himself that he would much rather it was Alan Yates that Frances was going out with.

'Everything all right back there?' Peter asked as James sat down next to him.

'Yes, absolutely smashing. Mary looks so sweet, good enough to eat I'd say.'

'I often feel that way about her myself,' her father said.

'Ellen and I think she's the best thing that could have happened to us.'

'The whole family think the same, you know they do. She has a way of worming herself right into your heart, doesn't she?'

'Couldn't have put it better myself, James.'

There were still people coming into the hall, and a lot of shuffling was going on as they squeezed by folk to find their seats.

James was still feeling very thoughtful, and suddenly he came out with a direct question: 'Peter, what are your instincts about Luke Somerford?'

Peter swallowed, turned to his nephew and whispered, 'I can guess why you're asking. To be honest, Ellen heard some talk about him that wasn't very nice. She asked me if she should tell Patsy and Eddie, or even your parents, but I advised her to keep it to herself for the moment. I know Alex would kill him if he hurt Frances. But after all, she is eighteen, she can pick and choose who she goes out with, and . . .' He hesitated. 'Afraid I thought it would only stir up trouble.'

'I know for a fact he gambles a lot, and he's quite a bit older than Frances,' James said.

Peter shuddered. 'Between you and me?'

'Yes, if that's how you want it. I promise. Though there is going to come a time when I will have to tell Mum and Dad.'

'What Ellen was told was that Luke is a heavy drinker, and not only that, he has suffered some big losses at various gambling clubs.'

James sighed heavily. 'This is just awful.'

'Yes, it is,' Peter agreed. 'But at the moment it is none of our business. It's his father's money that is going down the drain.'

'It's not the gambling that's worrying me, though it does

223

reflect badly on Luke and makes me even more certain he's no good for my sister. It's the drinking. He'd better not get our Frances used to alcohol,' James snapped. 'Not if he knows what's good for him.'

The lights were being dimmed in the hall and the show was about to begin as Peter very quietly murmured, 'Luke Somerford has serious problems, but we'll keep an eye on Frances and you come to me any time I can be of help.'

Soft music was playing and the curtains were being drawn back. A plump, slightly balding man in a dark suit appeared holding a microphone. 'Good evening, ladies and gentlemen,' he announced. There was a quiet murmur in reply. He shuffled a sheaf of papers and then began talking, taking the audience through the particulars of the coming show. He related how hard the children from three local schools had worked, as well as the older models who had volunteered, and described the generosity of folk who had lent or made clothes for the show. He finished with the fact that everyone involved was giving their services free and that all proceeds were to be donated to the Royal Institute for the Blind.

'There will be tea and coffee served during the interval and raffle tickets will be on sale. There are some very nice prizes, so please give generously. I think I have said quite enough, so, without more ado, let the show begin!'

There was a gasp from the audience as three beautiful girls stood centre stage twirling parasols. They were dressed as if they had stepped out of the twenties. Frances took the first step and, followed by the other two young ladies, slowly and gracefully walked the length of the catwalk.

James knew the whole family were seated in the rows behind him and Peter. Each and every one of them would be bursting with pride.

Later there was a standing ovation as six little crinoline-clad girls scattered rose petals as they walked through the centre of the audience. Ellen was sitting beside Patsy, directly behind Peter. As Mary drew level with her father and cousin, Ellen leaned forward and gripped Peter's shoulders. On each of their faces was an expression of deeply felt happiness and pride.

At the end of the same row sat Lily and George Burton. George was beaming; Lily was doing her best not to cry.

Oh, she was so proud of that wee girl.

Much later, when all the hugs and kisses had been given and the goodbyes said, James took hold of Sybina and Frances's arms, pulling them one each side of him.

'I've booked a table at the Strand Palace Hotel; now all we have to do is find a taxi.'

Sybina was the friendly type of young lady that everyone immediately took to. She was dark-haired with honey-coloured skin and the most beautiful big brown eyes that James felt he had ever seen.

During the meal Frances was very quiet. Sybina and James knew full well that she was disappointed that Luke had not put in an appearance. Sybina liked Frances a great deal, but she was not sorry that Luke wasn't there. He was nowhere good enough for her. At least that was Sybina's opinion. She had a sneaking suspicion that for all his charm and boyish manner there was something about him which did not ring true.

By the time coffee was served, Frances seemed much more like her normal self, and James made a decision. Tomorrow he would make a point of getting his sister on her own to make a brief mention of his suspicions about Luke, but he decided he must be casual and cautious. He felt he could not just stand by and say nothing, but on the other hand he must remember that she had a mind of her own and he didn't want to upset her unduly. His every sense told him it was important that she was alerted, put on her guard, since she seemed to be regarding Luke Somerford through rose-coloured glasses.

And the last thing he or the family would want was for Frances to be hurt.

Chapter Two

PATSY LIFTED THE CURTAIN and looked out of the window, then muttered miserably, 'Oh my God.'

It was a cold, dark, dingy November morning.

Why had the summer seemed to go so quickly? Because we've all had such great times, she reminded herself. They had been to the cottage in Cornwall twice. On both occasions Ellen had brought Mary with her, and the delight that child had found in playing on the sand and paddling in the sea had been a joy to watch. Each time they had arrived on a dazzling sunny day, seeing the sun shimmering on the calm sea, and Patsy felt she was as bad as the kids because she felt so happy and excited. Both times the fortnight had passed far too quickly. Besides spending hours on the beach, they had walked in the countryside smelling the wild flowers and always finding a small village shop where everyone looked forward to having an ice cream. They had called at farms where they were able to buy fresh eggs and vegetables and Mary was allowed to wander around and see the animals.

'If only the men had been able to come on holiday with us,' Ellen had said to Emma, 'I wouldn't ever want to go home.'

Such lovely memories, but this won't do, Patsy chided herself as she let the lace curtain drop. I'd better move myself and get washed and dressed. Then she said aloud, 'But not before I've had my second cup of tea.'

It was just turned nine o'clock when Patsy, looking extremely smart in her long camel coat, black ankle boots, and a bright red scarf wrapped around her neck, was ready to leave the house. Before she had a chance to close the front door the telephone rang. She stepped back into the hall and picked up the receiver, but before she had time to say a word, the caller was saying, 'Mum, is that you?'

'Oh, hallo, Vicky,' she replied, surprised. 'Yes, it's me. You sound awful. Whatever's the matter?'

'Oh, thank God! Thank goodness I've caught you.'

Instantly recognising the terror in Vicky's high-pitched voice, Patsy said, 'Vicky, take a deep breath, calm down and tell me what's happened.'

Vicky began to babble so hysterically that Patsy was unable to make any sense of her words. She sounded absolutely distraught. Patsy listened for a few seconds longer, getting more alarmed by the minute. Finally she cut in.

'Vicky, I can't understand a word you're saying. Please, dear, try and speak slowly. Is Alex not there with you?'

Patsy waited, heard Vicky sucking in great gulps of air. The long-drawn-out silence seemed to go on for ages.

Suddenly, and quite clearly, Vicky said, 'The police are here . . . It's our Frances.'

Now there was only the sound of Vicky crying bitterly.

Patsy went cold from head to toe. Endless questions were flashing through her mind. Why were the police there? Had Frances been in an accident? Was she dead?

Vicky's voice, when she did speak again, was a terrified whisper. 'Someone found Frances on Clapham Common. They've taken her to hospital.'

Patsy wanted to shake Vicky. So much information she

needed to know, and all she was getting were odd disjointed sentences.

'What the hell was she doing on Clapham Common? Is she all right?' she asked, sounding much sterner than she meant to.

'Well, she's not dead . . . but . . . her boyfriend Luke is.' The last four words came out in a rush.

Patsy gasped. This couldn't be right! What the hell was happening? Where was Alex? Oh, why wasn't he there? He'd know how to handle this ghastly mess.

'Vicky, listen to me. Do you know where Alex is?'

'No.'

'When he left the house this morning didn't he say where he was going?' Patsy asked sternly. Fear was making her exasperated.

'To the office first, something about seeing you and getting the post, but I don't know after that.'

Oh dear God. What should she do first? Go to the office? Phone David? No, he'd be gone to work by now. How about Donald? He might still be at home, but if she phoned there she'd frighten the life out of Emma. What could she tell them? What did she know herself? Patsy's mind was working overtime but it wasn't getting her anywhere. Knowing she wasn't going to get any straight answers from her daughter-in-law, not the state she was in, she said, 'Vicky, I'll be with you just as soon as I can, but first ask one of the policemen to come to the phone, will you, dear.'

There was what seemed like an awfully long silence at Vicky's end. Patsy sat down heavily on the hall chair. Her heart was beating like a drum against her rib cage.

'Mrs Owen?' a deep gruff voice asked.

'Yes. I'm Frances's grandmother.'

'We know that. I'm Inspector Walsh.' Although he didn't sound too keen, he gave her the essential details. The discovery of Luke Somerford's body had been made in the

229

early hours of that morning by a constable on his beat. He was in his own car and as far as they could tell he had been stabbed twice.

'It was much later when a milkman discovered your granddaughter.'

'Well how is she?' For Christ's sake stop beating about the bush and tell me straight, was what Patsy really wanted to say.

'Battered and bruised but alive,' was all the information that Inspector Walsh was prepared to give over the telephone.

'Thank you for speaking to me. I'll get someone and we'll be with my daughter-in-law as soon as possible.' Patsy spoke in a strong, calm voice that belied just how terrible she was feeling.

When she replaced the phone her mind momentarily went blank. 'Oh my God!' she cried out loud. What a mess. It was unbelievable. It couldn't be true. But she knew damn well it was. Shaking her head hard, she wondered where to begin.

Where were the men today? Ollie and Eddie had left together at about eight o'clock, but for the life of her she couldn't remember where they had said they were going today.

While she was trying to unscramble her thoughts, the phone rang again. She had hardly got the receiver to her ear when Alex's voice came down the line loud and clear.

'You all right, Mum? Bit late this morning, aren't you?'

Patsy gave a heartfelt sigh of relief. 'Oh Alex, I've never been more glad t' hear your voice. Can you get yerself down here right away?'

Alex arrived ten minutes later. He drew the car into the kerb and the wheels had hardly stopped turning when Patsy, who had been standing waiting on the pavement, wrenched the door open and got into the passenger seat.

'Are you going to tell me what is going on?' Alex demanded.

'I'll tell you on the way. Just drive,' Patsy ordered.

Alex put the car into gear and moved off, but he sounded angry as he said, 'Mother, I don't even know where we are supposed to be going!'

'Oh, I'm sorry, son.' Patsy was near to tears. 'We're going to Tolworth, to your house. Vicky phoned me just as I was leaving.'

'For God's sake, Mother, just tell me what all the panic is about.'

She had no option now. She turned, staring at his grim face and noticing that he was gripping the steering wheel so hard his knuckles had turned white. 'Frances is in hospital,' she said, her voice little more than a whisper.

'What?' He took his eyes off the road to stare at her. 'You mean she's been in an accident?'

'I don't know much more than that,' she lied. 'Just watch what you're doing and we'll get there all the quicker.'

Alex hadn't time to even put his key in the lock before Vicky pulled the front door wide open and fell into his arms.

The police had gone and Patsy thought it best if she left the two of them on their own for the moment. She went through into the kitchen, where she filled the kettle, placed it on the stove, struck a match and lit the gas beneath it. She was only doing what everyone did at a time like this, making a pot of tea. She did, however, leave the door wide open, as anxious as Alex to get the full details. She had lied when she'd told him that she knew very little, but it was only half a lie.

Vicky wasn't saying much, just sobbing bitterly, and Alex was holding her tight.

As quickly as she could, Patsy brewed the tea, set out a tray with cups and saucers, milk and sugar, and carried it

231

into the living room. 'Come on, both of you, come and sit at the table. A cuppa will settle all of us.'

After just a couple of sips of the hot tea, Vicky turned to Alex and told him what the inspector had told Patsy over the phone. Then, having wiped her eyes and blown her nose, she added a little bit more.

'The young constable was kind,' she began. 'The inspector was a bit of a brute.'

'Only doing his job,' Alex soothed her, taking hold of one of her hands and holding it tightly between both of his.

'Well, he told me that the police had two witnesses who had seen Luke and Frances in this club last night. Apparently they had been fighting.'

'Who had?' Patsy practically screamed. 'Surely Luke wouldn't have hit her, and I can't imagine our Frances fighting.'

'Hold on, Mother, let Vicky finish.'

'He did say the fighting was mostly verbal. One of the witnesses said Frances was shouting and screaming.'

Stunned silence followed that, until Vicky said, 'The inspector phoned Kingston Hospital before he left. He said our Frances was in the operating theatre but that we could go and see her later. Will you take me now, Alex?'

'Of course I will,' Alex said, drawing his wife near and kissing her forehead. 'Just let's all drink our tea and calm down a little, and then we'll go straight there.'

'When did you last see Frances?' Patsy asked.

'Last night. We had dinner, all four of us, about half past six or thereabouts. Then Alex and James started to play cards. Frances left the house about eight. Thinking back, she did seem a bit nervous. Not herself. But when I asked her if everything was all right she said she was fine. Promised me she wouldn't be late home.'

'Didn't you know she hadn't been home all night?' Patsy queried.

'No. Neither did Alex. And I feel so guilty. She always comes in very quietly and she often leaves really early in the morning. Always says it's the only way to get a seat on the train. Apparently she and her colleagues often have breakfast together in town before going to the office. When the police arrived I thought they were mad. I dashed upstairs hoping she had overslept, but . . . her bed hadn't been slept in.' Vicky broke off, sobbing as if her heart would break. Patsy tried to soothe her, reassure her, but Vicky started shouting.

'How could Alex and I have slept when she was lying out there injured? When the police said she was on Clapham Common I immediately assumed she was coming to you, Patsy.'

'Well if she had been you know either I or her grandad would have phoned you.'

'I know that, but if she wasn't coming to you, what was she doing on Clapham Common?'

Alex looked haggard. 'Thank God that milkman found her.' He turned to face Vicky. 'You said the police got her name and address from her handbag?'

'Yes, that's what they told me.'

'Well,' he said thoughtfully, 'if she still had her bag, the attack couldn't have been a robbery, could it?'

'Drink that tea,' Patsy ordered, 'and let's get to the hospital.'

'You coming with us, Mum, or do you want me to drop you off at your place or the office?'

'Blow the office, and as for being in our big 'ouse on me own today, I'd go barmy. No, get a move on, let's go and see 'er. I'm sure she'll be all right. A tough little nut is our Frances.' Patsy was hoping against hope that what she was saying would prove to be right.

There were still so many unanswered questions. Had Frances been trying to make her way to see her grandparents?

233

Wait till Ollie gets to hear about this, she thought. He will be so upset.

If some bloke had laid into Frances, given her a good hiding, then God 'elp them when her father and her uncles and cousins got hold of him. They'd make him wish he had never been born.

Alex had to help Vicky to put on her coat, and it was Patsy that found a hairbrush and saw to her hair. Poor Vicky. She couldn't stop shaking. 'Why would anyone want to hurt Frances?' she kept asking over and over again, and then she changed her mumblings to 'Please God, don't let anything happen to her. She's only a young girl. Please, dear God, let her be all right.'

'Come on, love,' Alex coaxed her. 'Come and get in the car and we'll soon be at the hospital, an' then you'll see she'll be all right.'

Once again Patsy prayed. This time it was that her son was right.

Chapter Three

'EDDIE, PLEASE TELL ME you don't think our Frances killed Luke.'

Eddie lifted his head sharply and stared at Patsy. 'Of course not. Whatever put that idea in your head?'

They were sitting facing each other on opposite sides of the fireplace. Ollie was at the table, shuffling through some papers, which he immediately let go of. Ever since they had got back home and Eddie had explained in great detail what had happened, Ollie had been afraid, not only that Frances might lose her life but that Patsy would go to pieces.

He turned his head and butted in: 'Where's yer sense gone, Patsy? A slight little girl such as our Frances capable of stabbing a big bloke like Luke? I don't think so, do you? Besides, how the hell did she end up miles away from the car? Ten to one she didn't bloody well walk. Not the state Eddie told me she's in.'

'Then why is there a policeman sitting beside her bed and another one on a chair in the hallway outside her room stopping anyone from going in to see her?' Patsy yelled out loudly.

Ollie cursed beneath his breath. The last thing he wanted was for any one of them to lose their temper. 'They don't want reporters and such-like swarming round her. You know full well she's been badly hurt, but they let her parents in and then they let you in, didn't they?'

Patsy didn't answer, but the sad look on her face was enough to break Ollie's heart. Over the years, all the love he had to give he had bestowed on Patsy and her family. And it worked both ways. Instead of being a lonely old man, he had the privilege of being not only a grandfather but a great-grandfather.

Now, although his heart was aching, he had to suppress a grin. They had let Patsy in to see Frances! There would have been trouble if they hadn't! Patsy on the warpath as she must have been at the hospital was the Patsy he knew only too well.

She was tough, having grown up as a kid of the streets. Even her mother's refined influence had been unable to suppress this trait in Patsy. She might wear expensive smart clothes now, but underneath she was still gutsy. To Ollie there wasn't anyone else like her.

Eddie sighed. 'I rang the hospital as soon as Alex let me know, but they weren't giving out any information over the phone and they said even I couldn't go in to see her yet.'

He had gone straight to Tolworth and stayed there until Alex, Vicky and Patsy had got back. When he finally heard from Alex what the police and then the doctors had told him, his stomach had turned over and it was hard to keep his feelings under control. There was no way he could give all the details to Patsy. It had been hard enough telling Ollie.

'You know what I'm thinking?' Eddie asked, looking first at Patsy and then at Ollie. 'We never did get to know Luke all that well, did we? And we knew even less about what went on in his private life.'

'It was different from ours, that's for sure,' Ollie murmured softly.

Patsy looked up. 'Frances brought him here quite a few times. I always found him a pleasant young man even if he was a bit upper-class, although Vicky was telling me today that she and Alex never got to spend a lot of time with him. I do remember Frances telling me that she met him up town at some club.' When neither Eddie nor Ollie made any comment, Patsy added, 'I can't help feeling sorry for his family. God knows what they must be going through.'

At that moment the door opened and David and Tim came in.

David bent low and kissed his mother, while Tim knelt down beside her armchair and put his arms around her, asking, 'Are you bearing up all right, Gran?'

'I'm all the better for seeing you and yer father, but I'll be even better when we get some good news from the hospital. Frances was still unconscious when we left her.'

Eddie was busy pouring drinks, and when everyone was seated Ollie raised his glass and said, 'To Frances making a speedy recovery.'

Silence followed the toast.

'The national press are going to have a field day,' was David's opening remark. 'I've only just left Alex. He'll be along shortly. We've both talked to the family solicitors, felt we had to have some legal advice.'

He broke off and smiled at Ollie. 'Harry Forrester sends you his regards, said over the years we've been loyal to their family firm and that they'll work their socks off for our Frances.'

'Best thing you could have done, lad,' Ollie answered seriously. 'There's been many a time since Jack died that I've been glad to fall back on that firm. They earn their fee, but it's gone beyond that now. I look upon them as family friends.'

At that moment Vicky, Alex and James came in. James was a broad-shouldered nineteen-year-old, but he still made

237

a bee-line for his grandad. Eddie held him in a great bear-hug, feeling the silent sobs shake the lad's body. Eventually he released him, and with tears trickling down his cheeks James murmured, 'They let me go in on my own to see Frances . . . Oh, Grandad . . . she looked lifeless, and her poor face . . .'

'James, come on, you have to be strong for your mum an' dad. Your sister is getting the best treatment possible. Go give yer granma a kiss but don't let her see you are too upset.'

Patsy got to her feet to put her arms around him. All the men in her family were so tall. She hushed and soothed him. 'James, my luv, we must thank God that they found her so quickly. All we can do is wait and pray. They'll make her better, you'll see.' But her voice sounded weary.

Only minutes behind came Ellen and Peter, and with them Emma, Donald and their youngest son, Sam, now a lanky, good-looking seventeen-year-old. 'We haven't been able to contact Edward and Tom yet,' Donald said by way of an explanation.

'And we thought it best not to bring Mary,' Peter said quietly as he bent to kiss Patsy. 'We've left her with our next-door neighbours. You know Mary likes to get in there and play with their two youngsters.'

The twins went first to Vicky, and though uncertain as to what to say, they went through the motions of telling her how sorry they were. The three younger women made a circle, arms around each other. 'I can't believe it,' Vicky sniffed, her hands trembling. 'Who the hell would want to beat up my daughter and murder her boyfriend?'

'Take a deep breath, darling,' Ellen said, stroking her hair.

Eddie passed a glass to Emma. 'It's brandy,' he said. 'Try an' get her to drink it.'

'Come on, Vicky,' Emma pleaded. 'Have some of this. It might help to calm you down.'

Vicky half emptied the glass in a single gulp, not even

noticing the burning in her throat. 'If our Frances dies I swear I'll kill the bugger that attacked her. I won't rest until I get him an' that's a promise.'

Ellen said gently, 'Frances isn't going to die. She's a fighter, she'll pull through, you'll see.'

Vicky broke free from their embrace. She loved every member of this family, but at this moment if looks could kill then the gentle Ellen would be dead!

'What the hell do you know? You haven't seen her. She was kicked and punched, but worst of all she was hit over the head. The police reckon the bastard hit her with a tyre-lever . . .' Vicky shook her head. She couldn't go on.

The twins both gasped. Ellen swiped at her tears with the back of her hand; Emma buried her face in her hands. They both murmured, 'I am so sorry.'

Vicky swallowed more of the brandy.

Out of the blue Alex very angrily said, 'I can't believe that the police even hinted that Frances might have had something to do with Luke's death.'

It was a horrible thought and no one had an answer to offer.

Over an hour later everyone was making a move to go home. Nothing more could be done tonight.

Suddenly Ollie stood up and, sounding very serious, said, 'The two cases might not even be connected.'

Everyone stared at him in astonishment.

'Well, it's a thought,' he said sensibly. 'Luke was found in his car outside a club. Frances was almost here, just over on the common. What does that tell you? Anyway, we shall have to wait until they find the fellow who supposedly offered to bring our Frances home. Also they'll need to find out who bore Luke Somerford a grudge bad enough to want him dead.' Then, very quietly but in a voice of steel, he said, 'We have to wait to see what the doctors have to say about Frances in the morning.'

As her family made to leave, Patsy was very near to tears as they each in turn hugged and kissed her.

If only Frances hadn't gone to that club.

If only she had never met Luke Somerford.

But then life was full of if onlys.

Four days had passed and it might just as well have been four weeks. The hours dragged. Nobody wanted to go to work. No one seemed able to sleep and meals were a very haphazard affair. And still it was only Frances's parents and her brother who were allowed to visit her in hospital. Patsy felt as if she were going out of her mind half the time.

It was barely ten o'clock in the morning of the fifth day when Donald and Emma came into their mother's house. Hardly had Patsy finished greeting them than Alex and Vicky came in close on their heels.

Patsy felt the colour drain from her face. Why was everyone appearing and yet saying nothing?

'Will someone please tell me what's going on?' she pleaded.

Emma gave her husband a look and nodded her head, and so it was Donald who spoke first.

'My men are doing some work on the Brittany Club, in Soho. The owner is having the whole place renovated and I popped in there early to see how the job was coming along. I couldn't believe it! The police were all over the place like a swarm of locusts. Apparently they've paid a visit to most of the clubs in the area. I hung about hoping I might pick up a bit of gossip, and luck was on my side. One of the plain-clothed guys, Reg Harris, is a neighbour of ours. Course, he'd already heard that Frances was our niece and so he came over, shook hands with me and said how sorry he was and wasn't it a shame that a young man like Luke had met such an untimely death. A cleaning lady offered us both a coffee and so we sat down and had quite a chat.

'Reg Harris said they've interviewed everyone who was at the Brittany club where Luke's car was found. Off the record, he told me that they think they've found the man who supposedly offered to take Frances home.'

Patsy was getting tired of Donald being so long-winded in getting to the point. 'Why would another man offer to take Frances home if she were there with Luke? It doesn't make sense.' She sounded cross but everyone understood. The strain was telling on all of them.

'It's been said that the fellow made the offer because Frances was having a row with Luke and according to him it was turning nasty.' Donald did his best to sound gentle.

'Do the police believe him?' Alex asked his brother-in-law.

'Yes, apparently. But they've given no reason as to how Frances ended up on Clapham Common.'

'I think we've all guessed that by now,' Eddie said wisely. 'If someone other than Luke was bringing her home, Clapham is a darn sight nearer to London than Tolworth. She was coming to us to stay the night, and she knew we'd phone Alex the minute she got in. But why in God's name didn't she phone us in the first place? She knew it wouldn't have taken me long to go up and fetch her.'

'With hindsight we can all be wise,' Ollie said sadly.

'Reg Harris did tell me one thing I suppose we should be grateful for. At least they won't be charging Frances with Luke's murder.' Donald still sounded half afraid to say too much. What Reg had told him was that they were looking for someone who had a good enough reason to want Luke Somerford dead. This last he kept to himself.

'Didn't Frances have a girlfriend with her?' Patsy queried. 'Luke never picked her up from your house, did he, Vicky?'

'No. She was on her own when she said goodbye to us and I told her not to be too late because it wasn't as if it were a Saturday. She had to get up for work next morning.'

Vicky realised what she had said and burst into tears.

'Didn't make any difference, did it?' she said, wiping her eyes with the back of her hand. 'She never got to work next day or any day since.'

A silence fell between them as they each concentrated on all that had happened.

Donald was arguing with himself as to whether he should say any more. He loved his wife dearly and they had three fine sons. The family he had married into couldn't be closer; each would do for the others whatever was needed at any time.

Hurt one and you hurt them all.

He had always felt it was a privilege to be part of such a great family. However, what he knew about Luke Somerford didn't reflect well on that young man, and if it should come to light and he hadn't said anything . . .

Taking a deep breath, he said softly, 'I think I'd better tell you all what little I know about Luke Somerford.'

Every eye was on him and Donald felt his face flush up.

'It's not much, and I don't know that it will have any bearing on this matter with Frances.'

'For Christ's sake, Donald, spit it out!' Alex shouted. 'My daughter is lying in hospital, she hasn't come to yet from the beating she got, and anything you know . . .'

Donald stood up, held his hands out in a helpless gesture and then said to his father-in-law, 'All right if I carry on, Eddie?'

Eddie nodded. 'Whatever it is you know, I certainly think it should be brought out into the open. Carry on, Donald.'

'All of you say that Luke had a certain charm about him,' Donald started off cautiously, 'but that wasn't the way I saw him. That was all on the surface. I always thought he was a cold fish and devious with it. Insincere, scheming all the time.'

You could have cut the air with a knife. No one said a

word, but their looks spoke volumes. Once started he had no choice. He had to go on.

'A lot of my work takes me into the West End. I was in a bar up town recently, discussing a business matter with my foreman, and Luke was there with a few of what I'd call his cronies. They were noisy, ill-mannered and well aware of the effect their presence was having on other customers. Luke in particular showed he had a terrific ego, playing the ladies' man to the hilt.'

'Was Frances there?' Vicky asked.

'No. No, she wasn't, but several young women were. Not that that should mean anything, but on the other hand, the way Luke was carrying on struck me as . . .' Donald didn't finish the sentence.

'Thanks, Don.' Alex walked across the room and put his hand on his brother-in-law's shoulder. 'Quite a picture you've painted. Did you tell this to the copper you know?'

'Yes, I did, and I gave him the name of the bar. He said that information may prove to be useful. Seems, though, that the police were already aware that Luke was known for being a lad about town.' He kept to himself the fact that Reg had said the girls were making a fortune. They were young, lovely, with firm bodies, and Luke and his type had money to burn.

Patsy's blood was boiling but she made a great effort. Going to Vicky, she pulled her head close, kissed her cheek, which was wet with tears, and softly said, 'We all make mistakes in this life, and as Florrie would have said, experience is a very dear commodity but we all 'ave t' buy it. I'm sure when Frances is better and comes home she'll realise what a lucky escape she has had.'

Patsy couldn't have known at the time how often those last words were to come back and haunt her.

It was a case of being wise after the fact.

Chapter Four

EDDIE LOOKED DEAD TIRED as he walked through the door.

'Bad day?' Patsy asked.

He didn't reply, but gently took her into his arms and laid his cheek against her soft hair.

'Not really,' he said at last. 'I heard today that the coroner's court will be holding the inquiry into Luke's death a week tomorrow.'

'Oh God, more waiting,' Patsy muttered, moving towards the sideboard. She took out a bottle of whisky, poured a good measure into a glass and handed it to Eddie, saying, 'I guess you can use this. Dinner won't be long. There will only be the two of us. Ollie phoned to say he is eating out tonight with a friend.'

'Good for him,' Eddie smiled. 'And great for us, make a nice change.'

'And while I think of it, Peter phoned. They're coming here for Sunday dinner. He said he'd had a long talk with Ellen and they've decided to tell Mary the truth. None of the gory details but enough for her not to worry as to why Frances hasn't been around. You know that child loves us all, but Frances spoils her and Mary loves her t' bits.'

Eddie laughed. '*Frances* spoils her? Come off it, Patsy, you're a right one to talk. Mary smiles at any one of us and we'd give her the moon and the stars to go with it if it were possible. She's such a great little kid.'

'Yes, she is, but we'll all have to watch what we're saying on Sunday.'

'I've some good news on Frances.' Eddie smiled.

'What?' Patsy's eyes were popping out of her head. 'And you didn't tell me the moment you got in.'

'I was waiting until we were both relaxing, but I can't keep it from you. You can go to the hospital tomorrow. Frances is out of the intensive care unit and Vicky said she'll phone you tonight and arrange a time to pick you up. She said it would be nice for you both to go together.'

Patsy heaved a great sigh of relief. 'Thank God! Do you know any details?'

'Not a one. But it was enough for me when Vicky said Frances was out of danger. You can ask all the questions you want tomorrow.'

'Oh, Eddie, I'll sleep a whole lot better tonight than I have been doing. It's like having a great weight lifted off your shoulders, isn't it?'

'It most certainly is. But don't go jumping the gun. Frances might have a long way to go yet.'

'I do realise that, but at least we know she's on the mend and we aren't going to lose her. Oh, Eddie, it's been a real nightmare, hasn't it?'

'For the whole family, but especially for Vicky, Alex and James. That lad thinks the world of his sister.'

'Oh, I am so relieved. By the way, what does a coroner do?'

Eddie sighed under his breath and reached for his Scotch. He peered into the glass, looking thoughtful. After taking a sip he turned to Patsy.

'Well, he has to be a barrister, or at least legally qualified, and his duty is to inquire into the cause of all deaths which occur in his district from violence or unnatural or unknown causes. If at the inquest anyone is found guilty of murder or manslaughter, the coroner commits him or her for trial.'

This gave Patsy food for thought.

She dished up the casserole that had been slowly cooking all afternoon, brought the dishes of green vegetables to the table, and the two of them ate in an unfamiliar silence. When Eddie's plate was empty and he'd refused a second helping, Patsy got up, removed the plates and dishes and replaced them with a bowl of fresh fruit and a cheese board which held a good selection.

'Oh, I've forgotten the biscuits,' she murmured.

'Sit down, Patsy, I'll fetch them. Do you want a drink or coffee?' Eddie offered.

'Coffee for me, please.'

'Right, I'll put the percolator on. We'll both have coffee,' he said.

Patsy had buttered two crackers and was nibbling a piece of very strong cheddar cheese when Eddie suddenly said, 'We never did get to the bottom of Luke Somerford.'

'What do you mean by that?' Patsy asked, sounding surprised that he had brought that subject up again.

'Like where he worked. I presume he did work for a living. I know you told me where Frances met him, but I'm blowed if I know what she saw in him.'

'Certainly different from Alan Yates,' Patsy said slowly, staring into space. 'I'm sorry he doesn't come around here any more. Nice dependable young man is Alan. Yet Luke didn't seem a bad lad. He always appeared to be friendly when Frances brought him here. I don't like to think it was all an act.'

'I wonder how much information the police do have?' Eddie said, thinking aloud. 'But I'd take a bet we'll have a long wait till they get to the bottom of all this.'

★ ★ ★

Come Sunday and the family gathering for Patsy's roast dinner still took place, though the atmosphere was not the same. The news on Frances was good. There was no brain damage. Her bruises and cuts were healing slowly, but her right leg had been broken and was still in plaster. Auntie Vicky had promised Mary that she would take her to see Frances some time during the week. Now James was demonstrating how poor Frances was learning to walk with the aid of crutches but that she wasn't very good at it. His acting set Mary off into peals of laughter, and as she rolled about in her chair her mop of fair curls tossed prettily from side to side.

'Perhaps we could get a wheelchair for her, then she could come home and I could take her for a walk.'

Everyone laughed at Mary's suggestion, except Patsy. The very thought of this dear little girl pushing Frances in a wheelchair out in the street made their grandmother recoil in horror.

The meal was over, everything washed up and stacked away. The whole family were in the vast front room, with Edward Junior, Thomas, Sam and James all sprawled on the floor helping Mary, amidst a great deal of laughter, to put the pieces of a huge jigsaw puzzle together on a big tray.

The telephone rang.

Ever since they had had the first news of Frances being hurt, Patsy had felt herself go cold every time she heard that sound.

Eddie got up to answer it, feeling very much as his wife did. Was this call going to be about Luke? Had it been a case of revenge? Had the same person that had killed Luke beaten Frances and left her for dead on the common? All these questions were running through his mind as he snatched at the receiver.

Before he had the time to say anything other than 'Hello', the caller was saying, 'Eddie, is that you?'

'Yes, who's that?'

'It's me, Valerie. I've heard about Frances and for days I've wanted to ring. I hope you don't mind.'

'Oh, hallo, Valerie,' he said, sounding as surprised as he felt. Then, recognising the anxiety in her high-pitched voice, he quickly said, 'No, of course I don't mind.'

'How is Frances?' she asked timidly.

'We've heard she is out of intensive care, but it's too early yet to really know how she is.'

'I am so sorry.'

Eddie wanted to ask what exactly she was sorry for. After all, it was she who left David, and it must be well over eight years since they had heard a word from her. Instead he murmured, 'We all are.' Then, kindness taking over, he added, 'David is here, would you like to speak to him?'

Eddie couldn't mistake the sound of her sucking in her breath.

Valerie hesitated, then haltingly said, 'Yes please . . . I would . . . if he agrees to talk to me.'

David came willingly to the phone, nodding his thanks to his father as he passed the receiver over to him. 'Hello, Val,' he said kindly.

There was an awkward pause at Valerie's end and complete stunned silence in the room. Everyone was wide-eyed. David had never bothered to start divorce proceedings, and so much time had gone by that everyone had assumed Valerie would never reappear. Patsy didn't know how she felt, but she was wishing that she could hear both sides of this conversation!

When Valerie did speak, her voice was little more than a whisper and David had a job to hear what she said.

Softly he said, 'Val, could you try and speak up a bit, please?'

'David . . . what can I say?' Then, without waiting for an answer, she hurriedly said, 'I know which club Frances was

248

in that night and I know quite a bit about Luke Somerford.'

'Were you there?' David almost gave way to a burst of anger but managed to restrain himself.

'No, I wasn't. I gave up clubbing a long while ago.' She paused again. 'Suppose you could say I saw the error of my ways.'

'Well, from the little you have told me, I think what you know could be of help to the police. You should go to the station and talk to them.'

'Maybe.' She sounded reluctant. 'I'd rather talk to you first.'

'That's OK,' David readily agreed. 'Where shall we meet?' He ignored the gasp that came from his mother, his sisters and his sister-in-law.

'You mean it?' Valerie asked quietly.

'Yes, of course I do. Just tell me where you are.'

'I'm in the phone box at Tooting Broadway tube station. Is that all right?'

'Yes. Yes, of course. Take me a little while, but I'll be there as quick as I can. You go over to Lyons, get yerself a cup of tea.'

'I don't want any tea. I'll be waiting in the tube station.'

She sounded calmer as she stammered, 'Th-th-thank you, David.'

'Goodbye,' he said and hung up.

The whole family had got the gist of the conversation and were not the least bit surprised when David said, 'I'm going to meet Valerie. Seems she knows a bit about Luke and she definitely knows which club Frances was in that night.'

Tim got up from his chair and very quietly spoke to his father. 'Did she sound all right, Dad?'

'A bit uneasy, but that's only to be expected. I think she's been very brave to phone me. She sounded very concerned for Frances.'

'Where is she?' Tim asked.

'Only at Tooting.'

'Shall I come with you?' Alex quickly offered.

'No. I'll go alone, I'll deal with it. See what's what and get back as soon as I can.'

Alex was a bit put out, and as soon as David had left he let his feelings be known.

'It's my daughter that she's talking about and she should be talking to me, not t' David.'

Patsy looked at Eddie. But as usual it was Ollie who poured oil on troubled waters.

'Give her a chance, Alex lad. It took guts for her to get in touch with this family after all this time.' Then, turning to Tim, he smiled and said, 'You'll maybe get to see yer mum now.'

'I'm not sure I want to,' Tim muttered.

Patsy rose and went to stand alongside him. 'Life is full of regrets,' she told him. 'Don't make any hasty decisions. Let's all just wait and see what David has to say when he gets back.'

David was shocked to see Valerie's drawn white face, and she was so thin. Nevertheless, old feelings stirred within him. She had hurt him and her son badly but he had never wanted anyone else. He could not stop himself; as their eyes met, he opened his arms and after a moment's hesitation Valerie slowly went into them.

A dry sob racked her body as he silently held her close to his chest.

When he let her go there was an uncomfortable minute as they gazed at each other. How could I have been so stupid? Valerie was asking herself. Just look at him. No rejection, after all I've done to him. He's such a good man. Steady, quiet, but oh so dependable.

'Come on,' David said at last, 'let's go to the Greek café. Bit more private than Lyons.'

Quite soon they were seated with mugs of steaming strong coffee in front of them.

'David, before I start, do you mind if I ask you how Tim is?' There was a note of pleading in her voice.

'A son to be proud of,' David told her seriously. 'He's very well. A great mate to me, and the whole family love him t' bits.'

'Thank you,' she murmured, brushing at her eyes with a handkerchief.

David let her be and it was a while before she spoke again. When she did it was with sincere sympathy.

'This must be a terrible time for Vicky and Alex. I do feel for them.'

David nodded. 'The whole family are feeling it. Mum especially. You know what she's like!'

Valerie gave him a wry smile. 'Don't I just. Hurt one of her brood and she's ready to kill.'

David grinned. 'Things are nowhere near as bad as the doctors feared at first. While Frances was unconscious there were two policemen at the hospital at all times waiting to question her. Mum somehow got it into her head that they were going to charge our Frances with Luke's murder.'

'What!' Valerie felt goose pimples run up and down her arms and her heart was racing. 'That is so ridiculous. I was told that Frances was found miles away from where Luke was murdered in his car.'

'That's what we were told too.'

Valerie sighed. 'What I can't understand is why Alex and Vicky let Frances go out an' about with that Luke. Didn't any of you know that he has a wife?'

David was obviously amazed. 'Christ Almighty, this gets worse. I'm sure none of us did.'

'Well he did. From what I've heard, Luke's family were trying to buy her off. They wanted their son to get a quiet divorce. It was supposed t' be all cut and dried. Then she changed her mind a couple of months ago. Refused to go ahead with it. She's much older than Luke, so the gossips say, and the story goes that she's been behaving horribly. Done some dreadful things. She has made his parents' life hell. Rows, violence even.'

David's face was drained of colour and he gulped.

'Our poor Frances. How on earth did she get tangled up with the likes of him in the first place?'

'That's easy. To a lass like Frances he was God's greatest gift. Tall, good-looking. Great charmer, and he could dance well. Plenty of money to splash around. Fast flashy car. I'd say, though, that Frances was only one in a long queue.'

David shook his head in utter disbelief. He was wondering how he was going to tell his brother all of this. And yet he had the feeling that Valerie was holding back. She hadn't told him everything she knew. Not yet.

Determined to find out as much as possible, he asked, 'Do you know what happened during the evening all this trouble took place?'

Valerie took a gulp of her coffee, and shook her head. 'Like I said, David, I wasn't there. But two women I know work in that club. One is a barmaid, the other what they call a hat-check girl. I've worked there with them on the odd night when the club has been short-handed. It's about a week since I met up with them. They knew that Frances was related to me and they couldn't tell me quick enough what had happened. You know what women are like.'

'And you've only just got round to contacting us?' David questioned, breathing hard.

Valerie looked ashamed. 'I felt I ought to, in fact I knew I should, but I didn't know how you would take it. It's been a long time. Besides, you haven't heard the half of it yet, and when you have maybe Alex and Vicky will wish they'd never heard from me again.'

'Jesus!' David made a fist. He badly wanted to thump the

252

table or even shake Valerie until he got all the details out of her, but he knew he had to take a hold of himself.

'Valerie, please go on, I need to know.'

'All right, if you say so. According to these two women, it was our Frances that started it, shouting and screaming at Luke. She finished up throwing her drink in his face. After that, well, I've heard two or three different stories. It appears all hell broke loose. Luke hit Frances, some blokes hit him, and the club manager phoned the police. By the time they arrived things had quietened down and Luke told the police that he had only pushed Frances and she had slipped and fallen.'

'Are you telling me the police were called to this club earlier in the evening?'

'So I've been told. Apparently Luke went mad because a few young men had decided to come to Frances's aid. The police didn't stay long. Just long enough to calm the situation down.'

'And that's it, is it? You've no idea how Frances came to be miles away from her own home?'

'No, my friends said she was still in the club when they left at about half past one. But David, there is something else.'

David puffed his cheeks out and blew hard but didn't say anything.

Valerie shook his arm. 'There's a bit more to tell,' she said sadly.

He sighed heavily. 'Well, spit it out. It can hardly be worse than what you've already told me.'

'Oh yes it can,' she warned.

'For God's sake tell me,' he shouted, getting really agitated as Valerie hesitated again.

'OK,' Valerie said reluctantly. 'Frances was heard screaming that she was pregnant and her baby was not going to be born a bastard. She was demanding that Luke marry her.'

'Oh, Christ!' David's heart sank. Why did he have to be the one to find all this out? This news would break Vicky and Alex's hearts.

He signalled for the waiter to bring two more coffees and on the spur of the moment ordered two brandies as well.

Despite the brandy, David still sounded very miserable as he asked Valerie, 'How on earth am I going to tell all of this to the family, and especially to Vicky and Alex? I'd better get back to them soon.'

A sudden thought came to him, but it took a minute or two before he found the courage to voice it.

'You wouldn't come back with me, Valerie, would you? Please. It will help if you're there to fill in any details I might forget. Besides, it will be better all round if you're there to explain how you come to know all this.'

Valerie backed away from him. 'David, you don't know what you're asking. Your mother and I didn't exactly part on the best of terms. She'd go mad if I were to walk through her front door.'

Out of the blue David asked, 'Did you know that Florrie had died?'

'Yes, I did. And I was sorry. Really I was. I still think one had t' be a saint to get along with her, but she did have a heart of gold.'

'Well, as you know, Mum loved her dearly. We all did. But Mum's never got over not being there when she died. Still misses her like hell. One thing I do know, she'll be pleased to see you.'

'Wish I was as sure,' Valerie murmured under her breath, remembering with regret some of the nasty things she had said to Patsy when she had last walked out of her house. Still, she had wrestled with her conscience for days as to whether or not she should telephone David. She sighed. I've got past that hurdle. But now to be asked to go with him to face the whole of his family . . .

254

David half smiled. 'Tim will be over the moon. First thing he asked when I came off the telephone was how did you sound.'

Valerie sighed the deepest of sighs but was only able to murmur, 'Oh, David!'

David let her be, remaining silent while a host of different emotions crossed her face. Foremost among them, he knew, was regret.

Tim was her son. God, thought Val, she had behaved so badly. Her treatment of him had been so shabby. How she would love to see him! But would he want to see her?

The Owen family had not disowned him. They had kept him within the family, cared for him and loved him. What must they think of her? How could she possibly face them all?

Well, like it or not, she knew she'd have to go and face them.

But it would be like putting her head in the lion's mouth.

Chapter Five

'YOU'VE NO IDEA WHO attacked our Frances then?' Vicky asked the first question.

Valerie lifted her head sharply. 'Of course not.'

She was pleased with the quiet way the family had greeted her, and really thrilled that Tim had hugged her. At the moment she did not feel too uncomfortable to be back in her in-laws' house. Only very upset as she had listened to David relate to the others what she had told him. The reactions on the family's faces had been hard to cope with.

Patsy was sitting on the opposite side of the room and Valerie was watching the tears roll down her mother-in-law's face. She nearly jumped out of her skin when Alex, her brother-in-law, said, 'You don't think Luke was murdered before our Frances left the club and that it was his killer that offered her a lift home, do you?'

Valerie frowned. What a question!

'No. From what I've learned I don't think that for one moment. Why, do you?'

Without hesitation, Alex exclaimed, 'I'm buggered if I know what t' think.' He paused and bit his lip. 'You say you weren't in that club that night, yet you know all about Frances yelling at the top of her voice that she was pregnant.'

Valerie nodded. 'Only because two women I know were working there. They came round to see me, whether it was out of kindness or just to spread gossip I don't know. They were aware that Frances and I were related. Actually, both of them spoke kindly of your Frances. They reckoned she was really and truly upset. According to them, another girl had just told her that Luke Somerford already had a wife, and that bit of information pushed her over the edge.'

The room fell silent. Patsy stared at her daughter-in-law. Val looked very drawn but was dressed very much more suitably than when Patsy had last seen her, and there wasn't a trace of make-up on her face.

Very quietly Patsy said, 'Valerie, we're all very grateful, you getting in touch and coming here with David. Over the last few days I think we've all panicked at some time or another, and Vicky and Alex have been at their wits' end. At least you've been able to tell us something about what's been going on.'

Vicky turned to face Valerie. 'I haven't thanked you yet for coming here. It couldn't have been easy for you. I want you to know that Alex and I are grateful.'

'I wish I could have been more helpful,' Valerie answered sadly.

'I'm going to the hospital to see Frances. James has said he wants to come with me,' Alex said to his wife. 'Would you like me to run you home first or are you going to stay here with Mum till I get back?'

'I'll stay here, for the night as well. It's so much nearer the hospital.' Vicky sounded weary, drained. 'You don't mind, do you, Patsy?'

'Vicky. As if you need t' ask.'

* * *

David came back into the room, having seen his brother and his nephew set off for the hospital.

'Where's Ellen?' he asked Peter.

'Mary's half asleep so she's taken her upstairs and is going to put her down to have a nap. Mind you, she wouldn't have agreed to go except that Ellen bribed her by telling her she could get into Gran an' Grandad's big bed.'

Vicky couldn't help herself; she began to cry.

'Oh darling, don't break down now. You've been so brave. But I do realise this last bit of news has been a terrible shock,' Patsy told her softly.

'You can say that again. I can't take much more,' Vicky said harshly. 'To learn that my daughter had been beaten up and left half dead was bad enough, but to find that she might be pregnant by some toffy-nosed sod who already has a wife is just too much.'

Patsy was about to say that that toffy-nosed sod was dead, but thought better of it. After what had happened to her daughter, who could blame Vicky for the way she was feeling?

Valerie's mouth went dry. Had she said too much? Me and my big mouth, she chided herself.

Patsy got up and went and knelt in front of Vicky, putting her arms around her. 'Oh, Vicky, we are all with you, it's going to be all right. There, there,' she murmured with the utmost gentleness, just as you would to a small child. 'Don't fight the tears, my love, you have a good cry.'

Vicky clung to Patsy, sobs racking her body, and Patsy stroked her hair, soothing her. Eventually she quietened. Soon she straightened up, blinking the tears away and shaking her head desperately. 'If anything happens to my Frances . . . I don't know what I'd do. I pray t' God she'll come through all this OK.'

How they got through the rest of that day Patsy felt she would never know. Endless cups of tea, and drinks for the men. She wasn't sure if she was glad that Florrie wasn't

258

here to hear all these terrible things, or wishing like hell that the wise old woman, always a rock to be relied on, had not left them.

It was a relief when Alex and James returned.

'We've been lucky.' Alex half smiled. 'There was a very chatty sister on duty this afternoon, and while James sat with his sister I managed to corner her. She'd heard from one of the policemen that Luke Somerford was still in the club when another young man offered to take Frances home. Apparently it was a bouncer at the club that gave the police this information. And the copper who talked to this sister said the bouncer was unshakable in that he saw Frances leave first.'

'Oh, thank God,' Vicky cried, rushing into her husband's arms for comfort. 'Maybe now they'll be able to catch the fellow who hurt our Frances so badly. But how was she today?'

'I thought she was breathing more easily, well propped up with pillows. Her face is still black an' blue. She didn't say two words. I thought it might be because her lips are so swollen, but the sister said because of the knocks to her head she probably doesn't remember what happened. I told her I'd be back later tonight and that you'd be coming with me to see her safely tucked up for the night.'

'What did she say? Was she pleased?'

'She didn't say anything, I thought she couldn't hear me but the nurse assured me that she could and will talk when her memory begins to come back.'

'All those bruises will heal,' James told his mother. 'It will take time but we can rest a bit easier now she's on the mend.'

'The police have still got to find out who killed Luke,' Ollie said sternly. 'To make sure they've got the right man who gave Frances this lift home and then attacked her.' He shook his head in despair. 'Helluva mess. But it does begin to look like the two cases are not in any way connected.'

A silence fell on them all as they dealt with their thoughts.

It was going to take a long time to get to the bottom of what exactly did happen that fateful evening.

It certainly wouldn't be sorted overnight.

Nobody seemed to want to go home. Patsy's eyes met those of her husband and she nodded her head towards the kitchen. A knowing smile touched Eddie's lips as he followed her out of the room.

'Shut the door,' Patsy said, laughing when she realised Eddie probably knew what was bothering her.

'The question is . . .' Patsy began.

'How are we gonna feed this lot?' Eddie finished the sentence for her.

'Well, they don't all usually stay for tea, do they?'

'No, but I'm sure your cupboards are not bare, my love. I'll send Ellen and Emma out to start making sandwiches while you see what you've got in those cake tins of yours.'

'Don't go empty-handed,' Patsy called as he made to leave the kitchen. 'Take a clean tablecloth with you, and a pile of plates from the dresser.'

'Yes, ma'am,' he grinned, giving her a mock salute.

Two minutes later Valerie put her head round the door. 'I ought to be going, let you all get on with your tea. It's late enough as it is,' she said.

'You certainly won't, not before you've eaten,' Patsy told her kindly. 'Besides, you can give me a hand, grate a load of cheese to start with and wash the salad while the twins make a start on the bread and butter. Good job I boiled a big piece of gammon bacon yesterday.'

The four women busied themselves in the kitchen, making regular trips into the living room to put bowls and dishes on the big table.

'This takes me back a bit.' Valerie spoke softly. 'You always gave us cold meats and bubble an' squeak if we popped in on a Saturday. God, how my Timmy loved your bubble an' squeak.'

'He still does. You could see for yourself if you care to start coming again. That's if you're not tied up with anyone else,' Patsy answered equally softly.

'No. There's no one else. I live in a bedsitter back of Paine's firework factory.' Valerie's cheeks were flushed and her voice was little more than a whisper.

'Well then, you'd be welcome.' Patsy still spoke softly, but there was a conviction in her voice that let Valerie know she was happy to have her back in the fold if she wanted to come.

The late meal was quiet, but happy. Mary, better for having had her nap, was talking away nineteen to the dozen, which helped to ease the tension.

Alex asked Vicky to get ready to go to the hospital, and everyone else made their preparations to leave.

'I'll take you home,' David offered, but Valerie looked very embarrassed.

Sensing this, Eddie quickly said, 'We'll both take her, and then you and I can nip in for a pint on the way back.'

The house suddenly seemed empty, and so quiet. Ollie and Patsy were seated one each side of the fireplace.

'Wasn't it nice that Valerie turned up after all this time?' Ollie asked.

Their eyes met but there was no smile on either of their faces as Patsy gently nodded her head. Then solemnly she remarked, 'As long as things don't go wrong again.'

Ollie's voice was soft as he said, 'David looked so happy when he helped Valerie into her coat. And as for Tim, his face was beaming as he watched his mother help to get the tea ready.'

'Well,' Patsy gave a soft sigh, 'they've never divorced. Legally they are still married.'

When Ollie answered it was as if he was talking to himself.

'If only I had taken the plunge and asked Ellen to marry me when we first met. All those years wasted. I always meant to, always wanted to, but your mother was out of my class.'

They both sat silent . . . remembering.

'You're too nice for your own good. Always have been.' Patsy looked over at him with a loving smile.

'That's as maybe.' This big, kind man who to Patsy never seemed old had a tear in his eye as he spoke slowly now. 'I can't help thinking how incredible it is the things that happen in people's lives. The suffering, the pain, the tragedies . . . even miracles sometimes. Something happens out of the blue that changes a person's whole life.' He sighed heavily, then his eyes brightened as he said, 'If Valerie hadn't heard about Frances she might never have got in touch with David again. And if your mother hadn't got pregnant and your father hadn't died before they could wed, she and I would never have met. It's odd to think Ellen lived in Tooting, worked on the market stalls and took care of you for nearly fourteen years without asking for help from anyone. It wasn't as if she had been born into that sort of life. Much later we were to learn just how well off her parents really were.'

It was still as if he were talking to himself, reliving the past, so Patsy kept quiet, not daring to interrupt.

'Your mother was too young to die. I had a good job at the time but didn't earn enough to be able to pay for her to go to a sanatorium. None of us had much money in those days. Florrie and I did our best for you, and the Day family were great. They took you to their hearts as if you were one of theirs. Then, years later, my brother Jack died. What a turn-up for the books that was. He was rich beyond our wildest dreams. Why couldn't we have had some of that money when Ellen needed it? Yes, I loved your mother dearly and I've never wanted any other woman for my wife. To this day I am grateful that she came into my life, bringing you.

262

You made a few mistakes, like we all do, but then you found Eddie and had your children and gave me a real family.

'So you see, out of bad does comes good. Please God it will be the same for Frances. We shall have to wait and see.'

For a long moment Patsy closed her eyes, then she leaned forward and touched his cheek.

'Whatever would I have done without you? You've been a darn good father to me all my life.'

'Well,' he said quietly, 'it works both ways. You are still the light of my life. If Frances is pregnant then what happens to the baby will be up to her, but let me tell you something, my darling Patsy. Your mother had the choice to stay with her well-off family, but only on the condition that she gave you up. Never, not for one day, did she ever regret holding on to you. That's the truth. The years she had with you were happy ones. Hard, yes, but incredibly happy. She loved you so much; you couldn't put into words the way she felt about you.'

Tears were now running unashamedly down Patsy's cheeks. Thinking of her mother still made her sad, but to hear the way that Ollie spoke about her was beautiful. He held out his hand, and as Patsy clung to it his look of love and gentleness said it all. After a while she wiped her eyes and smiled.

The terrible events of the past weeks didn't seem quite so bad right now.

On the other hand, Frances was by no means out of the woods yet. And what about the inquest? Would anyone be charged with Luke's murder?

At least she felt safe in the knowledge that all her family would stick together. And who knows, maybe Valerie and David would have a future together.

How good that would be.

Especially for Tim.

Chapter Six

THE LAST FEW WEEKS of anxiety and strain had taken their toll, and both Vicky and Alex looked exhausted, near to total collapse.

Gratitude was evident in Vicky's voice as she quietly said to her mother-in-law, 'I don't know what we would have done without you and Eddie.'

'It will soon be all over,' Patsy said, trying to sound reassuring. 'Just try and stay calm.'

'I'm fine, really I am. Just a little tired. Afraid Alex is the same.'

'I know, I know, but it's only t' be expected. I was thinking of you all the morning. It must have been a terrible ordeal attending the coroner's court. Once they had found out who had killed Luke I didn't think it would be anywhere near so bad. Good job it was decided beforehand that Frances had nothing to contribute to the proceedings.'

'Yes. Such a relief. You'll never know what a weight that was lifted off our shoulders. But Alex still felt we should put in an appearance and I'm sure now that he was right.'

'Was it really bad?'

'Oh, Patsy, I can't describe the tension in that room. It

was Mr an' Mrs Somerford that I felt the most pity for. They had to sit and listen to the coroner say that Luke's wife was under severe mental strain, brought on by acute depression, owing to the fact that her husband had left her for a much younger girl. Two witnesses said that only days before she killed Luke she had tried to cut her own wrists. A doctor testified that she died only hours after stabbing her husband. Then a pathologist gave evidence from the post-mortem that both alcohol and barbiturates were in her bloodstream.'

A silence descended on them all that no one felt able to break.

Eddie leaned back in his chair and let his thoughts drift. This whole mess had been a disaster, and he and indeed the whole family should now be relieved that it was over.

But was it?

What troubled him was Vicky's physical appearance and her state of mind. After all, Frances was her only daughter, and from day one he had been conscious of her worry and misery. The last hour had confirmed his feelings. Finally he said, 'You're very quiet, Vicky. You're still worrying about Frances, aren't you?'

'I'm afraid so, Eddie.'

'Nothing was said in court about the attack on her?' he asked.

It was Alex who answered his father's question. 'No. When the fact came to light that Luke had left his wife and taken up with a young girl, I felt sure Frances would be named. But I had mentioned the fact to the police beforehand and they said they had drawn the conclusion that the two cases were in no way connected. As soon as Frances was able to tell the police that it was Mark Philipson that had offered to drive her home, it became a different case altogether. Except maybe Mark was trying to score one over Luke when he made the offer. After all, the two men were friends.

Frances apparently knew Philipson pretty well or she would never have agreed to go with him.'

Eddie looked thoughtful for a minute. 'So what was the coroner's verdict?'

Alex looked at his wife and they both sighed sadly. Again it was Alex that replied.

'Muriel Somerford murdered her husband and then died by her own hand whilst under the influence of alcohol and drugs. Pity that's not the end of it all.' Alex took a deep breath before telling his father, 'We still have to face the court when Mark Philipson comes up for trial. He's out on bail now, charged with grievous bodily harm. We haven't told Frances he got bail; she hasn't asked and we thought it best to keep quiet. She's been through so much and we've been so worried about her.'

'We know you have,' Patsy answered for the two of them. 'I really didn't pay much attention to what was written in the local paper, to the things that were said about that club, about underage girls being allowed in and young men buying them far too many drinks and such like, but I must admit I was a bit thunderstruck when I heard Philipson had been granted bail.'

'So were we,' Vicky replied.

Minutes ticked away as each wrestled with their own thoughts.

Suddenly Vicky spoke up. 'But d'you know, Patsy, even now we haven't been able to get Frances to talk about it. Don't suppose we'll ever know from her what actually happened that night.'

'No. Don't suppose you will. But there is one relief to hold on to; the police doctor did say there had been no sexual intercourse at the time, didn't she?'

'Yes, and Alex thinks that's probably why Mark Philipson laid into our Frances. He thinks Mark knew she was pregnant. Easy touch, you know, slice off a cut loaf wouldn't make no difference or so he thought. Got a shock probably when Frances fought him off. He, like the rest of them in that club, had drunk far too much and his temper got the better of him.'

It was a very thoughtful Eddie who asked the most important question. 'What about the baby? Any decision yet?'

Both Vicky and Alex sighed heavily.

'Frances is much better; we've been told she may be able to come home soon. But she seems strange. Withdrawn. If only she would show some emotion. Even getting angry would be better than having to watch her staring into space and never saying a word.' Vicky took a deep breath and looked across at Alex. 'We've met Luke's parents, you know,' she admitted self-consciously.'

'Yes, an' we told them no involvement,' Alex cut in quickly. 'They had ideas that they would take the baby on the minute it was born. Had the bloody cheek t' say our Frances need never see it.'

'I hope you put them straight,' his father said angrily.

'You bet yer life I did, Dad. If he hadn't been an old man I would more than likely have thumped him.'

'Does Frances know about this?' Patsy was curious; this was a turn-up for the books. Up until now the baby had only been spoken about in whispers.

'Yes, we told her all right, hoping she'd say what *she* wanted to happen.'

'And didn't she?'

'No, Patsy, she just burst into tears. Sobbing as if her heart was going to break.'

Patsy was surprised. 'Well, well, maybe she wants to have the baby and bring it up herself.'

'I wish I could believe that you are right. She won't utter a word on the subject. Both her father and I have pleaded with her. Does she want to have it adopted? Does she want to keep it? Either way we have promised she will have every bit of help we can possibly give her, and still she doesn't answer.'

'I'll be glad when you do get her home and she starts coming here again.' Patsy smiled. 'I popped in to see her yesterday afternoon on my own. I thought she might have opened up a bit to me.'

'But she didn't.' It was more a statement than a question from Vicky.

'Everything went well. She seemed really pleased to see me, never let go of my hand the whole time I sat there, but from the beginning she made it perfectly clear that Luke Somerford was a taboo subject.'

'Tell me about it,' Vicky said sarcastically. 'There is one thing, though, Patsy, that I think you should know.'

'Oh, and what's that?'

'Well, I got the surprise of my life one morning when I opened the front door and Alan Yates was standing there with a really nice bunch of flowers and a card. He didn't even ask if he could go and see Frances; just enquired how she was and asked me to give the flowers and card to her.'

'Alan always was a nice lad,' Eddie said.

'Well, he must be if he came all the way out to Tolworth. He lives in that block of council flats at the bottom of Fountain Road in Tooting, doesn't he?'

'Now you're sounding a bit snobbish,' Vicky told her mother-in-law. 'But yes, he does still live with his parents. Our James and Frances and Emma's three boys were often round there when they were all at school. Mr an' Mrs Yates are nice people. They always welcomed the children.'

'We did the same,' Patsy protested. 'Whenever we had a party or a gathering of some kind or another I seem to remember Alan was always here. And I still say he must think a lot of Frances to come all the way out to you to bring her flowers.'

Alex grinned. 'Distance is no obstacle to youngsters today. Reach eighteen and they all have to have a car, even if it is an old banger. When James heard that Alan had been to the house he told us that Frances and Alan were pretty thick at one time. He was quite cut up when she ditched Alan for Luke.'

There was something about the way that Alex had made that statement that prompted his mother to ask, 'Do you like Alan Yates?'

'Yes, I do,' he said. 'He's a down-to-earth bloke, open and honest. After he left school he went to night classes, got himself a job in the print. Fleet Street no less. Deserves t' get on, he does.'

'Yeah, I think so too. Alan is the sort of bloke you can rely on,' Eddie quickly agreed.

Patsy gave her husband a warning look.

Eddie got to his feet, pulled Patsy up out of her chair and said, 'About time we all had a cup of tea.'

Out in the scullery Patsy turned on him. 'Since when did you ever offer to make the tea?'

'Since you were about to tell me off because you thought I was match-making.'

'And of course you weren't? It was as plain as a pikestaff that you were implying that Alan Yates would be a good bloke for our Frances to take up with. Vicky and Alex are old enough to draw their own conclusions,' Patsy said crossly.

'Well surely they must see what's going on under their noses? A young man doesn't go all the way out to Tolworth to take flowers when he could have sent them by Interflora if he wasn't interested in the girl. But what you're saying is they don't need a gentle shove from either of us,' Eddie said, grinning, as he filled the kettle from the tap over the sink. Having placed the kettle on the stove and lit the gas he laughed as he said, 'Florrie will never be gone all the time you're around, Patsy. But go on, now we're on our own, tell me what you really think our Frances will do. By the way, do you think anyone has told Alan Yates that she is pregnant?'

Patsy, setting out cups and saucers on a tray, threw a teaspoon at him. He ducked and it landed in the sink with a clatter.

'You, Eddie Owen, love a bit of gossip as much as the next one. I was going to tell you something but I've a good mind not even to discuss it with you now.'

'All right then, don't.' He grinned, knowing full well that was the best way to make her talk.

Having set a home-made jam sponge out on one plate and a fruit cake on another, she couldn't hold out any longer. Playfully she punched him in the ribs.

'Ollie told me this morning that when he was driving past David's house he saw Valerie going in there with two bags of shopping.'

'Did he now? Well, perhaps David had asked her to get him a few things.'

'And perhaps,' Patsy mimicked, 'he just gave her a key to let herself in and told her to leave the groceries or whatever on the kitchen table. No, I bet she's back living with David.'

'Well I hope you're right,' Eddie said, sounding serious. 'I'd be more than pleased if those two are back together again. Where *was* she living, do you know?'

'Not when she first cleared off, but when she was helping me get the tea she told me she wasn't with anyone, just living on her own in a bedsitter behind Paine's firework factory. Hold on, though, you went with David to take her home, so you must have seen where she was living.'

'Well that's not exactly true. I was sitting in the front of the car, with David driving and Valerie sat in the back. As we were going towards Mitcham, Val leaned forward and told David to turn off left at The Swan. It dawned on me then that I was playing gooseberry and that they might need to talk on their own. So I asked David to drop me off. Said I'd wait for him in The Swan – get the drinks in is what I really said. David wasn't very long; he'd watched her go in and she waved from an upstairs window. No sign of any bloke, and the house was a bit shabby, he said.'

It was Patsy's turn to laugh. 'I'm glad Ollie told me what he saw.'

'Yeah, well. Hold yer horses. Don't go asking David any questions. D'you hear me?'

'As if I would!'

'Yeah, as if.'

'What about our Frances and this Alan Yates? A bit strange, isn't it, him visiting her? Especially as she's having a baby.'

Eddie poured the boiling water into the big brown teapot and banged the empty kettle back down on to the stove.

'There you go again. What's it got to do with you?'

'Oi, why are you 'aving a go at me?'

'Because as usual you're putting the cart before the horse. We none of us know yet what Frances may decide. She might want to have the baby adopted. Whatever, it will be her decision and we must all of us support her all the way.'

'Oh, and you don't think I will? You told me the other day that I was kind, generous and fair-minded. Where 'ave I gone wrong today?'

When Eddie didn't answer, Patsy decided to well and truly tease him.

'I was going to suggest that me and the twins make some maternity dresses for Frances. And I was thinking of buying a load of wool and taking it down to Ramsgate. All our old ladies in the Maplehurst will be in their element if we ask them to knit and crochet baby clothes. On the other hand, maybe we should be thinking of a wedding dress if Alan still cares enough for Frances.'

271

'Heaven help me!' Eddie came behind his wife and lifted her off her feet. 'Is there no stopping you plotting and planning where our children and grandchildren are concerned?'

'Would you 'ave me any different?' she asked very quietly.

Eddie pretended to think for a moment before saying seriously, 'No. I don't think I would.'

Then he turned her round, kissed her lips and held her close.

Chapter Seven

CHRISTMAS MORNING AT THE Crawford house started early as ever. Mary was climbing on to her parents' bed to open her stocking with shouts of 'Father Christmas has been!' Chocolate money, a doll's tea service, doll's clothes, a tiny teddy bear, a rosy apple and a tangerine. And then came a trumpet, which had Mary puffing her cheeks out to tootle it loudly, making Ellen and Peter fall about laughing.

Traditionally the whole family would gather after breakfast at Patsy and Eddie's house, the family home as it was regarded by everyone. Not this year. With Frances still in hospital, the mood was not so merry. It was Emma and Donald who were hosting the festivities this year.

First thing that morning Vicky, Alex and James had been to the hospital to see Frances, and James had promised to come back later that afternoon bringing her cousins. A much more cheerful Frances had teased James that they were only coming because of the pretty nurses.

By eleven o'clock everyone had arrived in Tolworth. Cars were parked and everyone came into the house armed with presents which had all been prettily wrapped and hidden for weeks. David was the last to arrive, and Patsy smiled broadly at Eddie when she saw that Valerie was with him.

It had taken a lot of persuasion on David's part to get Valerie to agree to come with him. Within minutes of being in Emma and Donald's home she felt at ease, and the biggest and best Christmas gift that she felt she could have received was that her son Tim came forward to take her coat, kiss her cheek and hold her close for a long minute. He was twenty-eight years old and had shied away from the idea of marriage mainly because of how his mother had treated David. Recently he had met a young lady, Peggy, such a delightful person that he felt he could spend the rest of his life with her, and looking round the room this Christmas morning he thought maybe, just maybe, there might be another special occasion later on in the new year when all the family would be together – that's if he ever plucked up courage and asked this certain young lady to marry him.

Everyone had been given a warming drink and lunch came next.

Donald and Emma had excelled themselves with the salmon and prawn starter and the roast turkey with all the trimmings. Patsy had made the Christmas puddings weeks ago and Ellen had brought a huge trifle and endless mince pies. David and Valerie had provided a lovely selection of cheeses together with a rich and showy tin of assorted biscuits.

The table looked really festive with all the matching china, green and gold serviettes and a cracker on each side plate that exactly matched the serviettes. Red and green candles were placed at regular intervals along the long table and little Mary's eyes shone brightly as her Uncle Donald turned off the overhead light, lit the wick of each candle and then switched on the three sets of fairy lights that adorned the tall Christmas tree which stood in the centre of the bay window.

As always, Ollie had been asked to carve the turkey, and

the lads all fell about laughing as he made a great show of sharpening the carving knife by manoeuvring the blade up and down a shiny rod of steel.

An hour and a half later they all trooped back into the sitting room and started on the presents which were piled under the tree. Excitement rose, with young Mary screaming with delight time and time again. Great-Grandad Ollie had bought her a doll's house. It was so large that she needed help to remove the wrapping paper.

'Oh, I love you, Great-Grandad,' she said, throwing herself at him and putting her little arms around his neck. 'Look, everyone, it's got real furniture and beds and four people – well, little dolls really, but they do look like real people, don't they, Mummy?'

'Of course they do,' Ellen told her. 'And you must give each one of them a name.'

Soon the floor was covered with paper, cardboard boxes and brightly coloured ribbon, and the air was filled with cries of surprise and satisfaction.

Patsy had set Eddie's present aside and left it to open last of all.

'Grandma.' Mary tugged at Patsy's sleeve. 'You've still got one present to open.'

'Yes, darling, I know. It's from yer grandad.'

'Open it now, please.'

With all eyes on her, Patsy untied the bow and carefully undid the red and silver paper. Inside was a long white box. She took the lid off and saw the most beautiful peach-coloured underwear set in folds of tissue paper. One by one she removed each article, not unfolding them but laying them gently into the lid of the box. The last two items had her blushing, and she lowered her head to hide her smiles. They were a nightdress and a dressing gown. Not meant to keep one warm, that was for sure! They were lacy, luxurious and almost transparent. At the bottom of the box

275

was a peach-coloured envelope. Patsy removed this and slid it into the pocket of her cardigan. Later, when everyone was helping to clear up the littered paper, she went upstairs to the bathroom and opened the envelope and read the card.

To my darling Patsy, with all my love. Without you life would hold nothing for me.

Eddie x x

PS I thought this gift would assure my wife that I still fancy her like mad.

Happy Christmas.

When Patsy came back downstairs, with her hair redone, her face powdered, and smelling of Eddie's favourite scent, she looked at him and was rewarded with a gleaming grin of amusement.

It was ten days into the new year and Patsy was at Tolworth, waiting in Vicky and Alex's house. They had gone to the hospital to bring Frances home.

Vicky was on tenterhooks. This morning she had had a heart-to-heart talk with her mother-in-law.

'I mean it, Patsy,' she had begun. 'Our Frances still looks as if she's at death's door. I know the doctors keep trying to reassure us that she is not actually physically ill. They just keep saying she's emotionally disturbed, but if she would only talk about what she is going to do about the baby I feel we'd be more able to help.'

'At least she's told her father that she doesn't want an abortion, hasn't she?' Patsy asked.

'Yes, that's true. It's too late anyway. It would be dangerous, she's almost four months gone now and nothing has been decided. I've tried over and over again to bring the subject up, but she just gives me funny looks and retreats into herself, or changes the subject and starts to talk about something else.'

'Hasn't she given you any indication at all?'

'No, I've told you. She won't even discuss it.'

Patsy just couldn't make it out. Frances had always been such an open girl. Close to her parents and brother, and Patsy liked to think that there would never come a time when Frances didn't feel she could come to Eddie or herself if she needed help or advice of any kind. She wondered if being the only girl in the family when she was growing up had made any difference.

That Luke Somerford must have spun her a right old story, and she had swallowed it, hook, line and sinker. And who could blame her? He had been a real charmer.

The trouble was, Frances had always led such a sheltered life. With her cousins and brother to look out for her, she had trusted young men. And she was so lovely, a pretty girl who had grown into a beautiful young woman, but too innocent and trusting for her own good.

Patsy had already filled the kettle and laid out a welcome-home tea for the four of them when she heard Alex's car turn into the drive. She lit the gas beneath the kettle and went to open the front door.

She stood there waiting for her granddaughter to get out of the car, her arms flung wide. Frances walked slowly but straight into those waiting arms and laid her head on Patsy's shoulder.

Not a word did either of them say, and Vicky and Alex squeezed past them and left them to it. Minutes ticked away as Patsy patted Frances's back and repeatedly kissed the top of her head.

Finally Frances broke away and said, 'I hoped you'd be here, Gran.'

'Why?'

Her voice little more than a whisper she said, 'Because

after I've been home for a couple of days I wanted to ask you if I can come and stay with you for a while.'

'If yer mum an' dad agree, there's nothing I'd like better. I'll put it t' yer mum that she could go back to work knowing you'd be fine with me.'

'Oh, would you, Gran? I've so many questions I want to ask you. I don't know why, but I can talk to you so much more easily than I can to Mum or Dad. You don't mind, do you?'

'You soppy 'apporth, of course I don't. I'll be thrilled to 'ave you. Now then, let's get you indoors.'

All our children have lovely homes, Patsy had been thinking to herself as she had opened cupboards and found china and a tablecloth edged with fine lace and matching serviettes. She had set to, and with all the good things that Vicky had bought she'd no trouble in setting out a feast.

When Alex finally said, 'Seeing as how I picked you up this morning and you haven't got a car, I'd better run you home, Mum,' Patsy couldn't believe it was a quarter to six. Both Ollie and Eddie would be wanting their dinner.

She kissed Vicky goodbye and promised to phone her in the morning. Gently holding Frances in her arms, she whispered, 'Get a good night's sleep and I'll see you in a day or two.'

Frances had been staying in Navy Street for five days, and come the weekend her brother, who with his father called in every day just to see that she was all right, pleaded with her to join him, Sybina and some of their mates and go to a birthday party.

It had been a little after midnight when Eddie and Patsy heard them arrive home. It had already been agreed that James would stay the night, seeing as he was bringing Frances back here.

They heard footsteps come up the stairs, James whispered, 'Night, Fran,' and two doors closed.

'Now will you put the bedside light out and let us both get some sleep,' Eddie snapped.

Patsy gave a tinkle of a laugh. 'Oh, you haven't been lying awake listening for our youngsters to come home safely, have you?'

'No I have not.'

'Not much you haven't,' Patsy said, giving him a sharp dig in the ribs. Then, rolling over until she was almost on top of him, she teased, 'Do you really want to go to sleep?'

'You are incorrigible, Patsy Owen, you know that, don't you, and the older you get the worse you get.'

Patsy just had time to say, 'And you love it,' before he tugged her close and kissed her passionately.

'Did you have a good time at the party last night, Frances?' her grandmother asked as she handed her a cup of tea. It was still cold and very frosty outside. Seated side by side on a settee drawn up close to the fire, Patsy was more than pleased to have her granddaughter to herself for once.

Frances took a sip of her tea, put the cup and saucer down on a side table and turned to look at her gran. She nodded her head and said sarcastically, 'Oh yeah, wonderful! There was my brother and Sybina who couldn't keep their hands off each other, all my cousins with their girlfriends, not to mention the fact that I hardly knew anyone else there. I stuck out like a sore thumb and wished to God I had never let James persuade me to go with them. Naturally nobody asked me to dance. They all knew I was pregnant, even though you keep telling me it doesn't show yet. Oh yes, Gran, I had a great time.'

'So you're saying you weren't the belle of the ball then?' Patsy said teasingly.

Frances began to laugh, seeing the funny side of last

night's party, then snuggled into the corner of the settee and stretched her legs out. She put her feet in Patsy's lap and said, 'But the food was great, and I have to say Sybina was really nice to me. The worst thing was the mother of the lad whose birthday it was, she kept coming into the front room and telling her son to turn the music down. And that wasn't all. She was a nosy old cow.'

Seeing the look on her gran's face, Frances grinned widely. 'Well, she was! She came and sat beside me and had the cheek to give me a lecture about keeping the wrong kind of company and accepting lifts from strangers.'

'Didn't you set her straight?'

'No. For one thing I couldn't get a word in edgeways. She finished up by advising me to put the past behind me, get myself a job and get on with my life. I did manage to tell her I already had a very good job.'

'And?' Patsy pushed her.

'And nothing. Sybina saw and heard what was happening and came and rescued me.'

Patsy's face straightened instantly. 'Wish I'd been there. I'd 'ave told her a few things an' all.'

'Can't really blame her, Gran. I shouldn't have gone in the first place. It wouldn't have been so bad if Alan had been there. He was invited but he was working.'

Patsy thought hard for a minute. She had tried to bring this subject up several times lately, but each time Frances shied away from it. Alan had called at the house three times since Frances had been staying here. Only once had he asked to see her; the other times he merely said he was on his way to work and would Patsy give her whatever it was he'd brought for her. Once it was a book, another time chocolates. On the one occasion that he had come into the house Patsy had left them alone and he'd stayed for an hour and a half. 'Just talking,' was all that Frances had said when she'd tried to draw her on why he'd stayed so long.

This couldn't be allowed to go on. It wasn't fair on the lad.

Patsy breathed deeply and took the plunge.

'How about you and Alan?'

She saw the colour drain from Frances's face and her eyes glisten with tears.

'Oh, Gran, there is no me and Alan. How can there be, with this?' She prodded her belly. 'It's got nothing to do with him.'

More's the pity, Patsy said to herself.

'Alan thinks a great deal of you, luv, you must know that by now. Why else would he keep coming to see you and bring you all sorts of presents?'

'I know, I know, Gran, and I realise now what a fool I've been. I was so starry-eyed because Luke paid me so much attention that I forgot what a great bloke Alan really is. It's like you're always telling me, Gran, we can all be wise after the event.' She shook her head and almost beneath her breath muttered, 'Alan's worth a hundred bloody Luke Somerfords.'

Patsy felt a bit shocked. After all, the poor fellow was dead, cruelly murdered by his own wife. Christ, it had all been such a mess!

She struggled to pull herself together and said gently, 'Come on, Frances, cheer up. You'll feel different when the baby is born.'

'Will I? You can guarantee that, can you, Gran? 'Cos I'm still not sure that I shouldn't have had an abortion.'

Patsy was horrified. 'Oh, darling, don't talk like that.' Then, having taken herself in hand, she began to speak quietly and gently. 'It may be difficult for you to believe me, Frances, when I say that I do know exactly what you are going through, but I do, without a doubt I do. You've heard how I was married at sixteen, an absolutely disastrous affair that never should have happened. It was never a real marriage and for months my life was sheer hell. If it hadn't been for your aunt Florrie and your great-grandad I would never have survived it all.

'In the end it was because Ollie inherited a lot of money when his brother died and used some of it to move heaven and earth and get things done that I was able to get a divorce and marry yer grandad. But before all that happened, Grandad had my name changed to his by deed-poll and we lived together and had four children before we were legally married. There were times when people scorned me, called me awful names. But nothing mattered just so long as your grandad an' I had each other.'

A sob racked Patsy's body and Frances felt guilty; she'd upset her gran, and she wouldn't willingly do that for the world.

'I'm sorry, Gran, for so many things. I never wished Luke dead. And it was so awful the terrible way he died, but it's me that's left to pick up some of the pieces. It's me that's having to pay the price.'

Patsy took Frances's hand and held it between both of her own. She stared at her granddaughter's lovely young face and her heart ached.

'If only we could put old heads on young shoulders' was what Florrie used to say, and by God that was exactly what she was wishing at this very moment.

'When I was young I got myself pregnant.' The words came out of Patsy's mouth in a rush. This was a subject she never spoke about and had always done her best to block from her mind. 'I was younger than you are now and in those days you were shoved into a home for unmarried mothers, made to work hard to earn your keep and treated as if you were not only shameful but the scum of the earth.' Abruptly Patsy stopped, sat waiting, watching her granddaughter.

Frances sniffed her tears away. 'But you had Grandad to look after you.'

'No, darling, I never. I told you, I was married at sixteen. I hadn't even met your grandad then.'

'Well who did look after you? Oh, Gran, don't tell me you were sent to one of those homes!'

'No, Frances, I was lucky. I had yer aunt Florrie and yer great-grandad.' She paused and smiled. 'And we didn't have two pennies t' rub together. At least Florrie and I didn't have.'

'What happened to the baby?'

'Well, I never had an abortion, but I never had the baby either. I had a miscarriage. I had to put that tragedy behind me, and now you must try and do the same. Think how lucky you are to have such a lovely family. Each and every one of us love you t' bits.'

Frances sank back against the cushions, and the sadness in her eyes made Patsy's heart ache with love for the girl. She let the minutes tick away before she spoke again.

'Frances, you've been devastated by Luke's death, the terrible circumstances of it, and that is understandable. However, it was not your fault. You've told us you were not even aware that he was married. If you allow Luke's murder, and what happened to you, to fill you with guilt, you will never be able to love your baby in the way that you should. Because even if you did marry someone else Luke would always be there driving a wedge between you. Besides, what you have to remember is that when Luke made love to you, and you conceived that baby, you didn't hate each other. More likely than not, my pet, you imagined you were deeply in love with him. And of course you will love the baby when it comes. It didn't ask to be born, just you remember that.'

Frances was crying softly, but she nodded her head slowly. 'How wise you always are, Gran.'

'Not always, my love. Had a good teacher in yer aunt Florrie, though. Rough an' ready she certainly was, but a great lady for all that. In every sense of the word. God, if she was here now there wouldn't be a hint of talk about abortions or adoptions. She'd want you to get on with it, and she'd open her heart to yet another baby in this family. Whatever you decide to do, you mustn't let this child suffer for lack of love. As I've said, it didn't ask to be born. It will be a tiny innocent little thing, entirely dependent on you.'

'Not so little.' Frances laid a hand on her tummy and smiled through her tears.

'Well, he or she is going to need you, and just remind yourself you have something I didn't have: a mum and a dad. You've also got yer grandad and me, as well as all the rest of the family.'

Patsy's voice had grown sterner, and for a moment Frances felt scared.

But Patsy hadn't finished yet.

Remembering so much of her early life, the love and loss of her mother when she'd only been thirteen years old. How the authorities had tried to put her in the workhouse. And that is exactly where she would have ended up if it hadn't been for Florrie and Ollie. All the hate she had had to endure from the Jackson family and from Johnny in particular. Not to mention the good hidings. These were memories that she never usually allowed herself to think about.

She looked hard at Frances. Oh, she loved her dearly and was well aware that she had suffered badly, but she just could not let her go on feeling sorry for herself.

Quickly, before she changed her mind, she got to her feet.

'I'm going to make us a cup of tea,' she murmured. And then, much louder, she added, 'And you, young lady, should try counting yer blessings.'

284

Chapter Eight

FRANCES STARED INTO SPACE for a long time, doing her best to curb a flood of tears.

Her gran had as good as said she was to stop feeling sorry for herself.

She laboured to her feet, took Gran's thick cardigan from the back of her chair, wrapped it tightly round herself and walked off down the garden, staring ahead but seeing nothing.

The things Gran had told her!

While she had been in hospital, she had gradually learned all the facts about Luke. First off she had felt responsible for the break-up of his marriage. But even that was not true. When she had been moved into a general ward, Mr and Mrs Somerford had come to visit her, and at that point they had been extremely kind. Even going so far as to fill her in on a great many details.

Luke had been their only child and they had been devastated when he had married a woman eighteen years older than himself. When Luke and his wife had parted, he had moved into a flat in Chelsea to live with a young lady he had known for most of his life. Because he still liked to play the field where women were concerned, that partnership hadn't lasted very long. His parents were bitter. They felt all would have been so different if only he had married the younger woman in the first place.

By the time the ward sister told Mr and Mrs Somerford that it was time for them to leave, Frances had felt they were nice people and she had great sympathy for them both.

But the very next day they had paid a visit to her parents, stating quite openly that they were the right people to bring up Luke's baby. That was just awful. She should have been the one that they approached. Not that the answer would have been any different. It was appalling what they had said to her mum and dad. They'd take the baby the minute it was born and Frances need never see it!

IT, mind you. Not the baby. Not the child. But IT.

Frances felt herself getting angry. She turned and walked back.

Patsy was just putting a tea-tray down on a side table. She turned her head as Frances came through the door and smiled.

Frances went straight to her gran, reached out and grabbed her hand, saying, 'You are something else, Gran. It must have hurt you to be forced to remember all those horrible things that happened to you, but thank you for telling me. I promise I will take to heart all you've said about the baby.'

'Good,' Patsy murmured as she poured milk into each cup and then lifted the teapot to pour out the tea. Frances plonked herself back down on the settee and, taking the cup and saucer from Patsy, asked loudly, 'What have you got to eat, Gran? I'm absolutely starving.'

Patsy straightened up and burst out laughing.

'Course, I have to remember you are eating for two now.'

This bit of banter broke the ice. Patsy put her arms around her granddaughter and it was hard to say which of them was laughing the most.

* * *

Frances had eaten a sandwich and a slice of fruit cake and drunk two cups of tea. Now she was fast asleep. Patsy was watching her, her mind a mixture of emotions, when the shrill ring of the doorbell disturbed the peace. She hurried through the house, anxious for it not to ring again and wake Frances.

Patsy's face lit up the minute she saw the delivery man in his white coat holding out a floral arrangement to her.

'For Miss Frances Owen.' He smiled.

'Oh, that's my granddaughter. Thank you so much,' Patsy said, taking hold of the lovely little wicker basket. She stood and watched the delivery man walk back towards his van, and smiled as he turned at the gate and waved to her.

Now she turned her attention to the flowers: three African violets, two deep purple and one pale lavender-coloured one set in the middle. The small basket was padded out with green moss and the glossy dark green leaves of the plants. The handle of the basket had been entwined with lilac ribbon and finished with a pretty bow.

How lovely, she thought, noticing the tiny envelope tucked in between the flowers.

By the time she got back to the sitting room Frances was awake and sitting up. Patsy set the basket down on the nearest chair and handed the envelope to her.

Frances opened it, took out the card, read it and sighed deeply. Looking across at her gran she said, 'It's from Alan. All it says is "Sorry couldn't be there last night".'

How thoughtful, Patsy thought, just a dear little gift, nothing grand, but so very like Alan. Once again it had her mind going round in circles. He so obviously cared for Frances. But where was it leading? Where could any relationship between these two go?

Frances was having another man's baby. In normal circumstances she would have said it would be asking too much of any young man to take on a girl in Frances's position.

287

Their case was a hundred times worse. So much had been written not only in the local press but in the national papers as well. There was no getting away from it. The local gossips had had a field day once they'd got on to the fact that the murdered man was the father of the child that Frances was carrying. And as if that wasn't enough, they still had to face the court case of Mark Philipson.

Patsy shuddered. What would the press make of that? Frances had been miles away on Clapham Common with another man when her boyfriend was murdered. And the two men had been best friends, so why would he want to hurt Frances? Patsy was in no doubt that he would claim that Frances had led him on, and a lot of folk would believe him.

Suddenly Patsy felt herself getting angry again. I've had enough of this. I'm sick an' tired of worrying over problems that I can do nothing about. Alan and Frances have been friends since they were toddlers, but it's not up to me t' start asking questions now. What they do in the end has to be their own decision. If anyone is entitled to know what's going on it has to be Alex and Vicky. Come to think of it, what about Mr an' Mrs Yates? Bet they won't be over the moon if he goes home an' tells them he's taking Frances on.

Every evening Eddie warned her to keep her own counsel.

'Don't you dare confront them,' he ordered. 'Just be there for our Frances when she needs you, bide your time and let matters take their own course.'

Fond of giving me advice is Eddie, and that's all very well for him. It's me that's staying away from the office, doing my best to cheer Frances up. He goes off to work with other matters to occupy his mind.

It was a right old mess from start to finish. But that was half the trouble. The matter was nowhere near being finished, and God only knew what the final outcome would be.

Although it was a heavy burden, it was only natural that

Frances should turn to her grandmother for help and sympathy. And Patsy was glad that she did. She just wished she could see a way out of all this. I'm an old woman, Patsy thought. I shoud be well able to handle this situation. Surely there must be a solution of some kind!

It was a sure bet Florrie would have found one.

A few miles away, in the City, Alan Yates was taking his lunch break. He had decided weeks ago that he could not hide his love for Frances Owen. He was picturing her now. She was so beautiful. Her colouring was startling: the distinctive chestnut hair, her green eyes so big and with such thick lashes, and that healthy glow to her skin all set her apart. He'd been told that she got her looks from her grandmother, and he could see that for himself, although Frances was a couple of inches taller than Mrs Owen.

He had adored Frances when they were at school together but had been too shy to tell her so. Then, during their early teens, she had seemed to regard him as another brother, which hadn't worried him because they all seemed to go everywhere together.

Everything had been fine until Luke Somerford had come on the scene.

Flashy git!

That wasn't a very nice thought, but it was true. Fast car, plenty of money, expensive clothes, marvellous on the dance floor. What girl wouldn't have been thrilled to have him pay her attention?

Now Luke had lost his life and Frances's life was in ruins. What with all the muck that the papers had raked up, he knew darn well that at the moment most fellows wouldn't touch Frances with a barge pole.

He himself had been badly hurt by the events of the past few months, but now things were slightly better and Frances seemed to be telling him that she wanted them still to be friends. She had certainly made the effort, letting him know how much she regretted her affair with Luke.

It's different for me, he told himself. I love Frances, always have, ever since we were kids. If he couldn't have her, and even now he wasn't sure that things would work out for the two of them, then he wouldn't want anyone else. He wondered if she could learn to love him. Would he settle for friendship? Because that was what she seemed to be offering now. Or was that only because at the moment there was a shortage of friends rallying around?

She wasn't short of company. She had a very large and extremely loving family. Each and every member of it adored her. Any one of them would lay down their life for her, but would that kind of love be enough to carry her through the rest of her life?

Alan got to his feet, silently cursing himself, aware that the more he thought about Frances the more it made his head swim.

She was having a baby.

Luke Somerford was the father.

Couldn't he just think of it as Frances's baby? Now you're being bloody daft, he told himself. The situation was hopeless.

Sighing deeply, he decided that all he could do for the moment was be her friend, be there when she needed him. As he left the canteen and went back to work, he was thinking of the old saying, 'Time is a great healer'.

He hoped that might prove to be true for both of them.

Chapter Nine

OLLIE WOULD NEVER ADMIT it, but he had not been feeling well for some time.

Patsy needed no telling. She watched him like a hawk, and this cold February evening she was particularly worried about him. Seating herself in a chair in front of the fire, she tried to relax. Ollie was sitting to her right and Eddie and Tim were seated at the table playing cards. She noticed that Ollie's eyes were closed, and despite the heat from the fire he looked cold. Her heart sank.

'All right, Ollie,' she said briskly. 'First thing in the morning I am ringing the doctor's surgery to make an appointment for you.' When no reply came, Patsy leant forward and put her hand on his shoulder. 'Don't make out that you haven't heard me.' She gazed at him miserably. 'If you won't go and see the doctor, I shall ask him to come here.'

Ollie sighed. Eddie laughed. 'Getting at you again, is she?' he said, passing the pack of cards to Tim to shuffle.

Patsy swallowed. She decided to take a different course, wanting to force Ollie into being honest. She didn't need any telling that he was not at all well, but Eddie seemed to think she was imagining it all. 'Ollie, I'm sorry, I don't mean to sound as if I'm nagging you, because I'm not. I'm only pointing out that you aren't your normal cheery self, and a visit to the doctor can't do any harm, now can it?'

Ollie began to laugh. 'Oh, Patsy, you're like a mother hen the way you worry over every member of this family. But if it pleases you I will go up to bed now, have an early night, and go to the surgery if you make the appointment.'

Eddie looked across at Tim and in a stage whisper muttered, 'Poor Ollie, he's no different from the rest of us. Knows when Patsy's got him beaten so gives in and agrees to anything for a quiet life.'

'Now we've come to an agreement I'll say good night.' Ollie stooped and kissed Patsy, then squeezed her shoulder and stood looking into her eyes for a while.

Patsy watched him say good night to Eddie and Tim, and when he turned away her eyes followed him. It felt as if there was a stone in her heart as she watched him walk across the room. The door clicked behind him. She heard his footsteps crossing the hall and then she imagined him climbing all those stairs to reach his rooms at the top of the house.

She sat very still in her chair for a long time after he had gone, filled with despair. Ollie seemed suddenly to have aged. They would have to make some other arrangements; he wouldn't be able to manage those stairs for much longer.

Finally she roused herself from her troubled thoughts, pushed herself up out of the chair and asked, 'What would you two like to drink?'

'Cocoa, please,' Eddie and Tim said in agreement.

'As if I needed to ask,' Patsy muttered.

'And we wouldn't mind a lump of your gorgeous bread pudding if there's any left.' Eddie grinned.

The cards were packed away and the three of them sat comfortably around the table with their mugs of cocoa and hunks of bread pudding. 'You staying the night here, Tim?' Patsy asked, smiling because she already knew the answer.

'If that's all right by you, Gran. My place is like a fridge compared to this old house.'

'That's 'cos you're hardly ever in it,' Eddie commented drily.

'See you in the morning then, Tim,' Patsy said, kissing his cheek. And to Eddie she said, 'I'm going up, don't be too long.'

Slowly, wearily, she climbed the stairs to the first floor.

This *was* a lovely old warm house, and if the bricks could talk they'd have many a good tale to tell.

Ollie could not sleep. He tossed and turned, dozed and woke again.

He wondered what would happen to Frances and young Alan. It was almost as if history was repeating itself, for the third time. He thought fondly back to Ellen Kent arriving pregnant and unmarried in Tooting all those years ago, and then remembered his beloved Patsy's nightmare marriage to Johnny Jackson, and how well her life had turned out in the end.

And now there was Frances. The third generation. And look what a pickle she'd got herself into!

Several times he turned the light on to look at the bedside clock. The darkness was never-ending. Two o'clock. A quarter past three. A quarter to five. He couldn't get comfortable. His legs and his arms ached. His chest was sore and felt so tight.

Dawn came at last. There was no sunshine, merely a shadowy light sky.

At ten minutes to seven he climbed slowly from his bed, slipped his feet into his slippers and put on his dressing gown. Every single movement he made was an enormous effort. He went slowly and carefully down the stairs because he did not want to disturb Eddie or Patsy. Maybe he would surprise them and take them up some tea later on. At the kitchen sink he washed his face and hands, and cleaned his teeth as best he could with his forefinger. He needed a shave, but that would have to wait; he couldn't be bothered to go back up to the bathroom yet. He combed his hair. Folk marvelled at the amount of silky hair he still had, although now it was snow white.

When the kettle boiled he made himself a pot of tea. Gratefully he drank a full cup, for his mouth felt as dry as a bone. Then he unlocked the back door and took a few steps into the garden. God, it was cold! But refreshing too. The grass glittered with a covering of frost. His memory was telling him what good times they'd spent in this big garden. He looked further down to the two sheds that had stood the wear and tear of time. The things the boys had got up to in there! Mending old bicycles, chopping up boxes and selling the wood for a penny a bundle, collecting newspapers and selling them to the fishmongers. Those boys would never starve. They knew how to work and earn money.

Boys? They were men now. All big men and successful. Married with children of their own. He felt as he had always felt, honoured to be part of this family. No one had ever been turned away from this house. Folk down on their luck had known that help was at hand wherever Eddie and Patsy were. They'd both known what it was to struggle against the odds.

Ollie shivered. Suddenly he could see Florrie. A bit misty like, but Florrie it was, of that he was quite certain. He'd better get himself back into the house; he was feeling very cold. He reached the back door, went into the warmth of the kitchen and turned to close the door behind him. But it seemed that even this task was too much, for as he tugged at the door handle he felt light-headed.

He heard Florrie say, 'Let go, you've done enough. Our Patsy will be fine. You've earned yer rest.'

He reached the table, managed to pull out a chair and lowered himself on to the seat.

Far away, and faintly now, he heard Florrie say again, 'Let go, my dear friend.'

There's still so much I need to do, he wanted to tell her. It felt as if a band of steel was bound around his chest and it was getting tighter every minute.

All in all he, who had never been married himself, had the most loving family that anyone could wish for. Could he leave them all to fend for themselves?

He had no choice.

Chapter Ten

EDDIE STOOD AT THE side of the bed holding a tea-tray and feeling that he had never had to face a harder task.

Patsy stirred. He set the tray down on the bedside table and very gently shook her arm.

'I've brought you up some tea, dear. Sit up and I'll prop your pillows behind your back and then I'll pour it out for you.'

Patsy sat up, flexed her shoulders, stretched her arms above her head and gave him the sweetest of smiles. 'You're a darling man, what a lovely way to start the day.'

Then she saw the look on his face as he bent to kiss her cheek. She needed no telling that something was wrong. 'Is everything all right?' she managed to ask, knowing already that it was a daft question.

'Patsy, my darling, I'm so sorry . . . Well, it's sad news . . . and there's no other way to tell you. Ollie has died.'

Patsy's jaw dropped and her mouth hung open. She covered her face with her hands and it seemed to Eddie ages before she spoke.

'How? When? Are you sure?'

'I'm quite sure, though I have phoned for the doctor to

come. I think it must have been a heart attack. I found him, just sitting there at the table. There was mud on the bottom of his slippers and the back door was unlocked. He must have been for a walk outside in the garden. He looked very peaceful, just as if he'd fallen asleep.'

Eddie handed her a cup of tea and poured one for himself before sitting down on the side of the bed.

'I knew he wasn't well, I kept telling him *and* you. Why didn't he call me?' Patsy moaned.

'I don't think he got a lot of warning, though he must have felt strange or something when he was outside because he came in and got himself to a chair.'

'You said his feet were muddy,' Patsy said, trying hard to smile even though her eyes were brimming with tears. 'That's not like him. Not to wipe his feet.'

Eddie took the cup from her and drew her into his arms, and that was when the tears came.

'I must go to him,' she sobbed.

'It's all right. Tim's there, he'll let the doctor in.'

Patsy felt her head was about to burst. Ollie dead. She had dreaded this for ages now, and yet she felt the un-imaginable had suddenly happened. If he really were dead he would be gone for ever, and Patsy, who had been in contact with him almost every single day of her life, felt such an agonising sense of loss she didn't think she could bear it. Ollie was more than a father to her. He had chosen to love and protect her from the moment she came into this world.

'How can I live my life without him? I don't know how to. He was as wise as Solomon, and he loved me more than any other person on this earth. He proved it time and time again.' Suddenly she was crying like a baby and shivering from head to toe. All Eddie could do was wrap her dressing gown around her shoulders, take her on his lap, and gently rock her back and forth.

It was a long time before she quietened down enough for Eddie to suggest that she have a bath and get dressed. 'The weather's not going to be too bad today. At least it's not raining,' he told her, doing his best to sound cheerful though his heart was aching too.

He had lost the best friend he'd ever had.

Patsy was saying to herself, I don't give a damn about the weather.

Ollie was dead. Oh, dear God, there wouldn't be a day of her life that she wouldn't miss him.

That night when Eddie at last persuaded Patsy to come to bed, her feet dragged as she climbed the stairs and she was wondering how on earth she would have got through today without her family.

With the dawning of a new day, Patsy and Eddie knew they had a lot of business that had to be attended to.

'We'll have to get in touch with an undertaker,' Patsy whispered.

'We can safely leave all of that to Edward. It was his men that took Ollie away yesterday.'

'Do you mean Edward Towner?' Patsy asked. 'I know his father has been in the business for a very long time, but I didn't know that Edward was involved in the firm.'

'Yes, his father is getting on a bit and the family have such a good reputation that Edward decided to follow in his father's footsteps. Their main premises are at Bexhill in Sussex. His father runs that. They have another premises in Hastings which Edward's brother is in charge of, and Edward has taken over the one in Clapham High Street which was the family's first one. If you agree I'll give him a ring and we'll go together this afternoon and talk about what you would like for Ollie.'

'The sooner the better,' Patsy murmured. 'But I don't want to look at coffins; you can do that.'

Eddie sighed as he left the room, but when he returned his expression was one of satisfaction. 'That's it, then. I said we'd be at his office at two thirty. We have to go to the town hall first to get a death certificate. Don't look so worried, Patsy, it will be easier dealing with someone we know.'

'Yes,' replied Patsy. 'You've known Edward for a long time so it should be much easier. I didn't want strangers dealing with Ollie.'

They continued to sit at the table, where Eddie was making lists. 'Next person to get hold of is the priest,' he said, half to himself.

'Please, Eddie, let's wait until we've seen Edward. He'll know exactly what we have to do; after all, he must deal with these matters day in, day out.'

'You're right, pet. I'll make us some toast and a pot of tea, and you stay here and think about where you want Ollie to be buried.'

'Somewhere near to Florrie, he'd like that.' Then a thought struck her and she called out, 'I thought we already had a plot.'

At exactly two thirty Edward Towner was standing at the door of the funeral parlour. He shook hands with Patsy, then with Eddie, saying to him that it was some time since they'd met. Then he ushered them both into what seemed a very comfortable sitting room rather than an office. As soon as they were seated, a very smartly dressed young woman, aged about thirty-five, came in carrying a tray which held three glasses of a dark rich sherry. Handing a glass first to Patsy and then to Eddie, Edward Towner took one for himself.

'Funny how we both had the same Christian name yet even at school you were always known as Eddie while my name was never shortened. Still Edward to this day,' he remarked doing his best to set them both at ease.

299

Patsy had been afraid that coming here would be all gloom and doom. She had thought that Edward would be dressed in black, with a sorrowful expression on his face, and God knows what she had imagined the office would be like. Somehow her thoughts had centred on a darkened room with a vase of huge white lilies that gave off that horrible heavy smell one associated with funerals.

This was like sitting in someone's front room. There were two vases of sweet-smelling fresh flowers, and Edward was dressed much as Eddie was in dark suit and plain tie. They sipped at their sherry before Edward started to speak. From the start he was both saddened and sympathetic. He told Patsy that Ollie would be sadly missed. Not least of all for all the several charities that he had worked for and supported. Suddenly a smile lit up his face and he said, 'Only the other day an old chap was telling me how bad things were when he was a lad. At one time two thirds of the coal miners up north had been locked out of their pits because they wouldn't agree to accept lower wages. Their wages were already so low that men with families just couldn't manage to make ends meet, never mind take a cut. It caused a general strike. True, it only lasted nine days, but by God it caused great hardship.'

He paused a moment and gave Patsy a reassuring smile. 'It seems Mr Berry helped to make things happen at that time. Farmers had brought their milk up to Hyde Park in London but had no means of delivering it to ordinary families. It seems that Mr Berry somehow got hold of a horse-drawn cart, collected several milk churns and went around the streets to be greeted by women with jugs of all shapes and sizes into which Mr Berry and your husband carefully ladled out the precious milk. His great kindnesses will never be forgotten. I'm sure that must be of some comfort to you.'

Eddie shook his head at the memory and Patsy thanked Edward for his kind words.

'Well, now we had better get down to business.' Edward spoke kindly but firmly. 'Would you like to see a few coffins and make your own choice?'

It was all too much. Patsy covered her face with both hands and began to cry quietly.

'Edward, do you mind if I ask you to deal with everything?' There was a note of pleading in Eddie's voice. 'Just do the very best for Ollie, because he was in every sense of the word my wife's father. Doesn't matter about the cost, just send the bill to me.'

'I should be very honoured to be entrusted with the arrangements for Mr Berry's funeral,' Edward said sincerely. 'However, there are a few questions I do have to ask.'

'That's all right,' Eddie assured him, and Patsy wiped her eyes, blew her nose and sat up straighter.

From his briefcase Edward produced a notebook. 'The first thing we have to do is settle the day and the time for the funeral.' He looked at Patsy. 'You'll want a church service and a Christian burial. You will also need to choose the hymns.'

'I think we own a plot in the cemetery, next to where we laid Florrie to rest,' Patsy again reminded Eddie. 'You said at the time to buy two plots, although I didn't want to know about it then. Have I got it right?'

'Yes, now I come to think of it, you are right.'

'If you let me have the deed, that will help, and I'll ask Father Jonathan to call in on you. As you know, the church nearest to you is a high church, very well attended and very friendly. I'm sure Jonathan will be only too happy to take the service. And how about hymns?'

'Nothing mournful, please. Did Father Jonathan know Ollie? He was never exactly a regular church-goer,' Patsy told Edward.

'I'm sure he did, though perhaps not very well. But Mr Berry was always generous when the church needed funds.

By the way, you will need to put at least two notices in the papers. Would you like me to deal with that for you?'

Patsy and Eddie both nodded and Edward made more notes in his book. Looking up, he asked, 'Shall I ask the Women's Institute to do the flowers in the church? And what about family flowers?'

Patsy was quick to answer. 'Yes please to the church flowers, but as to other tributes, only from the immediate family, please.'

'Others will want to show their love and respect, Mrs Owen. A great many will send cheques, believe me.'

'Really? Well, what do you suggest?'

'How about we state in the newspaper announcement that all donations be sent to Towner's Undertakers, and we can forward them to whatever charity you prefer, though we should also state in the announcement which charity will benefit.'

'No problem, The Royal National Institute for the Blind,' Eddie told him. 'Ollie always said sight was one of God's greatest gifts.'

'Fine. We'll send all cheques on and you will in due course receive official acknowledgement. That only leaves the solicitors, bank accounts, that sort of thing.'

For the first time Eddie truly smiled. 'Knowing our Ollie, there won't be much to do in that department. I'd lay my life on the line that everything, down to the very last detail, has been dealt with in the most explicit terms.'

Even Edward allowed himself to smile before asking Eddie, 'How many cars do you think you will need?'

Eddie pondered for a moment. His sons had cars, and so did Tim and Donald, but it didn't seem right for a procession of different-coloured vehicles to follow Ollie's coffin. He deserved a better mark of respect than that. He made a quick count. 'Four, I think . . . no, better make it five. I'm sure there will be folk that we haven't thought about that will want to attend from the house.'

'Right, we'll make it five. You can always let me know should you not need the extra one.'

Patsy felt she knew now that Edward Towner was a true professional, and not only that, he was sincere. He meant every word and his sympathy was real, and for this she was deeply grateful. When he finally closed his notebook, and returned it to his briefcase, he looked at Patsy and said, 'I promise you, Mrs Owen, you can safely leave everything to me. However, there is one more question that I do need to ask you.'

Patsy felt faint. She had the weirdest feeling that this question was going to be of the utmost importance.

'Will you be coming to see your father here?'

Eddie was about to say no thank you, we shall remember him as he was. But Patsy was quicker. She cut him off.

'If it's all right with you, Edward, yes please . . . I dearly want to see Ollie; there are things I want to say to him.'

Edward came forward and took Patsy's hand between both of his own. 'I shall let you know the date as soon as possible. Meanwhile you come as often as you like. Could you please bring Mr Berry's clothes, everything, even shoes and socks. I promise you, he will not be in a coffin. He will be in a room very similar to this one, lying on a chaise-longue. We will place an armchair beside him and you may talk to him for as long as you like.'

'Thank you so much,' Patsy managed to say, even though tears were streaming down her cheeks. 'I only want to come the once, but it is something that I badly need to do.'

The house, with Ollie no longer there, felt so different. Frances had gone home with her parents, and although the family still popped in and out, every room was strangely silent. Only once had Patsy climbed the stairs to Ollie's rooms. When she came face to face with closed doors she knew beyond doubt that he had truly gone out of her life.

He had always left doors open, allowing her to see which book he was reading because it lay open on a small table which stood beside his armchair. His jacket would be hung over the back of a chair, and the windows would always be open.

Downstairs was no better. His chair stood empty by the living room fireplace. She'd turn to say something to him but he wasn't there. He hadn't always answered because at the end of a busy day he would rest his head back, close his eyes and doze. Even so, there wasn't much he missed. And if you accused him of having been asleep, his denial would be firm. 'I'm only resting my eyes,' would be his excuse.

Now there was no friendly chatter, no more warm and spontaneous embraces. Ollie was gone, and he'd left her feeling so lonely.

Repeatedly Patsy told herself she was not alone. She was so lucky, she had a large and loving family, and she had Eddie. It made no difference. Knowing that she couldn't talk to Ollie, that he was never going to walk through the front door ever again, was terrifying.

Without saying a word to Patsy, Eddie packed a suitcase: underwear, grey socks, black shoes and a pale blue shirt. He deliberated for quite a while as to which suit he should take. Finally he settled on a light grey, carefully folding first the trousers then the waistcoat and lastly the jacket and a plain navy blue tie.

The same lady who had provided the sherry took the case from Eddie and told him that Ollie would be ready any time after tomorrow. She spoke so kindly and so naturally, just as if she were inviting his friends to come and visit him. Eddie had to stand in Clapham High Street and compose himself. What he really wanted was to have a damn good cry.

Two days later he told Patsy that he would take her to

see Ollie at eleven o'clock in the morning. She nodded her head but made no comment.

They walked, arm in arm, the short distance to the funeral parlour. Edward was again waiting for them. 'Would you like to go in together?' he asked.

Quickly Patsy answered, 'No. If you don't mind, Eddie, I'd rather do this on my own.'

Edward led her down a short hallway, opened a door and motioned for her to go in, then closed the door behind her.

A number of emotions ran through Patsy's mind, but the main one was a feeling of peace. The room was softly lit and the smell from two vases of carnations was lovely. Ollie looked exactly as if he were having a rest before going somewhere nice. He was lying full length on a long, narrow sofa, exactly as Edward had promised. His head was raised, resting against the curved back of the couch.

Slowly Patsy lowered herself down into the armchair which Edward had promised would be there. Now her face was on a level with Ollie's. She leaned forward and placed her lips on his forehead. He felt cold but he looked so well, better than he had done for weeks. She slid her arm beneath his shoulders and started to talk to him.

'Ollie, please, don't go too far away. Be there for me as you always have. I keep thinking that at last you and my mother will be together. That's as it was meant to be. There will never be a day that I won't miss you. And how can I begin to thank you for all you have done, not only for me and Eddie, but for all our children. We will all miss you so much.'

Through her tears she smiled.

'You're going to meet up with Florrie. She'll be waiting, I know she will. Wish I could hear what she has to say to you. And after all these years you'll see your brother again.'

For a good ten minutes she sat in silence, just staring at that well-chiselled, beloved face. Then she slid her arm out

305

from beneath him, stood up, leant across him and kissed him full on the lips.

How she wished he could have responded.

Eddie was pacing the floor by the time she came out, and she quietly asked if he was going in to say goodbye.

'I don't think so,' he murmured.

'You'll regret it if you don't. He looks really well and peaceful.'

Eddie looked towards Edward, who nodded his agreement.

Reluctantly he went.

His visit lasted no more than five minutes, but he was half smiling when he came back to Patsy. 'You were right as always, my love. I feel so much better for having said my goodbyes like that.'

On the morning of Ollie's funeral, the house in Navy Street felt as if it was bursting at the seams. George and Lily Burton were the first to arrive. It had been agreed that Mary was too young to sit through the church service, so Patsy had asked Lily and George if they would mind coming to stay with Mary, keep the fires going and lay out the food and drinks for when they all returned. George looked very smart in a dark suit and black tie. Lily, dressed comfortably and suitably for all the jobs that she would be doing, was wearing a dark grey skirt and a jumper of a slightly lighter shade.

Patsy was thrilled to see them. She kissed George first. Then she found herself wrapped in Lily's arms and being given a great bear hug as well as several kisses.

When they finally broke apart Lily said, 'I've brought me pinny.'

Patsy just had to laugh, and wherever he was at this moment, she knew Ollie was laughing too. 'Lily Burton,' she said, 'you are not only a sight for sore eyes; you are a damn good tonic.'

The house was full of love. Each of their children had

kissed their mother and held her close. Her in-laws too, and that included Valerie, a fact that both Eddie and she were truly thankful for.

Time was getting on. Lily had taken Mary out into the kitchen and sat beside her at the table with a new jigsaw puzzle she had bought her. Mary was a very bright child, and she was well aware of what was going on.

'I don't mind staying with you, Auntie Lily, while all the family go to church to say goodbye to Great-Grandad. Mummy said she'll take me to the church next week and I will be able to take him some flowers then.'

Lily let out a great sigh, did her best to smile and said, 'Well, that will be nice, won't it, pet?'

All the same, she was more than pleased when George came into the kitchen saying, 'And where's my bestest girl?'

Mary was off her chair in a flash and throwing herself into George's arms.

The women were putting their hats on, pulling on their gloves. Tim was standing near the window, and as the fleet of funeral cars came slowly into view he turned and said, 'Grandad's here.'

Edward came into the house. Now he was dressed in black, and in his hand he carried a black top hat. Quietly he organised in which order they should get into the cars.

Patsy felt light-headed, and for a minute she stood frozen to the spot. Eddie was beside her in two strides, putting his arm across her shoulders and leading her out of the house. He loved her with all of his heart, and if he could have borne the anguish she was feeling today he would willingly have done so.

Ellen and Peter rode in the first car with Eddie and Patsy. The second car held Alex, Vicky and their two children. James was being very attentive to his sister. Their parents had done their best to persuade Frances not to attend the funeral, because she was still far from well. No matter what they said, nothing swayed her. 'He was my great-grandad too,' she'd told James in no uncertain terms.

David, Valerie and Tim travelled in the third car and the fouth brought Emma, Donald and their three sons. The last car held four stern-faced gentlemen each of whom had not only had business dealings with Alexander Berry, but had liked and respected him too.

For the length of Navy Street, Edward Towner and a colleague walked slowly in front of the glass-sided limousine which bore Ollie's coffin, their tall top hats held in their hands. The sides of the car were filled with floral tributes from all members of the family. Resting on top of the coffin was a solitary sheaf of spring flowers and green fern; this was from Patsy and Eddie, and the words written on the card would have made a grown man cry.

Cars slowed to a crawl, neighbours bowed their heads and men removed their caps. The curtains at every window of every house they passed were closed tightly as a mark of respect. Once they reached the main road, Edward and his associate took their places by the drivers of the first two cars. It took about fifteen minutes to reach the church.

Six of Edward's men carried Ollie to rest in front of the high altar. When the coffin was firmly in place, each member of Towner's removed his top hat, held it in front of his chest and bowed his head to where Ollie now lay.

As they followed down the aisle, Patsy was amazed at how full the church was. Already folk were standing at the back. The three front pews stood empty, and with Eddie leading Patsy, the family filed in to take their places.

This was the moment that Patsy had dreaded, for the coffin holding her dearly beloved Ollie now lay directly in front of her.

Soft music began, seeping into the silence of the church. Father Jonathan had done his homework. His tribute to

Alexander Berry was so true and so moving, it was more than Patsy could bear. All morning she had kept her tears at bay, but now she could cope no longer, and she let them flow.

Hymns were sung, prayers were said. Patsy kept the big white handkerchief that Eddie had passed to her firmly over the lower part of her face.

'Jesus said, "in my Father's house there are many mansions. If it were not so I would have told you. I go to prepare a place for you."' Father Jonathan was looking at Ollie's coffin as he said these last words.

Patsy's final prayer was that when the time came for her and Eddie to go, Ollie would have saved a place for them to be with him.

The house was even fuller than the church. Old neighbours from Tooting had deemed it right and proper that they should come, not only to say goodbye to Ollie, but to show their sympathy to Patsy, whom they had known from the day she'd been born.

The men ate and drank, Lily Burton made endless pots of tea for the women, but at last it was all over. Goodbyes were said and promises made to stay in touch.

Peter and Ellen were the first of the family to leave, because young Mary was tired out. The others soon followed.

Patsy and Eddie, seeing them off, watched the last car turn the corner and then, with a sigh of relief, turned and went back into the house. Lily was at the sink, her work-worn hands deep in soapy water, while George was still bringing empty dishes out from the dining room.

'It was a fantastic spread, and hardly a crumb left. Me an' George are almost finished. Why don't you an' Eddie take yerselves into the front room an' put yer feet up?'

'Oh, that sounds a marvellous idea, and I'm not going to

argue with you,' Patsy told Lily. 'As long as you and George promise to join us for a drink. I've made a bed up for you and Eddie will drive you home in the morning.'

A few drinks and none of them were sorry to climb the stairs and go to bed.

'Good night, Lily, you've been a treasure t'day,' Patsy murmured as Lily held her tight.

'My pleasure, gal. Wish it could 'ave been under different circumstances, but at least me an' George got to 'ave Mary all to ourselves.'

Patsy smiled. 'See you in the morning, an' thanks again.'

Eddie was already in bed when Patsy came back from the bathroom. She climbed in beside him, snuggled into his arms and immediately thanked God that she and Eddie had each other.

Chapter Eleven

ONE WEEK LATER, AT ten thirty in the morning, Eddie, Patsy and their children were seated around a long table in the offices of Barwell and Forrester, Solicitors.

Having greeted everyone, Harry Forrester adjusted his spectacles and began to read.

'This is the last will and testament of Alexander Berry, dated the first of March 1972.' He glanced up. 'To begin with, there is only one bequest outside the family. To Mr and Mrs George Burton, 5 Ariel Court, Kennington Lane, London, five thousand pounds. Mr Berry's comments on this gift were because Mr and Mrs Burton were instrumental in helping Mr and Mrs Crawford in their application to adopt their daughter. He goes so far as to say that in his opinion they actually saved the child's life.'

'Oh, that's marvellous, and so like Ollie,' said Ellen.

'So we can go directly to the residue of the estate,' Harry Forrester said. 'When the Ace Trading Company was formed, the shares were divided three ways between Mr and Mrs Owen and Mr Berry himself. Mr Berry's wish is that his shares be equally divided and given to his two grandsons, Alexander and David. His portfolio of stocks and shares also go in four equal parts to Mr and Mrs Owen and their sons Alexander and David.'

No one said a word, and the silence hung heavy.

'Now we come to Mr Berry's private bank accounts. There are two of them, and these mainly concern his grandchildren. Listed by age they are Alexander, David, Ellen and Emma. To each of these he has bequeathed the sum of twenty thousand pounds.

'Next are legacies for his great-grandchildren. We will start with the eldest, David and Valerie's son Tim. Then Alex and Victoria's two children, James and Frances; Emma and Donald's three sons, Edward Junior, Thomas and Sam; and lastly Ellen and Peter's daughter Mary. All seven great-grandchildren will receive ten thousand pounds each. In the case of the minors, Mr Berry's wish is that the parents shall be called upon to be trustees to this bequest either until the child becomes of age or until it should be deemed that a sum of money should be released for a special purpose.'

David and Ellen each reached for the other's hand, and their smiles were soft.

'How like Ollie! So kind and considerate to treat the two adopted children just like the others.' Ellen spoke the words quietly but she meant them from her heart.

Mr Forrester coughed discreetly.

'I'm sorry,' Ellen said, 'I thought you had finished.'

'Not quite. He sent her a grateful look, and resumed reading from the papers which lay in front of him. 'Four weeks ago Mr Berry came up to town and added a codicil to his will. I will read it aloud.

'"After my death there will be four shareholders of the Ace Trading Company. I hope and pray that the company will always see to the needs of any member of the family, male or female. No doubt you may come to wonder why I am placing my wishes with our family solicitor. At the moment it is Frances and her predicament that has caused

312

me to take this step. Should Frances need any special hospital treatment or anything at all that will help her, given that she, like all of us at some time or another, has made a terrible mistake, please, all of you, make sure that she does not have to pay too dearly. The company can well afford to set any of our youngsters on the right road and I trust the shareholders to take it upon themselves to do exactly that."'

Patsy pushed a stray strand of hair off her face. It was a weary gesture and both Ellen and Emma smiled at her sympathetically. There wasn't one of them that would not miss Ollie, but none more so than their mother.

Eddie was the first to get to his feet, and as he shook Harry Forrester's hand he turned his head and said to Patsy, 'What a man our Ollie was.'

She visibly shook herself before giving him a smile so brilliant he needed no telling that she was grateful that her dear Ollie had done his best for each and every one of them.

Once they were all back in the house, Eddie asked, 'What do you think was going through Ollie's mind when he added that bit about Frances maybe needing special help?'

'More than likely he was thinking that there is still the ordeal of Mark Philipson's court case to get through.' Alex was thinking aloud. Bad enough that his daughter was having a baby. The sooner this other court case was over, and a good many other things besides sorted, the better he would feel. He tried to put his feelings into words, but failed. Yet his brother and sisters knew exactly what he was going through.

'How many people are going to have to give evidence in court?' David questioned.

'I haven't the foggiest idea. But Frances will be treated with kid gloves, I'm sure.'

David hoped his brother was right, but he wouldn't take bets on it.

Vicky stood up, gave her mother-in-law a tight, strained smile and made for the kitchen, saying, 'I'm gonna make a pot of tea. I'm sure we could all use a cuppa.'

The day of the court case had arrived. Frances and her parents had been advised that Mark Philipson was being charged on two counts: sexual assault and actual bodily harm.

Only her father and grandfather had accompanied Frances to the court. She was wearing a loose-fitting maternity suit of a soft pink colour, with a large white collar which tended to make her look even younger than she was. They say women bloom when carrying a child; well, it was certainly true of Frances. She looked so much like Patsy had looked, Eddie thought, when Alex had been on the way. Today, with her clear skin, big green eyes and gorgeous chestnut hair, Frances did look truly beautiful.

Alex heard his daughter's name called and sighed with relief.

This case was dragging. The magistrate took one look at Frances and ordered a chair to be brought in for her. He listened as Frances quietly answered every question that was put to her. Then he held up his hand, and when silence reigned he asked Frances to turn her head and look directly towards the bench.

'Miss Owen, you have nothing to fear. My role as a magistrate is to get the facts straight, so I am going to ask you just a few questions. Are you all right with that?' His tone had been vastly softened and he sounded kindly.

'Yes, sir,' Frances answered clearly.

'You and your young man were in a club when you had a difference of opinion. For various reasons, he was unable to take you home.'

'That's right,' Frances said, nodding her head at the same time.

'Mark Philipson offered to escort you. You knew this young man, knew also he was a friend of your boyfriend and so had no qualms about accepting a lift in his car.' He did not give Frances time to answer; he was now on his favourite subject.

'This young man drove that car with enough drink in him to knock out a prize fighter . . .' And he launched into a diatribe on the failings of the judicial system that allowed young drunk drivers to be on the roads.

The magistrate's flow of words was halted as the clerk of the court stood up and handed him a folded piece of paper. He adjusted his glasses and read the note. It was a while before he raised his head. Then, looking at Mark Philipson, he said, 'You finally did the decent thing and have changed your plea to guilty. However, this case is beyond the bounds of this court, and therefore we are referring it to the crown court for sentencing.'

Alex and Eddie had been clenching their hands so tightly that their knuckles showed white. It would be hard to say who was the more relieved. When their solicitor told them that because Philipson had changed his plea to guilty, Frances would not have to attend the next hearing, they were even more relieved. Each of them was thinking that now, perhaps, Frances could get on with her life again.

What a hope! was the next conclusion. A few weeks' time and she'd have another life to be thinking about.

Alex's eyes were stinging with unshed tears. Frances was his little girl. For years she'd been the only granddaughter, the apple of everyone's eye.

Now, like it or not, she'd soon be a mother herself.

Chapter Twelve

ALICE YATES WAS A small, dumpy woman. She had been born within the sound of Bow bells, which made her a true cockney. She and her husband Fred had had two sons when they were offered the flat in which they still lived today, even though now the number of sons had doubled to four. When they had first moved in, Alice had thought she had everything that anyone could wish for. Coming from the East End of London to live in a brand-new dwelling in Fountain Road, Tooting, was, to her, like moving into the country.

Although Alice was small, quietly spoken and amiable, she could still hold her own when it came to the crunch. She loved all her sons and would do anything in the world for them. Although her husband Fred was large, and sometimes a bit brash, she adored him. For years he had worked in the docks, but found the travelling a bit of a bind as he got older. Lady Luck had shone on him one weekend when he'd been offered a job on Wandsworth Council. Foreman now at the main council yard, he was a man to be reckoned with. Any employee who needed help or even time off to see to a personal family matter knew they would be able to talk to Fred about the problem and he would do all he could to help. Play him for a fool and they soon learned that he knew every trick in the book, from a fake illness or accident to any one of the countless ways in which some of the men thought they could make a few dishonest pounds.

Alice cooked and cleaned the flat, grew plants on her kitchen windowsill and herbs outside on the balcony, and cleaned at the local infants' school three mornings a week. A drink and maybe a sing-song in the Fountain pub in Garrett Lane with Fred and their mates every Saturday night was the one thing she looked forward to. A week's holiday with Fred at Butlins holiday camp for the last three years running had helped to make her feel she was a very lucky woman.

She had known the Owen family for years. They were well respected around here, but when the older children bought brand-new houses out at Tolworth and moved away from Clapham, rumours had run rife as to where all their money had come from. Jealousy breeds evil, but it was a fact of life. Some wanted for nothing. Others worked their guts out and seemed to get nowhere.

Alice had no quarrel with the Owens; in fact as a family she greatly admired them, and as for Patsy Owen, they'd been friends from the day they'd first met. Like herself, Patsy hadn't been born with a silver spoon in her mouth, and had learned early on in life that if you wanted something you had to work for it.

The whole Owen family certainly stuck together, and Alan and Joe, her two oldest boys, had been made welcome at their home whenever the mood took them there. The Owen children came to her flat on the odd occasion, but with no garden it was a different kettle of fish having kids round to tea. Frances Owen had always tagged along with the boys, and they had been protective of her. Being the only girl among so many boys had made her into a bit of a tomboy.

317

Not that you could tell from her looks. Pretty as a picture, and so like her grandmother, with that mass of chestnut-coloured hair.

Alice couldn't help worrying.

For years she had seen it coming. Ever since Alan had laid eyes on Frances when she was knee high to a grasshopper she had affected him. As they had grown up, this knowledge had unnerved Alice. It wasn't that she didn't like Frances; she did. Very much so. But could her Alan ever provide the girl with the kind of life that she had grown up with?

The last few years Alan had slogged away at night school, doing his utmost to better himself, and by golly he had succeeded. Both Alice and his father were so proud of him. They'd even thought there might be a chance that he might make a go of it with Frances Owen.

Then, out of the blue, they'd split up. Alan had stopped bringing Frances round here for her tea, and they saw very little of her at all.

Alan was like a lost soul. She hadn't known what to do, let alone what to say to him. His father had shouted and bawled at him, telling him what a silly sod he was to be mooning over one lass when there were girls galore just begging to be asked to go out with a strapping lad that had a good job in the print.

'I think I'll put the wireless on, make a cup of tea, cheer meself up a bit,' Alice said out loud. Fred wouldn't be home for at least another hour, and it seemed a blooming long afternoon. She held the kettle under the tap, her thoughts miles away. Try as she would, she couldn't help it; her mind was full of Frances Owen and her Alan.

She knew darn well he was seeing her again. You'd think all the gossip and sleazy stories that had been in the papers about Frances and that toff of a bloke would have put him off. God knows there'd been enough of it to set folk's tongues wagging for weeks.

Just the opposite, it seemed. Alan wanted to protect her. Though only God Almighty knew how he was going to set about doing it.

It wasn't her place to make judgements. She didn't hold it against Frances. Everyone was entitled to a few mistakes as they grew up. And what's more, she *did* believe that Frances had not known that the bloke already had a wife. If it had been as straightforward as that, she'd be the first to go along with Alan trying his luck again.

But the girl was pregnant, and the father of the baby had been murdered! What kind of a set-up was that for her Alan to get himself mixed up in?

Not that she was going to put her oar in, nor yet offer any advice. Fred had dared her to. Not that that would have made any difference. If she'd wanted to mouth off, tell her Alan to steer clear of the whole mess, Fred's opinion would have counted for nought.

But this time he was right. She would keep her mouth buttoned. Why? Because if Alan wants to take up with Frances Owen again, there's nothing I or anyone else can do about it, she told herself sternly.

Besides, she knew her own son only too well. Alan would make up his own mind, and to hell with anyone that didn't agree with him.

Alan had driven out to Tolworth, worried because he hadn't seen Frances for almost a month. They had talked on the telephone but it wasn't enough to reassure him that she was coping as well as could be expected.

Vicky opened the front door and her face lit up. 'Hallo, Alan, we were beginning to think you had deserted us. Come in, lad, Frances will be more than pleased to see you.'

'Oh, Mrs Owen, I hope you're right, and before we go any further I would like you t' know I would never willingly desert Frances. If she doesn't want me around, well . . . that's another matter.'

Vicky gave him a smile, but her look was so sad he wished there was more he could do. She sighed softly. 'I know, Alan, I know. We can't thank you enough. You've been as solid as a rock where Frances is concerned, and it isn't as if she deserves it from you.'

'Oh, Mrs Owen, we all make mistakes,' he said, thinking at the same time that if Luke Somerford was not already dead, he would be tempted to kill him himself.

'There aren't many young men that would look at it like that,' she said, more to herself than to Alan. Then she said hesitatingly, 'I was just going shopping. I've tried my best to persuade Frances to come with me, but she won't budge, and these days I'm a bit wary of leaving her on her own.'

'That's all right, Mrs Owen. Today's me own. I'll stay, only too glad to.'

'Right. I'll get some lunch for us all later on, if you're sure you don't mind me leaving you on your own with Frances now. Mind you, I have to warn you, she's not in a happy mood this morning.'

Can you blame her? he silently asked himself. Aloud he said, 'I'll do my best to cheer her up.'

'I know you will, Alan, I know you will. She's in her bedroom, go on up.'

He tapped on the door and turned the handle gently.

Frances was seated by the window in her dressing gown, staring aimlessly down the garden. She turned her head and smiled, showing her pleasure at seeing him, then said softly, 'My, how smart you look.'

He was wearing fawn corded trousers, a dark brown shirt, a checked jacket which combined the two colours, and a fawn silk tie. He did look extremely well dressed.

Frances pulled her dressing gown more tightly across her belly and felt the colour rush to her cheeks.

320

'Please, Frances, don't worry about not being dressed,' he said, catching hold of her hand when he reached her side.

She kept her eyes lowered, and in a voice that was little more than a whisper murmured, 'I feel awful, you seeing me like this. Even my hair is a mess.'

'Well, perhaps these will help.' Alan smiled as he handed her a very smart shiny carrier bag. 'They are all free samples; the beautician on a very popular magazine gave them to me.'

'Why would she do that?' Frances asked, at the same time pulling out one pretty bottle after another from the bag.

It did Alan's heart good to watch her eyes widen with pleasure.

'Oh, Alan, how thoughtful of you to bring these for me. They really are very nice.'

She touched his hand, overwhelmed by this unexpected gift. She was near to tears as she remembered the little presents he had sometimes given her when they were at school. A penny bar of chocolate, a new whip when hers had broken; oh, how they'd loved to bowl their tops down the middle of the road, whipping them continually to keep them spinning. Once James had said she had to sit on the kerb and watch the boys' game because she hadn't any marbles, and Alan had given her three of his.

'What's the matter, Frances?' he asked gently.

She shook her head, blinking. 'I don't know. Yes I do, everything. This baby will soon be born and I don't know what I'm going to do.' She groped in her dressing gown pocket, found a handkerchief, blew her nose and gave him a watery smile.

'I was thinking of when we were kids. You always stuck up for me. My brother and my cousins never really wanted me tagging along, but you didn't seem to mind.'

Silence reigned between them for several minutes, until Alan sighed.

'Frances, why don't I go and wait downstairs while you

get dressed? Your mum will be back soon. She said she'll get us a bit of lunch, and then . . .' He paused, but eventually plucked up courage and said, 'Why don't I take you for a little drive this afternoon?'

He got no answer, but at least he had planted the thought in her mind.

Vicky was thrilled when she returned from her shopping trip to find her daughter in the lounge. Well done, Alan, she said silently. Frances had had a bath, washed her hair and even put on a little make-up. She was wearing a pretty, flowing maternity dress that Vicky had bought for her weeks ago and which up till now hadn't even been out of the wardrobe. It was in a shade of soft green which suited her colouring astonishingly well.

As Vicky bent over to kiss her she had to say, 'My, you smell gorgeous.'

'It's all down to Alan. He brought me a whole lot of beauty products,' Frances answered shyly.

'I'll make us all an omelette,' Vicky muttered quickly. She felt choked; she couldn't have said more to save her life. She needed no telling that the transformation in her daughter was down to that loyal young man. She shook her head in disbelief. All the pleading that had gone on endlessly from her and Alex hadn't got Frances to budge out of her room for days.

Now look at her!

'What am I going to do, Alan?' Frances stared at him, her expression woeful.

'You're going to take one step at a time, get through each day as best as you can until the baby is born,' he said confidently, giving her one of his reassuring smiles. 'And I'll be on hand whenever you need me.'

It had taken a great deal of persuasion on Alan's part to

get Frances to agree to leave the house and come for a ride in his car. He felt as they drove along the side of Mitcham Common that the fresh air was doing her some good. Already there was a little more colour in her cheeks.

However, he hadn't won her over. Not by a long chalk.

He had brought the car to a halt outside the tenement in Tooting where he and his family lived and tentatively asked her to come inside and have a cup of tea with his mother. She just sat and glared at him for what seemed an endless time. Then she blew her top. Told him it was a hellish thing to do. 'You've tricked me. You had it planned all along for us to end up here. You couldn't tell me outright because you knew I wouldn't have come.'

He was about to give up, turn the car around and drive her back to Tolworth when a window of a first-floor flat was thrown open and Alice Yates leaned out over the windowsill, calling down, 'Are you two gonna sit there all day? Twice I've boiled the kettle, I don't need to waste a Saturday morning baking everything I could think of 'cos you said you were bringing Frances t' tea. Now stop playing about an' get yerselves up 'ere.' The window shut with a bang. Frances looked very sheepishly at Alan and said, 'You never told me your mother was expecting us.'

Alan shook his head. 'I wasn't sure you'd believe me.'

Both of them were afraid as to how this meeting would go, though neither would admit it.

It was a very sheepish Frances that allowed him to help her out of the car and hold her arm as they climbed the two flights of stairs to where the Yateses lived . . .

Alice had the front door open and there was nothing dour about her greeting.

'Nice t' see you again, luv, after all this time. Come on in and sit on the settee, put yer feet up if yer like. How are yer?' And then, without giving Frances time to answer, she said with a laugh, 'Silly bloody question that was, eh? You'll be a darn sight happier when you drop that great lump.'

Frances smiled. 'I most certainly will.'

Alan led her to a big settee with squashy cushions that stood near the window and took her handbag while she made herself comfortable.

'D'yer fancy a cup of tea now before we eat?' Alice asked.

Frances nodded delightedly. 'I'd love a cup of tea, Mrs Yates, my throat is parched. But first I would like to thank you for having me here.'

'My pleasure, luv. I don't know why my son ain't brought you before. I've missed you.'

'Really?' Frances's heart was banging against her chest.

'I wouldn't say it if I didn't mean it,' Alice assured her.

Alan smiled, a happy smile that lit up his face and heightened his good looks, then raised his eyebrows and said gently, 'I told you Mum would be more than pleased to see you.'

'I'm gonna get that tea,' Alice said, disappearing into the kitchen.

Minutes later she was back with a tray holding two steaming cups of tea and a plate of biscuits. Alan pulled a coffee table closer to the settee and his mother set everything down in front of Frances.

Turning his back to Frances, Alan grinned at his mother, nodded towards the tray and mouthed, 'I see you've got the best china out of mothballs.'

Alice shook a fist at him, but she was smiling broadly as she left the pair of them alone.

Alan came to sit close to Frances on the settee. They each drank their tea and nibbled a biscuit.

'Shall I get you a refill?' Alan asked.

Frances shook her head. 'No thanks, that one was enough. It was lovely.'

He put his arm around her shoulders. 'Don't you feel better for having come out?'

'Yes. Yes, I do, but I still can't fathom why you bother with me.'

When Alan made no answer, she sighed heavily and said, 'I get bigger and more clumsy every day.'

'Come on, love,' he pleaded. 'Try not to be so gloomy.' He watched, waiting for her to smile. But she didn't.

'I can't help wondering why you are so good to me. Your mother too. Fancy her letting you bring me here today. Most people have washed their hands of me. The neighbours won't let your mum live this down.'

'The day when my mum worries what people have to say about her will never dawn. You can take it as gospel, Frances, my mum does her best as she sees it, and if that doesn't fall into line with what other people think, then tough. I promise you, she's not judging you. Besides, you, your brother and your cousins have been coming to this flat since we were at school together, and you've always been made welcome, haven't you?'

'Yeah,' she murmured. 'Seems ages ago . . . all those lovely summers when we went up the common or to Ravenbury Park. You and the boys used to fish. Only caught tiddlers, though, didn't you?' Before she could stop herself she added, 'Me, I brought it all to an end, thinking I could mix with the upper classes, and look where it got me.' She patted her belly and struggled to sit up straight.

Alan put his hand over hers. 'Oh Frances, don't be so hard on yourself. Everyone who really knows you realises it was not all your fault. I'll tell you something you might not believe, but my mum is knitting baby clothes for you, and my gran is crocheting a shawl for the baby. They would have sent them to you when the time comes whether you had come today or not. I'll tell you something else an' all. My dad is a rough diamond, everyone knows that, but he's always thought the world of you. He phoned your dad weeks ago t' say that you'd always be welcome here.'

'Alan! I don't deserve you or your parents. I never for a moment thought they would be so kind.'

'And why not? No one goes through life without making a few mistakes. So why wouldn't they want to see you?' Squeezing her hand, he added slowly, 'Besides, they know how much I care about you.'

'Oh, Alan! How can you say that when I've got myself into this awful mess? I am so sorry. If I could turn the clock back . . .'

'What's done can't be undone,' he said sorrowfully. 'But no one should have to spend the rest of their life saying sorry.'

At that point there was a lot of noise as Fred Yates and his son Joe came through the front door, calling out to ask Alice if she'd got the kettle on. Joe was just one year younger than Alan, then there had been an eight-year gap before Alice had had the younger two boys.

Frances watched closely as the two men came into the front room. Being almost the same age, Joe and Alan had been close pals all their lives, and Joe had been part of the gang that Frances had always trailed around with.

Seeing the two of them sitting close on the settee, Fred Yates laughed loudly then came forward and smacked a kiss on Frances's cheek. 'Blimey, gal, you're a sight for sore eyes.'

'It's nice to see you again, Mr Yates,' she said, smiling and really meaning it. This man was larger than life but he had always had time for her, and they had never gone off to play somewhere without him slipping each of them a couple of coppers to spend.

Joe felt a bit muddled. He didn't know how to treat Frances or what to say to her. It was she that put him at his ease. She looked him in the eye, hoping her thumping heart wouldn't let on that she was scared as to what reception she was going to get, and said, 'Trust you to turn up just in time for tea, Joe. You always were a hungry beggar.'

'Hallo, Frances.' He grinned. 'Nice to know that you

326

remember me. It's great t' see you again, but I still 'aven't worked out how you came t' prefer my daft brother t' me.'

Alan threw a cushion at his brother's head just as Alice called out for everyone to come and sit up because tea was ready.

God, the sight that met Frances had her eyes brimming with tears, and she nearly choked as she did her best to hold back a sob. Alice was beside her in a flash. 'Whatever's the matter, luv, does the sight of food make yer feel sick?'

'Oh no, Mrs Yates, it all looks wonderful. It's just that I suddenly remembered how we used to sit around this table when we were youngsters, and how well you used to feed us.'

'Well, if that's all that's wrong, sit yerself up and get stuck in. The two young 'uns are off to camp with the Scouts this weekend, so we've got ourselves a bit of peace.'

Mrs Yates really had made an effort. There was a nice cloth spread over the big kitchen table, and it was covered with food of all sorts. Besides the fruit cake, the jam sponge and the trifle that Alice had spent the morning making, there was a huge bowl of salad topped with slices of hard-boiled egg, a meat dish covered with well-carved slices from a lump of bacon that she'd slowly simmered until it was tender, and a dish of tinned red salmon. Thin slices of both brown and white bread completed the feast.

Alan passed the salad bowl to his father, but soon got short shrift. 'I don't eat rabbit food, as yer muvver knows darn well. I'll have some of that bacon or ham or whatever yer call it, a great lump of cheese, please, and some of your home-made chutney if yer don't mind, Alice.'

'Pickles,' Alice grumbled as she got to her feet and went to the cupboard. 'Why in God's name yer have to have pickles with everything I'll never know.'

Fred took the jar from her hand and grinned. 'These are no ordinary pickles. They were made by your own sweet hand, weren't they, my luv?'

'Sweet talking won't get yer anywhere with me.' Alice winked at Frances, who was already enjoying the salad and salmon that was on her plate.

It was a great tea party with lots of banter and laughter, and it came to Frances that her Granma Patsy would have enjoyed this. It was the kind of thing that went on in Patsy's house very often.

Frances was very tired when eventually Alan stopped his car outside her house.

He got out, came round to the passenger side, opened the door and helped her to get out. Using both hands, he made her stand still for a moment, steadying her. Then he led her up through the garden to the front door. She placed her key in the lock, turned it and opened the door.

'Are you coming in?' she asked.

'No, I won't today. You've had quite enough to tire you out good and proper. So in you go and get a good rest. I'll see you again soon.'

He bent his head and very gently kissed her cheek, then turned and started back down the path. When he reached the gate he looked back over his shoulder. Frances was still standing in the open doorway, and he smiled, calling, 'Good night, Frances.'

'Good night, Alan,' she replied.

Alan's thoughts were very mixed as he drove back home to Tooting.

Now that Frances had been to his home, seen that his mother and father weren't against her, should he get his hopes up? Well, maybe she might begin to take him seriously. By which he meant that she might eventually say yes if he asked her to marry him. He would willingly accept the baby as his own.

With Luke Somerford dead that was not a problem.

He loved Frances so much, he knew he could love the

child she was about to bring into this world. After all, he would know the baby from the minute it was born. He would look upon it as his own son or daughter. His feelings for Frances ran so deep that he knew beyond any doubt that they would last.

He wondered whether or not she could come to feel the same way about him.

That was some question.

All he could do was wait, hope and pray.

Chapter Thirteen

As THE DAYS DRAGGED on, Frances grew heavier with the baby and always seemed to feel weary and exhausted. To her dismay, her legs continually swelled up, even though she spent a good deal of time with her legs propped up.

Her mum and dad were so good to her, never laying blame, never harping on about what she should or should not have done, doing their utmost to keep her spirits up. All the family were a comfort to her, especially Grandma Patsy. Frances wondered every day what she would have done without their support and devotion.

The weather had been grand these past few weeks. Everywhere you looked, spring bulbs pushed their way up through the grass. After all the April showers were behind them, the May sunshine was such a joy. Frances spent a lot of her time sitting in a deckchair beneath the apple tree that stood near the fence at the bottom of the long garden.

She had never mastered the art of knitting, but she could sew. Her mother had come back from town one day with yards of white cotton material, bundles of different-coloured ribbons and a plentiful supply of narrow lace. She had also remembered to buy patterns for babies' long nightdresses and cotton petticoats.

'There is nothing to stop you setting to and making up some garments for the baby,' she had coaxed Frances. 'We'll lay it out on the kitchen table and I'll help you cut them all out from the patterns.'

'You're presuming I'm going to have a girl, aren't you, Mum? I know you've bought yellow, blue and pink ribbon, but petticoats and nighties?'

'Well, even baby boys sleep in nighties to begin with, and a petticoat is a must under a romper suit.'

Frances laughed to herself. She'd see about proper baby clothes when she could get to the shops. Meanwhile, if it made her mother happy and gave herself something to do, why not?

In the early hours of the last Sunday in May, Frances felt she had to get herself out of bed and to the bathroom. She had only got about halfway along the landing when a pain gripped her so suddenly it frightened her. She clung to the banister rail and held on. Oh no! she thought, she was wetting herself, she couldn't control it. Water was running down her legs, staining the carpet.

She did the only thing she could do. She yelled for her mum.

Vicky was beside her in seconds. She put her arm around her, holding her so tenderly, and said, 'Don't worry, love, it means your waters have broken.'

Then, 'Alex,' she called loudly. 'Quick, phone an ambulance and bring Frances's case, then come and help me to get her downstairs.'

Alex, out of bed and wide awake now, was tempted to shout back and ask what he was supposed to do first. He took one look at his wife and daughter and jumped the stairs in leaps. Reaching the telephone in the hall, he dialled 999 as quickly as he could.

The ambulance came and the two-man crew asked what

seemed to Frances a load of daft questions. Were the pains severe? How often was she getting them? At last she was strapped on to a chair-like stretcher and gently lifted into the vehicle, which would convey her to Epsom Hospital.

Her mother and father stood in the road, and as the driver moved off she lifted her arm and waved to them. They gave no answering smile or wave, and tears stung the back of her eyes. She was about to give birth and there was no one with her. No one that really cared.

One of the ambulancemen knelt down beside her and held her hand. Smiling he said, 'It's not that they don't care, my dear. You can see out, but they can't see in; the windows of this ambulance are just dark glass from the outside.'

And that's supposed to make me feel better? Frances asked herself, clenching her teeth as another wave of pain racked her whole body.

The journey did not take long, but the hours that followed were worse than anything she could ever have imagined.

She was washed with Dettol, her nightdress was removed and a shapeless white gown was put on her. Both doctors and nurses examined her, but all they kept saying was, 'You've a long way to go yet.'

But the pain! It was getting worse. She was sweltering. The sweat was pouring off her forehead. She'd been left in a small room with a huge light directly above her head shining straight down into her eyes. She was alone. No one cared whether she lived or died.

This is my punishment for having made love with a married man.

She actually believed what she was saying to herself.

She couldn't take much more. She wanted her mum. She wanted to die, get it all over and done with.

It was late Monday night, ten minutes to eleven to be exact, before she gave birth to a baby girl who weighed six pounds and one ounce.

332

Only Vicky and Alex were allowed in to see her. They raved over the baby, and the fact that they were now grandparents didn't bother them one little bit. In fact Alex was so proud as he stared through the window of the nursery at the wee little girl that one would have thought she had been made to order just for him.

The time dragged. Frances was doused with Dettol twice a day, and her nipples were sore because the nurses would insist on pinching them to form a point in order for the baby to be able to suck more easily.

Frances wasn't sure, but it felt to her that she wasn't being treated with the same respect as the other mothers in the ward. She wore no wedding ring, was referred to by everyone as Miss Owen, with the emphasis always being on the Miss.

The only joy she felt during the eight days she had to remain in hospital was when they brought her baby daughter to her to be fed. She had got the hang of it now, and just to hold that little being in her arms was something she was unable to describe, even to herself. So tiny, so perfect, so beautiful.

There was one point for which Frances felt she would be eternally grateful.

Her baby had all the hallmarks of being an Owen.

'I wouldn't change a thing about you,' she whispered as she placed her lips gently on the soft golden down that covered the tiny head. The baby's eyes were a very pale blue, but a nurse told her they would change colour within a few weeks. She needed no telling; her baby would have green eyes just the same as her own and those of her grandmother. Frances also knew that she could safely forecast that as the child's hair grew it would have the same chestnut glints as she and her gran had.

★   ★   ★

Frances had been home for three days.

Every member of the family had been in to see her and Olivia. After a long discussion, she herself had chosen the name for the baby because it was the nearest she could think of to Ollie. He might not be around any longer, but he would never be forgotten, and she felt that he was watching over her. She felt exactly the same sentiment regarding Florrie, and Grandma Patsy had been really pleased when she had told her that she would like her baby to be christened Olivia Florence.

It was three o'clock in the afternoon, and Frances and the baby were in the house on their own. Olivia lay sleeping, propped in safely by a pillow, at one end of the settee in the front room. Frances couldn't take her eyes off her. She still found it hard to believe that in spite of all those hard times she had given birth to a child who was so beautiful. She wasn't just any baby. She was hers. Her very own little daughter.

The door bell rang, and reluctantly Frances went to answer it. Alan stood there, his arms full of parcels. He took a step towards her and stopped.

'Please, come in,' Frances said, doing her best to sound normal.

He looked marvellous, well dressed but in a casual way.

'How are you, Frances?' were the first words he managed to say.

'I'm all right, really I am.'

'May I put all these parcels down?' he asked, smiling. 'They're from me gran and me mother. Just a few things for the baby.'

'Oh, Alan, I'm sorry,' she said, relieving him of them and placing them on the hall table. 'It really is so good of them. You will remember to thank them both for me?'

'Course I will. Mum said she was so thrilled when your mother rang to say you'd had a liittle girl.' He laughed. 'Both her and Gran have been busy adding pink ribbons to everything.'

'Would you like to see her?' Frances asked hesitantly.

'Frances, you don't know how much I've been hoping you'd say that,' he admitted.

'Well, come along then, she's sleeping in the front room.'

Alan had always thought this was a lovely room. Now, in the second week in June, the french doors were flung open, giving a full view of the garden. There was a bird bath standing on the edge of the lawn, fancy bird feeders swung from the branches of two trees, and the flowerbeds were bursting with colour.

'New life out there and in here,' he joked. 'Where is she?'

Frances smiled and pointed to the corner of the settee. In three strides he was there, staring down at the baby as if he couldn't believe his eyes. He was momentarily at a loss for words.

'Well?' Frances asked quietly.

He got down on his knees, the better to see her. He reached out and touched her tiny hand that lay outside her shawl. Immediately her fingers curled around his index finger, and he couldn't have been more pleased, though neither he nor Frances spoke, because each was lost in their own thoughts.

'We've settled on a name.' Frances finally broke the silence. 'She's Olivia Florence.'

Almost as if she recognised her own name, the baby stirred, bunched her fingers into fists and opened her eyes. From that very moment Alan was captivated.

'Please, may I pick her up?'

Frances had been watching the emotion on his face and she felt incapable of answering. If only it was Alan who was the father of that tiny baby, how much better she would feel. But all the wishing in the world wouldn't make it so.

She bent low, carefully picked her daughter up and placed

her in Alan's open arms. He held her gingerly, his heart pounding. Never for one moment had he realised that he would feel like this.

Frances felt her throat tighten and the back of her eyelids prickled as tears threatened. To see the way Alan was cradling her daughter in his arms tore her heart in two. It seemed a long time before he gave her back to Frances to settle her down again.

Alan felt out of his depth. So much he wanted to say. But where would he start?

And then, slowly, he felt a new and wondrous feeling. A peacefulness, as if things had been sorted out for him and he knew that now was the right time for him to speak.

As Frances straightened up, he reached out and stroked her cheek very, very gently. She looked into his face and cautiously smiled. He put his arms around her and held her close for what seemed a very long time. And then, slowly and tenderly, he began to kiss her, her eyes, the tip of her nose, the top of her head and finally her soft lips.

The kiss was deep and lingering, yet there was compassion in it and a depth of feeling that told of the months of pain they had both had to endure.

When he finally released her he spoke softly. 'Frances, have you any idea how much I love you? For as long as I can remember I have loved you. I was still at school when I promised myself that one day I would buck up enough courage to ask you to marry me.' He held her at arm's length. 'Seems today is the day that I've found that courage. I want to spend the rest of my life with you, if you'll have me. Please, Frances, will you be my wife?'

Frances pushed his arms out of the way and flung herself at him. Clinging to him she murmured, 'Oh Alan, I don't deserve you. How could I have been so daft as to not realise a long time ago that I love you. But how can I marry you? I did everything wrong and I have Olivia to think about now.'

'Shall I tell you a secret?' he whispered.

Frances nodded her head.

'Well, when I was holding Olivia I asked her if she would be my daughter. I promised I would love her dearly and take care of her for as long as I live, and I also promised her that I would do the same for her mummy, if she would let me.'

Although tears were trickling down Frances's cheeks, she managed to smile and ask, 'What did she say?'

'Well, she didn't keep me waiting like you are. She said yes, straight away, and she called me Daddy.'

'You're mad. You know that, don't you?'

'I don't think I've quite got to that stage yet,' Alan said solemnly. 'But if you don't give me an answer soon, I really will get mad and that won't be a pretty sight for our young daughter to witness. So for the second time of asking, Frances, please, will you marry me?'

'Yes, yes please, Alan. I would very much like to become your wife. Especially as you say Olivia has agreed that you may be her daddy.'

'She not only agreed; she said it was what she wanted.'

'Oh, you daft so-and-so, I do love you.'

'Well, that suits me fine. Don't ever change your mind, will you, Frances?'

'Most certainly not,' she said with conviction.

He went straight to where the baby was lying and, on his knees again, told Olivia that everything was going to be fine.

Frances just stood stock still and listened.

He was the same old Alan, steady and reliable. It was she that was different. She had learned her lesson and she appreciated what she now had more than words could say. She was deeply in love with Alan Yates. It had started off with needing to renew their friendship. Being grateful for his understanding. Now she knew that talk was cheap. Actions speak louder than any words.

337

And she was quite sure Alan was the only man she wanted.

And what about Olivia?

It seemed she had already made her choice of who was going to be her father.

There wasn't an evening that Alan didn't come out to Tolworth straight from work. This fact not only pleased Alex and Vicky more than words could say, it gave them a great sense of relief, because since Alan was back in Frances's life she was a changed girl.

One morning, whilst having a quiet cup of coffee together, her mother had taken the opportunity to tell her, 'It's up to you what you decide to do. But don't rush into anything. Remember, this is your home, yours and the baby's, for as long as you want.'

It was Monday morning, and Alan arrived at the house at nine thirty.

'Gentleman of leisure now, are you?' Frances teased.

'I have today off for a very special purpose which only occurred to me yesterday though I wouldn't mind betting that it's been worrying you sick. So today we are going to settle the matter.'

Frances wasn't the least bit surprised when Alan added, 'We're going in to Kingston to register Olivia's birth.'

He was quite right. She had been worrying, because it had to be done, but what was she going to put on the certificate? She knew Alan did love Olivia and meant what he said about taking care of her, but this business about registering the birth was a delicate issue.

Alan held the baby while Frances settled herself into the back seat of his car. Then he placed Olivia into her arms and set the bag which held all the paraphernalia necessary for the baby's needs down on the floor by her feet.

Kingston was teeming with people for it was market day. It took a quarter of an hour before Alan was able to find a parking space that was anywhere near the register office. There were at least six other people sitting in a line. 'Take a seat, you'll be seen in turn,' smiled a lady clerk as she hurried by.

As each person rose and went to the counter, behind which two male clerks were working, the waiting queue moved up a seat, and Alan laughed and whispered to Frances that it was like playing musical chairs.

Now it was their turn. Together they went forward and Frances gave the baby to Alan to hold. 'I'd like to register the birth of my daughter, please.'

'Fill out this form,' grunted the older of the clerks, thrusting a document at her. 'You can use that writing table over there,' he said, pointing with the end of his pen. 'Then when you've completed it, bring it straight to the desk, no need to queue again.'

Olivia had started to cry, and Alan was slowly walking up and down, rocking her gently to and fro. Frances watched for a minute. He was looking at Olivia with such tenderness that she felt she should be pleased, but as she sat down at the table and picked up a pen, her heart was aching. She did her best to fill in every line on the form, but her writing was terrible, her hand was trembling so much. Then she came to the space where it said, 'Enter the father's name.'

She couldn't take the liberty. It would be presuming too much. Oh dear God, what should she do?

She felt rather than saw Alan come up behind her. His head leaned over her shoulder and he quickly read what she had written. He took a step backwards and told Frances to stand up, and as she did so he passed the baby to her and sat down.

He started to read from the top of the form, and when he came to the space requiring the father's name, he wrote without any hesitation, 'Alan Frederick Yates'.

Together they went back to the desk, and it was Alan who

handed the clerk the form, which he quickly scanned. 'Bit late registering this child, aren't you?' he grumbled.

'Better late than never,' Alan quipped. 'Registered for life now, isn't she?'

Later they sat at a table in the market café with a steaming hot cup of coffee in front of each of them. Frances was nursing Olivia, giving her a drink from a half-size bottle that contained boiled water. Alan had his arm across Frances's shoulder, and suddenly he started to kiss her cheek.

'Stop it, you dopey thing,' she whispered. 'People are looking at us.'

And they were. But Alan didn't care.

'Are you happy, Frances?' he asked, encircling both her and the baby in his arms.

'I never thought I'd be this happy again,' she said.

He kissed her again, and everyone in the café could tell just by looking at him how much he adored her. One woman was so moved by the sight of this young couple with their new baby that she clapped her hands, and soon every customer in the shop had joined in.

For a moment Frances was embarrassed, as good wishes were called from all corners of the café, and even from the proprietor who stood behind the counter.

Then Alan began to laugh, and she laughed with him.

Chapter Fourteen

IT WAS A TRULY beautiful Sunday afternoon in August. There had been no roast dinner today. It was far too hot. Instead a full-scale picnic in the long garden, with everyone bringing a contribution.

Patsy was sitting in a deckchair, watching her grown-up children and their children larking about. She felt so happy and relieved as her eyes roamed over the happy scene.

She turned her attention to where a huge blanket had been spread just a few yards from her feet. Eddie was sitting facing her, and with him were Frances and Alan. The three of them formed a semicircle with baby Olivia in the centre, lying on a long pillow.

Frances was a different girl now, carefree again, and her eyes, which for so long had shown how sad and troubled she had been, now sparkled with laughter. There was a new tranquillity in her face, and as always when she had Olivia with her her manner was gentle and loving.

Eddie had been making funny noises and shaking a rattle at Olivia, thrilled to bits when she smiled and gurgled at him. Suddenly he stopped playing and crouched over her, looking into her now solemn little face, regarding her intently.

'We're fixing up a date for your mummy and daddy to be married. Won't that be lovely?' His voice was quiet but determined.

Patsy hadn't heard exactly what he had said, but when he raised his head, looked directly at her and gave her a thumbs-up sign, she could have made a jolly good guess. That subject had been the main topic of conversation every time she spoke to Vicky or Alex.

Her heart was bursting with love. She could hear Ollie saying, 'See, I told you, out of bad *does* come good.'

Oh, that baby was such a darling. If only Florrie was here to see her. She'd be saying, 'It's history repeating itself all over again.' And that would be true. At least in some ways.

Olivia's eyes *were* green, and already her hair had a burnished gold look to it. Thank God she looked every inch an Owen. Not that Alan would have let on that he minded if she had looked different, but he was as pleased as Punch when folk stopped to look in the pram and remarked how like her mother the baby looked.

Coming up behind her, Ellen said, 'Daydreaming, Mum?'

'No, darling, just thanking God for the way things have turned out for Frances and Alan. And for all my loving family,' she added thoughtfully.

After planting a kiss on her mother's cheek, Ellen said, 'The men have rigged up that old tennis net. They've found some bats in the sheds and a bag of tennis balls and they're going barmy down there. I'm going to drag Emma into the kitchen with me. Time we all had a cup of tea, and some of the youngsters might prefer a cool drink.'

Youngsters? Patsy queried to herself as she watched Ellen go into the house. There were only two of them now, young Mary and baby Olivia. Even Emma must be getting old, because she still regarded her three boys as being young.

Well what does that make me? Patsy grinned to herself. She would be glad when Frances and Alan were legally married and the baby christened. They had to find somewhere to live first, though. Alan was still living with his parents and Frances was still at home in Tolworth with the baby.

Patsy knew she was a terrible worrier. She wanted so much for each member of her family. Always felt she was not able to shelve problems. They had to be tackled there and then, not put off till tomorrow. Still, life was good. They'd put the last nine months behind them and she'd no complaints at the moment.

Her grandchildren were all doing well. James worked in the family business, though only one of Emma and Donald's boys had elected to do the same. That was Edward Junior. Named after his grandfather, they were as alike as two peas in a pod. Thomas and Sam both worked for Donald, and very prosperous they all seemed to be.

Only Tim still worried her a little.

She supposed that once they got Frances and Alan married it wouldn't be too long before the family had a spate of weddings. James and Sybina would be the first. Even young Sam liked the girls, so he wouldn't be far behind. But not Tim. She somehow couldn't be sure about him. He didn't appear to be lonely, though there was a time when he'd talked about a young lady named Peggy. Most likely nothing ever came of it, because they'd never got to meet her.

He did seem a whole lot more settled now that his mother and father were happily back together. He still lived in what had been Ollie's house in Strathmore Street and it had been agreed by the family that the deeds of that house should be changed into Tim's name so that he owned it outright.

He could easily sell that property and buy something a whole lot more modern, were Patsy's thoughts on the matter.

Eddie's reply to that proposition was, 'Why would he want to move when most of his time is spent in Navy Street where he has a gran who spoils him rotten?'

343

Eddie had also set her thinking. He had stared at her for a few seconds before saying, 'If Tim does get married, you realise you'll be stuck with only me to cook for in this great big house.' He had put this to her one evening when they had been in on their own.

'Are you suggesting we move to a smaller house?' she'd cried out in alarm.

His answer hadn't helped.

'Would that be so terrible, Patsy? There is always so much work to be done here, and you spend hours cleaning, besides insisting that you still come into the office some days. Besides, we'd rattle around in all these rooms like two peas in a colander.'

Patsy's voice was loud and unusually aggressive now.

'And what about weekends? Where would the family gather if you shove us into a modern two-bedroomed place? You'll be telling me next I can't manage stairs and we'd be better off 'aving an old folk's bungalow.'

By the time Patsy had finished stating her case, Eddie had wished he had never brought the subject up.

Ellen came to the kitchen door and shouted for Peter to bring some folding tables up from the shed.

Patsy didn't move. She sat back for once and watched as everyone else pitched in, and soon a lovely spread was laid out. Emma came down the garden carrying a tea-tray which held two family-sized teapots and two jugs of hot water.

'Tom, you can go indoors and fetch the cups, saucers and plates,' Emma said to her middle son, but as she turned and noticed that Sam was smirking at his brother, she quickly told him, 'And you, clever clogs, can go with him and fetch the milk and jugs of lemonade.'

Patsy laughed to herself. Emma sometimes still spoke to her lads as if they were ten years old.

The years had slipped by so quickly. They weren't children

344

any more but fine-looking, intelligent young men with a quick wit and inbred charm.

She thought the world of all her children and grandchildren. Yet it was her twin girls that intrigued her the most. She would sometimes look at the pair of them and catch her breath, seeing such a striking resemblance to her own mother in each of them. She had only been thirteen years old when her mother had died, but her memory of her had never faded.

Both Ellen and Emma were real beauties, willowy, graceful, their lovely faces surrounded by the same thick head of hair as Patsy's own. But above all they were sweet-natured. Kindness and caring came naturally to them, for which Patsy was more than grateful. Thinking back to her own childhood had Patsy sending up a prayer that hopefully the nightmare that Frances had suffered was over, and her life would now take a turn for the better and she would be able to experience a great deal of happiness in her future life with Alan.

The Ace Trading Company had continued to grow. They now owned three hotels and the rest home, besides a fleet of coaches and the cottage in Cornwall. By following Eddie and Ollie's shrewd instincts and listening to Peter Crawford's advice, they had sold off most of the company's foreign interests and invested the money wisely.

Within reason there was nothing that she and Eddie or any of their children were unable to have. Despite all the hard work her boys and their wives put into these business enterprises, they all seemed perfectly happy.

Patsy's main interest was still the family. The very thought that the family might break up, or the social gatherings cease, sent cold shivers down her spine. Each and every member of her large family she loved dearly, and their interests would continue to obsess her as they always had.

She shook herself as Ellen handed her a cup of tea, telling

herself to stop looking back and look to the future.

They were tucking into the sandwiches and cakes, the men sprawling out on the grass, when a head appeared over the back gate and a gruff voice called out, 'Would we be intruding if we come in?'

Both Eddie and Alan jumped to their feet, but it was Eddie who moved the fastest. He unbolted the gate, swung it open and said, 'Mr an' Mrs Yates, come on in, you're more than welcome.'

'You're sure now?' Alice Yates looked across at Patsy, who was already on her feet and coming across the grass to meet them.

'Sure? We're absolutely delighted. Come an' have something to eat. I don't think this lot have scoffed everything yet and Emma will soon make a fresh pot of tea.'

Everybody was shaking hands, and a few introductions were necessary because not all of the in-laws had met Alan's parents before.

'I'm Fred and this is me wife Alice,' Fred stated in no uncertain terms. 'We don't want no more of this Mr an' Mrs lark. We've 'eard nothing else for days from our Alan except how beautiful this baby is, an' what with Alice nagging on about when was she gonna get t' see her, I took the liberty . . .'

Eddie cut him off short. 'No liberty, Fred. None at all. We should have thought of asking you, we would have as soon as the date for the christening is settled, but you turning up today is a godsend, gives us all a chance to get to know each other.'

Alice was already seated in a deckchair next to Patsy. Frances shyly came towards them and timidly held out the baby to Alan's mother, saying, 'Would you like to hold her?'

'Would I?' Alice exclaimed in delight. 'Makes a change from so many lads.'

She peered at the baby in wonderment and rocked her

back and forth. Olivia gurgled and kicked her bare legs. 'Oh, she's so sweet, a real little cherub.'

After a few minutes Frances said, 'Shall I lay her down, Alice, while you have some tea?'

'Not before I let my Fred 'ave a look at her. You don't mind, d'yer?'

Both Patsy and Frances were amused. Fred Yates was such a big, burly man; what would he want to be looking at babies for?

But Fred not only looked at the baby, he stroked her cheek with his forefinger and beamed, saying, 'My goodness, Alan wasn't wrong, you really are gorgeous.'

Alan stood beside his father. 'You are staying, aren't you, Dad?'

'Course I am, son. 'Ave yer ever known me refuse a cuppa tea?' He settled himself on the grass opposite Eddie and took the big mug that Alex was holding out to him.

'Better than one of my mother's dainty cups, eh, Fred?'

'You're a lad after me own heart.' Fred grinned as he took hold of the steaming mug of tea.

Alice had already drained her cup and eaten a slice of fruit cake when she picked up a big bag which she'd set down by her feet. Taking out some parcels, she gave them to Alan to pass to Frances.

'It's just a couple more things that my mum and me 'ave made, but the soft toy is from our Joe.'

Frances smiled. 'Oh, Mrs Yates . . .' Then, remembering what Fred had said, she quickly changed it to, 'Oh, Alice, you're too generous. You've already given me so much.'

'It's nothing, luv, gives me an' me mum something t' do. Besides, I 'aven't seen my Alan so happy in a month of Sundays. You're a good girl and that's a sweet baby you've got, an' I pray t' God that from now on things will go smoothly for the pair of you.'

She wanted to add that her son had told her that he and

Frances were to be married, but she didn't want to speak out of turn. He had also told both her and Fred that he had been named on the baby's birth certificate as the father of the child. Neither of them had made any comment at the time, and for once in her life Alice had kept her own counsel ever since.

That's not to say that she hadn't prayed that he had done the right thing.

'Come on, Frances, open the parcels,' Alan urged. 'Here, start with this one.'

He handed her the largest packet. Frances sat down on the grass beside him and unwrapped it.

'Oh, Alan, isn't this lovely?' she exclaimed, lifting out a soft white teddy bear that had a wee baby teddy clutched between his paws.

Alice grinned. 'Joe said he hoped you'd like it.'

'Oh, I do, and so will Olivia as soon as she's big enough to appreciate it. I will thank him myself as soon as I see him.'

Alan was grinning like a Cheshire cat at the thought of his brother buying a teddy bear.

'Unwrap these two now, they're bound together so I guess that's what you're meant to do.'

Having carefully taken the paper off, Frances lifted out a knitted coat of the palest pink trimmed with mother-of-pearl buttons, followed by a bonnet and a pair of booties to match.

'They're from me mum,' Alice said. 'She's made them a bit big because by the time the winter comes the baby will have grown.'

'How thoughtful.' Frances was really pleased, and it showed. 'They are perfect. I don't know what to say, Alice.'

'Unwrap this one. It's the last,' Alan said.

Frances couldn't believe her eyes. It was a shawl. Not white and not wool; in fact, the only word that came to

Frances's mind was gossamer, because it was like a flimsy cobweb and the shade was a paler pink even than that of the coat and bonnet. She was touched by such kindness from Alan's family, and for a moment was too full of emotion to find any words that would show her true feelings.

Alice was so pleased that Frances liked their gifts.

'I know me mum already sent you a shawl, but that was a heavy warm one, do for the winter. I thought this would look so sweet for when she is christened. Light as a feather, isn't it? And before you ask, no, I didn't make it. I'm not that clever. Actually, it was Fred that bought it.'

Fred looked very uneasy. 'That's not strictly true,' he piped up. 'Alice went shopping and she saw it. I merely gave her the money.'

'Oh, Alice and Fred, thank you so much. We'll make sure we have a photo taken of you both holding Olivia in the shawl at her christening.'

'As long as yer like it, luv,' Fred said, 'it's our pleasure. Believe me it is.'

The christening was grand.

First Emma and then Ellen had cradled Olivia in their arms, for they were both godmothers. Her godfather had been thoughtfully chosen. Joe Yates had been bursting with pride when his brother had asked him, and had willingly agreed.

The vicar was now holding the baby.

'This baptism is taking place in the spirit of love, for God's own son Jesus said, Suffer little children to come unto me and forbid them not.'

The vicar turned his head to look at Frances, asking, 'The child will be named?'

And voicing her wishes aloud, Frances murmured, 'Ollie and Florrie,' for it was these two dear people who were filling her mind this day.

The vicar was staring at her and she quickly corrected herself: 'Olivia Florence Yates.'

He dipped his fingers into the font, and trickled the holy water over Olivia's head. 'I christen thee Olivia Florence Yates, in the name of God the Father, the Son and the Holy Ghost.' He dabbed at the water on Olivia's brow with a cloth, and as she started to cry he made the sign of the cross on her forehead.

When Frances had her safely back, she soothed her gently. 'Don't cry, pet, please, smile for Mummy,' she was murmuring as she cradled her in her arms.

Alan placed his arm across Frances's shoulders, bent his head and kissed the baby. Then he stared into Frances's face, smiled and kissed her too.

'Do you feel happier now that she is christened?'

'Yes, I do. Thank you, Alan.'

He looked at her and his face seemed very serious, and his words were even more so.

'All we need to do now is make sure your mother's surname is the same as ours, eh, Olivia?' His voice was soft and caring, and Frances knew just how sincere he was.

As if on cue, Olivia stopped crying and smiled.

The whole Owen family were there, and the Yateses too. The baby looked absolutely adorable in her long white lace-trimmed christening robe, with the soft pink gossamer shawl resting lightly round her tiny shoulders.

True to her word, Frances made sure that her father made a point of taking at least two photos of Alice and Fred holding the baby with her special shawl well on display.

Fred Yates was enjoying himself, and he was pleased that his missus was so proud of their Alan and this dear little baby. And the Owens seemed a real nice family, no side to them, just straight talkers. The type of people he could get on with.

All the same, he had his doubts.

True, his son was named on the birth certificate as being the father of this baby. But that didn't make it so.

Frances was a real nice girl. And no one was more sorry than he was that she'd gone off the rails for a time. It wasn't even a matter of whether or not his son loved her. He had not the slightest doubt on that score. He was convinced that he adored her. But what about in years to come?

Someone, some time, was bound to tell the child the truth, that her real father had been murdered.

Then what?

He had no answers to that question.

Chapter Fifteen

PATSY WAS WORRIED. OLIVIA was now four months old and nothing more had been said about Frances and Alan getting married. At least not to her it hadn't!

The funny thing was that both James and Tim had come out with an item of news that had made everyone sit up and take notice.

'Sybina and I are getting married next Easter, but we're moving into a house we've bought next week,' James said casually.

It was a Monday afternoon, and Patsy and Vicky had been working all day in the office at Stockwell. At four o'clock, as they were thinking about packing up for the day, James had come in with his grandfather. When he'd imparted his news, Patsy didn't dare look at his mother's face. Instead she looked at Eddie, and they both raised their eyebrows.

These young people of today, Patsy was thinking. They were quite relaxed about living openly together until it suited them. All those years ago, when Eddie had changed her surname to his, she had lived in terror that folk would find out that they were not legally married. They had even contemplated leaving all their loved ones behind and emigrating to Australia, where no one would know her history.

Things were certainly very different today.

It was Vicky who recovered first. 'Where's this house you've bought, then?'

Eddie didn't wait for James to reply. Ever the sensible one, he came straight out with his question. 'Have you bought this property in your own name?'

'No, Grandad. Sybina put up half the deposit and we're buying it in our joint names, and to answer your question, Mum, the house is at Shannon Corner, not too far from Tolworth, so you and Dad will be able to pop in for tea.'

Vicky wasn't sure if she wanted to laugh or cry. She looked at him, her face serious.

'Have you told your father yet?'

'No, I haven't had a chance. We only exchanged contracts on Friday. Would you like to tell him for me?'

James took one look at his mother's face and took a step back.

'Only joking, Mum. Honest. I thought I'd bring Sybina round at the weekend.'

Patsy was sitting quietly at her desk, but she was well aware of what Vicky must be feeling. It was Alan and Frances who should be looking for somewhere to live and thinking about setting a date for their wedding. She hoped to God that one or even both of them had not suddenly got pre-wedding nerves.

That very same evening Patsy's jaw had dropped when Tim had said he would like his grandparents to take a look at the house in Strathmore Street and give their opinion as to whether he should sell it and buy something a bit more up to date, or spend money and modernise the place.

'Why the sudden decision?' Eddie had asked.

''Cos I'm thinking about getting married,' had been his quick reply.

353

For the rest of the week Patsy had kept saying to herself, there must be something in the water. Three weddings coming off!

Well, she hoped it was going to be three.

Saturday afternoon, and for once Patsy was not sorry that it was going to be a quiet weekend. Eddie and Alex were in the front room, watching the football on the television. Vicky, Frances and she were in the big living room drinking the inevitable cup of tea.

Suddenly it was as if the house had been taken by storm.

Everyone seemed to arrive at the same time, though none of them had been expected. David and Tim went straight into the TV room and were soon joined by Donald, Edward Junior, Thomas and Sam. Valerie and Emma made for the living room and the teapot. Peter, Ellen and Mary were the last to arrive. Peter took one look at the room full of women and beat a hasty retreat to join the men. Mary gave a squeal of delight at seeing all of her aunts together and the fact that her aunt Vicky was nursing baby Olivia.

Of course the conversation was about weddings.

Valerie turned to her mother-in-law. 'Has Tim spoken to you about the house?'

'Yes, luv, he asked if me and Eddie would look it over, but Eddie is so busy. I thought I might go down to Tooting on Monday morning.'

'Would you mind if I came with you?'

'Course not. I'd rather have yer company than go on my own. Years since I set foot in that house.'

'Well, Patsy, I can tell yer now, my Tim won't 'ave done much to the place. Figures and bookwork and he's as happy as Larry, but decorating and such like, no, not him.'

'All the more reason to go together. I'll meet you at the Broadway underground station at ten o'clock. That suit you?'

354

With that settled, the room went quiet and everyone's attention was on the baby. Vicky was still nursing her, but Frances had given her half a Farley's rusk and it was quite funny to watch what she was doing with it.

Patsy was wondering if she dared ask Frances when she and Alan planned to get married when she found herself listening to Frances saying, 'Listen, everyone, I hope you'll all be free to come to my wedding.'

Her mother looked up from wiping the baby's face and asked, 'And when will that be?'

Frances's face was radiant and her eyes sparkled.

'The weekend after next, Mummy, if that's all right with you.'

Everyone was hugging her so hard that Frances winced.

'And where is this wedding going to take place? You've not given any of us much time to arrange things, have you?'

'I didn't want a lot of fuss. Just a quiet ceremony at the registry office.'

The silence that followed Frances's statement was such that you could have heard a pin drop. She looked at her mother's face, then her grandma's, and finally she gazed around at her aunts. Disappointment, even shock, was apparent on all of them.

Frances smiled to herself and took her time before saying, 'But Alan had other ideas.'

Vicky felt that at any moment she might slap her daughter. Why the hell was she being so unreasonable?

'So, are you going to let us in on this big secret?' She was beginning to sound angry.

Frances decided she had provoked them all far enough.

'All right, I'll get to the point. Alan said point blank that he wanted us to have nothing less than a church wedding. Said he wanted to show me off. Do things properly.'

Both her mother and her grandmother heaved a mighty

sigh of relief. Not to mention her aunts, who were all smiling broadly.

Monday morning, and Valerie was waiting as Patsy crossed the main road. Five minutes later and they were walking down Selkirk Road.

Nothing much had changed here, still the fish and chip shop on the right-hand side of the road and the pie and eel shop on the left.

'Oh, how I used to love a penny basin.' Patsy grinned, looking into Harringtons and seeing the same marble-topped tables.

'What on earth did you get for a penny?' Valerie asked in disbelief.

'A bowl full of parsley sauce, or green gravy as we kids used to call it, and a great big dollop of mashed potatoes. Plenty of chilli vinegar an' pepper an' salt and it were a feast fit for a king.'

Valerie wrinkled her nose in disgust, but all the same she was laughing. Patsy Owen, company director, eating a penny basin!

Then they were walking down Strathmore Street and Patsy's heart was pumping nineteen to the dozen. God, how the memories came surging back.

Much had altered here, from the look of the front gardens, and even more so the front doorsteps. The tenants, or maybe the owners now, of these old houses must have a different sense of pride. Or more than likely a different set of values.

As she passed number 22 everything became blurred. The tears stinging the backs of her eyes were really painful. This had been the house that Florrie had rented. The upstairs rooms where she herself had been born and had lived with her mother for nearly fourteen years. And with Florrie for a good few years after that.

The lump in her throat was threatening to choke her.

356

Even in those days this street had been narrow, with back-to-back houses almost pressing against each other, but folk had done their best, kept the windows clean and the lace curtains crisp and white. Now most of the low fences had been knocked down, the gardens concreted over, and cars were parked in front of several windows.

In minutes they were outside Tim's house. Oh, the happy times Patsy, her mother and Florrie had spent in this front room with Ollie.

She wouldn't cry. She wouldn't let herself cry.

Life had moved on for her and she had so much to be thankful for. All the same, her insides were turning over. It was a funny feeling.

The front door always used to be on the latch, or at least a key dangled on a length of string and one only had to pull it through the letter box.

Not so today.

Patsy passed the key that Tim had given her to Valerie, and it was she who turned it in the lock and opened the front door. Immediately another load of memories flooded Patsy's mind.

She had to force herself to take that first step over the threshold. Pity she hadn't given more thought as to how she would feel. At this moment it felt as if she were stepping back into a time which was long gone.

They had only looked at the ground floor so far and already Patsy was aware that this house had seen better times. Going into the kitchen, where Tim had a load of papers set out quite tidily in different piles on the same old wooden-topped table that had served Ollie for years, she wasn't at all sure she had done the right thing in coming here.

Valerie was already filling the kettle. 'I'll make us a cup of tea. From the look of the dresser Tim has some decent china. I suppose that's one thing in his favour.'

As Valerie set out the cups and saucers, Patsy stood feeling awkward and looking anxious. The kettle boiled and Valerie made the tea.

'At least he's got a fridge,' she said, taking out a milk bottle and sniffing the contents. 'Smells pretty fresh.'

While the tea was brewing, Val found a tray and, placing everything on it, led the way back into the sitting room. Ollie's old settee still stood beneath the window, but there were two fairly new armchairs placed one each side of the tiled fireplace.

'Might as well sit ourselves down.' Valerie waited for Patsy to make herself comfortable, then settled herself in the other chair. There wasn't any other furniture in the room, just a nest of tables with a radio on top.

Patsy sat sipping her tea, quiet and sad, remembering so much and yet wanting to forget. She didn't speak.

She shouldn't have come.

Reading her mother-in-law's thoughts, Valerie said, 'You don't want to bother to go upstairs. When I've drunk my tea I'll pop up an' have a quick shufty. This place is not as bad as I thought it might be. At least my Tim keeps it reasonably clean, but he certainly hasn't spent much money on the property. I'll come back another day and give the whole house a good going-over. I should have offered before now but I haven't liked to interfere. My Tim's made a good life for himself and that's down to you and your family. I can't take any of the credit.'

Patsy smiled at her. 'Valerie, my luv, don't be so 'ard on yerself. None of us get through this life without blotting our copybook at some time or another. And I've wanted t' say this to you for ages. Both me and Eddie were thrilled when you and our David got back together again. Look at yer now. You're dead smart. Yer hair is cut in the latest fashion and you're a damn good wife. I only hope you don't think that it's me what has encouraged Tim to live away from home.'

358

'Course not, Patsy. There was a time when I would 'ave given the world to have him back under our roof, but not now. He's a grown man, he pleases himself *and* he knows where he's best off.'

Patsy nodded. 'You're saying the same as Eddie, that I spoil him, ain't you?'

'A bit of spoiling never hurt no one. And my Tim doesn't get singled out. You spoil everyone in the family, young and old.'

Patsy nodded in agreement. She and Eddie did spoil their children and their grandchildren, and so had Florrie and Ollie, yet they had all turned out well. They lived good lives, worked hard, surrounded by nice kind people, and most of all she hoped they were happy.

'Like you say, Val, there's no need for me to go upstairs. You go up on your own, then we can get off.'

It wasn't long before Valerie came back down the stairs. She had gathered up a few old newspapers, but as she said to Patsy, 'For a fellow living on his own, the place is not too bad at all.'

Patsy stood up abruptly. 'So what are you going to recommend that Tim does with this house?'

His mother grinned. 'I haven't a clue. All I do know is if he meant what he said, he'd better start shifting himself, 'cos there's no way he could bring a new bride home to live in this house. Not the state it's in.'

Patsy had to bite her tongue. She knew things had altered. Today young people getting married handed out lists requesting some very expensive items they would like as wedding gifts. Val had just said that Tim couldn't bring a bride to live in this house, yet to Patsy and her mum, Ollie's house had always seemed to be a palace. Warm and comfortable, with an inside lavatory.

Keep yer thoughts t' yerself, she chided herself, because she didn't want to cause a scene by telling Valerie that she thought Tim was very lucky to have been given this house outright. She could hear Florrie saying, 'Think what yer like, gal, but keep yer lip buttoned.' So she managed a smile and said gaily, 'Let's be off. Think I'll stay out of it, leave the men to give Tim their advice.'

She watched Valerie tug the front door to close it and then pass the front door key over to her.

'I think Tim should sell up and buy somewhere in a better neighbourhood. But in the end I suppose the decision will have to come from him.' Val's voice was hard; she sounded as if she meant it.

Patsy swallowed down what she would have liked to say.

On the doorstep she brushed a tear away from her eye and looked back at the front room window, and to herself she said, You've been a happy house, and nobody ever had a better friend than you, Ollie.

I won't forget.

Not ever.

Chapter Sixteen

DESPITE FRANCES'S WISH TO have a quiet wedding, Alan was adamant that they should be married in church. He made it clear that he wanted everyone to know that from the moment the ceremony was over Frances would be his wife until death did them part.

All the female members of the family were absolutely thrilled. They backed Alan all the way. After all, this was the first wedding of a grandchild that the family had experienced. If it were to be a white wedding with all the trimmings, then no expense should be spared, was the unanimous vote.

All the same, talk about a rushed job. Other families took months arranging all the details. Not the Owens.

What was accomplished in that short time was unbelievable. However, there were enough of them to pitch in, and every aunt chose a job for herself and carried it through as if her very life depended on it. Not that a few tempers didn't get frayed along the way, or women didn't get edgy, but somehow it all came together very nicely in the end.

★ ★ ★

The great day had arrived.

Much to Mary's delight, Ellen and Peter had taken baby Olivia home with them the night before the wedding.

'That's as it should be,' her grandmother had declared. 'It's your day, Frances, you spend the early hours getting yourself ready and then it will be a day that you remember for the rest of your life.'

How could Frances argue with that? To tell the truth, she didn't want to. Much as she loved Olivia, she couldn't have wished for two more caring people than Aunt Ellen and Uncle Peter to take her baby for the night.

It was the bride's mother who was the most nervous. Vicky got herself into a right old stew. The flowers hadn't arrived. What time were the cars due? Was the hairdresser coming to the house to do Frances's hair? What about her own hair?

Also, much as she tried to prevent it, her mind would keep wandering back over the past year. How ill Frances had been. How they'd learned that their daughter was pregnant. Alan had been like a knight in shining armour riding to their little girl's rescue. But he wasn't really like that. He was an ordinary young man who had worked hard to get himself a decent job. That he loved Frances dearly there wasn't a shadow of a doubt.

But would it all work out? Or could there come a day when he'd feel sorry that he'd taken on another man's child?

Vicky was surprised that Alan's parents hadn't protested when he'd told them he was going to marry Frances and take and bring her baby daughter up as his own. They were good people, Alice and Fred Yates. Frances was very lucky to have such decent folk as her in-laws. But she was sure that there must be times when they questioned as to whether or not their son was doing the right thing.

All right, Luke Somerford was dead, and his so-called

friend was in prison for what he had done to Frances.

The very thought of Mark Philipson and she felt herself start to sweat.

Only once after coming home from hospital had Frances broken down and told her mother some of the gory details of what had happened that night. She had begun by saying, 'Mum, Luke was so drunk that night there was no way I was going to let him drive me home. When Mark made his offer I thought how kind he was and that I would be safe with him. Honestly, I had no idea that he too had had so much to drink. It was only when he drove towards the common instead of making for the Kingston bypass that I began to feel a sense of panic.'

She had been unable to continue until she had taken several deep breaths.

'Mark stopped the car and I knew then that I was in trouble. I pleaded for him to take me to Gran and Grandad's; we were so near their house, and yet so far. He just laughed, pulled me into his arms, and brought his mouth down on mine so hard it hurt. I struggled with him, but his grip was so firm. I bit him, scratched him, but he was so much stronger than me. There wasn't enough room in the car to move away from him. He tore my dress, ripped my tights. It was when I started to scream that he punched me in the face. I remember that he got out of the car and came round to the passenger side, and as he opened the car door I shot my foot out and kicked him hard right in his crotch. I couldn't move, couldn't run away, because he was doubled up in pain and I couldn't get past him to get out of the car. I remember we struggled and he started to hit me, but after that nothing. Not until I woke up in hospital.'

Vicky's heart was aching as she took her daughter into her arms, soothing her as best she could.

'You won't tell Daddy that I've told you all this, will you?' Frances had pleaded, and her tear-stained face was something that Vicky thought she would never be able to erase from her mind.

If only Frances hadn't been attracted to London night life; if only she hadn't met Luke Somerford, hadn't accepted a lift home with Mark. How different it would all have been. Yes, hindsight was a marvellous thing.

That subject had never been mentioned from that day to this.

For Christ's sake stop it! Vicky said to herself now. She was so worked up and it was showing.

Alex came into their bedroom and took one look at his wife, who was sitting on the edge of the bed, holding her head between her hands. Then he turned on his heel and went downstairs. Five minutes later he was back, holding two glasses in one hand and a bottle of brandy in the other.

Vicky hadn't moved. He sat down beside her and poured a generous amount of brandy into each glass. When Vicky took the glass he was offering her, he put his free arm around her shoulders.

'Been a rough year, hasn't it, love? What with one thing and another. But today is a fresh beginning for our only daughter, and you and I both know she's found a good bloke in Alan, so let's drink to them, calm our nerves and get ready to go to their wedding.'

Vicky looked up adoringly at her husband. All these years, the Owens had been there for her. To have had Alex as her husband and James and Frances as their son and daughter was like a dream come true. She sipped her drink and began to feel much calmer.

'Here's to Frances, Alan and Olivia,' Alex said, touching glasses. They drank and then he added, 'Here's hoping that they will be as happy over the years to come as you and I have been.'

She put her glass down on the bedside table and he did the same. Their arms went around each other and silently they sat hugging tightly, until at last Alex said, 'Come on, we've a wedding to go to.'

Alex watched his daughter come slowly down the stairs, and his breath caught in his throat.

His little girl was a beautiful woman. Her shining chestnut hair was coiled up at the back of her head with tiny white flowers intertwined, and she wore tiny sparkling earrings. Her dress had been made along the lines of the antique dress she had worn for the charity fashion show: a creamy-coloured silk underslip with flimsy material over the top; high stand-up neckline, padded shoulders, wide sleeves with long fitted cuffs that had a row of pearl buttons reaching halfway up to her elbows. It was nipped in tightly at the waist, and the full skirt fell in straight folds down to her satin shoes. The hem of the dress had a band of heavy beaded embroidery to weigh it down. She carried only a small spray of the palest pink roses.

She looked sensational.

'Don't you dare cry,' her father said, holding her hand tightly as the limousine, decked with long white ribbons, took them on their journey to the church.

Grandma Owen stood with Ellen in the stone porch, keeping their eyes on Mary. She was clutching a basket of pink rosebuds as she hopped from one foot to the other, waiting for the bride to arrive. Mary too was wearing a replica of the clothes she had worn on the day of the charity show. Even down to the poke-bonnet, which was trimmed with the same rosebuds as were in her basket.

She looked as pretty as any picture.

Lily and George Burton had both been moved almost to tears as they passed the only bridesmaid, who was blowing them kisses as they made their way into the church. Lily had to wipe her eyes before they took their seats.

'Whoever would 'ave thought that weak, scraggy little baby would 'ave grown so beautiful, bless 'er,' she sighed.

Both she and George felt so grateful that despite the difference in their circumstances, Ellen and Peter had always kept in touch with them, and had taught Mary to regard them as her aunt and uncle.

'The bride has arrived.' The murmur ran round the church as the organist started to play the wedding march.

To Frances, the walk down the aisle on her father's arm felt endless.

In front of the altar stood Alan, with his brother Joe as his best man. They both looked sleek and well groomed, in well-cut dark grey suits and crisp white shirts with grey silk ties.

When the priest finally declared, 'You are now husband and wife,' Frances gave Alan a smile so brilliant that he felt choked, and at that moment he couldn't have said a word to save his life. Instead he took his bride into his arms and kissed her.

It was a long, lingering, tender kiss.

There was a lovely reception at the Spread Eagle pub just outside Epsom, and then Frances and Alan departed for a three-night honeymoon at the old Ship Hotel on Brighton's sea-front. Neither of them wanted to be away from Olivia for too long. Frances's parents had taken on the task of caring for her whilst they were away.

Patsy could hardly believe that so much good had finally come about after the disastrous events of the last year. She hoped with all of her heart that Frances and Alan would be just as happy as Ellen and Peter were. The circumstances of the two couples were somewhat similar. There had been many doubts when Peter had proposed to Ellen, mainly because of Ellen's sad experiences. But look at them now – they were inseparable. If Ellen said she wanted the top brick off the chimney Peter would have got it for her. Although he worked within the family firm he was wealthy in his own right, mainly due to Jack Berry. If and when he did travel he took Ellen with him and she and Mary always accompanied him on his annual trip to Australia. The only one thing Ellen had longed for was a child of their own. It was not to be.

But she took great pride in Mary, and even though she was reluctant to admit it even to herself, she would never mention the word adoption. Mary was their child. Hers and Peters. They loved her dearly, and that love only became stronger with time. By nature Mary was sweet and loving, and because of the affection and attentions showered on her by all of the family she was a self-confident, outgoing little girl, yet she was utterly unspoiled and natural with everyone. If Peter could bring himself to love and cherish a baby which he had not fathered, Patsy just prayed that the same would be the case with Alan.

Chapter Seventeen

ALMOST BEFORE ANY OF the family could catch their breath, a great number of decisions had been made.

To start off their married life Eddie had suggested that Frances and Alan use Ollie's flat at the top of their house in Navy Street, just for the time being. The young couple had been thrilled, and Frances had thrown her arms around her grandad's neck in sheer joy. But that was only the half of it.

James and Sybina had moved into their house at Shannon Corner and the company had agreed to pay a part of the asking price so that only a small mortgage would be required. Tim and Peggy were looking for a suitable property, and when they found a house which they both liked, the company would pay half because Tim had offered to give up his house.

Already Eddie had set up a contract with a reliable firm of builders to modernise Ollie's old house in Stratton Street. No expense was to be spared, and this house, when ready, would be given outright to Frances, Alan and Olivia.

Patsy was over the moon. Ollie's house would come alive again. She would be able to visit. Go into rooms in which she had sat with her own mother and with Florrie and Ollie.

She would hear laughter ringing in that house again.

Alice and Fred Yates were more than pleased. Strathmore Street was only ten minutes' walk from where they lived.

Alan too couldn't have been happier. He was near the tube station and so able to get to work that much quicker, and the Owens had been so generous. He and Frances weren't saddled with a mortgage, and what money they had saved could be used to buy furniture when the time came for them to move in.

Frances wasn't too far from her gran and grandad, and that was a bonus. Also, she knew her gran would always drive her out to Tolworth to see her parents whenever she wanted to. Not that they, and all members of the family, wouldn't be dropping in at Strathmore Street from time to time, Olivia of course being the main attraction.

So one way and another everyone seemed to be happy.

Patsy, Eddie, Alex and David agreed that the company had carried out Ollie's wishes to the letter, and that he would be more than pleased with the results.

Then Donald and Emma decided that as the summer was drawing to a close it was time they hosted a party. 'We'll even have a bonfire if you like,' they whispered to little Mary.

Patsy grinned. 'What you mean, Donald, is that your garden is well overgrown and you're getting us all over there to help clear it.'

'Trust you to suss me out,' he laughed, 'but as usual I'll lay on a big chair for you, Patsy, and you can sit and oversee what everyone is doing and make sure your orders are carried out.'

'Well I'm blowed. Donald, you're a cheeky whelp. I've a good mind to stay away from your party,' Patsy declared huffily.

'Go on with you.' He grinned. 'Wild horses wouldn't keep you away. You do know James is bringing Sybina and Tim is bringing Peggy? You'll have to be thinking about buying new hats again if we get more weddings.'

Although it was the last Saturday in October, the weather was still really great, something Emma was more than grateful for. A few years ago Donald had set his men to building a conservatory on to the back of the house. It was twenty-seven feet long and twelve feet wide, and Emma loved it. It was something she had wanted from the moment they had moved into the house, and it served so many purposes.

Today was no exception. In the conservatory were tables laden with food and extra comfortable chairs for the older adults who didn't want to get roped into what was going on in the garden.

The whole family was there, including Alan's parents, and Ellen and Emma laughed together as they heard Fred Yates's voice above everybody else's, giving out orders. Mary was sitting astride his broad shoulders, both of them lording it over everyone as Mary sang, 'I'm the king of the castle'.

It was five o'clock and things had quietened down, mainly because everyone was eating. At the bottom of the garden the pile of old wood, rotting shrubs and half the contents of two old sheds had grown to huge proportions, and all Mary kept asking was, 'Please, somebody tell me when we are going to light the bonfire.'

The conservatory rang with laughter and friendly but unmerciful banter. Sybina was giving as good as she got. She was a friendly girl, the type that got along with everyone, and a good-looker with it. But then that was to be expected, seeing as how James was a handsome young man. She had acquired a gorgeous sun-tan and her bare arms glistened in her sleeveless dress. She had dark hair, thick and straight as a die, but sleek and smooth, cut so skilfully that it bounced as she moved her head.

Now Peggy was the opposite. Having observed her for

370

the last hour or so, Patsy decided that she was the ideal young lady for Tim. He was not as outgoing as James, and Peggy hadn't so much to say for herself as Sybina had.

Tall and slim, with fair hair and a pale complexion, Peggy would not be one to sit in the sun. However, it was her hands that attracted Patsy's attention. She had smooth skin, and the longest fingers Patsy had ever seen, with lovely nails that were varnished a very pale shell-like colour. All in all she was very charming and ladylike.

For Emma, being the hostess, Peggy had brought a gift of a small floral arrangement. It consisted of only five white roses intertwined with greenery, and stood in a Royal Doulton bone china dish. It was exquisite.

And no wonder.

Patsy later learned from Emma that Peggy worked for a florist in the West End of London and did floral arrangements that were either in the entrance halls or on the reception desks of many of the better-known London hotels.

The talk had turned to housing and was getting noisy.

Edward Junior, Thomas and Sam were determined to have their say. 'After all, we aren't guests, this is our home.' So said young Sam.

Donald was on his feet in a second. He only had to look at his son and say one word: 'Sam!'

Sam's voice was a harsh whisper. 'Well, I am sorry that I was rude, but there are three of us boys and everyone else seems to be getting a property compliments of Great-Grandad while we're left out in the cold.'

Emma looked serious as she walked across to her youngest son and hugged him.

'Listen, Sam, and your grandad will explain.'

Eddie got to his feet. 'The thing is, Sam, you each got the same amount of money. I can understand that you feel you are being left out when it comes to where you want to live.'

371

Sam looked defiant. 'Not only me, what about Edward and Thomas? Seems no one in our family gets a look-in.'

'I'm sorry to hear you talk like that, young Sam. Why couldn't you have come straight to me and we could have talked it through?'

Sam shrugged and carried on staring at the carpet.

Eddie was more upset than he cared to show. These family gatherings had always gone off so well. He didn't want any animosity to spoil today.

'Tell you what, young man, I'll get you a copy of your great-grandad's will and you can take your time and read it very carefully, and then you will realise that when the time comes for all three of you, or indeed any other member of this family, the company funds are there to be used for that particular reason. So far not one of you three boys has shown the slightest inclination to flee the nest, which suggests to me that your mother spoils you all by waiting on you hand and foot.'

Sam loved his gran, and his grandad was his role model. He hadn't meant to upset them. The fact that Grandma hadn't said a word worried him more than if she'd had a go at him.

'All right then, Sam? I won't forget, we'll go through that will together if you like. You'll see you'll be able to buy a property when you decide you've had enough of living at home.'

Sam felt better now that his Grandad had put his arm around his shoulders. He looked up into Eddie's face and grinned.

'OK, I'll start looking tomorrow. I'll have a mansion with a swimming pool and about six acres of land.'

The tension was gone. Everyone laughed.

Fred Yates got to his feet and followed Eddie out into the kitchen.

'Fancy a beer, Fred?' Eddie asked.

'I most certainly do, mate, but that's not why I came out after you. I wanted to say well done. You handled that bloody well. A diplomat, that's what you are. We could do with someone like you in our union.'

They touched glasses and each took a good swallow of his beer.

'We're gonna light the bonfire now, Grandad. Come on or you'll miss it.'

Mary was tugging at his sleeve, and he and Fred each took one of her hands and together they joined the mob that was walking down the garden. Cheer after cheer went up as the fire burnt merrily and Donald brought out his surprise.

Two huge boxes of fireworks.

'But it's not November the fifth,' Patsy complained.

Donald laughed. 'No, it always rains on Guy Fawkes night, so I thought we'd have our show a few weeks early.'

The expression on Mary's face as sparklers were lit, rockets soared up to the sky and fireworks exploded in a shower of coloured stars was a joy to be seen and caused great excitement.

Very late that night, when Eddie climbed into bed beside Patsy, she kissed him and said, 'Good night, my darling.' Then sleepily she added, 'All in all it's not been a bad day.'

'But it's not over yet,' Eddie said, kissing her and drawing her into his arms.

Suddenly Patsy wasn't tired any more. As they began kissing and his hands were gently moving over her body she whispered in his ear, 'Do you realise, my darling, that I am a great-grandmother and you are a great-grandfather?'

Eddie laughed. 'Well, you're not exactly acting like a geriatric.'

'Neither will I. Not ever, all the time I have you to love me.'

They made love with the same passion and devotion that had carried them through the years.

Later, when Patsy lay fully contented in his arms, her green eyes were shining with joy. Eddie was such a good man, a decent man, and she loved him to bits. Loved him so much it frightened her to think what she would do if anything were to happen to him. Almost from the first day that she had clapped eyes on him she had been in love with him, and in spite of all the problems they had had to contend with, their love had grown stronger over the years.

'Eddie,' she said, 'we've come a long way together, 'aven't we?'

Eddie held her close as he answered. 'We have indeed, my darling, and please God we've still got a long way to go.'

She looked into his face and smiled, murmuring, 'If only Florrie and Ollie could see how well all the children are doing, how well the whole family has stayed together.'

He touched her face with great tenderness. 'I'm sure they can, Patsy. I'm sure they can.'